THE TRUTH EFFECT

RISING WORLD
BOOK 1

ANNE MORTENSEN

PUENTE PRESS

Puente Press

United Kingdom
First published
October 2021 © Anne Mortensen
Written by Anne Mortensen
All rights reserved.

Cover Design by Nick Castle

British Library Cataloguing in Publication Data.
A CIP catalogue record of this book is available from the
British Library

ISBN 978-1-907688-03-4 (ebook)
ISBN 978-1-907688-02-7 (European paperback)
ISBN 978-1-907688-05-8 (US trade paperback)
ISBN 978-1-907688-01-0 (international trade paperback)

PUENTE PRESS

In memory of my grandmother.
1923-2021

RETRACTION

FRIDAY, 9 JUNE 2028   THEDAILYTIMES.COM

An editorial piece titled, "Illegal Narcotics Ring Thrives in Central London," published on 8 March 2028, contained a major error. The article named Mr. Ian Smith as a suspect in an illegal narcotics exchange.

New facial recognition evidence has since come to light, proving that the person involved in illegal narcotics activities was not Mr. Smith. In addition, the Biometric Unit of the Metropolitan Police has confirmed Mr. Smith was in Stockholm, Sweden, at the time the crime took place. Mr. Smith has been released from police custody and is no longer a suspect.

The Daily Times is dedicated to printing factual information. In light of the Truth Laws currently being discussed in the wider public, we have deleted all articles citing allegations against Mr. Smith.

We have also removed the reporter who originally investigated the allegations from her position at the Daily Times, effective immediately.

We take our reporting seriously.

The Daily Times online newspaper apologizes to Mr. Smith for its erroneous reporting.

- ROBERT GREAVES,
EDITOR-IN-CHIEF

The reporter's name was redacted, but in the shadows of Lambeth, South London, Kelly Blackwell knew the price of one wrong thought. One slip, and the echo chambers would turn her doubts into a noose.

WEEK 1

ONE

KELLY BLACKWELL SAT cross-legged on the edge of her sofa and watched the anonymous whistleblower's file drift, tissue-like, across her screen. Watching his gift of gigabytes travel at a crawl, heat mounted in her stomach. They had only thirty minutes to complete the transfer. Thirty minutes to get the hard evidence for the scoop that would restore her reputation. Thirty minutes before the entire Internet switched over to the Truth Laws system. At that point, what she was doing now would be illegal.

Come midnight, the new Truth Laws would give the government what it craved: full power to comb the web for untruths, hunt down the posters, and prosecute them. This transfer would put her squarely on the wrong side of the law.

The minute hand on her wall clock snapped forward.

Her nerves frayed, but no way would she let this chance pass. After living under the stigma of being a discredited journalist for two years, the risk was worth it, and she still had time. Just.

She pulled the duvet snugly around her shoulders and dragged the hot water bottle closer. It dragged across the cushion like a lifeless fish. Ready, she clicked open the last file, a JPEG, that had landed on her desktop.

A profile of a greasy-haired man tainted her screen. His hand rested on the hip of his pinstripe trousers, looking way too smug for the criminal he was, is, and would always be. "Mr. Smith."

Saying his name coated her tongue with a sour taste. It had taken her months to find a sliver of evidence that could take him down—and exonerate herself—and now the full evidence was nearly in her grasp. She was so close.

She clicked on the amber minimize button at the top of the photo. If this transfer failed again, the libel scar on her record would become a noose —the sender's evidence buried, her career finished.

The computer didn't respond.

She hit escape.

The zombie file hung static in the middle of the screen, taunting her.

Sweat trickled from her armpits. She hadn't moved in the last hour, so no way could she have tripped the connection. Those files—her fate— were trapped somewhere in the Ethernet void between London and the whistleblower's cloaked location.

She poised her fingers over Control, ALT, Delete, but then hesitated. If she shut down the computer, she might lose everything. She raked her hair with both hands and dropped her bare feet to the floor.

The modem hummed warmly, its indicator glowed hazel green, and the power cable was bundled tight and tidy in a clip. The fault had to be elsewhere. If Josh were there, he'd immediately identify the problem and fix the proxy chain coupled with the makeshift VPN. After all, it was his setup. But he was on a photoshoot, and Kelly was running out of time.

She breathed in deeply, her belly stretching as far as it could go. "Whistleblower, you still there?"

Silence buzzed.

She pressed her temples. "Think, think, think." If news articles could be shadowbanned, so could proxy servers. Didn't mean they disappeared, just that they went offline or invisible. The interrupted transmission had to be because of the proxy. Try a different server address.

Simple. She leaned into the mic. "If you can still hear me, hang in there."

From the list of proxy IP addresses next to her, she hammered in a fresh set of numbers. Loud clicks ricocheted off her studio's walls. She held her breath and hit enter.

The screen didn't flicker.

She flung off the duvet and typed in another IP address, then another, and another. "Please be there."

The whistleblower's avatar flashed on the screen—the only one she'd ever seen. "Kelly, I send—" his digitized voice said.

Her heart pounded.

"Chris—" he said.

"Did you say Chris?"

"Mallow—"

"Christopher Mallow?" Kelly leaned in. "What about him?"

The screen froze over. Neon pink squares sugarcoated the whistle-blower's avatar eyes.

"No!"

The clock ticked closer to midnight, closer to the Truth Laws going into effect.

Her heart quickened. She steadied her aching fingers on the keys and entered each number of the last IP address on the list—her last hope. "Hang in there. I'm finding a stronger connection."

The speakers went silent, the screen dark.

Her body felt numb. She clenched her long hair, limp like velvet rope.

Out of nowhere, a crackle of dry leaves crunching underfoot streamed through the speakers.

She drew back.

The screen flicked to life, and she could see two men traipsing through woodland at night, clouds of vapor emanating from their nostrils. Woolen coats, leather gloves, tweed caps. Each held a shotgun, butts tucked under their arms, long barrels angled toward the ground. They halted between stark trees and came into focus.

One man had acne-scarred cheeks. He stood in front of a younger man with a sleek, smooth face. The moonlight cast a blue-tinged shadow over their eyes.

The IP address on the screen matched the one on her list, but two hunting buddies taking a nighttime stroll with their shotguns wasn't what she had paid for. "What the hell is this?"

"The AI is moving to its ultimate phase," the scarred man said.

The mention of AI snagged her attention. Anything connected to online crime did, but time was running out. She reentered a used IP address and punched enter.

The screen reloaded, and the view crash-landed on the same distant spot—the hunters in the woods. "Whistleblower, are you directing the feed?"

The smooth-faced man shoved a cartridge into the chamber. "There might be a crazed saboteur threatening the project." His lisp scratched the speakers.

She winced and tapped down the volume. Threatening the project... those were the words the whistleblower had used in his first email to her. She boosted the screen's brightness.

"They have it in hand."

The man's accent was English, but the woodland location could be in any number of countries. Nighttime hunting? An activity easily dismissed as something eccentric Englishmen would do. Apart from the vague mention of AI, there wasn't much to go on. Except...

She jumped off the sofa, her knees buckled. Limping to the window, she pulled back the curtain. The moon's silver glow filled the night sky like a splendid mistress walking through a troubled room. Its fullness and position in the sky mirrored the one in the video. The men's private meeting was taking place somewhere in the south of England. She edged up to the screen and pumped the volume.

"I wouldn't worry about it," the scarred man said. "They won't let anyone hinder the goal. You'll make your investment back a hundredfold."

The feed ended.

Cobalt blue light burst onto the screen, flooding the room, and it punched a hole right through her.

Deadly spikes of despair started to invade her soul. Her heavy head dropped back. Maybe the whistleblower had connected her to these hunters for some strange reason, she thought. Didn't matter. Whatever the feed showed her still didn't replace the missing gigabytes of evidence she needed. And then that mention of Christopher Mallow...made no sense at all.

She sighed, but deep inside, she could feel herself reaching out, as if to grab hold of the frazzled tip of thread the whistleblower had thrown her way. She turned toward the ceiling. "Jerko, where is Christopher Mallow?"

The machine's red eye pulsed. "Current whereabouts unknown. However, he's scheduled to be at the INNS in Covent Garden in the morning."

She massaged her scalp. The Internet News Network Service, or what most journalists called the echo chambers, was integral to the Truth Laws system and the worst place to talk.

The analog clock on her wall snapped to midnight.

The modem's light flipped red.

Now, every written word on the Internet was legally regulated. Now, all content on the Internet was monitored. Now, the truth was a dangerous thing.

It was over. Or maybe not. Though Christopher Mallow was a bite-sized hope so far away as to be a fantasy, he was a lead. And lead meant the story, her story, wasn't dead. If she pursued this, she'd have to get Christopher out of the chamber, away from the cameras and mics, and she wasn't sure how she'd pull that off. She hadn't seen him—in fact, actively avoided him—for months.

Her voice wobbled in her tight throat. "Jerko, book me a slot at the INNS. Same time as Christopher Mallow."

TWO

7 January. 6:30 a.m.

KELLY UNBOLTED THE FOURTH DEADLOCK, her backpack in tow, carrying the whistleblower-sourced documents. If not entirely comfortable with her upcoming meeting, at least she was fully prepped to meet Christopher Mallow.

"Happy Birthday, Kelly," Jerko blared.

She stiffened and drew back. Weeks earlier, she'd instructed the bot to delete her data from her personal calendar as well as from every genuine online profile, but it had been acting up lately. It had been a freebie—of sorts—so what could she expect?

After she had been charged with libel, the State offered her a choice. A State-appointed digital deputy or a fine she would never be able to afford. She opted for the digital deputy, christened it Jerko, and repurposed it as her personal assistant. It hung from the ceiling like an all-seeing eye ever since. "Jerko, search and destroy all of my personal data online. I don't want to say it again."

She slammed the front door.

A gust of icy wind stung her face. The cold wrapped around her arms and legs and then whistled around the concrete columns of the Eden Council Estate. She blinked hard, wringing out the water in her eyes, and pulled her woolen hat over her ears. It failed to block out the sound of the pedestrians' rhythmic footsteps, summoning like a pied piper.

Under the dim sky, Kelly fiddled with her backpack and noosed the drawstring tight as an airlock. At least a year had passed since she last saw or talked to Christopher Mallow, and that wasn't the way to treat a man who had nurtured her career into existence. She wasn't sure how she'd explain her silence or whether she'd mention the whistleblower, but she expected he'd be surprised to see her standing in front of him.

In search of some insight, some guidance, she looked up at the sky, hoping that an inspired piece of advice would magically parachute down. But the elevated road blocked her view, and all she could see was its cracked underbelly—in harmony with Lambeth's concrete columns and mile-high, brutalist buildings. Extracting a morsel of enlightenment from this environment was futile, Kelly thought, as she tugged once more on the backpack's strap.

She stepped onto the path and merged with the pulse flowing up Black Prince Road—the primary artery in and out of Lambeth. At this hour, most of the traffic was going out.

An SS—a street-level State surveillance camera—flashed an image of a curly-haired woman, polka-dot mug in hand, sitting in front of a fireplace. "Good morning, Kelly Blackwell. Would you like chamomile tea?"

Kelly huffed. "I'm in no mood."

She walked on and brought her wristwatch in line with her face.

A pedestrian knocked into her.

Her backpack fell to the ground.

"Hey!"

She clocked the navy coat, white beanie, black scarf. Pinned inside his ears were bone-conducting earphones—the preferred option for people who wanted to block out the world. He was engaged in a chat with a three-dimensional hologram woman beaming from his watch. Navy Coat would listen to Kelly whether he liked it or not. "You, idiot! In the navy coat."

He carried on walking.

Kelly could almost hear her late Aunt El speaking sage words in her ear: *Pick your battles, Kelly. Soon, you'll be free.* Reluctantly, she dropped it, scooped up her backpack, and walked on.

Once again, she lifted her wristwatch to her face. It beeped and displayed ID number 2.689XF alongside her profile pic. She had snapped the photo back when she had short, wispy hair. Her pale skin and guarded crescent smile hadn't changed, but every time she saw that pic, she thought the same thing: ask Josh to take an updated photo of her. And every day she put off asking because having her picture taken, yet again, had become rather like having blood drawn.

A confirmation button popped onto her watch, and she logged into the citywide max octave Wi-Fi. She pressed enter. A fresh window opened like a doorway to the cosmos and immediately directed her to the Global Wires check-in window. Small Star Trek spaceships danced on the window frame—Harry White's personal touch. She smirked, and her face felt like it would crack.

Harry had set up the portal, under Spence's order, shortly after thugs had raided Newswire's editorial offices. They kidnapped an editor and beat him in the back of a van. Hours later, they dumped his body, black and blue, in front of the building.

A horrified Spence installed the check-in protocols for Global Wires as a kind of mental safety pin for himself. Being Editor-in-Chief, he claimed it as his duty. Personnel about to enter the echo chamber, or working a beat, had to check-in. Kelly pressed the green check mark under the INNS. Done.

At last, she arrived at the conflux between north and south, east and west, otherwise known as the chokepoint, and the light was predictably red. She huddled with the mass of pedestrians.

Just across the road stood the State's sparkling jewel, the INNS, the echo chamber. Glass and carbon and steel housed the system that transformed her thoughts into code and eventually into money at the end of the month. Wasn't it Christopher Mallow who first branded it an echo chamber? Yes, it had been him. She could still hear the quiet, mocking anger in his voice as he pronounced the words.

The light flashed green.

If all went according to plan, she'd show Christopher the docs, he'd verify details, and she'd be finished in no time. Kelly drew in a deep breath and swung her backpack behind her. The air tickled her throat as she marched forward.

KELLY SHOVED the QR code tattooed on her wrist under the scanner.

A laser glowed red against her skin. The glass door slid open.

Inside, the chamber had the feel of a library and the look of a space capsule. Frosted glass walls blocked out the city street, the hermetically sealed windows vacuumed out the noise.

Right up front in the first row, two screens beamed their light onto the eggshell ceiling.

Christopher had to be one of the users.

She hung her Everest jacket and woolen hat on a wall hook, and a mechanical shelf thrust out a pair of earbuds.

"Welcome back, Kelly Blackwell," a silky system voice spoke from the earbuds in her palm. "From your biometric readings, we calculate it will take seven deep breaths to upload your work. Please occupy cockpit number six."

Her first task was to find Christopher. When her business with him was settled, she'd upload the crime stats, her weekly task for Global Wires. She stuffed the earbuds in her jeans pocket and crept down the aisle. Rows of doorless cubicles lay barren, their pilot seats empty, their Fi headsets docked. Too early in the morning for most, she guessed.

She came to the front row and parked her backpack next to the semi-opaque divider in cockpit six. Even though the chamber was practically empty, her assigned cockpit stood too close to the exit for comfort. She tucked her backpack under the pilot chair. Feeling secure now, she pivoted toward the glowing screens.

A young man occupied cockpit three, his eyes closed, his arms splayed on the armrests. She brushed past.

There, in cockpit one, sat an old man topped with a tangled mess of gray hair, his eyes closed. It took her a moment to recognize him, but the mess of a man was none other than Christopher Mallow.

A softness came over her. Early in his career, he was a foreign correspondent reporting on government corruption; he had landed himself in foreign jails a few times and eventually won an award for bravery. Today, under the new Truth Laws, the articles that had brought him such acclaim would pass through the Zone servers for State approval prior to Internet publication. In a twisted way, the libel charges against him had saved him by confining him to writing up factoids.

The lights on his Fi headset glowed steadily, a sign that he was in the middle of an upload.

She resisted an urge to interrupt—there was nothing more annoying—and stood off to his side. But then, glancing at his screen, Kelly saw a jumbled disaster of mathematical equations interspersed with forward slashes, brackets, stars, and alphanumeric characters littered across it. Either his mind was a mess, the Fi headset was faulty, or a virus was on the attack. She tapped him on the shoulder. "Christopher?"

His eyes shot open. He yanked his earbuds out. Deep lines constellated his forehead, deeper than she remembered.

"Kelly? Is that you? How long has it been?" His tone was bright.

"Your screen..."

He glanced over her shoulder. "Guess I didn't get enough training."

Every journalist had undergone weeks of training in order to transmit thoughts via the Fi headsets with minimal text contamination. It involved breathing techniques, taming stray thoughts, and crushing emotional whims that might disturb the upload. Kelly hit a ninety-five percent success rate with a simple strategy: a pre-upload dose of the neutralizer and a dash in and out of the chamber. Christopher's strategy looked to be all over the place—if he had one.

He leaned in. "Truth is, I'm too old for all this shite."

He waved his hand in the air, at the tech all around, and struggled to his feet.

She offered him her hand.

"Thank you, dear." He stood straight, a single button on his disheveled overcoat holding him together. "You and I, we shouldn't even be in this damn place. Crime requires our full attention."

A warm sensation filled her chest. Life had been simple in the Daily Times days. A clipped sigh escaped her lips.

"You're at Global Wires, right?"

"Crime desk," she said. "They have me on petty crime for a few months yet."

"It'll zoom by. Before you know it, you'll be back in the game playing with the big boys."

If the whistleblower's files, hidden in her bag, proved her innocence, the judgment against her should be dropped immediately. She stepped close to Christopher and lowered her voice. "I need to ask your advice about...something." She glimpsed the ceiling camera. "Can we go outside?"

He scratched his cheek and looked toward the door.

The young man in cubicle three came up to them, and before she could even step back, he held out his hand. "Oliver Green. I work with Leeland and Partners."

Thick, wired glasses and a snooty tone never meant good things were coming. "Hello." She shook his hand out of politeness. "Leeland and Partners?"

"A start-up." He held onto her hand longer than necessary, longer than she liked.

She pulled out of his grasp.

"Sorry to intrude," he said. "I can't get my screen to work either."

A flash of heat spurted deep inside her. This damn kid was threatening to derail her plans. She rubbed the back of her neck.

"Now's not a good time, Mr. Green," Christopher said.

A spotlight illuminated Christopher's cockpit. "If you are encountering a problem, Christopher Mallow, please reset the Fi headset and start again," the chamber cooed.

Oliver glanced at Christopher's screen. "Who knows what goodies they snuck into the hardware overnight."

"A restart usually does the trick."

She reached for the console. The key was missing.

Oliver looked at Christopher. "Did you knock it trying to upload?"

She didn't have time for a diagnostic conference of the latest technology mishap. "The INNS was bound to be shaky on the first day of the Truth Laws."

"I don't trust any of this," Christopher said.

"You and me both," Kelly added. "Maybe we can call a tech guy to come around later."

"Yeah, c'mon. Let's get out of here." He knocked on a plastic panel with his wrinkled knuckle. "We have some catching up to do."

Oliver stared at Christopher. "You can't just leave your screen like that."

He shuffled past Oliver. "Oh yes, I can. I'm not going into battle today. It'll still be here tomorrow."

Kelly followed Christopher to the exit. A waft of tangy sweat lagged behind him. Something wasn't right.

"I still have my system of paper, ink, and filing cabinets, remember?" Christopher shuffled around and egged her to catch up. "Before your time, we had a trail of the records we could trace back to who handled what. Always keep hard copies of your final drafts."

He had told her this countless times when he mentored her at the Daily Times. The familiar phrase brought a smile to her lips.

The door buzzed.

Cool air whooshed through the chamber.

Boots slammed onto the tiled floor.

She jolted. That wasn't the sound of a typical chamber user.

"Users, please return to your stations."

Two elite enforcers of the Truth Laws marched down the passage toward them.

She narrowed in on their visored eyes and stepped back. "What are they here for?"

Christopher ducked. "Go to your station."

She dashed to cockpit six, whipped on the Fi headset, and fumbled for the earbuds in her pocket. "Kelly Blackwell, take twelve deep breaths."

She hauled in one breath, two, three, and tried to settle her mind long enough to focus on her weekly task, the crime stats. The white light overhead transitioned to tangerine orange reminiscent of summer evenings long ago. She clasped her eyes shut.

Moments later, the Fi headset was ripped off her head.

"What the—" Her words sank into the void in her stomach.

Two troopers towered over her. Wooden batons hung from holsters around their waists. Each held a K45 laser.

Her thoughts raced backward. Chamber, chokepoint, road, home. Had she said anything to anyone along the way? What about the crowd at the chokepoint? Could they have reported her for something? No, no—at least not that she could pinpoint. Did the Elite Squad find out about the whistleblower? Or maybe the SS saw the papers in her backpack with their X-ray capability. Her mouth went dry.

"Your ID," the taller trooper said.

She kicked her backpack deeper under her seat, by now certain that the file inside was about to create more problems than she ever dreamed. "I... uh."

The distance between her and the exit was short, but the troopers would be relentless. A grab and go was impossible. She extended her arm.

The shorter trooper grabbed her wrist and flashed his QR code scanner over it. "Kelly Blackwell, journalist for Global Wires. Please confirm."

"I...uh."

"Confirm." The trooper's clutch grew tighter.

Her throat tangled. "Yes. Yes." She twisted her arm free. "I'm Kelly Blackwell. Officer, I—"

They didn't nod. They didn't speak. As coordinated as a pair of robots, they marched to Oliver Green's cockpit.

She sank into the folds of the leather chair, the semi-opaque panels her only cover. Had the troopers known about the file, things could've been so much worse.

"Oliver Green?" The short officer's tone was no less harsh than when he snapped at her. "Recently employed at Stanley and Lee. Confirm."

She jerked upright. That was wrong, according to Oliver. He'd said he worked at Leeland and Partners. She gripped the armrests, slid to the edge of her seat, and leaned toward the panel.

Oliver glowered at the trooper's visor. "I confirm."

"Carry on."

She slumped back. A routine check. That's all it was. She had to stop thinking the worst.

The two marched to the next cockpit, Christopher's.

Her watch lit up.

She flinched. The opening chords of *Sweet Dreams* by Eurythmics rang out. The light in her cockpit pulsed to the beat. Spence, her boss, was calling. Worst timing ever.

The tall trooper marched back to her cockpit. "All watches must be turned off in the INNS."

"I know. I'm sorry, officer." She fumbled for the off switch, her fingertips slippery with sweat. "They moved my slot at the last minute and—"

"Powered-on watches in the INNS incur a fine of bits."

That was coin she didn't have. She tried to detect if a smidgeon of sympathy existed behind his dark visor, but it was clear he didn't want an explanation. He wouldn't have cared less if her studio flat had blown up this morning. She licked her bottom lip with the tip of her tongue. "I'm sorry. It won't happen again."

The trooper paused a moment. Behind the visor, unexpectedly, something shifted in his demeanor. "I'll let it go this time."

"Thank you, sir."

She actually felt grateful to an Elite Squad trooper. What was the world coming to?

He rejoined the other trooper hovering at Christopher's station.

"Christopher Mallow of the Daily Times. Please confirm."

Silence seized the chamber.

"Sir, please confirm your identity."

Christopher Mallow sat motionless in his seat, staring straight ahead.

Oliver poked his head over the edge of the panel and waved his hand at Kelly. He mouthed, "What's he doing?"

Kelly shook her head, wishing she knew.

"Sir," the trooper repeated.

Oliver was right. Why didn't Christopher just answer the trooper and be done with it?

He launched off the chair and dove through the gap between the troopers. He crashed into the wall, breaking his stride with his palm. He propelled toward the exit.

The troopers spun around. The taller trooper grabbed Christopher by the neck and threw him to the floor, belly down, while the other whacked him with a baton across his back.

A bone cracked.

Christopher howled.

Kelly sprang up. "Get off him!" She waved her hands at the cameras housed in black domes on the ceiling and pointed at the troopers. "Are you getting this? He's just an old man!"

"Kelly Blackwell, remain seated," one trooper ordered. "This is State business."

"You call this State business?"

"Stand back." He held out his arm. "Unless you want to be arrested." His visor turned transparent and his dark eyes shot through, laser-like.

Her resolve melted. They could crush her between their hands—if they wanted to—and the algorithm in control of online information would telegraph her demise in seconds. Her job, her voice, her independence—all gone before she had a chance to fight. As much as she wanted to stop the madness and be by Christopher's side, no good would come from getting arrested.

She stepped back, shame burning through her chest. Christopher had taught her to stand up to power, to ask the questions no one else would ask. And here she was, watching him bleed while she did nothing.

The trooper turned back to Christopher and flipped on his radio. "We have apprehended the fugitive at INNS location six."

Indignation plumed inside her. "A fugitive? For what, resisting arrest?"

"I said, step back!"

The ceiling cameras beat down on her. She should move, retake her seat, but she didn't. She couldn't. Pursuing underground criminal networks was what she lived for, and she knew what to expect, but taking on the State and its Elite Squad would come with untold consequences. She backed up, feeling like a coward.

The troopers hoisted Christopher up and slung his arms over their shoulders, like Jesus Christ on a black cross.

Kelly looked skyward to drain the tears welling in her eyes.

"I'm innocent," Christopher said. "Like Mr. Smith."

His words stunned her into stillness. What was he talking about? Smith was guilty. As night was dark, Smith was guilty. Through her tearful blur, Christopher's bloody face was so swollen it looked deformed. She wanted to call out to him, to tell him she'd heard, that she understood— but his message made no sense. These could be his last words to her, and she couldn't even decipher them.

The crackle from a taser whipped him into submission.

A violent tremor rattled Christopher. His head jerked back. "Don't let them get away with this!"

The troopers lugged him out the front door, his feet dragging along the floor. The sound of his shoes scraping tile would stay with her forever.

She stood rock still, her mind sputtering with the shock of what she had just witnessed. What she just witnessed was illegal, wasn't it? But who would she report it to? The Elite Squad answered to no one. Christopher was gone, and she had stood there and watched it happen.

A scratchy sound, like a rat gnawing on a wire, pulled her out of her daze.

Oliver Green was on his hands and knees, his arm reaching under the seat, the one where Christopher had been stationed.

Disgust quivered through her. "What the hell are you doing?"

"I just wanted to see if the old man left anything behind." Oliver stood, empty-handed.

A prickly sensation crawled up her spine. She should have known when she first saw those beady eyes hiding behind his fancy glasses. "Vulture."

"Me? Not me. But some of them pay well." He rubbed his thin fingers over the hair plastered to his forehead. "I'd split it with you."

He was a snitch, probably working with a petty crime network. "It's all fine and dandy while you work with them," she said. "But after they're done with you, they'll chew you up and toss you—"

He raised his hand. "Got to go, they're waiting." He ran for the door.

"I'll be cheering them on when they throw you to the wolves!"

The door slid shut and muted the sound of his fleeing footsteps.

Now alone, the chamber felt like it was creeping in on her, quiet as a morgue. She wanted to flee, too, but her legs were rigid, unable to move. Witnessing the beating, the potency of the Elite Squad, up close and personal, had shocked her limbs stiff.

A thin spatter of Christopher's blood stained the floor. If he was a fugitive, why was he in the echo chamber, their domain? Why did he say Ian Smith was innocent?

Questions swirled and her fingers itched. Then, the crime stats popped into her mind. She shook herself, trying to dislodge the confusion, the tension between her shoulder blades. It was no use, she was in no shape to upload crime stats. Certainly not here.

She fished out her backpack, grabbed her coat and hat, and rested her trembling hand on the door. Shadows lurked on the other side of the chamber's door. Still feeling the ordeal of what she had just witnessed, she pushed against the glass.

"Kelly Blackwell, please scan your code to exit."

She bared the underside of her wrist, and the door swung open.

The cold air cleansed her mind, making room for one single question to plant itself. What had Christopher been working on that got the attention of the Elite Squad? She stepped into the square, tapped her watch, and logged into Jerko.

She paused. She couldn't let the Elite Squad find her digital fingerprints all over this case. From now on, old-fashioned face-to-face questions out in a park, in the middle of nowhere, was the only way to go. But would

Jerko's upcoming search assignment be considered a digital fingerprint? If articles were online, she rationalized, they had official clearance. "Jerko, email me links to all of Christopher Mallow's online articles."

She remembered the first article she'd written under his supervision—how he'd made her rewrite the lead seven times until she got it right. "Journalists don't ask permission," he'd told her. "We ask questions."

Her resolve fortified, she started in the direction of INNS location five. The trek would give Jerko time to compile the list and give her time to offload tension before uploading the damn crime stats—a task she never expected would become her cover.

THREE

IN SOHO, central London, in the newsroom of Global Wires, Spencer Wyatt sat at his oak desk in his office. A picture frame rotated between images of his five-year-old daughter and his beautiful wife in their garden. He remembered taking the photos as though it were yesterday, and he wondered what the world would be like when his daughter started her own family. The thought made him shudder.

He glanced at his watch. Thirty minutes had passed since he had called Kelly, the first of his staff to upload under the Truth Laws, and he wanted to see how it went. It wasn't like her to refuse his call, but she must have had a good reason. She was rigorously precise, and of all his staff, he worried about her the least. As for the others...

He turned back to his screen. The notes for the editorial meeting were already too long and needed paring down, dashing his hopes of getting home before dinner.

He typed, "Remind staff they must inform The Zone immediately if they discover anything that might endanger State Security. If not..."

He leaned into the back of his chair and crossed his arms. Never in a million years had he thought the Truth Laws would get the votes in the Houses of Parliament. All the editors fought hard against the bill. It didn't get enough public support either, according to the polls. How this day came to be, he'd never know. What he did know was that his job was now to keep the newsroom functioning and intact at all costs. He tilted forward. "Prep staff for change in desks."

A bark of laughter leaked through his closed door. He resumed typing.

Seconds later, he heard metal clinking against a ceramic mug.

He rose from his chair and opened the door. Nothing but bare desks, dimmed lights, black screens, and empty swivel chairs. Murmurs dribbled out of the break room. He could use a break himself.

As he approached the kitchen's entrance, he could hear two people in a hushed discussion. He slowed his pace. The voices were coming from a man and woman he didn't recognize. He stepped into the kitchen.

The chatter ceased.

The man and woman stared at him, their brown eyes set in blank faces, their round bodies, clothed in ice-white uniforms, swayed in their thick-cushioned shoes.

Sweepers, the guardians of buildings. They scavenged for planted mics, cameras, and trackers like owls in the night. It was unusual to spot sweepers during the day like this.

"Morning," he said. "I'm Spencer Wyatt. I don't think we've met."

Their heads bobbed in unison.

"Sorry if we made too much noise," the man said. "We didn't think anyone was here." He placed his mug in the sink.

The woman followed his lead.

"I thought you came in on Fridays." Spence opened the cupboards. A half-eaten packet of digestive biscuits. A box of cereal. Beetlebug Bars. He grabbed the canister of instant coffee crystals on the shelf, next to the powdered milk and sugar cubes, and flipped the switch on the kettle. "Can I make you a cup?"

The man shook his head. "Mr. Damian asked us to come in every day now."

"Ah." He kept his tone light. It was a smart decision, but Damian hadn't notified him. He brushed a sprinkling of crumbs from the counter and put his mug down. "With so many changes happening, it's hard to keep track."

"We hope you are happy with our work."

"Of course. In fact, I'd like your opinion on something."

They nodded.

"Given your experience in...security matters, do you think it's absolutely necessary to come in every day? I mean, I wouldn't want to alarm my staff unnecessarily."

"Whatever you like, Mr. Spencer. Maybe you talk to Mr. Damian?"

"Of course. Would you like a biscuit?"

"Our shift is over," the man said. "Time to get home."

They grabbed their coats and dashed out the door. The kettle popped.

He hated it when Damian took action over his head. And without so much as a courtesy email. Spence rushed back to his desk.

He swiped the notepad and opened his email. He lasered in on the email Damian had just sent. Two minutes ago. "His ears must have been on fire." He clicked on the message.

Spence,

I'll be in this week to go over some changes.

Joanne will be in touch with the exact time. See attached.

Damian

He double-clicked the PDF. A colorful pie chart popped up, each slice named by topic: taste flavors of the month, sunny places to holiday, fashion trends, technology gadgets. He scrolled down the page. More detailed graphs listed demographics of potential purchasers.

"That's it?" On the first day of the Truth Laws, the owner of Global Wires gives the editor-in-chief of the biggest news outlet in England a PDF of fluff to cover for the week? What a sad joke. He tossed the tablet aside.

His protocols, solid check-in protocols, kept his staff safe and productive so they could investigate hard news topics. Stories the public needed. Not fluff pieces. He pressed Damian's number on his watch.

A knock pounded his door. He pressed pause. "Come in."

Harry White poked his head in. "Any idea when the crime stats will be uploaded?"

Harry was the all-rounder every office depended on, and Spence's proud reminder of the best promotion he had made. He moved Harry up from IT in the basement to the civil notices desk. On the side, he did light office management, and he was going to hate hearing that fluff was in, crime was out, and that Kelly still hadn't called.

Spence suppressed his growing paranoia on that last subject. He pinched the skin between his eyes. "I'm sure Kelly will get the upload done soon."

"It's not like her to be late."

Harry sounded the way Spence always felt but could never show: worried. "It's probably a glitch or upgrade error holding up the transfers."

Harry drummed his fingers on the door and popped his lips. "Righto. I'll keep the ticker tape running as is." He closed the door.

Spence's neck ached for all the tension and the blood pulsing through his body. Kelly was going to hear from him. And so was Damian.

He rolled his chair away from his desk and surveyed the newsroom. The last time a journalist went missing was...he shook away the ugly thought and scooted up to his desk.

He opened a fresh message and addressed it to Harry. "Look into procedures for reassigning the desks. Get back to me ASAP."

FOUR

The elevator brushed open to the Global Wires newsroom. The lingering aroma of toast and coffee, personalized ring tones, and beeps comforted Kelly as she strode down the walkway toward her desk.

Harry popped up, his red hair glistening under the halogen lights. He snapped off a chunk of green apple. For once, his mouth was doing something useful, she thought.

"Thanks for the stats," he said. "You look haggard."

"Spence should've kept you in the basement," she said.

"Count yourself lucky you don't have to log all the death certificates." He swiveled in his chair. "It's a bit late for you. Where've you been?"

She dropped down in her chair. "Who needs to know?" She wiped her forehead and unexpectedly mopped up cold sweat.

He dangled his arms over the connecting panel. "Did you hear about Christopher Mallow?"

Kelly switched on the computer screen and the projection keyboard. The desk glowed green.

Harry hunched in close, and she could feel the heat in his eyes scanning her face for a reaction, but she stayed focused on the screen. She hadn't yet decided how deep she wanted to dig into Mallow's arrest; her next step depended on whatever Jerko sent her.

"So you know. How did you find out?"

"You're not the only one with a direct line to the Prime Minister."

"Never mind." He pulled back. "Sources tell me the Daily Times was going to shit anyway. It was just a matter of time."

The Smith Affair had chipped off the first chunk of the Daily Times's reputation, and now, with Mallow's arrest, their reputation shattered. Her cheeks heated.

"Maybe Spence'll talk about it in the editorial meeting today. Want some coffee?"

She shook her head. "I'm not feeling so hot. Do you have vitamin C, extra strength, and zinc?"

"Samantha has that sort of thing."

He ambled toward the kitchen.

Being the lifestyle journalist for Global Wires, Samantha's drawer was usually packed with vitamin and wellness products companies had sent her to review. During the cold season, people raided her stash of goodies and left behind the scraps. Kelly feared she was too late. She opened the drawer. Sure enough, it was empty.

Stoic in the face of a fever, or whatever was bringing on the ache in her bones, she turned back to her computer. The fluorescent green light speckled her knuckles, giving them a mottled, diseased look.

She typed in her Internet ID and opened her email. Jerko had sent her Mallow's online profile and hundreds of hyperlinks to his published work. She rolled her shoulders and clicked on Mallow's online profile. Verified: data journalist. The Elite Squad hadn't arrested Mallow for being a basic data journalist.

She scanned the hundreds of links to factoids on human behavior collected off smartphones, step counters, card readers, vehicle computers, and AI PAs like Jerko. Other articles covered online polls, surveys, personality tests, and bio-data from blood drives. Unable to decipher which was the most revealing, she clicked on a random line. In a fingertip second, a page popped up, listing factoids similar to data Harry gathered. A quick scan failed to reveal anything personal to Mallow. She skipped down the search and spotted a name she recognized.

Heather Mallow, Christopher's wife. She worked at the Daily Times, covering Health and Science. A flurry of trepidation rippled through her chest. She hadn't seen Heather since Kelly had been fired from the Daily Times, and she wasn't sure what to expect if she contacted her. But Heather had a clean reputation, and she was known for her thorough research.

Kelly clicked on the first article, *Panic Epidemic Sweeps the UK*. Published in May 2028. It had received millions of hits since its publication.

One in three people had reported panic attacks to the Department of Health in the first quarter of 2028. Slightly more women than men, but the difference was negligible. The medication most commonly prescribed was MK860, a blend of herbs with no reported side effects. The medication was so frequently prescribed that the NHS released an over-the-counter version.

Kelly glanced around. The article's statistics—probably gathered by Christopher—meant eight of her colleagues had experienced a panic attack. Samantha was probably one, she thought, and Lily in Arts and Entertainment, for sure.

Kelly turned her attention back to the article and clicked on the cross-links for the online health forums. All the links were dead. The State was the likely killer, but why?

A journalist like Heather, one who researched in-depth articles with genuine and independent sources and managed to keep her work online, would know what her husband had been researching that got him arrested. Kelly opened the media personnel intranet.

In the corner of her eye, she glimpsed Harry returning to his desk, mug in hand, and shot Heather a message: "Let's meet. Please contact me ASAP."

Harry plonked his mug on his desk. "Who are you looking up?"

Kelly closed the intranet window. "No one."

The screens pinged across the office.

A red alert D-notice, a media-wide gag order, flashed across her screen. In the center of the bulletin, a static black and white mugshot appeared. Christopher Mallow, his eyes burning with defiance, filled the screen like a most wanted poster in a Western film. The mugshot looked like a duplicate from an earlier arrest.

She recalled how Christopher Mallow relished flouting D-notices; his skirting along the forbidden had distinguished him as an adventurous journalist among his peers but an outright irritation to the establishment.

"Are you seeing this?" Harry asked.

"When you mentioned Mallow earlier, did you know this D-notice was in the pipeline?"

"My sources are good, but not that good."

"Mallow had it coming," Spence shouted as he trundled into the newsroom.

The journalists leaned back in their chairs and swiveled round.

He parked himself in the middle of the floor, his reading glasses balancing on his bald head.

"That's a bit harsh," Kelly said.

"I know you worked with him, but so did I, over at The Independent, back in the day. He was crazy then, and clearly, he's crazy now." Spence clamped his hands on his hips. "Here, we do things differently."

"Normally, they wait a day to issue a D-notice so they can get the facts straight," Kelly said.

"First day of the Truth Laws is the reason, I suspect," Spence said.

"How are we supposed to do our jobs if they keep gagging us?"

"If you were thinking of doing a story on this, Kelly, especially after the video they released this morning, forget about it."

"What video?"

"You didn't see it?" Harry looked surprised.

"My slot at the echo chamber got moved up, and I had to run out of my flat. Totally screwed up my morning."

Harry clicked on his watch.

"Mallow's arrest was a message to all of us," Spence said. "We follow protocol, keep our heads down, and we'll be good."

Spence and his damn protocols. They were nothing more than an insurance policy against thugs, the Elite Squad, criminals, missile attacks, you name it.

"Looks like the video got scrubbed," Harry announced. "So, Christopher Mallow was the famed Truth Laws fugitive." He bounced on his heels. "Mystery solved."

That's what the troopers called Mallow in the chamber. A fugitive. "When did they scrub it? Do you have a copy?"

"Don't answer that, Harry," Spence said. "As for any stories about this case, didn't you hear what I said? It's a no-go, Kelly." Spence tapped his finger against her desk. "Just to be on the safe side, we're freezing the crime desk."

Kelly reeled back. "Excuse me?"

"Please arrange for the move to happen, Harry."

"This is a joke, right?"

"Crime desks are going to get scrapped eventually, anyway."

"Are they forcing all news outlets to get rid of them now?" Harry asked.

"Not yet," Spence said. "But this whole thing with Christopher Mallow has put a nail in the coffin. With the Truth Laws, independent crime investigations will get buried or transferred elsewhere."

"Let's wait for the order," Kelly said. "Besides, you can't just pull the crime desk out from under me without notice or warning or anything. I mean, what is this? We might as well wheel up the guillotine, extend our necks, and release the latch on ourselves."

"Looks like that's what's happening already," Harry said.

Spence shifted his weight to one foot. "It's called being proactive."

Why was he caving in well before the Ministry made its move? "All I'm saying is we shouldn't stop investigating crime in this city because of something that might happen."

"There is nothing to investigate," Spence said, turning back to the other journalists. "The D-notice has been issued."

"By who?"

Spence swallowed. "You know who."

Yes, she did know, as did everyone in the media. She rubbed her sweating palms together. "I can't believe this."

Harry opened his mouth to speak.

"Harry, if you're worried about Kelly, don't be," Spence interrupted him. "I have something else lined up for her."

"I'm right here, Spence. You can talk directly to me."

Spence turned to Kelly. "I'll confirm your new position tomorrow in the editorial."

"Tomorrow?" Harry interjected.

"There's too much going on today. I've rescheduled it for tomorrow."

"Wherever you put me," Kelly said, "I already know I won't like it."

"Nothing new there," Samantha said.

"I don't need your two-bit opinion, Samantha, thank you very much. Oh, and your drawer is empty."

"Everyone, take a breather," Spence said. "It's a temporary freeze until this whole thing blows over."

This wasn't like a celebrity in a public toilet caught with his pants down. "How long is temporary?"

"As long as it needs to be."

"I can't fucking believe this."

"It shouldn't bother you since you aren't working on a Mallow-related story anyway, right?"

"Christopher Mallow isn't the only criminal in town, Spence. There's plenty of corruption out there. Who's going to track it all?" Had she shown her hand? "But, c'mon, it's my job."

"Don't worry. You still have a job." Spence turned to Harry. "Please start reassigning the phones and setting up permissions."

"I think this is a bit drastic," Harry said.

"You too? Maybe I should send you both to the basement until you cool down."

Harry rolled his eyes.

She studied Spence's face. He was the sort of boss who never made sudden, unconsidered moves. Someone else had to be behind this. "I'm sure you have it all in hand, Spence."

"I hear the sarcasm in your voice, Kelly."

"I just lost my goddamn desk in the deep freeze. Forgive me if I'm a little upset."

"Take the rest of the day off. Just make sure you come at 9 a.m. tomorrow for the editorial and your new assignment."

Spence trundled back to his office at the far edge of the newsroom. His gray shirt and slacks blended with the gray walls.

Spence and whoever put him up to this would not stop her that easily. There was a video out there with clues. Yes, it was scrubbed, but there were ways to find it.

She scrolled through numerous contacts on her watch—a lot of dead data—and came to Josh Munro. She pressed the call button.

He wasn't answering. Most weekday mornings, the paps hung out on the pavement in front of the Canary Hotel in Mayfair—an unofficial marketplace of sorts where they traded jobs and gossip while earning coin capturing celebs leaving the hotel's gilded gates. That's exactly where she'd find him first thing in the morning.

FIVE

8 January

THE SUN WAS LIGHTING the sky just as Heather Mallow's train neared King's Cross, St. Pancras International. She slipped the frayed strap of her leather satchel over her head. The satchel should have been tossed years ago, but her husband had given it to her on their second anniversary, and the worst she could bring herself to do was retire it to the back of her closet like much-loved, overworked shoes. But then the D-notice came out, followed by a call from Commissioner Lydia Rackham. She was asking to see Christopher's work notes. At that point, the trusty bag came out of retirement.

Satchel in hand, Heather stepped onto the platform. The bag clung to her body as she weaved through winter-season tourists and made her way to the main hall. Briefly, she glanced behind her and then descended two flights of stairs.

In front of a row of lockers, she rummaged through the bag, her fingers brushing the cool steel of the freshly sharpened switchblade. She stuffed the knife in her back pocket and clamped down the bag's flap, safeguarding the two notebooks her husband had filled with code he'd collected over the last twelve months.

So many times he'd tried to explain the equations, the numbers, the dates, the connections, and the broad implications, but she never really understood. Didn't want to either. It was probably because she never agreed with his method of executing the Resistance's plan. Exasperated at her reluctance to grasp the information in the notebooks, he'd said, "If all else fails, Kelly Blackwell will know what to do with this." And now he was in custody.

She pulled the strap over her head and stuffed the bag into the locker. At that moment, a new plan rolled into motion. She didn't know if her plan would work, but she would do what she could to nudge Kelly along, enticing her to collect the crumbs of hard evidence against the State that could put an end to the Truth Laws once and for all. Heather punched in the locker code 1-2-1-0, the date she first met Christopher on the train coming back from Paris, and slammed the locker door shut.

Footsteps echoed down the stairs.

Heart as tight as her grip on the knife, she removed the switchblade from her back pocket. She kept still and waited. All this intrigue and hiding...she never wanted to be part of the Resistance. Certainly not at her age. She tilted her head from side to side, listening.

A backpacker struggled down the steps.

She exhaled as though blowing out all her birthday candles at once. All she'd hoped for was a quiet life with her husband, perhaps back in Paris. Every muscle aching, she climbed the stairs and stepped into the light.

The only thing she could do now was wait for Kelly to find her.

SIX

IN THE CRISP MORNING AIR, Kelly balanced on her tiptoes and scoped the crowd of paps occupying the road. Their tripods like stakes on the tarmac. They were clutching their cameras in front of the gilded gateway of the Canary Hotel—a cornucopia filled with celebrities that provided photographers with steady work. She was so glad she didn't have to work the Arts and Entertainment desk, especially after her investigation of Ian Smith and the seedy world of the rich and famous. But somewhere in the crowd of celebrity chasers dwelled the only person she trusted to get counter-surveillance equipment and who knew where to find the maker of the Truth Laws fugitive video. Unfortunately, Josh was nowhere in sight.

She spotted the doorman, George Barry. She wouldn't call him a friend, but he had tipped her off to foreign and domestic politician check-ins, and in return, she sent him his favorite sweet tea, gifts for his kids, and chocolates for the staff. Most smart news-hungry journalists did.

George Barry was picking up stray bits of plastic and cable and twigs from off the marble steps. Kelly nodded at him as she filed through the patch of paps.

Deep inside the crowd, Josh spoke into his watch, his free arm battering the air. He was probably arguing with his agent, Percy, which was nothing new. She'd never met or seen Percy but had heard plenty about him.

Josh's camera hung around his neck—just like the first time they met when they were nine years old, the day Kelly and Aunt El had moved into their council flat in St. John's Wood. They were unloading boxes when Josh turned up on the side of the white van, camera resting on his chest. He offered to help carry in some boxes, and Aunt El gave him her instant approval. All in all, Kelly was a council kid, and he was a rich kid, but none of that got in the way of a solid friendship that eventually developed into a brief teenage romance.

From within the crowd, he nodded at her, gestured five, and turned back to his watch.

Kelly checked her watch for messages. Plenty of reader complaints packed her inbox, but not a peep from Heather Mallow. She hovered over the forward button. Under normal circumstances, Kelly would be pounding on Heather's desk at this very moment, but with the Truth Laws and the newly issued D-notice, Mallow's story was too hot. Maybe Heather was taking time to process it all herself.

There was always Ian Smith to track down. In a way, he was the one she had more questions for. She scrolled her contacts list and stopped on his name. Her breathing shallowed. She had held on to his number in a deluded fantasy that one day she'd charm a confession out of him. Never once had she dialed the number, but it was now or never. Her neck muscles tensed. She hit the call button.

"The number you are calling is no longer listed."

"Can you believe it?" Josh's voice boomed from somewhere behind her.

Her hand flew to her heart, and she spun around. She'd never once reacted to Josh's closeness like this, but right now, everything felt too on the edge. "You scared me," she said, trying to keep her voice light.

He smiled, exposing the small gap between his two front teeth.

She stepped back. "Believe what?"

His lips kinked. "Those idiots lost some of my images." He pointed at a drop of blood on her jeans. "What's that?"

She cast around for the nearest SS and exhaled. "Did you see the latest D-notice?"

He cradled the N16 camera in his hands and shook his head. "D-notice over what? And what's that got to do with the blood on your jeans?"

"Let's get some coffee."

They moved to the edge of the sidewalk where a vendor had set up his coffee stand, a permanent fixture in front of the Canary.

Kelly glanced again at the SS, turned her back to it, and ordered a cup of black tea. "Do you remember the journalist who trained me at the Daily Times?"

Josh squinted.

"Christopher Mallow," she said. "The Elite Squad arrested him this morning. Brutally arrested him." She paused and glanced at her jeans. "A D-notice was issued, preventing any write-ups on the matter."

Josh squeezed his temples between his index finger and thumb. "Christopher Mallow?" Josh's hand muffled his voice.

The vendor placed their drinks on the counter, and a tiny tremor traveled up Kelly's arm.

Grabbing the drinks, Josh led her away from the vendor, the hotel, and the paps, who would be all too eager for a story about a reporter breaking a D-notice. "Isn't he a data journalist these days? What do they want with him?"

"The whole thing was strange," she said. "One minute, he's uploading, next minute, the Elite Squad took him in. Beat him up pretty good too when he tried to escape." The hot tea warmed her hands. "Right in front of me in the echo chamber."

Josh's brow shot up as though a jolt rattled him. He studied her face, and for a moment, she thought he might reach out to her, offer some gesture of comfort. Instead, he looked away. "The Elite Squad aren't just enforcers. They have an investigation unit, too. They'll be crawling all over the Daily Times. Might shut it down by week's end."

Kelly's throat tightened. She'd watched Christopher bleed, and all anyone could talk about was not investigating it. Spence, freezing the crime desk, had been steering his staff away from a dangerous future, she now realized, and she felt a stab of guilt for giving him a hard time. "Daily Times staff had nothing to do with whatever Mallow was up to."

Josh glanced at her sideways. "What happened to Kelly-logic?"

She scratched her neck. Faulty logic got her in trouble in the Smith Affair. "This time, I have to consider all the angles before I jump into this thing. I don't need another retraction on my record."

"For what it's worth, I still think you were on the right track with Smith. That whole facial recognition trick was...well, let's not dwell on that." He looked at her directly then, and she saw something in his eyes she couldn't quite name. Concern, maybe. Or guilt. "Did you work with Mallow while he was a foreign correspondent?"

She shook her head. "He'd come back from Syria by then and got himself in trouble tracking down former ISIS fighters in London. By the time he was training me, he was relegated to desk duty." She sipped her tea. "Why do you ask?"

"Knowing him...," Josh said, "he was probably onto something having to do with the Truth Laws, but I wouldn't get involved if I were you."

A lump settled in her gut. "Rooting out corruption was his real gig," she said.

Josh rocked on his heels.

"Apparently, there was a video aired online this morning. Something about a raid," she said. "The Truth Laws fugitive was Mallow."

Josh flicked on his watch. "Let's have a look."

"It's already been scrubbed."

He squinted. "That was fast."

"As fast as the D-notice." Kelly shifted the paper cup to her other hand. "Can you find out who might've filmed the footage?"

"We're all under an NDA of some kind. No one's going to talk, not on the first day of the Truth Laws."

"I need to find out what was on that video and what Mallow was working on." Kelly sneezed. "If you hear something, let me know."

"You need to be careful snooping around. Someone isn't going to like it."

The paps' voices suddenly amplified. Josh and Kelly whirled around. Two paps were fighting over a patch on the pavement.

"Too much caffeine," she said.

"Too much cocaine."

A scratch tickled Kelly's throat, and she slurped down more tea. "I keep wondering who has the most to gain from keeping Mallow quiet."

"You can probably contact some of the people Mallow worked with, find out what they know."

"Everything Mallow is off-limits. Spence shut down the crime desk."

Josh raised his eyebrows. "Who got to him?"

"He says he made the preemptive decision himself. At first, I thought that was a bunch of bullshit too, but now that you reminded me of the Elite Squad taking on investigative powers—"

"I'd go with your first impression. Don't let that shit with Smith derail you. Just think carefully about it. But the closer you get to the truth, Kel, the darker it can get."

Josh's sentiment tallied with her exposé on Smith, the exposé that Greaves had retracted. But this time, her lead was in prison, guarded by the Elite Squad. "If I decide to look into Mallow's case, I'll need...equipment."

"You still have the neutralizer?"

As of today, that little biorhythm converter had become more valuable than the Blue Moon Diamond. She nodded.

"For extras, go to the Luntan," he said.

Kelly sneezed again.

"You okay?"

"Just a cold coming on. The bank's damn algorithms drained my account. Paid all my bills except the heating bill, of course." She pinched her nostrils. "The Luntan. Isn't that a hackers' haven?"

"Still is, but it has evolved. You'll find all sorts there now, and you're gonna need money. You'll also need money for equipment, so this is what you do. When you get into the Luntan, ask for Roseman. He's got every-thing, even if he says he doesn't. The counter-surveillance stuff can get pretty pricey, so charge it to the Channel."

She laced her hands in front of her. The Channel was an unofficial pool of donations made by anonymous journalists and photographers. In exchange, the donors received on-the-ground intelligence. George Barry's network was peanuts in comparison.

Kelly had stayed away from The Channel because she never had cash to spare. And the whole group thing, even if it was anonymous, didn't feel right. Not to mention, if anyone found out she was associated with a network of undercover journalists, she'd be done. Worse, she'd have no one to blame but herself.

A flash flared against the Canary's gilded doors. The legion of paps dropped their lattes and cappuccinos. Hot liquid splashed onto the road and formed a steam bath of toffee-colored liquid. Video cameras and recorders took center stage.

"I have to get to work." Josh grabbed his camera. "Message me."

She gave him a thumbs-up, and he merged with the crowd.

Peter Lajay stepped out of the gated entrance of the Canary, his eyes hidden behind sunglasses, his body wrapped in a fur coat. A wall of light flared.

The flashes blinded her. She squinted and, for a moment, wished she had chosen the camera as her weapon. Their work was simple. Point. Focus. Shoot. Words and thoughts balanced on the edge of the Truth Laws abyss. Deep down, she knew she wouldn't have it any other way.

She set off at a brisk pace, generating much-needed heat in her cold limbs. As she hurried along the street, unbidden, the memory of that day in Greaves's office flooded back. How he'd looked up from reading the piece she'd written on Ian Smith, shaking his head. "Kelly, you're chasing shadows," he'd said. "There's nothing here."

Holding herself back from digging into Mallow's arrest was killing her. But the whole thing stank; she knew in her gut there was more to it. Shivering against the cold, she hurried away from the still-clamoring crowd behind her.

SEVEN

RIGHT NOW, Josh wanted nothing more than to bolt from the steps of the Canary. That news about Christopher's arrest had changed everything —but worse was the lie he'd just told Kelly. *I don't know anything about that footage.* The words sat like acid in his throat. He glanced over at Kelly, who was still making her way out of the crowd, still too close. Making a sudden move now would alert his fellow paps to something being up— undoubtedly, word about the failed mission was already making the rounds. It wouldn't be long before his crafty colleagues sniffed his connection to Christopher's arrest, however tenuous. When they figured it out, they'd set upon him like rabid dogs.

Paps hollered around him, cameras clicked. "This way, Peter!"

Josh set his camera to auto-focus, pressed the shutter button, and took cover under the Peter Lajay spectacle. The gravity of Christopher's arrest grew heavier with every click. No self-preserving journalist would touch the story, and as for Kelly, she'd be shut down in an instant. Now more than ever, the Resistance Network was the only fighting chance the country had to subvert the Truth Laws and wrestle freedom back from the State. Assuming his footage was used to track down Christopher, the Network would eventually find out and turn on him, too.

He checked his watch. Not a message from anyone in the Resistance about Mallow's arrest today. Their silence stung.

Peter Lajay's bodyguards stretched their arms in front of the clicking cameras. The paps ducked and dodged around them, flashing away for that special, final shot. Unfocussed shots meant less money, but Josh played along and clicked the last round of useless photos. Josh's eyes shifted—something unsaid about the source, a lie in the shadows. His lie. To Kelly. A limo pulled up to the curb and squeezed the paps onto the narrow sidewalk. The show was almost over.

Kelly wouldn't let another truth die buried—her redemption started with that raid footage. She'd looked him right in the eye and asked for his help. And he'd lied to her face. Worse than exile from the Network would be Kelly's reaction once she discovered the footage was his. He'd be forced to choose between her and the Resistance—a choice he could never make. He stumbled back.

Recovering, he refocused on Lajay and held down the shutter button. The only way to keep himself out of danger—the only way to bury what he'd just done to Kelly—was to get his footage of the Elite Squad's raid on Christopher's building back from Percy.

He let the charged-up paps jostle him from his position as Peter Lajay ducked into the back seat of the black-windowed limo. In the distance, Kelly's silhouette was but a dark speck at last. The lie walked away with her. Josh let go of the shutter button and lowered his camera. He drifted to the back of the crowd, pulled the flashgun off of his N16, and slipped it into its case.

Lajay's limo door shut with a low, soft thud. A frenzy of flashes bounced off the pavement and blacked-out windows. The limo drove off.

It was time to get his footage back.

Josh worked his way to the edge of the crowd.

"Hey, Josh." He tensed and turned. It was Quentin, a hard-core pap who sold photos by the dozen. "Coming to the pub?"

"Not today, mate." Josh hoped his tone sounded casual. "Got some work to do."

"Who for?" Quentin could be part of the Resistance, but it was doubtful. Missions were time-consuming and sporadic, and Quentin was bent on making every daylight hour pay.

"Corporate," Josh said.

"If you need a second camera, give us a shout."

"Will do." Josh locked the camera case in the seat of his bike, exchanged the case for his helmet, and revved up the engine.

TWENTY MINUTES LATER, he ran up the stairwell in Percy's office block, rushing past its peeling paint and skid marks on the walls. On the second floor, a light glowed through Percy's frosted office window. Josh barged in and swept past Angela. Her chair legs scraped the floor as she stood. Her nail file clinked on the concrete floor.

"Hey!"

He ignored her and burst into Percy's office. Percy was sitting behind his desk, munching on a white bread sandwich. Paper stuck out of manila folders piled in the corner, cables and wires cut across the floor.

"My footage from last night. Where is it?"

Percy leaned back in his chair. "I can't disclose that information."

Josh whipped off his helmet. "Did they use my footage in the newscast that was wiped off the web this morning?"

"They're always wiping footage off the web."

"You know which one I'm talking about."

Percy finished chewing the bite of sandwich and swallowed. "It's now considered evidence, so I can't return it to you if that's what you want."

"Evidence?"

Percy took another bite of sandwich. "I don't want any trouble, Josh."

"You're the one who called for the shoot last night."

Percy swept his tongue over the white bread glued to his front teeth. He brushed it off with his finger and wiped it on his shirt. "You should've recorded the newscast before they took it down."

"Wouldn't be here if I did."

"That's too bad. It was damn good."

"I want my raw footage back."

"No can do, my friend. If you're worried about the money—"

"It's not the money."

"Not the money?" Percy put down the sandwich. "How can it not be about money?" He waved his hands in the air as if praying.

Josh stretched across the desk and leaned into Percy's oily face. "It's for my portfolio."

"I shouldn't need to remind you, your contract prohibits you from disclosing what happened last night." Percy's breath reeked of cheese and onion. Josh nearly gagged, and he stepped back. "You lied to me about what I was filming. You lured me with the story of a football player getting nicked at a drug den. That's the only reason I was there."

"You're not an idiot." Percy chugged down water and smacked his lips. "When you saw the Elite Squad bulldoze into that building, you should've known."

Josh grabbed Percy's t-shirt. "A drug bust. That's what you said." His eyes widened. "But you saw all those people hustled out of the building and that little kid crying."

Josh released Percy. "You fucking sold me out."

"I didn't sell you out." Percy smoothed his t-shirt. "Hell, I would've got more money for you had I known the Ministry of Information was...." Percy's breath hitched, his jaw clenched.

The slip almost knocked Josh out. "The Ministry of Information?" He paced the room. "MI fucking 5?"

"So what? Happens all the time. It's me you should be worried about. If you find my dead body floating in the Thames—"

"You'd do a deal with the devil if it saved your ass."

Percy cocked his head. "I take that as a compliment."

"It's not meant to be." Josh stopped pacing and grappled with the reality that MI5 was involved and that his footage was sitting on someone's desk inside that building, metadata and all. "So, who in MI5 has my video footage from last night?"

"How the hell should I know? It's MI5. They probably don't even know their own names." Percy rolled his shoulders. "Good news, though

An NGO who advocates for journalists got wind of the Elite Squad raiding the building. They told the ICO, and now the Commissioner is looking to protect me, well, us."

"Fuck the Commissioner and fuck the NGO."

Percy's face scrunched up as though someone were pulling out his toenails. "I need to know who ordered my footage to go offline."

"Keep your voice down. I'm just the bag man, okay?" Percy shuffled papers on his desk and found one he had scribbled on. "The Commissioner's name is Lydia Rackham. She might know."

No way in hell was Josh going to call some bureaucrat.

"She's on our side," Percy pleaded. "But I know what you mean. After the Truth Laws, it's been a fucking circus. Actually, it's been a fucking circus for a while." He shook his head and shoved the paper at Josh. "But the Commissioner lady can help."

"Was my name cited on the webcast?"

Percy shook his head. "Then how did they know the footage came out of your office?"

A flush crept across Percy's cheeks. "When I saw the footage online, I made some noise about it. We got two million hits and no cash." His voice traveled up a few octaves. "An NGO called me to verify if the footage came from this office. Then, I got an email from an assistant to the Commissioner. I didn't give your name out." Percy pulled his belt over his potbelly. "I protect my talent."

"You protect your paycheck."

"Same thing. I have standards."

Didn't matter that Percy didn't disclose Josh's name. His name and address were in the metadata—standard procedure when submitting footage. Busting on Percy was futile at this point. He stepped back. "NGO, ICO, MI5, Jesus Christ, I don't care who asks, don't give my name out, Percy. I want this whole thing to die."

"What's this got to do with, Josh?"

"Don't worry about it."

"Don't worry about it? You come in here, frickin' all over me, and I'm supposed to forget it?"

There had to be a better way to find that footage and destroy it, or at least wipe Josh's ID off. Before Kelly found out what he'd done. "Percy, do me that favor."

"But—"

"Stick to the usual vetted contacts. If anyone calls asking about me, tell them you don't know where I am."

Josh stormed out of the office.

EIGHT

9 January

KELLY SWIPED her card at the entrance of Global Wires, and hot air blasted her like a sandstorm. Her face prickled in the heat. Heather still hadn't responded to her messages for a meetup. She shook off the tension in her shoulders.

She climbed the last flight of stairs and reached the double doors, her lungs pumping, her thighs throbbing. Huffing, she pressed in the code to unlock the doors and stepped into the newsroom.

The smell of hot toast hung in the air. Fingertips tapped on virtual keyboards that projected their pin lights onto any and every flat surface. A mash-up of foreign languages blared through speakers. Some journalists dictated directly into laptops.

Spence was striding across the newsroom in the direction of the fish-bowl—their nickname for the conference room. Upon seeing her, he halted in midstride. "Blackwell, what do you call this?" He was clutching a bundle of papers in one hand and a cup of coffee in the other.

She froze. "What do I call what?"

He scrutinized her over the rim of his glasses. "The time."

She glanced at the large digital clock in the center of the ceiling. Fifteen minutes to nine. "I'm early."

His eyes narrowed. "Didn't you get the message?"

Slowly, she rotated toward the clear glass windows of the fishbowl. Samantha, Lily, Trevor, Hassan—the main desk editors—were sitting around the oval conference table. They were all facing the owner of Global Wires. "Shit!"

Kelly rushed toward the fishbowl, Spence right behind her. The editorial meeting was in full swing. She tiptoed along the floor-to-ceiling glass windows. Her cheeks burned as she took the seat next to Harry and dumped her backpack under the table.

Damian Winters's charcoal-colored suit hugged his athletic physique. The gray hair at his temples added a sophisticated, wise air to the man who already possessed an aura of hard-earned power. A rare visitor to the newsroom, he provoked an almost reverential response from his employees, probably because he could change everything with two simple words: you're fired.

"As I was saying..." Damian Winters stood shoulder to shoulder with Spence. "Everyone, meet the new compliance officer, Geneva Winters."

A young woman sprang off the sofa behind Damian. She was clad in a silver, oversized man's shirt tucked in at the waist of her black slacks. Her blue eyes glimmered. "I'm so excited to meet you all."

She greeted the journalists one by one. When she got to Kelly, her gaze lingered for a tad longer than was comfortable. Kelly broke the young woman's gaze and turned her attention to Damian.

"She will oversee office activities." Damian closed in on the conference table like a conquering warlord. "She is only here so that Global Wires remains a respectable news outlet. As such, Geneva will oversee computer activities, and she'll report back to me at the end of every day."

Kelly looked at Geneva and back at Damian. Their resemblance was unmistakable. Somewhere deep inside, Kelly recoiled. She didn't know Damian well, but she didn't expect the media mogul to be just another crony businessman handing his daughter a job Kelly had worked her ass off to keep. She pulled in her chin.

Lily cleared her throat. "We have confidential sources on our computers."

Spence stepped forward. "And they will remain confidential."

Damian nodded. "Correct. Geneva will also be tasked with trailing all the heads, one at a time."

The journalists stared at Damian, their breaths soundless.

Spence clasped his hands in front of his chest. "The first one she will trail is Kelly."

Hearing the words come out of his mouth was a gut punch that forced a nod, but Kelly would not be cowed by Damian or his little spy. First, her desk stowed in the deep freeze, and now this. She threw a caustic look at Spence. "I have a lot on my plate at the moment."

He stepped back. "It'll only be a couple of months."

Kelly's facial muscles tightened, but she hardened her smile. Her most recent searches were all on Christopher, the subject of the most recent D-notice. Her mind raced for a justification for why her computer should be left alone. She came up empty.

The air around Kelly constricted. They probably already knew about her internet searches on Christopher Mallow. Something else was up. Maybe they were downsizing—making the workplace so unbearable that the journalists would be forced to resign. Maybe they didn't want to pay benefits. Kelly bit her lip for fear she'd explode in front of everyone.

Geneva edged toward Kelly. "Nice to meet you, Kelly." She held out her hand.

Reluctantly, Kelly shook it. "I wish I had been told about this earlier. I would've lined up a juicy story to work on."

All around the table, the journalists sank into their seats, as if to protect themselves from the brewing trouble.

Spence piped up. "Everyone will be trailed. No exceptions."

A murmur filled the fishbowl.

Damian stepped forward. "Our primary goal for Global Wires is to remain compliant with The Truth Laws." He turned to Kelly. "I think Geneva will learn a lot from you."

She'd heard this kind of flattery before, and it was usually a cover for something else. She could challenge him, but instead, she placed her hand over her heart. "I'm honored."

"I'm a fast learner, and I won't get in your way," Geneva said.

Kelly gave her one of her crescent moon smiles. "How long will I be trailed again?"

"A couple of months."

"Perfect timing. Right after the crime desk got frozen."

Harry cowered in his chair, sinking his head into his shoulders.

"Kelly, the truth is...," Damian said. "We have no alternative."

Her blood simmered under her skin. There was always an alternative, but she held her tongue. "Are there any other surprises I should know about?"

"I'm reassigning you to arts and entertainment."

She felt her jaw drop. "Just shoot me now."

Lily shot up from her seat at the end of the table. "No way. I can't work with her."

Spence raised his hands. "Now that we're on the desk reshuffle..."

Chairs squeaked as the journalists whipped around, looking at each other.

Damian tipped his head toward Spence. "Geneva and I will wait outside."

Spence clapped his hands. "We have to stay focused. Kelly will be covering the Live Earth Concert now. Lily, be sure to give her the contact details."

"I've been working on securing the Shiva interview for the past three months—"

"Things change, Lily. We all have to get used to it."

Kelly sat in a daze while Spence reassigned all the heads with new duties, their voices laced with disappointment and frustration.

"Blackwell."

Spence's voice snapped her out of her daze.

"I want to see you in my office in ten."

NINE

RETURNING FROM A BRISK WALK OUTSIDE, Kelly came to her desk. A dusty imprint was all that was left of her computer.

"What the hell?"

"New girl," Harry nodded at the fishbowl.

Kelly's computer was sitting on the conference table where Geneva was setting up her new station. Everything she'd worked for, every source she'd protected, every story she'd built—sitting there for someone else to sift through.

Blood shot to Kelly's face. "Screw this." She dumped her knapsack onto Harry's desk and strode toward Spence's office. She barged in.

"You're late again. Close the door."

She slammed it shut. A pile of black tablets was stacked along the edge of his desk like sandbags lining a trench.

"Where's my computer?"

"Please, sit down."

She was tempted to swipe the pile of tablets, which would surely provoke him, get him to feel like she felt—sidelined, discarded, ignored. Instead, she took a deep breath, marshaling every bit of control she possessed, and placed a pile of tablets on the floor. "Where is my computer, and what is really going on?"

The deep grooves on Spence's forehead ironed out to faint lines. "It's being scanned for Truth Laws compliance. You'll get it back when Geneva's done with it. In the meantime, you'll be given a new one, temporarily."

Over the years, she had faced down threats, intimidation, slashed bike tires—the reason she now chose to walk everywhere—but Spence's sagging posture behind the desk, that sorry look in his eyes, she could barely stomach. He looked beaten down. "Ever since I've been here, I've followed the rules."

"No one's disputing that, Kelly. You're a good journalist. The best at what you do. That's why Geneva is trailing you first."

"Remind me not to be employee of the month next time."

His hands tapped on the table. "Don't worry. You won't be getting any awards for your attitude." He pulled his hands toward his chest. "Lucky for you, celebrities love the spotlight, can't help themselves, so they'll actually want to talk to you as long as you're on A&E, the safest place for you at the moment." He unclasped his hands and leaned forward. "Under that desk, you can do what you need to do."

He seemed to be implying he knew about her undercover investigation into Christopher's arrest and that she could use the A&E desk as her cover, but she wasn't sure. "You mean—"

His head bobbed ever so gently, it was almost imperceptible. Then he turned his weary eyes toward the ceiling. "I want you to comply—" his voice raised, "to the new rules."

She sighed. "Everyone will comply," she said, for the hidden mics that were being heard by others.

Spence exhaled as though releasing deep-seated tension.

She rested her hand on her lap. Maybe Spence was adjusting to the new reality better than she had given him credit for. After all, he had managed to gather a bunch of stray journalists and formed a news team that kept people reading serious news to this day. But the melancholy of what the news was becoming hung heavy in her chest. First Christopher, now this. Everything was being taken away, piece by piece, and all she could do was watch it happen. "I guess we did it to ourselves."

"Did what?"

She blinked. "The sweepers. The echo chambers. The Truth Laws. The frozen crime desk."

"We're in a new era." Spence's tone hinted at despair.

"At least Christopher Mallow went down fighting."

"And look where it got him." He leaned in. "No one here will put this office at risk."

She stared at Spence, each protected by the oak desk between them.

"Tell me you understand," he said.

She pressed her lips together. It's not like she could resign and find a job somewhere else. Choices had narrowed for everyone, especially for Kelly. She should feel grateful for having a job at all, but all she felt was a sharp pain deep in her gut. She'd tell Spence what he needed to hear, what anyone else listening needed to hear. But not one of them could stop her from asking questions. She squared her shoulders. "Of course, I—"

"One last thing." He tapped his hands on the desk. "I know the girl is an irritation—you didn't hear that from me—but do us all a favor and just cooperate with her. It's only a few weeks." He stared at Kelly for a long second.

The last thing she wanted was to make Geneva's life easy, but Spence wasn't just her boss. He meant more to her than just a boss. In the Winter of 2028, after months of not selling a single story, Kelly had come home to a headhunter on her doorstep. Under Spence's order, the headhunter hired her on the spot. He never divulged his reasons for hiring her, but that didn't matter. He had hired her when no other media outlet would even meet with her, and for that, she owed him. "I'll cooperate," she said. "But only because you're the one asking."

"Good. Now, go. A & E awaits."

FAINT TAPS on a keyboard cut through the somber atmosphere in the newsroom. Lily slouched at her desk, stone-faced. Samantha's seat was abandoned. Today marked the moment that all their work got taken from them, reconstituted, and forced fed back, whether they liked it or not. All because of the Truth Laws. Kelly knew she could only pretend to go along with the new demands for so long before some part of her died. She wasn't going to let that happen. She'd rather go down fighting, like Christopher.

She walked down the middle aisle, passing rows of empty desks. The person she wanted to talk to most was Heather, but with the crime desk frozen, she would have to find a sideways angle into the Christopher story without tripping the algorithmic alerts.

She slowed her pace. Several of Mallow's articles had been coauthored with a guy named Stan Bletchley, published weeks before Christopher's arrest. They had questioned the zettabytes of data collected by the Ministry of Information, MI5. Stan Bletchley could be her in, and the person who could confirm that was Trevor, head of the tech desk. Plus, an in-person search didn't tip off the algorithms. She made a beeline to Trevor's desk.

"Hey, Trevor, can I ask you something?"

His hands froze over his keyboard. "Can it wait?"

"I'll be quick."

He smacked his lips and looked at her through yellow-tinted glasses.

She leaned toward him. "When was the last time Global Wires did an article on data collection devices and the amount of data collected by the government?"

"That's more like a thesis." His brows furrowed. "Months of work for one person."

"And if two people worked on it?"

"Fewer months." He shrugged. "With so many new devices being introduced all the time, the article would be out of date within a week."

"Does the name Stan Bletchley ring a bell?"

"I'm not in tech anymore." Trevor let out a scornful snort. "Remember?"

She leaned in close. Christopher's freedom, and her own sanity, depended on her pushing through all the despair. "It's prep for Live Earth."

"Right." He pursed his lips. "He works over at TechTonic."

Her watch vibrated against her wrist. She flinched. It was Omar, her few-times-a-month lover, who claimed to work in the Ministry of Transport. "Thanks," she said to Trevor and started down the aisle.

"Hey," she said into her watch.

"Do you want to do dinner tonight?" Omar's voice sounded light, a contrast to the morose silence surrounding her.

"I'm not—"

"My treat."

She walked toward Harry. The only rule she and Omar had was to keep work talk to a minimum, confining their conversations to food, fashion, and culture—very little conversation at all. "I have too much going on."

"We'll keep it low-key. How about if I drive over with some food, bring some wine?"

He shouldn't drink, and she couldn't drink, but she arrived at Harry's desk and wasn't about to deliver a lecture in front of the town crier. She nodded at Harry and slung her backpack over her shoulder.

"You know I don't drink."

"Is there anything you do need?"

She paused in midstride. He had contacts. The right phone call could get her information about the Elite Squad and the Zone, the place where Christopher Mallow probably ended up. Who knew what Omar would let slip under the influence of a glass of Burgundy? "I can do tomorrow. Can you bring decaf coffee?"

"Tomorrow's good. Coffee though?"

She started walking again.

"All right. Let's say eight-thirty."

She closed the line and slumped in the chair next to Lily, who was talking to someone on her watch. The smell of gardenias and powder filled the air surrounding the former A & E editor. Kelly actually sympathized with Lily's plight until she remembered how capable Lily was of stabbing someone in the back with an engraved letter opener.

Lily got off the line and turned to Kelly. "What do you want?"

"If you have a problem with the new arrangements, take it up with Spence."

A scathing look flashed across Lily's eyes.

"I need your notes on Shiva so I can get up to speed in time for the concert."

"Saturday. The concert is on Saturday, the nineteenth." Lily's lips curled. "You better not screw this up for me. I will get back on A & E, and when I do, I don't want this desk's reputation in tatters."

Kelly fastened the backpack on her shoulder as Lily woke up her computer screen. "Just email it to me." She turned to the double doors.

"Where are you going? Don't you have to meet with the new compliance officer?"

"No."

Lily blinked.

Kelly's need to research Stan Bletchley, and eventually meet with him at TechTonic, moved to the top of her list. "I have something important to do. If compliance needs me, she can call me."

TEN

10 January

SWEAT ROLLED down Josh's back while he waited for his online footprint to travel from Morocco to Frankfurt and back to its final destination—his secret den in his home in London. First, he had to find, then verify, Percy's version of events. After that, the real work would start: locating the footage on someone's computer in MI5—a tall order.

At last, Percy's email account popped up on one of Josh's three screens.

Even though his connection was doubly encrypted, he held back from diving in. If the State found him hacking into Percy's email and destroying the footage, he'd be in no better position than Christopher. Maybe worse. He took a sip of his vodka-spiked black coffee.

"I can always change the IP address manually." He muttered self-assurances to himself, shoring up his anxiety. "Every five minutes if I have to."

He sat up straighter and placed the mug down among the mismatched keyboards, camera storage cards, and taped-up burner phones. He stretched his fingers and his knuckles popped.

In Percy's inbox, he found old marketing emails, a stock photo request from Lily Henderson of the Daily Times for shots of Peter Lajay, The Negotiator's Handbook PDF, and an email from CleanFluff groomers.

He chuckled, his neck muscles loosened. "Percy has a dog?"

He came to an email from the NGO, and then one from the Commissioner's office. Both on the same day, the morning after the raid, an hour apart.

His stomach hollowed. He manually changed his IP address and waited. When the connection was stable, he clicked on the email from the Commissioner's office.

Dear Mr. Percy Mandeville,

In accordance with The Truth Laws of 2030, please forward any and all footage your crew filmed of Building 10 on Monday, January 7, 2030.

In addition, please provide a list of the names of all the videographers present.

Sincerely,

Mr. Collier

Assistant to the Commissioner of Information

It was less of a request than a demand.

Josh clicked open the sent folder and scanned its contents. Percy's email response to Mr. Collier included a hosted link to download a sizeable encrypted file.

"Shit."

Breaking into the host of that downloadable file would be labor-intensive but doable. Only then would he know whether his name was on the list Percy had sent over, but so far, Percy's story checked out. Josh slumped back in his chair.

No doubt, Mr. Collier would have downloaded Percy's attached file—whatever it was—and it was now sitting on his computer.

The realization sent an alarm through Josh's mind. Collier's computer was hackable, but it was also at the Commissioner's Office, less secure than MI5 but still fortified. Hacking into two heavily secured computers—if he made it that far—was prison time. At best. Whatever bravery he had evaporated. He threaded a hand through his hair.

One of the burner phones rang.

His muscles rattled.

The ID was hidden. Could only be the Resistance, the only ones who had his burner numbers, but with the Truth Laws in full force, and Christopher in custody, he hesitated to answer. "Get a grip, Josh."

He pressed the go button and stayed silent, like he always did.

"Christopher Mallow has been captured," a man on the line said.

Josh pulled the phone closer to his mouth. "I'm aware."

"The plan has changed. We need to meet."

His fingers tingled at the thought of being brought back into the mission. Maybe they would ask him to lead it this time. "Who should I book?"

"Laura Cassavetes."

The name wasn't real. The connectors used aliases, and he never knew their real names. Sometimes a guy would show up. Sometimes a woman. But the message they delivered was always critical and trustworthy and free of digital fingerprints.

Maybe a raw copy of the footage would encourage them to task him with the mission. Correction, a clean copy of the raw footage credited to a nonexistent person. When the footage got circulated, it would cause confusion when compared to the edited version already in circulation. "I have something you might find helpful," he said.

"Oh? You know what to do."

The line went dead.

Josh brought his screen back to life, closed Percy's email, and inserted a hard drive labeled with the date of the raid on Christopher's house. He pressed play.

A weeping child crouched on the wet pavement in front of Building 10 and sent a quiver through Josh. That was the one. He pressed stop.

He opened the EXIF metadata bleaching software and wiped the data clean. Now, no one would ever link him to this version of the footage. He copied it to a clean hard drive. In the creator's ID line, he typed in Jack Smith.

The common name would have MI5 and the Commissioner hunting down every Jack Smith in the country. Could take weeks.

It would look too obvious now if he added the fake Jack Smith name to the Percy list. Better leave it. Having complied with the Commissioner's orders, Percy could talk his way out of any hole. Satisfied, Josh ejected the hard drive and opened a fresh window.

He clicked on the TrueLove bookmark at the top of the window. According to the website, Josh had been on five dates in December. Felt about right. In the search box, he typed in Laura Cassavetes.

The profile was of a twenty-eight-year-old single woman. One of her album photos showed her playing with a black cocker spaniel. In others, she rode a brown and white horse. Her other hobbies were scuba diving and cooking. Laura Cassavetes, a lover of the outdoors, looked way too happy to be living in this world.

Despite her shiny appeal, she wasn't someone he would date, even if she were real. He thought back to Kelly, the only one he had ever loved. Still loved.

He refocused on the Laura avatar and pressed the request connection button. Thirty seconds later, his request was accepted.

From under a nonworking tablet in his drawer, he pulled out a yellow silk pocket handkerchief—the signal indicating he was a member of the Resistance. The raw footage of the Elite Squad raid on Christopher's home, filmed by Jack Smith, was ready to be delivered.

ELEVEN

A FAN HEATER under one arm and her bag at her hip, Kelly flipped the deadlocks shut and leaned against the door, defeat weighing heavily on her shoulders. Stan Bletchley had been too afraid to talk to her, despite being outside, far away from the SS. Her bag slid down her arm; she set down the heater and closed her eyes.

Even now, in the safety of her studio flat, she still saw Christopher's bloodied eyes flash in her mind, his cheek bruised, his arm broken. She couldn't shake the image lodged in her mind, but the neutralizer might help balance out the erratic impulses she was sending out.

"The Kendra Thompson search is complete."

She startled and spun toward Jerko.

Its red eye pulsed.

She groaned. It usually did a decent job of getting her search results on time, but lately, it had been out of sorts, and she made a mental note to shake up its algorithms. "It's a little late for that now."

She opened a drawer in her kitchenette, dropped her watch in, and grabbed the dome-shaped eyepatch shell. Next, she hauled a chair in from the bedroom and placed it under Jerko. Shell in hand, she reached up and snapped it onto Jerko's red pulsing eye. "Penalty for the pain and suffering you are causing." She hopped down.

She made her way to the bathroom and pulled out a wicker basket from under the basin. The basket overflowed with spray-on shampoo, deodorant, micro-soap flannel cloths—guaranteed for twenty body washes —and it was all there to mask the jewel in the crown: the neutralizer.

She picked up its plum velvet pouch and let the hard plastic case, two small electrodes, and cotton pads slip out onto her palm. This delicate thing was powerful enough to gloss over the rough edges of her biometrics until she looked sleek as liquid steel to the eye of every SS. But Josh had warned, more than once, that a missing digital footprint was as suspicious to the SS as an erratic one, so she should only use it once a week. But most people hadn't had her kind of week. After this baby was done with her, she'd be restored to being an average person having an average day. She picked up an electrode and fiddled it into the tiny hole at the top. *Click*!

The assuring sound filled her with calm. She stretched out on her bed and slid her fingers along her rib cage until she came to the hollow of her solar plexus. She flattened the sticky side of the pad against her skin and set her watch to go off in thirty minutes.

The phase one mapping process began, and a soothing warm ripple radiated from her center. A flicker of a smile passed over her lips, her arms dropped to her sides.

Minutes later, a loud bang shook her front door.

Kelly's eyes shot open.

Another round of bangs. "Kelly Blackwell." The voice on the other side of her door sounded urgent.

"Who is it?" She kept her voice as light as she could.

"Metropolitan Police."

She stiffened. "Shit." She cleared her throat. "Can you come back later?"

"We just have a few questions to ask," he said. "It won't take long."

Her heart rate quickened. They weren't going away. "One minute!"

She cradled the neutralizer and electrodes and eased her sweater over her torso, careful not to snag the delicate wires.

Making her way toward the door, she tucked the body of the neutralizer under her armpit.

On the other side of the peephole, two uniformed officers waited. Like the troopers in the echo chamber, one was short, the other tall. Too tall. Too muscled. Kelly straightened her back and swung open the door.

"I'm PC Blake and this is my partner, PC Wainwright."

His deep, mellow voice jumbled her defenses. She glanced down the corridor. "Is something wrong?"

He ran his eye down all four deadlocks as if counting them. "Are those legal?"

After months of having them, had someone reported her? She put on her most innocent smile. "Why wouldn't they be?"

"They're manual."

It had taken her quite a lot of research to find deadlocks that operated independently of computer security systems. She stepped in front of the locks. "I wasn't aware manual deadlocks were illegal." She crossed her arms, holding the neutralizer in place. "As I'm sure you are aware, crime is getting worse and being a single woman, I need strong deterrence."

Wainwright glanced at Blake. "Building regulations stipulate only certain types of locks can be bolted onto the door."

Kelly had to get them on their way and a tit-for-tat over deadlocks would defeat the goal. "I'll look into it and replace them if I have to. Is that all?"

"We have a case of a missing person who we think you might have seen," Blake said.

Wainwright peered over her shoulder and into her studio flat as Blake presented a photo on his tablet. It was the kid from the chamber, the scavenger. Oliver Green. Something in her hardened, and she was tempted to turn him in, here and now, but if the police were here asking about him, maybe the kid wasn't a rat after all. "Who is he?"

"So you did see him?" PC Wainwright asked.

The neutralizer vibrated against her ribs, sending a flutter through her body. If they saw it, if they asked what it was, everything would unravel. She jerked. "He looks like an average kid, so I can't be sure."

"You seem nervous, Ms. Blackwell."

Her watch buzzed behind her. "I'm pressed for time. I have a deadline to meet."

"We all have targets to meet," Blake said.

Kelly's stomach heated. "Yes, of course."

"Is everything all right?"

"Yeah." Something was going on with the neutralizer because the skin against her ribs throbbed hot. "I'm just in a bit of a rush." She softened her tone, hoping a touch of submission would move them along faster.

Blake fixed her with a stare. "We all have important things to do, Ms. Blackwell."

She took a long, deep breath in. "If I remember anything specific, I'll send you a message if you leave your contact details. But—"

"You seem eager to go."

"Quite," Wainwright said.

"What's the man's name again?"

"Oliver Green." PC Blake dialed commands into his watch. "I've logged our visit to you and have sent you our details. If you see him, please get in touch as soon as possible."

"Most certainly."

The police officers turned on their heels. PC Wainwright stopped and looked back at her. "Make sure you check those locks with building regulations."

"Yes, of course, officer."

She shut the door, sucked in her breath, and ripped off the neutralizer's sticky patch. Her skin stung, raw and pink. Blood pooled under her skin.

She closed her eyes and breathed out the tension clogging her mind. Everything was piling on top all at once, and she needed to get it all under control.

"Jerko, start a search for anything on Oliver Green."

"You have a visitor due this evening."

She squeezed her eyes, remembering Omar was on his way.

TWELVE

Troy raced across the camp to the main tent, the Underground Freedom Fighters headquarters. When he entered the communal space, some Fighters were coughing violently, their faces sweating; others were doubled over, panting. They'd just returned from their mission in the city, and he could see something had gone wrong. He could see defeat in their eyes. War was hell, he thought, but necessary. He would never have sent them off on this hasty mission, but, as always, he would be cleaning up the mess. First, he had to find out just how big a mess it was. "Felix," Troy yelled in the direction of the kitchen. "Get us some water!"

The dusty ground, swirling like tear gas, began to settle. Eventually, Felix entered the communal room carrying jugs filled with water. The Fighters gulped the clear liquid between heavy breaths as though their lives depended on it. Within minutes, the jugs lay empty.

Rozlyn swept into the tent, her brown skin glimmering, her emerald eyes impenetrable. No matter the crisis, their leader's cool exterior never betrayed her emotions.

"What the hell happened back there?" Sinclair's Scottish-accented tone was brusque.

"Anyone?"

No one replied, no one explained. The men and women slumped as though the weight of failure was too heavy to carry.

"This isn't a spa, people." Sinclair's voice thundered through the tent. "Get on your feet!"

They assembled into a crooked line and stood at attention.

The doors crashed open. Troy whipped around. Catalina stood behind a dark-haired young man who had tumbled onto the floor in front of the line of Fighters.

"Is this the target?"

Catalina nodded.

"Get him up," Troy ordered.

She pushed the young man into a chair, his hands splayed. The chair rocked until the young man's bodyweight anchored it to the ground. His wide eyes flashed through his dark-rimmed glasses, his breath clipped.

Late last night, Rozlyn had received a tip about an alleged double agent playing the Underground Freedom Fighters off against the city-based Resistance. If the agent was left unchecked on the field, his actions could lead the two groups to face off, inevitably culminating in their mutual destruction. It was a good plan, no doubt engineered by someone in government. With both groups out of the way, the government would be unopposed and apply its power at will. Hastily, in Troy's judgment, Rozlyn deployed Sinclair and a few Fighters on an early morning mission to capture the double agent and bring him to the camp alive. But this young man before them seemed far from what Troy expected of a double agent.

Troy raised a laser-printed photo of the reported agent and held it up to the twenty-something man, now shaking on the chair. His green eyes, thin lips, and soft, round face matched the photo. Five feet, eight at a hundred and sixty pounds also matched. Troy lowered the photo and stared at the Prime Minister's nephew, one named Oliver Green.

Troy handed the photo to Sinclair. "The mission to retrieve Oliver Green from the city and bring him to the camp was successful." Troy clenched his hands in front of him. "But it seems we still have a problem."

Catalina shuffled her feet. "I had no choice. I had to fire," she said, her eyes steady.

Rozlyn stepped forward. "Did you shake off the Elite Squad when you came into No Man's Land?"

"Yes, ma'am."

Troy eyed Catalina. "We need a report from the perimeter cameras." Troy turned to Peter. "Get Luke in here."

Peter ran down the passageway toward the comms room.

"The comms crew will tell us exactly what went down," Troy said.

"I have every faith in comms."

Troy's jaw tightened. Rozlyn had glossed over Catalina's screw-ups too many times. At some point, in private, he would have to address Rozlyn's lenient attitude directly. "Comms'll need twenty-four hours to confirm how far the Elite Squad penetrated No Man's Land. I suggest we use the time to prep for all eventualities."

Rozlyn lifted her chin in his direction. "If the mission took a turn in the wrong direction, we'll decide what to do then."

Her angled chin sent a jolt of defiance through Troy, but he held himself in check. Now was not the time.

Luke sprinted into the tent and halted in front of Rozlyn. His spiked hair contrasted with the oversized, baggy clothes that hid his thin physique. "Reporting."

"We need to make sure the camp is closely surveilled for the next forty-eight hours," Rozlyn said.

Troy glanced at her. A face as stiff as stone, the look of someone who never backed down. In the early days of the Freedom Fighters, her stubborn nature was an asset, but now it was becoming a hindrance to their cause, and Troy's tolerance was running thin.

"Keep an eye on all surrounding cameras," she continued. "Especially the ones in No Man's Land."

"Yes, ma'am."

"I think it best we prepare to move location," Sinclair interjected.

"That won't be necessary," Rozlyn said.

Troy turned to the Fighters. "So what happened out there?"

"We masked the surveillance system en route to and from the city for this mission, sir, ma'am." Luke leaned back as if feeling for a solid wall where there was none. "It was all going well until—"

Catalina cleared her throat. "I take full responsibility."

"Endangered the rest of us, too," another mission fighter said.

"That bullshit you pulled could've gotten us all killed," Sinclair thundered.

"We'll settle this later," Rozlyn said. "For now, I'm assigning Catalina to comms with Luke and Michelle."

"Comms?" Sinclair sneered. "Might as well give her a paid vacation."

"And toilet duty," Rozlyn added. "Luke, reorganize Catalina's schedule to accommodate her new night shift duties, and please report to me with hourly updates over the next twenty-four hours."

Rozlyn turned to the Fighters. "Take the target to the holding cell. We'll start the interrogation this afternoon."

Two Fighters hauled Oliver Green off the chair.

He bucked against their grip. "What the hell are you people doing? I thought you were on our side!"

"We'll find out who is on what side, one way or another," Rozlyn said.

"There are only two sides. The government's or the people's."

She cracked a catlike smile as the Fighters dragged Oliver out of the headquarters tent.

Troy leaned toward Rozlyn. "We need to talk."

"I thought you'd say that."

———

TROY STEPPED through an indigo velvet curtain into Rozlyn's quarters. The rug covering the dirt floor lent her private space a majestic air. She leaned against the edge of her desk.

"It's best to plan missions rather than take on these hasty ones," Troy began. "There'll come a time I won't be able to fix the mess."

She swept her hair back with a flick of her finger. Her brown locks swayed stiffly. "We have another mission, but I'll let you run it." She picked at a groove on her wooden desk. "This one will be planned."

Skepticism split his mind, his resolve. Half of him felt the weight of his oath to his commanding officer, to his friends, to the camp that had become his home. The other half questioned her judgment, something that had been happening more and more. "What's the mission?"

"The mission is to kidnap a journalist by the name of Kelly Blackwell."

An angry question now danced on the tip of his tongue, but he caught hold of it before it escaped his mouth and twisted it into a harmless digression. "Isn't she the journalist who tried to frame an innocent guy for drug running?"

Rozlyn nodded.

"Why do we want to bring her here?"

"A source tells me she has valuable information."

Troy studied Rozlyn's face. "Who's the source?"

"You know I can't tell you that."

He backed up. "You don't need me. Get Luke to break into her watch and eavesdrop on her. Supplement it by tapping into the surveillance screens and monitor her movement. Job done."

"The SS won't give us what we need."

"I don't like this kidnapping trend that's suddenly become a thing around here."

"Some compromises are more expedient than others."

He glanced at her, his arms crossed over his chest. "I don't kidnap people."

"Call it whatever you like; it's your mission, your call."

He pulled back from the exit. "What's this journalist got to do with our cause? No, wait. I'm beginning to wonder what our cause actually is. I thought it was to fight the Truth Laws, not kidnap people and take hostages." He shook his head. "That's not what I signed up for."

She reached out to him and placed her hand on his arm. "Having the journalist here will get us a seat at the negotiating table."

He could feel her hand's gentle squeeze and was tempted to shake her off. "Seems to me this source is someone who wants us to do their dirty work."

She let go of his arm. "No."

"Then tell me one thing that would convince me this Kelly person fits into our cause."

Rozlyn webbed her fingers. "Kelly is a Fighter of sorts. She just doesn't know it."

Troy opened his mouth to talk, but Rozlyn raised her hand, signaling she hadn't finished. "Steer this mission in the right direction, and you'll be rewarded too."

Waging a quiet war against the State, a common purpose he shared with the Fighters, was in itself a reward. But he knew public support was key, and maybe Rozlyn's efforts had been designed to legitimize the Underground Freedom Fighters in the public's eyes.

Maybe having a seat at the table was the most efficient way of gaining full public support and city-based cells. That wasn't a compromise. It was strategy. How this Kelly person fit into the puzzle was a mystery, though. "We do this my way," Troy said. "Luke will lock eyes on Kelly, who she sees, who she meets, her pattern of movement. I'll assess the situation first. Depending on what I find, I'll abort or proceed. If she does come to the camp, she will be here of her own free will. She will be under my protection. Agreed?"

Rozlyn nodded casually, as if the subject hardly mattered to her. As if the request she had so delicately broached with Troy was of no real importance at all.

THIRTEEN

THE LIBRARY in the members-only Travellers Club in Pall Mall had been cleared of patrons on Omar's order. Now, two hours later, his boss, Lydia Rackham, sat next to him at a round table in the subdued room. They were buffered by eight-foot floor-to-wall shelves, holding books like *The Defense of the Realm* and *An Open Secret: My Life as a Spy*. Together, they faced the most important official in the country: the Prime Minister. A white-gloved waiter tilted a water pitcher toward the Prime Minister's glass.

He covered the rim with his palm. "This won't take long." He turned to the Commissioner of Information. "I need your help, Lydia."

She leaned into the table. Her dark brown eyes, framed by a high fringe and marbled gray hair, centered on the most powerful man in the country. "At your service, Prime Minister."

Omar felt her solar-flare power radiating. The Commissioner of Information worked out of a modest building on the south side of Westminster Bridge, but despite the humble location, important people knew what she really was: the de facto head of MI5. Omar knew his place in this triad: speak only when asked.

"The Underground Freedom Fighters are holding my nephew hostage."

"I'm sure MI5 is on the case."

"More than I'd like them to be." His eyes flickered. "They're sniffing around the Eve program. I need not tell you that's not a good development. However, stopping them at this point will rouse suspicion."

"I'll get on it. If there's anything specific you need…," Lydia said.

"Oliver is my nephew, and it's taken all the power of my office to keep his mother, my sister, from going to the press." He clinked the water glass with his fingernail. "We need to keep this out of the press and away from one journalist in particular."

Lydia gave a slow nod of understanding. "The journalist's name?"

"Kelly Blackwell. She works over at Global Wires."

Omar's fingers turned cold. Hearing Kelly's name felt like a grenade had landed right in front of him. Escape was pointless.

Lydia's face hardened. "I'll handle it."

She glanced at Omar. He gave a single nod to convey his consent. Anything less would be deadly.

The Prime Minister rose from the table. "I came to you because I know how you value discretion."

"I'm happy to serve," Lydia said. "Rest assured, it'll receive my personal attention."

After the Prime Minister had left, and now alone with Lydia, Omar's chest pounded in the quiet room. She had assigned him to Kelly twelve months earlier. Just another journalist to monitor, Lydia had said. His reports landed on her desk once a month ever since, giving her as much information on the journalist as any intelligence agent could hope for. What he kept out of the reports was his growing fondness for Kelly. With this latest development, he wasn't sure whether to protect Kelly or protect himself. He needed more to go on.

"I'm happy to take care of it," he offered.

"This is something I'll have to personally see to myself. Starting with Damian Winters."

Lydia's response made his scalp itch. Omar was already involved with Kelly, and Lydia could easily expand the scope of his case, but she had chosen not to. He had little choice. He had to go with it. "I'll walk you to the door."

Omar draped Lydia's shawl over her shoulders, tacking a miniature spy mic into the folds of the garment.

OMAR STOOD beside Lydia as the black door of the BMW glided open, windows as dark as the night. Her driver held open the door with his gloved hand. Having one of these vehicles himself, Omar knew it was packed with voice recognition commands that could outperform any human assistant, but she kept Collier around like a favorite toy.

She patted Collier on the shoulder. "Get Damian Winters on the line."

He returned to the driver's seat. Collier's bulletproof sense of duty to Lydia was admirable, and it sent a pang of shame through Omar. After tonight's meeting with the Prime Minister, his loyalty had wobbled for the first time. Though Lydia hadn't given him a direct order, eventually, she would.

He watched her scoot onto the supple leather in the back seat, the shawl wrapped around her body. "If you need anything—"

"We'll catch up in the morning." Her voice was resolute.

The door closed with a soft thud.

He started along Pall Mall and briefly crouched, pretending to tie a shoelace. Slyly, he clipped on the earbud that would pick up Lydia's voice as long as he remained within fifty meters of the still stationary car.

He could hear their voices transmitting clearly and resumed his walk at a crawl's pace.

"Damian Winters is waiting on the line," Collier said.

"I hope I didn't catch you at a bad time, Damian. This is a secure line, but it's still best if we meet in person."

Omar's heart sped up. Though limited, this one-sided conversation could give him more than he expected, namely a trail to follow. He pressed the earbud deeper into his ear. He knew Lydia wanted as much power as she could gather, but he also knew that Damian Winters wanted the same.

"This request is coming from the top," Lydia continued. "It has to do with one of yours." There was a long silence. "Kelly Blackwell." Omar heard Lydia take a deep breath. "The Oasis Cafe. In an hour."

He lowered his chin. Not enough time to set up a pair of eyes on the place. He vowed to be better prepared next time. And there would be a next time. He dropped the earbud to the pavement and stepped on it, crushing it into pill dust.

FOURTEEN

WATER, cold as winter rain, blasted out of the showerhead. Kelly cranked the hot water tap all the way, sat on the lip of the tub, and let her thoughts drift to her meeting with Stan Bletchley at TechTonic, a total bust. Speaking of busts, was she wasting her time emailing Heather Mallow? She still hadn't returned any of Kelly's messages. She needed a win.

Mist shrouded the bathroom.

She stripped down and stepped into the jet stream. Hot water splashed over her sore limbs, her tight muscles, and slowly, the day's frustrations began to drain away. If Heather didn't respond, for whatever reason, Kelly would go to the Daily Times, she thought. Simple. If that meeting proved to be a dud, too, that would be the end of the line. She couldn't keep risking her job, her freedom, her reputation—what was left of it.

The doorbell buzzed.

Her neck muscles twitched. Omar had arrived, earlier than expected. The rusty tap screeched at the sudden clockwise twist, and she snatched the terrycloth robe from the bathroom door hook. She wrung excess water from her hair and clipped it as she stepped out of the bathroom. The change of temperature sent a shiver through her, and she yearned to stretch her neck and shoulders, releasing the tension that the warm shower hadn't penetrated.

Another loud knock shook the door.

"Coming," she yelled out, tightening the robe's belt around her waist. She peered through the peephole.

Omar held a grocery bag in one hand and a bottle of red wine in the other. The fisheye lens distorted the size of his swaying head.

The time had come to get Omar to open up and give her the intel she needed. She hand-combed her hair and opened the door.

His dark brown hair was slicked back, his jawline overshadowed by dark stubble.

"You're a bit early," she said.

He pecked her on the cheek and headed straight to the kitchenette, placing the bag in the kitchen sink. His empty arms reached out and hugged her.

His strong arms seemed to squeeze out a deep ache in her back.

"What's wrong?" He fixed his gaze on her.

"I think I'm coming down with the flu."

He rubbed his black leather gloves together. "What do you expect when you don't turn your heating on?"

Central heating was a luxury. "Not this month, I'm afraid."

"Are you mad? It's freezing outside." He turned to the all-seeing eye. "Jerko, deposit ten thousand bits into Kelly Blackwell's account from Omar Betesh's account number—"

"Don't."

"Let me put it this way. I don't want to sit in the cold."

She glanced down. "I'll pay you back."

"Don't worry about it." He finished giving his account details and turned to Kelly. "When did you put an eye patch on your PA?"

"I must have forgotten about it when I was cleaning the other day."

Omar furrowed his brows.

"I'm not going to get up there now to take it off. It hears us well enough."

He rolled his eyes and ordered it to pay the heating bill. "Should fire up in a few minutes. Let's have a glass of wine. That'll warm us up."

Wherever he did work, it provided the perks of a driverless car and taxpayer-funded discounts in Whitehall's winery, among other things.

He peeled off his gloves and stuffed them in his coat pocket. "You look great, by the way." He rummaged through the utensils drawer.

"I do?" She glanced down at her terrycloth robe and rubbed her damp hair. "I had a really shitty day."

"So that's why you let me come over." He stopped searching through the cupboards. "Where's the corkscrew?"

"It's in the back of the top cupboard," she said.

"It's meant to be in a drawer."

"Be happy that I have one at all."

"Aha!" He held the corkscrew in one hand. "So what happened that was so bad?"

The swift topic switch caught her off-guard, or maybe her stuffy head was processing at a slower rate. The timing wasn't right. In order for him to let slip any helpful contacts or rumors about Christopher's arrest, he needed to be pliable. She waited for the wine to start flowing. "I'll tell you later."

The wine cork popped, releasing butter and oak aromas into the air.

He poured red wine into both glasses and placed one in her hand. "Happy Birthday," he said. "Twenty-seven is a solid number."

"Yes, it is, but then so is twenty-eight." For the sake of the celebration, she let a drop of wine coat her tongue. "And my birthday was on Monday."

"Twenty-eight...," he said, then kissed her neck.

Her body unexpectedly shuddered, surprising her. Normally, she fell into his embrace, loved his kisses. "It must be the cold."

He stepped back. "You're tense. Why not just tell me what's going on, and then we can relax?"

She dropped her hands to her side and narrowed her gaze. Impatience stretched across his face. So, who of the two was breaking their rule tonight? "Fine." She stepped away from him. "Did you hear about the journalist arrested for breaking the Truth Laws?"

He placed his wine glass on the coffee table. "I heard about it." He sat on the sofa.

"How?"

He clasped his hands. "Through Cicada."

The Cicada—named after the buzzing insect that flits around from tree to tree—was a halfway reliable forum that dealt in gossip, anonymously released government leaks, and news before it hit public awareness.

"I'm surprised your office lets you hop onto that website."

He shrugged a shrug that probably meant he scanned the site at work under disguise. He grabbed the glass of wine and sipped.

"What are you doing on Cicada anyway?"

"Just taking a look around."

She sat next to him on the sofa and let her thigh touch his. "Do you do that often?"

"More than I should."

After a year of trivial conversation, it was hard to believe he opened up so easily. Too easily. "Don't you think it's fucked up that the public has to rely on Cicada to get an idea of what's happening in this city?"

He nodded. "How often do you get on it?"

"I don't need another strike against me for visiting that website. So what did you see?"

He snuck a glance at the wine. "A D-notice leak."

His furtive look at the wine gave her the impression he wanted to take a sip to soften the edginess building up inside him. She topped up his glass. "If I had the name of someone who worked at the Ministry of Information—"

"My department doesn't have access to that place."

"I'm sure you could find something out. There's footage of a raid—"

He snapped his neck back. "If you start meddling, it won't take them long to figure out who's asking questions."

Irritation started to simmer under the surface of her skin. No authority would ever stop her digging for answers, digging for the truth, digging until life finally made sense, and certainly not him. She took a swig of his wine. It tasted sour, like vinegar. She smacked her lips.

He placed his hand on her thigh. "No one even knows who issues the D-notices."

"It's the Committee."

"So they say." He poured more wine into the glass. "But who really directs the Committee? They'll have you running in circles before you even get a hint of who that might be. Then, you'll need protection."

She batted his hand away from her thigh and propelled off the sofa. "Are you saying there's corruption to be investigated?"

He scooted to the edge of the seat. "Just drop it, Kelly."

"Don't you see it?" Her face tightened. "A journalist is forbidden from investigating the arrest of a fellow journalist. We live in a deranged world." She took another swig of wine. Her cheeks warmed.

"The media have proven incapable of investigating itself. That's why the Elite Squad does investigations now."

She swirled the wine inside her glass. The maroon liquid threatened to spill over the edge and onto the floor. "This is turning out to be a blast of an evening."

She gulped down more wine. The alcohol seemed to numb her taste buds.

"You need to cool down on that." He reached for the glass. "Let's just drop the whole thing."

She pulled away; her legs wobbled. "Don't tell me what to do." He was the one who opened up the work discussion, but she was the one who was going to finish it. "Instead of just sitting at your cushy desk in your temperature-controlled office, maybe you can actually do something useful for a change. Like, find out who scrubbed the Truth Laws fugitive video from the Internet." She drank more wine, and with every sip, her body felt lighter and lighter. "You have access to databases of everything on the streets and the money to throw around."

"I'm in a completely different office." He stood. "And I don't have that kind of clearance."

She cradled the glass in her arm and gave him a sideways look. "Back office admin, my ass. You've been spouting that story for as long as I've known you."

Even though her focus blinked in and out, she could see the focused fire in his eyes.

He seized his coat from the sofa and whipped it open. "I don't need to hear this. I should go," he said, his tone controlled but venomous.

She rocked back on her heels, growing more unsteady with every passing second. "You must think I was born yesterday."

"I'll remember to never bring a bottle of wine over again."

"It's not the wine."

"Look at you. You can't handle it."

She pursed her lips. He was right on that point. She couldn't process wine or any alcohol. She lacked the gene to metabolize it, but he knew that. Her condition, a gene anomaly, meant alcohol went straight to her head. But this wasn't the wine talking. She was fed up with a whole year of pretense. "So, why did you bring the wine over? I asked for coffee, and you brought wine."

"I shouldn't have come," he said. "In fact, I shouldn't even be seen coming here. If they see me with you, I'm done."

"Oh? Now my job is a problem for you? Well, you won't have to worry about it for much longer. You know why? Because soon there won't be a proper journalist left in the land, including me. The Truth Laws are yanking out our claws, one by one."

"Stop feeling sorry for yourself. Your egos are bloated, your news-rooms are riddled with spies pretending to be truth-seekers, and most of you regurgitate whatever the companies give you to write. You gave them the excuse they needed. If you lot had done your jobs, we wouldn't all be suffering under the Truth Laws."

She raised her hand. "I'm no spy. And I never took a single bribe."

"Oh? And what about Ian Smith?"

She dropped the glass. Millions of cutting blades scattered across the floor. Wine painted the floor blood red.

"Jesus Christ, Kelly!" He threw his coat back onto the sofa. "Get your shit together!"

She stood barefoot in a sea of glass, but she didn't care. He dared to bring Ian Smith into this, to humiliate her into silence. And, on this one occasion, where she asked for intel, he wasn't giving up so much as a hint. There was no point anymore. "It's best we stop seeing each other," she said.

"Don't be dramatic." He snatched the handy hoover from the wall. "Every couple has arguments. Doesn't mean we have to end it all."

He switched it on and pieces of glass clinked against the inside of the vacuum, sounding like coins in a slot machine on the verge of an explosion.

"We're not a couple, never really were."

He powered off the vacuum and shot her a hard look. "You're drunk, and you don't know what you're saying." He tossed the vacuum onto the sofa and grabbed his coat.

He bent to kiss her.

She turned her cheek. "I mean it."

He sauntered down the hallway.

She slammed the door shut and clamped the deadbolts.

The heating clicked on.

FIFTEEN

THE RED VELVET-LINED walls of the Old Red Lion stored the sounds of beer-filled glasses patrons had guzzled over the six centuries of the pub's existence. The musty air, sour with bitterness and sweet with sweat, danced around the room like an old prostitute trying to pick up a trick. "Mike was here" carvings scarred the dark wooden tables. Most important of all, for Josh, the thick walls blocked out the high-octave citywide Wi-Fi. This place was tracker-free, enabling him to send and receive a face-to-face message to the Resistance via the connector.

Josh ordered an espresso.

"That'd be 245 bits," the pub lady said as she fanned herself with her hand. Her tight, white T-shirt displayed her soft bumps.

Josh swiped his pay card. "I can bring in a fan if you need one."

"A fan won't fix me, love," she said. "What I need is a little less stress."

"Don't we all?"

She smirked and gave him his drink.

He turned on his heel. A handful of spaced-out drinkers took up residence on the pine chairs, feet away. In the era of fast-advancing technology, the Old Red Lion roared against time and protected the long-suffering patron who just wanted to exist.

No matter where Josh sat, he'd enjoy plenty of privacy to speak freely with Laura Cassavetes. He dodged a low-hanging lamp as he scooted into a booth at the back of the pub. Settled as comfortably as possible on a wooden bench, he pulled out the yellow silk pocket handkerchief from his back pocket and flattened it on the table.

Minutes later, a young woman, face buried in a hoody, stood at the table's edge. The smell of tobacco perfumed the girl's navy overcoat. "Josh Munro?" Her accent was posh Chelsea.

He nodded once and scrunched the yellow pocket square in his hand.

She scooted into the booth across from Josh. "The network's plans have changed," she said through dry lips.

"I gathered as much."

It didn't matter what she looked or sounded like. Her sole task was to deliver a message and, hopefully, to take one back.

"They want you to head up the next task."

Excitement squirmed around his body. He cleared his throat.

"You'll have time to get up to speed, but don't take too long." She rested her small hands on the table, her fingernails bitten to the bed. "You have to start sooner rather than later."

"What do they want me to do? If it's finding Mallow—"

She shook her head. "Don't worry about Mallow."

Josh jerked back. "What's going to happen to him?"

"We all know the risks."

"We can't just abandon him." He looked around and lowered his voice. "We have to get him out."

"They've located him. It's a bit... tricky." She tapped her clasped hands on the table. "The overall mission is greater than one man."

Josh rubbed his forehead. They were all soldiers gambling with their freedom. He had signed on knowing that, as had Christopher. He lifted his chin and gazed into the shadow concealing the woman's face. "So what do you want me to do?"

"They're going to handle this next task differently from last time. They might have to speed up the timeline, but they also can't afford to screw up. They're getting some final verifications. Be on standby."

"Understood." He was hoping they'd tell him his task today, but he could go with standby. He licked his lips. "One last thing." He slid his storage drive toward her. "Footage. Of the raid on Mallow's residence. The one from the Internet."

She didn't make a move to take the drive. "Your work?"

He shook his head.

"Where did you get it?"

"Got lucky. It happens. Someone slipped it in my bag while I was on a shoot."

"It could be doctored. Or worse."

"I already scanned it for viruses. Looks raw. But you're the experts. You decide."

She plucked the drive from his hand and studied it back and front. He had never passed off his own footage as someone else's, and the mild deception made him feel queasy.

Laura looked up at Josh, her blue eyes the color of a spring sky. "I'll give it to them. As for the task itself, you'll get a link or a message in a couple of days. Keep your VPN on."

She stuffed the drive into her coat pocket and scooted out of the booth. A sharp blast of cold air chilled the room as she stepped out the door and into the wintery morning sunlight.

Things were moving in the right direction.

SIXTEEN

KELLY WOKE up on the two-seater sofa, snuggled under a duvet she didn't remember grabbing. Still wearing the terrycloth bathrobe, her stomach heaved, and her throat felt parched.

"Your morning news briefing is ready," Jerko said.

She grabbed a cushion and hurled it at the hunk of metal. Pain ricocheted inside her head, down her neck. Had she drunk that much wine? Slowly, she lowered herself to relieve the thumping inside her skull.

The memory of Omar's visit barreled into her mind like a wayward train. She had kicked him out and broke up with him in one fell swoop.

For a moment, she considered calling him to apologize, but then remembered how he tried to dissuade her from pursuing the Mallow leads. Last night was the one time she had made a special request of him, and not only had he refused to help, he had insulted her by bringing up Ian Smith. "Asshole."

Despite her aching body, she eased herself from the sofa. Miscalculating, she went to stand and instead slipped onto the coffee table. The table tipped over, and the empty wine bottle crashed to the floor, rolled, and banged into the kitchen cabinets.

She picked up the bottle and threw it in the bin, never to be recycled. "Go to hell, Omar."

Ice-cold tap water enlivened her senses. She could almost feel her dehydrated cells plump with every gulp. She wiped her chin dry with the back of her hand. "Jerko, clear my schedule."

"You have several messages. One is marked as priority."

She glared at the dome over Jerko's all-seeing eye. "Not now."

"It is a request for your presence at the Zone, today at two o'clock."

"What time is it?"

"Ten past twelve."

Holy crap. She way overslept. It was that wine. She plodded to the kitchen sink. "Why do they want me at the Zone?"

"You are to give a witness statement in the Christopher Mallow case."

She jerked up from the sink. Her head throbbed, but she knew she had to go; she had to find out what they wanted. She grabbed her watch from the kitchen drawer.

"Jerko, who sent the priority message?"

"The message came from caller ID 7255698, Daniel, at the Zone. He has arranged a pickup point at 202 City Road. The Zone takes full priority, and your schedule has been rearranged to accommodate it."

The thought of climbing into a moving vehicle made her stomach wrench. "Who the hell is Daniel?"

Jerko remained silent.

She sighed. Talking to Jerko was a laborious game of twenty questions.

Her stomach heaving, she inched toward the bed. "Jerko, any other messages I can promptly ignore?"

Jerko's mechanical voice continued. "You have a second high priority message from Lily Henderson with an attachment entitled Shiva, Live Earth."

Kelly toyed with the idea of neutralizing before heading out to the pickup point. It would straighten her biorhythm for the Zone's cameras, but it was meant to be used only once a week, and she didn't know the consequences of a second full session.

"You have one other message, but I am unable to decrypt it."

"Send it to my watch."

She climbed onto the bed and glanced at her watch for the message. It was as though someone had rubbed a film of Vaseline over the watch face. She rubbed her eyes twice. "Jerko, project the message onto the wall." She turned her head to the blank wall. "Jerko, I said, project it onto the wall."

"The message is projecting now."

"How come I'm not seeing it?"

She glanced at eye-patched Jerko. "Damn it!" If she wanted to see the message, she'd have to get up, get a chair, climb up, and remove the flipping patch. "Just describe the damn thing."

"It appears to be a video."

"That's it?" She moaned. "It's probably marketing bullshit. Leave me alone and cancel everything."

"The video was originally uploaded on January 7 at four-thirty in the morning and removed from the Internet approximately three hours later."

She could feel the pulse in her throat. Could it be the scrubbed Truth Laws video? She held her head steady, grabbed a chair, laddered herself up, and ripped off the eye patch.

Her eyes widened, her breath quickened, unable to jump down from the chair. She stared at the black letters projected onto the wall.

Elite Squad Hunt For Rogue Journalist
As The Truth Laws Take Effect.

Beside the headline was a black square thumbnail video. She inched toward the dark, still image. "Jerko, play the video."

"I'm afraid the video is no longer available."

"You've got to be kidding. Who sent it?"

Its red eye pulsed. "I don't have that information. You must be at your pickup point in an hour."

Maybe the whistleblower was back, and he had pushed the link at her. If it had been him, she'd have to wait for his next communication. But how did he know she was looking for it? She shook her head. It had to be the algorithms sending her ghost text the web crawlers hadn't yet scrubbed. She cradled her face.

Having glimpsed this headline, there was no way in hell she could arrive at the Zone and risk a thought transfer. For all she knew, the Zone could've evolved into one massive Fi headset brain scanner by now. Considering the link she had just received, that would be problematic. A neutralizer top-up was unavoidable now.

"Jerko, keep me posted on the time."

She shuffled to the bathroom.

ALONE ON THE BACKSEAT, Kelly rocked side to side in the self-driving van ferrying her to the Zone—a panopticon that housed the echo chambers' servers, manned by the most sophisticated AI system in the country

Global Wires had toured the Zone when it first opened just over a year ago. She looked out the window.

Every twenty feet, a black SS was rooted on the pavement. With the amount of surveillance the city endured, there shouldn't be a pickpocket walking the streets. Yet, gangs of thugs came out at night and somehow never got identified. "What a joke."

"We didn't understand," the car's system said. "Can you please repeat?"

"Never mind."

Kelly faced forward. The Truth Laws called for immediate reporting of hackers' links. She was already a criminal for failing to report the fugitive headline and thumbnail Jerko had projected onto her wall. Dead link or not, she couldn't unsee it. All she could do now was hope that the image was burrowed deep inside her brain, barricaded by the neutralizer. She chewed on her nail.

The van took a sharp left eastward. Nausea swooshed in her stomach. The neutralizer, followed by a cold shower, had purged most of the hangover, but clearly not all. She clasped the handgrip.

The red brick walls of the Zone came into view. Though the overcast sky subdued its domineering presence, the Zone's invisible tendrils still crept outward through the city.

The van came to a barrier, and the backseat window rolled down. Kelly eyed the surrounding cameras, the size of little black eyeballs. They were smaller than the ones she remembered during the tour. Rumor had it the cameras were so sensitive they even tracked flies buzzing past. Plus, these upgraded ones had the add-on X-ray feature. The thought made her shudder.

The intercom scratched to life. "ID, please," a man's voice blared.

She startled and stretched her arm out the window. A red laser scanned her QR code.

The barrier lifted, and the vehicle drove over the red-and-yellow candy-cane-striped boundary etched on the tarmac.

A security guard idled in a checkpoint booth up ahead. When the van slid open its side door, he stood, grabbed a black wand, and quickly put on a face of concern. "Please stretch out your hands."

Kelly stepped out of the van, thankful that the nausea had dissipated. "The last time I was here, I didn't have to go through this."

"We have new procedures."

A sense of rebellion tugged on her. She pushed out her hands.

He glided the wand over her skin. "Palms, please." Next, he swabbed the soles of her shoes, her hair, her jeans, and her backpack.

She felt like a turkey being primed for Christmas. "Is this really necessary?"

"All visitors go through the same screening." He fed the swab into a scanner.

"They know I'm coming."

Boredom underlaid his serious expression. "If you return to the Zone, you won't have to repeat the full procedure."

"Hopefully, I won't have to come back."

Her profile photo popped up on his tablet, and he lifted it up next to her face.

On seeing her outdated photo, a familiar annoyance spiked inside her. "Before you say anything, I already know."

He raised his eyebrows. "Know what?"

She was about to explain her outdated photo, but, mercifully, his tablet beeped.

"Your data is now in the system."

The steel doors lumbered open to an atrium that smelled of lemon-scented disinfectant. Her sneakers squeaked against the shiny octagonal floor tiles, and the sound bounced off the high domed ceiling as she traversed toward the only other human in the room, a young man behind a broad reception desk.

He glanced at her. His nametag read "Daniel."

She gave a lackluster smile. "You sent me, Kelly Blackwell, a message this morning about giving a witness statement."

"Welcome." He moved out from behind the desk. "Please, follow me."

"How long is this going to take?"

"Hard to say. It totally depends on your interviewer. Let me show you to the room and I'll let Ms. Rackham know you're here."

"The interviewer?"

He nodded. "She's the one assigned to your case." He led her down a white corridor.

Kelly cocked her head toward Daniel. "My case? I thought this was about giving a witness statement."

He paused in front of the fourth door. "I'm sure Ms. Rackham will clarify it all when she comes." He motioned for Kelly to enter the room.

A fluorescent tube cast a hard light across the exposed cinder block wall. This small, simple room suited the grungy city of London better than the antiseptic, futuristic lobby.

"Would you like anything to drink?"

She shook her head. "I don't expect it'll take long."

"I'll bring some water, just in case. It can get a bit warm in here." He left the room and closed the door behind him.

The windowless room suddenly felt stuffy and humid. Kelly unzipped her jacket and hung it on the back of a Formica chair tucked under a raw metal table.

The sound of stiletto heels on the tiled floor in the hallway grew louder. A forty-something woman burst into the room. "Please, take a seat, Kelly."

Her silky long-sleeved blouse, buttoned up through the middle, outlined her slender arm muscles. A brown and gray bob rested on the edge of her collarbones. Her full lips were painted matte silver, like the raw metal table. So, this was Ms. Rackham.

Kelly sat on the hard steel seat; the cold penetrated her jeans, chilled her skin.

"Thank you for coming," Rackham spoke through perfect porcelain teeth. "We appreciate the time you're taking out of your, no doubt, busy day." She took up the seat opposite Kelly, placed her tablet on the table, and brushed a glance over her watch.

She studied a graph on the tablet's screen.

Kelly's legs buzzed, eager to get out of the Zone as swiftly as possible.

Rackham looked at Kelly, her steady gaze almost entirely obscuring the tempestuous energy coiled within. "We're asking people who were in contact with Christopher Mallow before his arrest to come in to answer some questions."

Kelly flashed her a fake smile. There was a knock at the door.

"Come in."

Daniel placed a glass pitcher on the table. Orange and lemon slices bobbed on the surface of the water. He scuttled out of the room.

"Let's get down to business, shall we?" Rackham said, seemingly annoyed at the interruption. "I understand you saw Christopher Mallow at the Covent Garden INNS unit on Monday. Is that right?"

"Correct."

"I'm sorry you had to witness his arrest."

"Where is he?"

"Being held on charges of subversion and possessing classified State information." Her eyes sharpened on Kelly. "You spoke with him before the Squad entered the INNS. What did he say to you?"

Kelly recalled the jumbled mess on Christopher's screen, but she had only glanced at it a couple of times. "He was having some trouble at his cockpit and asked if I could help."

"And you helped him."

"Well, yes." Kelly's forehead tensed. "I don't know a whole lot about computer systems, but yes, I suggested a reboot."

Rackham swiped the tablet screen. "From what I see, you're on your way to clearing your record of libel charges."

"What does my record have to do with anything?"

"Goes to credibility."

Kelly pulled her chin in. "I have to say I did find it odd that the screens at the INNS didn't work on the first day of the Truth Laws."

Rackham straightened up and flashed her eyes at Kelly. "It's been fixed now." Her lips pursed. "While you spoke to Mallow, did he give you anything?"

Kelly laughed. "You mean like slip something into my hand?"

"Nothing is funny about this, Ms. Blackwell." Rackham's cheeks appeared bloodless. "There was another person in there with you. An Oliver Green."

Heat rushed into Kelly's cheeks; her hangover flaring up at this moment was bad timing. She reached for the pitcher. "Daniel was right. It's getting a bit warm in here."

Rackham waited for Kelly to finish pouring water into a glass. "When Oliver Green left the INNS, did he tell you where he was going?"

Kelly chugged down a full glass of the cool liquid. A metallic aftertaste coated her tongue. "Ms. Rackham, you already know the answers to all your questions. You get the image and sound feeds from the echo, I mean, the INNS units. So, why am I really here?"

"You're right." Rackham lounged back in her chair. "We have all the feeds. Audio, visual, temperature, everything." She licked her steel-colored lips. "But there are some things computers aren't good at recording, not yet anyway." She leaned into the table. "Impressions. Gut senses. Those sorts of things aren't picked up by computers. For that, we rely on the surrounding biorhythms."

Kelly matched Rackham's gaze. "You mean, humans?"

"No. I mean biorhythms," Rackham said. "And you have been unusually even-keeled since that morning. It's unusual for someone who has witnessed a frantic arrest to be unfazed. Your emotions have been flat since that day. It's odd, wouldn't you say?"

Kelly pressed her tongue against the roof of her mouth, the metallic taste of the water lingering there. So, this was about the neutralizer. Unless she confessed to having it, they had nothing on her. It wasn't illegal to have neutral biorhythms. She needed to get Rackham on a different track.

"Maybe I'm so even-keeled because I think Christopher Mallow deserved his fate."

Rackham arched an eyebrow.

The brutal words had come automatically, astonishing Kelly herself into silence. There was a brisk knock on the door, and Kelly was grateful for the interruption.

Daniel entered the room and dashed over to Rackham. He whispered in her ear, his lips moving rapidly.

Rackham nodded. "Thank you, Daniel. Tell them I'll be right out."

He scampered out. His frantic energy sent an alarm through Kelly. "What's happening?"

"I'm sorry to have to cut the interview short." Rackham rose from her chair. "We've just received some unfortunate news. Mallow passed away."

Dizziness whipped through Kelly. He was onto them, and they killed him. She'd watched them beat him in the chamber, watched his blood spatter the floor, and she'd stepped back. Done nothing. And now he was dead. They wouldn't get away with it, but she had to keep her facade in place, her reactions under control. Kelly tugged at her cuff. "How did he die?"

"That's what I'm about to find out."

"Not just the first journalist to break the Truth Laws, also the first to die in Elite Squad custody."

Rackham glanced at her tablet, her eyebrows raised. "How curious. I don't like to jump to conclusions—"

"What?"

"Your biorhythm reads neutral."

The hair on Kelly's arms bristled. Kelly's biorhythms should have been bouncing all over Rackham's screen, but they weren't. The neutralizer was more effective than she realized, and Rackham would have her cornered unless she found an explanation—fast. "For all I know, you fed me a lie about Mallow's death," she said.

Rackham's face gave nothing away. "You have a suspicious mind."

"Blame my childhood."

Rackham shook her head. "It's true about Mallow. And no one is more upset about it than I. Not even you, evidently." She glanced at her tablet again. "You're free to go. Daniel will arrange your transport back."

"That's it? We aren't going to talk about the Elite Squad? Or—"

"I have all the information I need." Rackham paused at the door. "Being a crime journalist, you might have an inclination to investigate Mallow and what he was working on, but I want to remind you that his file is under the domain of the Elite Squad."

"In whose custody was Mallow?"

"*Our* investigation will be thorough." Rackham exited the room, the clip of her heels against the tiled floor fading into the distance.

Kelly sat in her chair, stunned at how coldly Rackham had talked about Christopher, as though his life was nothing more than the contents of a measly file. Then there were Kelly's heartless words from earlier in the interview. What had they all become? She inhaled and stared at the ceiling.

On some level, Kelly doubted Rackham's abrupt announcement, but why lie about Christopher's death? The uneasy interview felt like a test, and it left her wondering what it was really all about. She would never get answers here, but one person knew the gravity of what Christopher had uncovered. Heather. His wife.

She would also soon learn about her husband's death, and Kelly wasn't sure what effect that would have on her. Though she hadn't responded to Kelly's private messages, the time had come for a face-to-face. There was only one place Heather could be, the one place Kelly had been avoiding for the last year.

Soon, she'd be back inside the Daily Times.

SEVENTEEN

IN THE QUIET of his office, Spence perused the latest protocol reports. As long as the office checked in, swapped desks regularly, and stayed away from crime stories, at least for the time being, they would all get through this. Damian and his daughter would eventually leave.

A rap on the door cut through his thoughts. "Come in."

Geneva stepped in. "Mind if we have a chat?"

"Take a seat." She closed the door. Smooth face, slight smile, she could want anything. He tossed the report to his desk. "Everything all right at your new desk? I'm sure Harry could adjust things if needed."

She glided into the chair, graceful as a ballerina. "Thanks, but I'm not here about my new desk." She cleared her throat. "Someone in the office has been conducting unauthorized searches on government agencies."

Not even a week in, and the ballerina was stomping on years of work he put into his staff to make Global Wires the number one online news outlet. He crossed his arms. "Which government agencies would that be?"

"The Ministry of Information."

Not as bad as she was making out. He leaned back in his chair and bounced against the springy back. "The Truth Laws don't forbid anyone looking at the MI5 website."

"I know." She lifted her chin and was almost looking down at him. "But here at Global Wires, we've decided it's best to leave that particular government agency alone."

He suppressed the urge to raise his voice and sighed. What had the world come to when journalists couldn't investigate the nation's intelligence agency? "The guidelines only came out yesterday."

"Statistics show the likelihood of contravening our guidelines is quite high, if the person in question has been visiting certain websites."

"Oh, now we're in pre-crime territory. Who was the journalist in question?"

"Kelly Blackwell."

"That I don't believe." He clasped his palms. "You sure it was Kelly?"

Her head bobbed gently, probably because she knew she was about to leap her way to a standing ovation of triumphant success. "Several times over this past week."

"We shuffled the desks, sharing terminals. Was it under her ID?"

"Someone could have stolen her ID, I suppose."

He lifted his chin. "We don't have thieves in this office."

She wiggled in her chair. "I'm not accusing anyone. It just looks suspicious." She cleared her throat. "Especially since I also found searches on Christopher Mallow."

Spence dropped his gaze. "If the searches happened before Monday, then it doesn't count. You and I both know the Truth Laws weren't in effect." She opened her mouth, and Spence held up his hand. "If it makes you feel comfortable, why don't you conduct interviews with all the staff?"

"I'm not sure that's necessary. The searches were on Kelly's computer under her ID. On Monday. It might be more efficient if I zeroed in on—"

"Sometimes being efficient can send the wrong message. Let's be thorough in our investigation before we accuse anyone in particular."

She swallowed. "I understand." She stood abruptly and walked out of his office, her ballerina's grace slightly ruffled.

Spence drummed his fingers on his desk. It wasn't the searches that left him with an uneasy feeling. Kelly had been on a tangent since Christopher Mallow's arrest. She didn't talk to Spence about it, but the protocol report told him she had been there when it happened and had seen it all. The effect must have shocked her. Any real journalist worth their salt would want to know why he was arrested. No, it wasn't Kelly he was worried about. In time, she'd fall in line.

It was Damian. He was overreaching, hiding behind his daughter's tutu. His stringent rules, even stricter than the Truth Laws, would devalue this office, everything Spence had worked so hard to achieve. A sinking feeling lumped inside his stomach as he turned back, dispirited, to the protocol reports he had been examining with a lighter heart before Geneva's interruption.

EIGHTEEN

THE DAILY TIMES' offices were in a former residential building in the northern suburb of Haringey. Fighting an urge to turn back, Kelly approached the red brick building and slowed her stride. Robert Greaves, her former editor, the one who had fired her, would be there, and the only way to see Heather would be to face him.

A grid of knots lined her gut. She rang the buzzer. She wasn't sure what to expect, wasn't even sure Heather was in.

A beam of light flashed in her eyes. "Can I help you?" The voice belonged to Siren Susie, the fielder who looked at her nails more than she did the readers' messages.

Kelly looked into the camera. "I'm here to see Heather Mallow."

"Is she expecting you?"

The knots in her gut whirled into butterflies. Or were they rabid moths? "I sent her a message. Several, in fact. It's me, Sue."

The door buzzed. "Second floor."

Kelly made her way up the stairs. The small round table in the lobby still functioned like a roundabout: fielder typists to the left, journalists to the right, toilets straight ahead.

Siren Susie approached. She looked Kelly up and down through heavily mascaraed eyelashes. "This way." She motioned for Kelly to follow her.

"Did you hear about Christopher?" Kelly asked.

"Which Christopher?"

"Mallow."

"No."

Four journalists sat at their desks. The editor, her former boss, the man who fired her without so much as a debate, sat in his catty-corner office.

On seeing him, Kelly's throat went dry. Ten years younger than Spence, Robert Greaves was the youngest Editor-in-Chief in the city. His reputation as a workaholic—more nights in the office than at home—had earned him his position by the time he was thirty-five. He glanced up. She jerked her gaze away from his sharp eyes.

"Heather is over there." Siren Susie wiggled back to the lobby.

Heather's long silver hair clung to the back of her white striped shirt. She was punching words onto the screen. How would Kelly tell her Christopher had died? How would she explain she saw the Elite Squad beat him right in front of her eyes? And most of all, why hadn't she told her sooner?

Kelly passed journalists toiling at their desks and halted behind Heather, waiting for a natural pause in her typing. Her restless fingers moved in a flurry.

"Heather," Kelly said eventually, her tone hesitant. "Sorry to interrupt."

Heather swung around. "You scared me." Her fist clasped at her chest.

"Sorry. I thought Susie told you I was here."

"She's focused on her...job."

"I sent you a few messages."

"Yes, yes." Heather released a heavy breath. "Couldn't answer. Too many eyes, ears." Tension slipped into her voice. "I'm glad you came. Christopher was right about you."

An awkward silence filled the gap between them.

Kelly shifted her weight. There was never a right time to break the news about the death of a loved one. "Can we go somewhere to talk?"

Heather opened her drawer, pulled out a folded piece of paper, and shoved it in her pocket. "Come with me."

They walked out of the newsroom, past the lobby, and Heather held open the door to the stairwell. A camera flashed its red eye, and Heather pulled back out of its line of sight. They stepped in, keeping close to the wall. The door closed with a soft thump. Steeped in a cold, hard granite staircase, this seemed the worst place to deliver sensitive news.

Kelly's stomach fluttered. "I just came from the Zone." She couldn't bring herself to say it. "About Christopher, did you hear?"

"Everyone's heard." Heather's eyes glassed over; a shadow crept across her face. "He's been in these situations before. He knows how to handle himself."

A lump formed in Kelly's throat. By the look on Heather's face, Kelly could see she didn't know her husband had passed away. "I don't know how to say this..."

Heather's eyes narrowed. "Not here." She pulled the paper from her pocket. It was trembling in her hand. "Christopher said you'd know what to do with it," she whispered raggedly. "Everything you need is on there. Look at it without cameras around." She looked at Kelly. "Smith is involved."

"How? Smith ran a drug operation. What does he have to do with Christopher?"

"Christopher was trying to find out what that drug money was used for. I think he found out. Keep on investigating Smith."

"Smith has a restraining order against me."

"Just find a way. Other info you need is on that paper."

Goose bumps rippled up Kelly's arms, and a moment later, commotion echoed up the stairwell. Heather fixed her eyes on Kelly.

"Guard that information with your life," Heather said quickly. "Don't put it online, or they'll find it. If that happens, we're all doomed."

The hair on Kelly's arms stood to attention as though every cell in her being sensed the danger of the information written on the paper Heather had just handed her. She crushed the urge to rip open the paper immediately. "Who's they? What is it?" she whispered.

"Chris tried to explain it, but it's all about computer codes and viruses." Heather scraped back her hair. "He said that you are the only one who could do anything about it."

"I'm the last person—"

Chaotic footsteps clanged against the concrete steps below them. Garbled voices thundered. Whoever it was, it sounded like they were on the first flight of stairs. Heather whipped Kelly out of the stairwell and into the fielder's room. Siren Susie glanced up and turned back to her screen.

The sound of thudding boots was coming closer, drawing nearer to their floor.

Kelly's thigh muscles tightened. "Is that who I think it is?"

"Everyone, listen up!" Robert Greaves shouted. "Go to the fielder's room, lock the door behind you. I'll take care of this."

Kelly shoved the paper inside her jacket and grabbed Heather's hand, hauling her toward the fire escape. "Let's get out of here."

Her eyes wild, Heather pulled back. "It's too late. They're coming up in all directions."

The journalists piled into the fielder's room. Siren Susie screeched and crammed against the wall. Someone slammed the door and punched in the lock code. Their only protection was the door—a pitiful barrier against what was coming for them.

They were trapped.

FROM THE OTHER side of the walls came an almighty crash.

Journalists huddled tighter against the wall, their screams ricocheting through the air. Kelly squeezed her head, terror clogged her throat. She hauled a deep breath, desperate to survive.

Heather pulled her to the back of the room. Vaguely, she could hear Robert's voice booming on the other side of the door. "Leave now!"

Kelly frantically searched for an escape, but there was nowhere to go.

The sound of gunfire shook the door.

Kelly froze, and a wave of panic swept the room.

Robert's voice had gone silent. *Thump*!

"Robert!" Susie screeched. She tried to break free from the huddled mass, but someone pulled her back. She folded to the floor, the side seam of her skirt ripped up to her waist.

Three black-clad thugs burst into the fielders' room, their bootprints stained the floor with blood. They barked at the bunched staffers, taunted them with pistols, all the while searching relentlessly for whatever it was they had been sent to find.

Time stopped. The noise stopped. Kelly's breathing stopped. Her body dissolved into dreamlike air.

Outside of herself, she floated above the terrified crowd and drifted into the other world where the tangerine sunset never set. "Some people scream," a voice far away and inside her whispered. "Some run, some freeze, you must breathe, Kelly, breathe. You know this, remember the chamber."

Below, her eyes closed, her fists clenched, she nodded.

A thug lifted her chin. The smell of his sweat stung her nostrils. Her head jerked back, and she sucked air deep. He laughed and tightened his grip on his gun. Screams and chaos and wails returned in full.

Breath interrupts adrenaline long enough to regain control, Kelly remembered. She sucked in air so deep she could feel it infuse her toes. She held the air in, counted to five seconds, and exhaled through pursed lips. The fuzziness in her head cleared.

"Eeny, meeny, miney, moe." The thug pointed his gun at Susie. She sobbed, hugged her knees, and rocked. "Get up!" Fresh tension seeped through Kelly's skin. The red-faced thug turned his gun to Heather. "Bingo!"

Heather's eyes grew wide.

Kelly's breath caught. There had to be a way to defeat them. "No."

He grimaced; his silver teeth glistened like a rabid dog's. If she could inject just a drop of doubt, he might hesitate, she thought. Kelly raised her hands, showing her palms. All four thugs howled with laughter, their faces mangled and colored red to her eyes.

Her voice trembled. "You could be making a big mistake."

The lead thug stopped laughing, his face the reddest of all. "You'll be next if you don't shut up."

Heather tugged Kelly's arm, but Kelly inched forward.

The red-faced thug's lip twitched. "You stay right there."

Kelly halted. She had no idea where she was going with this. All she knew was that she was buying everyone time, and time opened up possibilities. "Imagine if your boss finds out you killed the wrong person."

He reached for her wrist, and she slapped his hand away. He mocked her with a howl and turned to the other thugs. "Take the watch."

One thug held her arms while the other ripped the watch from her wrist. Both reeked of week-old rubbish.

The red-faced thug ran his tongue across his silver teeth. His wingmen glanced at each other, their thick, tattooed necks oozing with sweat. He glanced at his watch as though he were checking something, lifted his gun, and pointed it at Heather's forehead. "Heather Mallow, you are done."

Kelly's body moved before her mind could catch up, but hands grabbed her arms, held her back. She opened her mouth to scream, but no sound came.

A single bullet tore a hole through Heather's head. Her neck cracked back. Her body crumpled to the floor, eyes open.

A shot of adrenaline surged through Kelly, and all she wanted to do was run.

WEEK 2

NINETEEN

13 January

LYDIA RACKHAM STEPPED out of the shower and reached for the silk robe hanging off the silver-plated door hook. Her arm trembled from post-workout fatigue.

She draped it around her wet shoulders and stood in front of the mirror, examining the gray in her roots. It was time to get in the private stylist.

The telephone in the bathroom buzzed.

She plunged her arms through the sleeves of the robe and swept her hair behind her ear. "Lydia Rackham."

"Holdsworth reporting, ma'am." The tone of the lead investigator held a note of confidence. "Kelly Blackwell has been located in St. John's Wood."

Lydia's moist skin tingled. "Did she go there right after the Daily Times?"

"Yes. She's been there since Friday."

She tapped her index finger on the marble sink. "Excellent work."

"What would you like us to do?"

"Keep the warm eye on her—all the way."

"There will be a bill."

Lydia stepped away from the basin. Using human trackers would rack up a healthy bill, but they needed to keep an unofficial tab on Kelly. "I'll take care of it." She made a mental note to call the Prime Minister. "Did you send me the files I asked for?"

"They should be in your inbox."

"From now on, send me paper copies."

She put down the phone and logged into the screen on her bedroom wall. Her government email portal appeared, and two files sat in her inbox.

"Open Oliver Green's file."

The file popped open. He was a nineteen-year-old man, registered at an address in East London. She skimmed the rest of his profile:

DOB: 20 November 2010
Nicknames: Oli, Olivier, Scat
Mother: Julia Green. Cohabitant.
Father: Deceased in 2024
Political Party: Unregistered
Ethnicity: French/British
Religion: None specified
Income: £10,000-£17,000
Net Worth: None
Relationship: Single
Children: None
Siblings: None
Work History: Manual labor jobs
Primary School: Primrose Hill Primary School
Secondary School: Prince of Wales Grammar School for Boys. Incomplete.
University: None
Properties: None
Vehicle: None

She turned from the screen and pieced together his story from the data. Smart, young man. Opportunities cut short when his father died in 2024, making him fatherless at the age of fourteen. The PM had to be helping the family out, she thought. But, by the look of those income numbers, not by much. Good. She liked the needy. They were easy bait. "Close Oliver Green's file."

The second attachment was the Kelly Blackwell file.

Already having memorized all journalists' files, Lydia shut the portal and ambled to her walk-in closet. She perused the array of suits. Kelly Blackwell, having witnessed Mallow's arrest, complicated matters, but that cold look in Kelly's eye when she talked about Mallow deserving the arrest, together with her neutral bio-reading, eased her. Then again, Blackwell had visited Heather Mallow at the Daily Times. Her best guess was that they discussed Christopher Mallow. Her lips wriggled. All the digital surveillance in the world, and she couldn't use it in this case. This wasn't the first time she had needed to keep a mission off the books. Lydia needed to see more of Holdsworth's handwritten reports before making a final decision about how to manage Kelly.

She reached for the red suit and paused, remembering the PM's order. "Discretion." She huffed. Discretion. "Blue blends in better."

She grabbed the blue suit, propped it in front of her, and stared at her reflection in the full-length mirror. Now, the cash problem. There had been cash incentives for parliamentarians, cash for the opposition to ignore proposals, even cash to convince the Prime Minister that the Truth Laws were a benefit to everyone.

Her belly tightened. Sometimes, loads of cash hadn't been impressive, not to the wealthy ones like the key cabinet minister, the chief whip. He didn't want or need cash. He wanted something different: his weight on top of her, his undulating double chin rubbing against her face as she lay on her back, staring up at the ceiling. She brushed away the memory and reminded herself just how small the price had been for safeguarding the nation.

Stoic, she reminded herself, as she recalled the most important choices she had made to get to this point were off the books. The Truth Laws were a reality, and she was in charge of the Elite Squad. She flexed her shoulders, tightened her tummy, and gave a small smile of satisfaction at the reflection in the mirror.

She dropped her head back. Now that Ian Smith was out of commission, only one other person could provide the kind of cash needed to release the Prime Minister's nephew from the Fighters, in addition to everything else.

Lydia laid the suit carefully on the bed, cinched the robe around her torso, and glided down the stairs to the ground floor. She picked up the yellow phone on her office desk.

"Prime Minister, good morning."

"Do you have news for me?"

"Shortly." She could feel the plush rug poking through her toes. "It could get costly, though."

"Can that Smith fellow step in?" he said.

"I know it's been over a year, but I wouldn't use him for this job anyway. We need to keep spending...time close to home." Asking for untraceable cash over the line somehow felt distasteful.

"Of course."

"We'll need a lot of time to grease the wheels of discretion."

"Naturally," he said, his tone curt. "It has to be returned, though."

"Next year."

He went quiet.

Of course, he would approve. He had no choice. His nephew's life was at stake.

"Send me a number, and I'll make the time available later today. Remember, Lydia. Discreet." He closed the line.

Lydia called Collier. "Have the car ready in thirty minutes."

"Yes, ma'am."

She shuffled up the staircase, her discreet black suit it would be.

TWENTY

THE LIGHT SNAPPED ON.

Gold lettering on the spine of a book glistened on the dark wooden shelf in front of Kelly. *Crime and Punishment* nestled beside *Beowulf* and *Inferno* and dozens of other hardbacks, their spines faded or broken. She had always loved this room. She sank into the leather sofa.

The smell of the musty room took her back to her childhood. Josh's father, the late Mr. Munro, read the classics in his green leather chair. When Kelly was a kid, she'd climb into his chair when they were gone and put on his reading glasses. Now that chair stood in the corner of the room, its leather arms cracked, its seat flattened.

She drifted back in time to Aunt El and Mr. and Mrs. Munro having grown-up talk over risotto with asparagus tips while Josh and Kelly checked out the latest online game or YouTube influencer. When called to eat, they'd moan.

Josh poked his head into the study. "The light was on."

She leaned against the sofa arm and hugged her knees to her chest. "Come in."

He slung his jacket across the back of the leather chair. "Want some coffee? I have decaf."

"What time is it?"

"Three in the afternoon." He smiled. "Didn't want to wake you."

The kettle popped in the kitchen, down the hall. The rich aroma of coffee infused the air. She dropped her feet to the rug.

"I'll be right back."

Minutes later, Josh returned with the French press, a couple of mugs, and a bottle of milk. Without asking, he poured the coffee and pushed a mug toward Kelly.

"Thanks, Josh."

He exhaled and cocked his head. "So, you're gonna tell me what happened yesterday?"

Images of the Daily Times staffers flashed through her mind. A journalist, comatose but alive. A dead body in the lobby. A gun. Heather. Dead. Kelly's hands trembled, and she couldn't seem to get warm, couldn't stop the cold from seeping into her bones. She shuddered and cradled the mug close to her chest, but the warmth didn't reach her.

Josh's eyes bore into her. "Do I have to play the twenty-questions game?"

The events collided in her mind, the fallout of which she was still piecing together. She went to speak but couldn't form the words. How do you say it? How do you tell someone you watched a woman's head explode? She opened her mouth, closed it again.

His watch buzzed from down the hall.

She put the mug down on the coffee table. "They took my watch."

"Did you get mugged?"

She shook her head. "Thugs."

"What?"

She pinched the bridge between her eyes. "It was probably just a psychological game they were playing. To scare me. To keep me quiet."

Josh started to speak, but another buzz from his watch interrupted him. "Let me go see what it is. Be right back." He returned, a dour look on his face. "It's a damn code red. The Daily Times is shut indefinitely because Editor-in-Chief Robert Greaves passed away this morning due to a fatal heart attack."

"That's all it said?"

He nodded.

Her mind reeled. There was no mention of Heather Mallow. "It's all lies."

Josh sat across from her. "Start from the top."

For a fleeting moment, she questioned whether she had imagined the whole thing. The events leading to the raid jostled in her mind. She could still see Heather's body crumpling to the floor, the red blooming on the wall behind her, the thug's silver teeth glistening as he turned the gun away.

Like a war correspondent in a distant land, she reported on Heather, the raid, the thugs, the fear, the screams, the tears. Saying it out loud should have made it more real, but instead, it felt like she was describing something that had happened to someone else.

She pulled out the paper Heather had given her in the stairwell. Blood stained the creases. Mindfully, she pried it open as though it were brittle parchment.

Scribbled notes lined the page in sentence fragments. If this had belonged to Christopher, as Heather had said, they looked like the notes of a man who had lost his mind.

"What the hell is this? Heather said it belonged to Christopher."

"It sort of looks like code," Josh said. "But then, maybe not. The lines are weird."

"A hacker will know."

Just as she was folding up the paper, she glimpsed a note at the bottom of the page. Neatly written in cursive handwriting, it said, "KX locker 512 code 1210." She finished folding it and put it in her pocket.

"We can't ask Christopher or Heather. They're both...dead."

A shadow darkened Josh's face. "Wait, what? When?"

She wrung her hands, squeezing so tight they turned white as she reached the part of her story she'd not yet been able to tell Josh. "Christopher died in Elite Squad custody on Friday." Kelly picked at the cracked skin around her thumbnail, inflamed and red, one layer away from blood.

Josh reached out and touched her hand. "You need to take some time to process all this, Kelly. You have to look after yourself; otherwise, you're no good to anyone. And, whatever you do, don't tell anyone about any of this. Not yet."

She pulled her hand away. "Fielders and journalists were there."

"They won't say a word."

"The thugs took my watch. God knows what information they'll release from it."

"Did the thugs take anyone else's watch?"

"Only mine. When they crack it, they'll have all my data."

He stood and paced the room. "I can track it down. See where it went." Josh's voice sounded determined.

"I always thought the thugs were just terror freaks. You know, psychos out for mayhem and random violence."

Josh nodded. "That's exactly what they are."

Kelly shook her head. "They could've easily killed everyone in that room if they wanted to, but they didn't," she said. "They were taking orders from someone."

He stopped pacing and crouched next to her. "They took your watch to spook you. That's all. I'll track it down. Roseman, at the Luntan, can get you a temporary replacement. As for what you witnessed..."

She sunk her face into her hands. The memory of the raid was like a black hole threatening to suck her in forever—if she dwelled on it. She leaned back and fixed her gaze on Josh.

"I know that look," he said. "You're doing what you always do."

She pulled her chin back. "What do you mean?"

"You're trying to work all this shit out in your head." He stood. "There are other ways of finding out who the thugs are working for without putting yourself in harm's way." His tone backed down. "Let me ask around, behind the scenes."

A twinge jabbed in her heart. If anything happened to Josh, she'd never forgive herself. "I don't want you to become a target. Just track my watch, shut it down if you can. That's it. I'll do the rest."

He nodded, a weary look in his eyes. "Before you start poking your paw into the wasp's nest, promise me you'll go see Roseman," Josh said.

"I'll send him a list of counter-surveillance equipment to get you started. But you'll have to meet him yourself."

Kelly shoved a foot into her sneaker.

"You're not going to find Roseman at the corner shop. There's a process."

"I'm not going to see Roseman. I'm going—" Dizziness overcame her.

"You need time, Kelly. It's the weekend. Rest here."

She finished lacing up her second shoe. "Ian Smith. Christopher was onto him." She looked at Josh. The white spots had disappeared. "Ian Smith is connected to whoever killed Christopher, Heather, and to those thugs who took my watch to fuck with me."

"Ian won't confess."

She exhaled and stood, her legs wobbling.

"You need time, Kelly. You've been through a lot."

"Whoever ordered Heather's murder is cleaning up. I need to find out what Christopher was onto before every avenue is sealed."

"If you're thinking of writing this up, what then? You won't be able to print it."

"Maybe not in this country..." The whistleblower popped up in her mind. "Somewhere, someone will take it." She headed down the magnolia-cream hallway.

"Hold up." He sprinted up the staircase. Seconds later, he came down with a watch in hand. "Use it to make one call, then throw it away." He shoved a piece of paper into her hand. "Fresh IP addresses. Give yourself plenty of time to find the Luntan's next location."

She pecked his cheek.

They stared at each other for a long moment.

He leaned in and kissed her, just like when they were seventeen. "If you don't get anywhere with Smith, or can't sleep or whatever, call me."

She opened the door. The fresh air brushed her face, enlivening her senses.

She stepped onto the road and glanced at the building next door, the one she grew up in. They were carefree back then—almost carefree.

"Do you think our parents knew?"

"Knew what?"

"Never mind." She walked southward.

"Yeah, they probably did," he yelled after her.

She twirled to face him, noticing how heavy her heart felt. She put on a brave face and waved her hand in the air. "Even at that age, we had something to hide."

He cracked a smile, the first that afternoon.

She pivoted and walked southward in the direction of King's Cross.

TWENTY-ONE

As much as he wanted to pull Kelly back inside, it was pointless. She wasn't going to listen to him or anyone else. He shut the door and walked down the hallway.

He'd seen her kind of shock in photographers who had come home from war. Fidgety at first, then a slow descent into anxiety, paranoia, and then, boom, they crashed. Sometimes, it took a day, a week, maybe a month. Standing in the study now, he poured some whiskey into a tumbler. Sooner or later, he thought, Kelly was going to crash. He swigged down the golden liquid.

And Christopher dead? He dared not believe it. He sat in his father's old chair and dangled the empty tumbler from his fingers. He'd done all he could to control his reaction in front of Kelly, but the news had settled inside him like a rock, and he could feel a slow-rising anger igniting inside. If true, then Christopher's death was the fault of the Resistance. They hadn't acted quickly enough.

He shot up from the chair and poured some more whiskey. They had teamed him with Christopher Mallow to work on code, but then, halfway through, the Resistance handed the project to another hacker to finish. They had said it was better to split the work to avoid detection. He knew how it worked. They all knew how it worked. The mission was bigger than one man; that's what the connector reminded him of the other day. Still, Christopher's death dealt him a heavy blow.

He laid the empty glass on the silver tray and marched to the living room. Not a single message from the Resistance. His jaw clenched. The one person who had sent him a message was Percy. Josh clicked it open.

It was an assignment, a spying job. Josh texted:

> Percy, this latest assignment. No can do. Give it to someone else.

He climbed the stairs to the second floor. His watch vibrated back on the dining table. Maybe it was Percy. Possibly Kelly. He scrambled back down and grabbed the watch. It was Percy.

> No negotiation. Take it or it'll be the last from this office.

> Who's the client?

> Anonymous

> This better not be like that football player bullshit you pulled. I need a name.

Percy sent through a photo of a woman with hard green eyes fixed in an angular face, brown skin.

> Rozlyn Abbott

> ??

> Underground misfit

> You can do better than that

Leader of the Underground Freedom Fighters.

The leader of the UFF was not a person he'd ever expected to spy on. They were an extremist group who kidnapped people for ransom, bending the government or corporations to its will. "Should be interesting," he muttered as he climbed to the top of the staircase.

Accepted

He punched his code into the keypad beside the door. The iron bolts clicked open, and the door to his den swung open. Hopefully, this new assignment came from the Resistance. If not, he'd soon find out.

TWENTY-TWO

A DISTANT PIANO echoed in the shopping hall of King's Cross station. Kelly made her way through the crowd with Heather's leather satchel; inside was a notebook. It had been inside station locker 512, which she had opened with the code 1210—the code at the bottom of the bloodied paper. The satchel smacked her hip with her every stride.

A camera flashed.

A prick behind her eye pained her as black and white spots clouded her vision. She leaned against a column, and all around her, watches beeped. A chuckle echoed through the hall. A domed camera in the ceiling's corner flashed its red eye.

She pushed off the column and shuffled toward the exit at the far end of the hall, the shortcut to Copenhagen Street, the road on which Ian Smith lived. As she stepped out, a burst of ice-cold air cleared her head and cooled her burning cheeks.

Electric motor taxis and tourists crowded the road outside the station. A car beeped.

Her heart thumped. She clutched the satchel against her chest.

A luggage trolley rolled along the pavement. "Oh, sorry about that." A woman with a bright purple jacket and snow boots repositioned her drag-along luggage.

Kelly hadn't even noticed the collision.

Moments later, she stood in front of a glossy red door, her heart pounding. Was he behind that door? Was he even there? She pounded on the door and stood back.

Feet shuffled on the other side. *Jesus Christ*. Her mind went blank. She straightened her back and stood firm, satchel in hand.

The door swung open. "What do you want?" Booze wafted off his breath. Standing before her was a man who hadn't shaven in days. Was this really the Ian Smith she investigated two years ago? This weathered man before her, reeking of alcohol? By the mere sight of him, she realized she had been nurturing a fear that needn't have existed. The bogeyman in her mind, the Ian Smith that nearly ruined her, was himself a ruined man.

He dropped his arms by his side in resignation, as if he had prepared for this long ago. "I was wondering when you'd find me." He swayed on his feet. "Come in."

She stepped inside.

The stale air inside Ian Smith's flat grazed her cheeks. She sidestepped pizza boxes, cans of beer, unwashed clothes, and searched for a clear surface.

He scratched his greasy salt-and-pepper hair, looking around for somewhere she could sit. He cleared tablets and empty pill containers off the sofa.

She sat on the edge of the cushion and rested the satchel on her lap, careful not to touch anything else.

"Would you like something to drink?"

She shook her head. "I won't take up much of your time." Kelly opened the satchel and pulled out the notebook. "Does this look familiar to you?"

Ian Smith flipped open a page and quickly handed the notebook back to her. "Does it look like I write code?"

She closed the notebook. "It was worth asking."

"Anything else?"

"You were drug running, weren't you?"

He glanced around the room, and his eyes eventually landed on a half-empty bottle of gin. He poured the clear liquid into a dirty glass and swigged it down. "Yes."

The word hung in the air between them. Yes. Two years she'd waited to hear him say it. Two years of professional disgrace, of sideways looks in newsrooms, of Spence having to defend hiring her. Two years of knowing she'd been right while the world called her a liar.

Kelly's throat tightened. She'd imagined this moment so many times—vindication, triumph, Smith on his knees admitting the truth. But sitting here in his squalid flat, looking at this broken man, she felt nothing close to elation. Just a hollow ache where victory should have been. Christopher had died digging into this. Heather had been executed for it. And here was Smith, still breathing, still free to rot in his own filth.

"And you were running drugs for someone in the government."

His eyes grew heavy. "It's not like I have much to lose at this point." He shrugged. "I don't know who, and the money ended up in an anonymous account. I suspect it was government-related."

"How much did you make for them?"

"Can't remember. Probably added up to billions in the end." He glanced around his flat again. "And look where it got me."

"Did you ever meet anyone that you can ID?"

He shook his head. "Give them some credit. They're smarter than that."

"How did you get roped in?"

He shrugged. For a moment, Kelly thought he might have decided not to talk to her after all, but then he shifted in his chair and rubbed his chin. "I was pulled out of Belmarsh, cleaned up, and my record wiped clean. In exchange, I was to do this job. I didn't ask who or what, I just played the part they wanted me to."

"They?"

He nodded. "I never found out who it was, but who else could pull those kinds of strings?" He gave her a knowing look.

"You must have gotten paid for your work."

"I did. Sold drugs in the celebrity world, and any other market that would buy. Lived the high life for a while because of it." A slight smile crept across his lips.

She remembered how she discovered his criminal activity. Smith had frequented the Mayfair bars, hobnobbed with footballers and celebrities, drove his yellow Ferrari around town—a real British John Gotti. But there was obviously nothing legitimate to back up Smith's showy activity. Anyone who paid attention would conclude he was a hustler, and Kelly happened to be the one who decided to find out. "You were living the high life until I came along."

"My cover was blown. They cut me off." The heavy look in his eyes returned. "These people are powerful."

"Are they still at it?"

"Probably. I set down some good tracks into the celeb world for them, but it's probably all done online now."

They probably used forums and code names to exchange information, but that wasn't what interested her right now. "Do you know what the money was used for?"

He slapped his hand on his thighs. "You name it!"

The obstacle normal people face when dealing with criminals is adopting their frame of mind. Criminals have asymmetrical logic. They don't reason like the average person with all the normal motivations of making a living, feeding their families, living in a secure neighborhood. Criminals search for undetectable ways to make money to subvert the law and hide their tracks. They're a creative bunch addicted to risk.

"Where does any of this money ever end up?" he asked but didn't pause for an answer. "Bribes, guns, contracts they want to keep hush-hush, honeypot mansions. Could be anything."

Satisfied that she heard what she needed to know, she stood. "Thank you for talking to me."

"Like I said, I don't have much to lose. But a word of warning before you start feeling too grateful to me," Smith said, casting his haunted eyes around his desolate flat. "If they find out you know what I know, you're going to end up just like me."

As Kelly walked east, homeward bound, Ian Smith's confession echoed with every step.

Everything he said confirmed her original allegations, and then some. All along, she had known the truth. She should have felt elated, but sometimes knowing you had been right doesn't set you free. Often, it just leaves a lonely numbness, a void for cold reflection. She trudged forward.

For a long time, nearly two years, she had endured professional disgrace for standing by what she had suspected all along—that the evidence that freed Ian Smith was bogus. After her meeting with him, she had all but the written confirmation of that fact.

Disappointment was settling inside her because the world, the weary, frightened world, still needed time to catch up with the truth. It felt a long way from any kind of victory or vindication. Christopher had known the truth and died for it. Heather had protected the evidence and been executed for it. And Kelly? Kelly was left standing, vindicated in a way no one would ever witness, walking home alone through a city that didn't care.

She felt alone.

To his handlers, Smith's true crime was the reckless folly that got him caught by a crime journalist. That's what they punished him for. Not the drug running or whatever criminal activities he engaged in.

They ruined him because he got caught.

Whoever these secret forces were, they had taken him down, and Christopher Mallow followed. In comparison, she had gotten off lightly. The realization comforted her, sort of. She shoved her hands in her pockets and started down Pentonville Road.

Whatever that money was for had to be something big. Could she unearth it on her own? Could she endure another two years of ruined reputation, ruined life, ruined everything? Truth was, the burden already weighed heavy, and more of the same could destroy her irreparably. There would be no coming back. Come Monday, she'd tell Spence what she had discovered about the Smith Affair. Spence had taken a gamble hiring her;

he'd given her a chance when no one else would. He deserved proof that he made the right choice.

She halted in midstride. What was she thinking?

Smith was connected to Mallow. Even though Spence didn't know about Mallow's investigation, eventually he'd put it together. She could just tell him upfront. She shook her head. He'd fire her on the spot. And the information would put him in a tough spot with Damian Winters. She pulled her jacket in tight and carried on toward the lights at the Angel junction.

She came to a stop. Maybe she should just stay quiet about everything.

The light turned green.

She shoved her hands in her pockets. Ian Smith's handlers were still out there. Somewhere. If she were to find them, she'd need equipment. Roseman. She picked up the pace.

TWENTY-THREE

THE DAY HAD BEEN LONG, and Kelly gladly stripped out of her jeans. The list of IP addresses Josh had given her jutted from the pocket. Someone on Cicada would know where to find the Luntan; that's what the IP addresses were for. Given that the Luntan's location changed regularly, she knew it would be smart to kickstart a quick request now and let it brew. A response would land by morning. Eking out the last of her energy reserves, she dropped to her knees and dredged up a box from under the sofa.

Laptop, a pre-configured router, cables coiled like a black python, and a piece of paper with various passwords and fake online IDs, courtesy of Josh. Without him, she'd be a bumbling fool roaming the Internet.

In one snip of the tie, the cables let loose across the floor. She turned on the laptop.

The prep to get online from her home network slowed her down, but entering the one site that could give her valuable information called for protection. Protection not just from the State, but from Cicada itself.

Cicada users weren't known for being scrupulous, law-abiding users— quite the opposite. Any normie needed mental fortitude to make a simple statement in the forum, which is why most people never entered. The site was only for the truly brave or the truly stupid. She clicked the tunnel icon and promptly entered the Cicada forum.

The site was populated with Japanese animation, porn clips, and ads for sex dolls. A window prompted her for a username.

Stormykitten would be her new alias, taken off Josh's list. She punched it in.

After a few minutes of scanning the site for a user to zero in on, nothing. With nothing to lose, she came straight out with a demand for the upcoming location of the Luntan.

After a few minutes, username FahKew claimed the Luntan did not exist. This was the first firewall. Several exchanges of scorn later, he confessed to having heard about the Luntan.

Exchanges between Lyn and DarkTimes filled her screen—presumably because FahKew was thinking things over. Finally, FahKew hit up Kelly for pro-crypto, the currency of choice for dodgy dealers. Pro-crypto was on the blockchain but in a way that would take tech police weeks to hunt down the sender and receiver. By then, the dodgy dealer would be able to change address, number, and business name. The amount FahKew asked for was reasonable, but getting hold of the hard-to-trace coin was all sorts of other trouble.

> Stormykitten: LOAN?
> FahKew: FUCK OFF.
> Stormykitten: SEX?
> FahKew: WHAT DO YOU THINK I AM? NO CRYPTO, NO INFO.
> Stormykitten: MATTER OF LIFE & DEATH.
> FahKew: KYS

"Fuck," Kelly yelled. KYS was the abbreviation for kill yourself, which was FahKew's way of saying forget about it. She needed to get crypto in a matter of minutes, or else FahKew would disappear into the ether.

"Jerko, find a small pro-crypto loan shark with the lowest interest rate, preferably no interest rate, secure and anonymous."

"Lowest interest rate is one percent a day."

"If I borrow bits, what am I looking at in terms of gas?"

"Two hundred bits."

"Jerko, how much will I get if I sell you?"

"It is illegal for you to sell me," Jerko announced.

FahKew was now bargaining with other users, half probably his own sock puppets.

Her neck muscles tightened. She couldn't believe she'd have to pay to get the location. "Jerko, arrange the loan."

The transfer confirmed; she received the Luntan's location.

The address was a short trek from her home, but the opening time was midnight, the night before the Live Earth concert. She groaned.

Stormykitten: IF DATE & LOCALE ARE WRONG, MY HACKER FRIENDS WILL FUCK YOU UP.

FahKew signed off with an emoji flip-off—a good sign that he was legit.

She logged off and stretched her neck. Her muscles felt as stiff as cold taffy.

"YOUR NIGHT NEWS BRIEFING IS READY," Jerko blared.

Kelly startled awake. She couldn't remember falling asleep.

"Elite Squad hunt for rogue journalist as the Truth Laws take effect."

She groaned. The ghost had returned, or Jerko needed to be recalibrated. "I really need to replace you. That's not a headline."

"Projecting now."

She turned to Jerko. "I said—"

A dark thumbnail displayed on the white wall.

A chill rattled down her spine. This wasn't a ghost. She made her way to the wall of black letters and darkened image. Up close, she detected a faint outline of a human head and stepped back, hoping the broader range would give her a better perspective, but the millions of grainy pixels still obscured the image.

"Play the video."

The thumbnail enlarged to a full screen of people huddling in front of a residential block of flats. One was a small child, no older than seven years old. The skin on Kelly's neck tightened.

An old woman in a robe shuffled in her slippers along the wet pavement. She looked disoriented, possibly due to dementia, or maybe it was just the stress of being in the middle of the street at night.

Kelly's heart grew heavy in her chest. She looked at the headline again. "What has this to do with the Truth Laws?"

The video played on. Masked Elite Squad troopers slunk out of the building. A blood-curdling screech pierced the doomed night.

The child's eyes grew wide, as if ready to pop, and his bottom lip quivered.

Like a swarm of locusts, the Elite Squad troopers surrounded the helpless souls.

"Jerko, stop," Kelly whispered.

The video froze on a trooper shoving an elderly man in striped pajamas out the door, his hands suspended in the air like a mime about to fall.

"The video ends in two seconds."

"Jerko, who sent this video?"

"The sender has no ID."

She pulled back. Josh and Omar were the only ones who knew she was looking for this video. Or, it was a fake sent by some anonymous person from Cicada. Or, maybe it was the whistleblower, but he hadn't made contact since the ghost text. "Jerko, make a copy of it and send it to my private email."

The self-combusting video had zero views—probably doctored. She sent a copy to her email before it expired.

"Who uploaded this file to the Internet originally?"

"The original poster of the footage was the PPA."

Josh worked for the PPA. He would've told her about it, wouldn't he? "Call Josh Munro."

"If you speak to Josh Munro, you will delay your schedule."

She tensed. What the hell schedule was he talking about? "Jerko, call Josh Munro."

The call tone reverberated throughout her studio. No answer. She tapped on her thigh. "Close the line and locate Josh Munro."

"Josh Munro appears to be offline."

She threw up her arms. "Do I have to do all the thinking around here? What time is the PPA open?"

"Tomorrow morning at 10 a.m."

She had no choice now but to wait for the morning.

A FAINT TAP, tap, tap stirred Kelly awake. Her eyes adjusted to the dark as she glimpsed the clock. Three o'clock in the morning. The noise was probably from one of the neighbors. She snuggled under the duvet.

The tapping grew into loud bangs. That was no neighbor, she thought, but she held her breath and listened anyway.

A slow creak echoed in the hallway.

Adrenaline pumped through her. She crept to the door, ran her hands over the locks, bolted shut, and leaned against her only shield from the outside world, wishing she had a weapon.

She tiptoed to the kitchenette and opened the drawer. Metal utensils clanged. Her heart skipped. She froze and listened for movement.

Quiet.

In the darkness, she ran her fingers over the mishmash of useless utensils she had collected, mainly from Secret Santa exchanges. She picked up a knife, duller than a sheet of paper. "This thing couldn't kill a ghost." She put it back in the drawer and picked up the corkscrew.

As a weapon, a simple jam and twist of this pointy spiral could cause a lot of damage if there was enough force behind it. She wrapped her hand around its sturdy handle and carried it back to the sofa, eyeing the door, hoping the movement in the light on the other side of the door was her mind playing tricks.

The doorknob rattled.

Sweat sprinkled her palms, and she rose from the sofa. Her heart pounded deep inside her chest, her nostrils flared. She gripped the corkscrew and crept over to the lamp in the corner.

If someone dared to enter, she reminded herself that she knew the layout better than them. She also had a weapon, however mundane, and with the force of adrenaline, she had the potential to be deadly.

Her hand trembled as she reached for the lamp switch. She snapped it on. The click of the switch sounded like a faint snap, a sound she feared carried through the walls.

The door knob stilled.

She held her breath and listened.

Footsteps pattered away down the hallway. She stood, frozen, letting soft breaths escape her lips.

When the downstairs door creaked, she darted over to the window and peered down, hiding behind the sash as she did so.

A man in a black coat stepped onto the path where a car waited, the engine thrumming quietly. He scooted in. A soft, muffled sound, one that belonged to an expensive self-closing door, started up. Moments later, the car drove off.

She slumped against the wall. This could have been a warning. Possibly from the thugs. Possibly from someone on Cicada. Maybe Ian Smith had tattled to someone about her visit. Or maybe it was a random criminal on the prowl in search of an opportunity. For a moment, she contemplated calling the police. Maybe that Officer Blake. What would she say, though? No crime had actually been committed. And given the connections of the people Smith had been working for, she couldn't be certain of trusting the police in any case.

She grabbed a sheet of paper and added a few weapons to the list for Roseman.

She glanced at the clock on the laptop. Hours before the PPA opened. Maybe it was a good idea to tell Spence everything after all. At least that way she wouldn't be on her own. Plus, he'd know the truth if she was found floating in Regent's Canal.

TWENTY-FOUR

14 January

KELLY SLUNG her bag on the A & E desk and headed for Spence's office. Under normal circumstances, Kelly wouldn't seek Spence's help, but after last night, she had little choice.

Jonathan rushed over. "You can't go in there," he whispered urgently. "He's in a meeting."

"I need to talk to Spence."

She nudged him out of the way and stepped into his office.

Spence, Damian, and Geneva all looked up sharply the moment Kelly stepped into the room. Spence's face was lined with deep crevices, the knot in his tie sagging below his shirt's collar. He looked as though a couple of pounds had melted off him. Damian Winters sat back in his chair, cool-faced.

Geneva's accusatory eyes bore a hole through Kelly. "I've been looking for you all over." It looked like the girl had far more to say but couldn't.

Whatever was going on in this office couldn't possibly be more important than the attempted break-in to her flat last night. "This can't wait."

Kelly said. "The Daily Times, Robert Greaves. He didn't die of a heart attack."

Spence pinched his eyes between his thumbs.

Damian leaned into the table. "How do you know?"

"A source contacted me last night about Mallow's arrest, and—"

"A source?" Spence said.

The three around the table exchanged solemn glances.

Kelly stepped back. "What the hell is going on in here?"

"We need everything verified by at least three sources," Damian said. "But in this case, it's irrelevant anyway because the Mallow story has a D-notice on it."

"It is a deliberate—"

"You're not on the crime desk anymore, Kelly."

"Can you just let me finish?"

"In case you forgot, the crime desk was frozen," Spence said. "More importantly, we got word you were over at TechTonic."

Kelly shuddered but tried to hide it as best she could. "So what?"

"Seems you were over there asking questions about Christopher Mallow."

She reeled back. That weasel Bletchley was cagey about the article he had coauthored with Christopher Mallow, but she never thought he'd take it so far as to make a complaint. "I wasn't asking him about Mallow. I wanted to know about an article Bletchley wrote."

"Right," Geneva said.

"The D-notice made it clear," Spence said. "I made it clear. No Mallow story."

She wanted to slink off and start all over again, but she stood in the center of his office, taking the hits, bearing the brunt of the fallout, and braced herself.

"If I catch you, or anyone in this office, you will give me no choice but to let you go. You've been assigned to Live Earth, and that's all. Geneva will now be accompanying you."

Kelly's throat tightened. "Of course."

"Have you written the teaser for it yet?" Spence said. "Lily gave you her notes, didn't she?"

Kelly had skimmed them briefly, but not enough to put together a teaser. "Yes, I'm on it."

"This is your last chance."

She gritted her teeth. It could have turned out a lot worse. Her shoulders sagged as she closed the door behind her.

What had she been thinking? This wasn't like her. The fear over the attempted break-in last night must have spooked her more than she realized. She was off-kilter. She rubbed her eyes and shook off the confusion.

She made her way to the A&E desk.

HARRY SWIVELED AROUND. "What happened to you?"

"It's been a long day." Kelly leaned against his desk.

"It's only nine fifteen in the morning." He swiveled back around. "The long day has only just begun. Remember what I said about the Daily Times? Now look at them. Kaput." He buffed his nails against his shirt. "You heard it here first."

Without a registered watch, she was out of the loop, and now she was relying on Harry for all the gossip and news. She nudged her long sleeve over her bare wrist. "What else have you heard?"

"That's all. Unofficially though..." He scooted toward her. "Some fat dude was spotted coming out of MI5 and got into a black chauffeured car."

"So?"

"So, no one knows who he belongs to. Which is a little unusual, don't you think? But fear not, Meister White is on the case." He scooted back. "Then, I saw the PM and the Commissioner at the Traveller's Club Library. It looked like a secret rendezvous."

She shrugged. That could mean anything. Government officials met up all the time. "Maybe they're having an affair." The thought of the old man naked in bed made her stomach flip.

"I doubt it. Some other guy was at the Club's library with them. I only got a flash of him before Justin blocked the view."

"Justin?"

"He's one of the waiters. I'm a member of the club. I know all the staff."

The door to Spence's office opened, and Geneva stepped out. She gave Spence and Damian a sharp nod before turning on her heel. It looked like they had more to say to each other, stuff Damian didn't even trust his daughter with. And by the look on Spence's face, Damian was conveying more than just idle gossip.

Geneva strode down the central aisle and caught Kelly's eye. "I've been calling you all morning, Kelly. Didn't you get any of my messages?"

The tone of her voice sounded like she was out on a mission, and that mission involved Kelly. "Technology has failed me all week."

"No excuse," Harry said.

Kelly glanced sideways at him and turned back to Geneva. The Live Earth concert teaser, the one Kelly had to upload, suddenly became an irresistible priority. She shoved off the desk and scooped up her backpack.

"I need to speak to you. Privately. Now."

Kelly was too tired to talk to the compliance officer and felt for an out. "Why do you want to work here, Geneva?"

Harry stopped tapping at the keyboard.

"I mean, the bots are taking over, the media is doomed. Not sure why you want to enter the fray." Kelly hoped her quick add-on covered up the dig.

"They won't be successful." Geneva stood in front of Kelly, her hands on her hips, her chest heaving up and down a little faster than it should be in an office. "They can't overtake the creative fields. Nuances are important."

"So, that's what we are now?" Kelly tugged at the strap on her shoulder. "Creatives?"

Geneva shook her head. "That's a larger discussion. Right now, we need to focus on something more immediately important to this newsroom."

Harry raised his eyebrows.

"Whatever it is you need to talk to me about, can it wait?" Kelly braced herself for a protest. "I need to get to the echo chamber."

"I'm conducting interviews with all journalists on staff. Best if we talk in the conference room." Geneva pointed her shoes in the direction of the fishbowl.

Kelly could see there was no getting out of it. She resigned herself to the fate that awaited her and started for the fishbowl. She could hear the girl's footsteps behind her, so she halted midstride and waited for her to catch up. "How long is it going to take?"

"Hard to say."

The elevator bell dinged behind her.

Harry stood, stretched his neck over the desks, and eased down into his chair, his eyebrows raised.

Kelly turned toward the elevator.

A wave of anxiety shuttled through her at the sight of Omar looking lost and bearing a bouquet wrapped in gold metallic paper. Caught between the spy and the ex-boyfriend, Kelly wished she could magically teleport to the echo chamber now. "I'm not trying to avoid this meeting, but I really need to do it later," Kelly said to Geneva.

"No. It's important. I'll meet you in the conference room." Geneva's footsteps pattered down the aisle like a hamster in a wheel.

Omar wandered over to the fielders. Kelly lingered, trying to decide how to handle this. He was the last person she wanted to deal with.

"Love is in the air," Harry cooed.

Kelly shot Harry a sour look and resolved to get rid of Omar as quickly as possible. As she drew near him, the sweet fragrance of the flowers assaulted her nostrils. The deep purple, red, and pink of the roses throbbed in the light. A headache teased the edges of her mind. Omar lifted the flowers toward her.

She winced and pushed his hand away. "What are you doing here?" She led him by the arm to the stairwell.

"I wanted to make up for the other night. Truce?"

He shoved the flowers at her. A headache teased her temples. "It's over, Omar."

"Are you still upset? I'm sorry about everything I said."

"Doesn't matter. We're through. Don't make this more difficult than it has to be."

Her rejection didn't seem to register. He offered her the flowers again. "Please, take them. They're for you."

Her stomach contracted. "I think I'm allergic."

"Since when?"

"Since now."

He placed the flowers at her feet. "Give it some thought." Slowly, he descended the stairs as though expecting her to call out to him.

Holding her breath, she scooped up the flowers and plunked them onto Jonathan's desk back in the newsroom. "Enjoy," she said, more an order than a gentle suggestion.

The nausea that had threatened to overwhelm her simmered to a low boil the farther she walked away from the flowers.

Harry was craning his neck out the window. "And he drives a car. Government issue." He pulled himself back and plopped down on his chair. "Kelly has hit the big time."

One irritant down, another to go. Kelly glanced at the fishbowl. "Where's Geneva?"

"Probably the ladies. So, who is lover-boy?"

"Don't you have work to do?"

From the corner of her eye, Kelly could see Geneva making her way to the fishbowl. She swung her backpack onto both shoulders. "Geneva, let's catch up later. I really have to get the Live Earth teaser done."

Geneva raised her hands in the air in exasperation. "You can't keep running, Kelly."

She pulled open the door to the stairwell and descended the stairs.

TWENTY-FIVE

15 January

Josh zoomed to East London, camera equipment in the hard case tucked in the compartment above the back wheel. A photographer of his caliber should be on his way to a celebrity wedding, capturing beautiful women in pastel-colored dresses, sunlight streaming through the windows. Or a model with perfect hair and makeup and a shiny dress falling down her shoulder. Instead, he was off to a greasy spoon café to spy on the leader of the Underground Freedom Fighters: Rozlyn Abbott. Still unsure of who the anonymous client was, he shook his head at the absurdity of it all.

Back in the day, when his father gave him a starter camera, a Sony DSLR, he never imagined he'd end up using his skills to surveil people. Lightweight for his young hands, the sweet Sony shot continuous bursts, making him feel like a professional. Most of his photos back then were of insects and rocks, and he loved it. At ten years old, he was selling his pics for a penny.

His first self-purchased camera was a Nikon D800, secondhand. It was all the rage because of its increased megapixels and full-frame digital sensor. It took crisp shots, especially in low light settings, rivaling the

Canon 5D Mark III, the camera most fashion photographers were using at the time. He took his secondhand baby out to the high street and captured paparazzi-style photos of beautiful girls, their hair billowing in the wind, frozen in time. What the hell happened?

Where were all the private eyes, the moonlighting cops, the kids with camera phones who wanted to make an extra bit or two? He came to a stop on Marylebone, in front of the iron-gated entrance to Regent's Park, and lowered a foot to the tarmac. He rested his hands on the tank, giving his wrists a break. The terrorist attacks hit London. That's what happened. It started a wave of restrictions that never let up.

The red light changed to amber.

He leaned in and revved the engine. On green, he took off ahead of the auto-cars. The early restrictions confined hobby photographers to public spaces. Eventually, hobbyists required model release forms in order to publish digital galleries of identifiable people. He got busy learning Photoshop, mastering the Gaussian blur tool.

Tourists were exempt from those restrictions because it was too cumbersome to prosecute them, but really, it was because the State wanted to preserve its image of a free society in the international community.

The pressure on local photographers, however, continued to mount. When it got too much, he joined the Photography Press Agency to get the necessary licenses. But then the Truth Laws arrived.

The Resistance network sprang into being, and anonymous journalists joined by the dozen. He still didn't know if the current assignment was from one of the Resistance cells. Regardless, they would still benefit when he handed over copies to them—an incentive to hurry it up.

The Oasis Cafe came into view. Faded palm trees embossed the grime-covered sign above the café, and its storefront was a dirty yellow.

He pulled up on the other side of the road, kicked out the stand, and studied the layout of the café through its large window. Apart from the staff, only two people sat inside, each at a different table.

A cashmere-coated lady—out of place in a greasy spoon—didn't so much as twitch. Given that the café wasn't far from a crematorium, maybe she was stealing a moment for herself in this dive. At the other table, a man sat alone, his face a mask of despair. He stared at the floor. It didn't look like either of these catatonics would be departing any time soon.

Visor down, Josh walked up to the café's dust-streaked windows. He picked up a flier from the rack on the windowsill and dropped a die-sized audio receiver; the little white cube would go unnoticed here. Whatever Abbott said inside the café would now be transmitted to him within a one-hundred-foot range.

He moved his bike to a spot with a line of sight into the café but also with enough distance so as not to be too obvious. Finally, he took off his helmet and surveyed the location. The overcast sky tinged the shadows blue, a natural filter that dampened highlights on shiny surfaces. Drizzle began to wet the tarmac, making surfaces shimmer and reflect the yellow signage. At least these images would pop.

He whipped open a collapsible two-legged pod. Its hefty suction cup foot safeguarded against any potential sudden gusts of wind. Secured to the pavement, he mounted a super telephoto lens, used for wildlife photography, onto the N16 camera and threaded the whole setup onto the pod.

Memory storage had enough space for three hours of continuous shooting. He doubted the Underground Freedom Fighters' leader would be there longer than thirty minutes—from the look of the café, he couldn't imagine what she would be doing in there at all.

He peered through the electronic viewfinder and scanned the shot.

Overhead, fluorescent bulbs drained color from the one face he could see, the man staring down at his shoes. He fired off three test shots and then quickly reviewed the images in the camera's viewfinder. The man's sallow, jaundiced face was crystal clear. Good to go. He waited.

The frame of the camera lens enlivened Josh's instincts like nothing else could. Now, seeing the cashmere-coated lady through the lens, it was obvious she was there for a purpose. He fired off the shutter, high-speed continuous bursts.

She wasn't turning around. Not an inch.

He switched to video mode and let the camera run while he surveyed the street.

There she was. That angular jaw. Rozlyn Abbott. The petite woman stood a head shorter than the guy walking with her—a blond, bulky six-foot man, possibly her bodyguard. Josh had expected a taller woman; that's how she came across in her picture.

At the door of the Oasis Café, she fixed on a smile, and they entered.

The woman in the cashmere coat tilted her head and curtly nodded at Abbott. The woman's movement was so economical that Josh couldn't even see the tip of her nose. "Who are you, lady?" he whispered to himself as he adjusted the camera to tighten the frame on Abbott and the cashmere-coated woman.

Abbott took up a seat. Her blond bodyguard stood behind, arms folded, guarding her back.

Josh popped an earbud into his ear, tuned the audio frequency, and pressed record.

"Must be important for you to call on me." Abbott's lips moved in the viewfinder. He logged her as the one with a monotone voice.

"I have a problem only you can help solve."

Abbott crossed her legs. "I'm listening."

"You seem to have a civilian in your territory. We want him."

A flicker of recognition flashed across Abbott's face. "I don't know who you are talking about."

"Don't play games, Abbott. We have eyes everywhere. We saw it all."

Abbott shifted in her seat. "He's one of ours. We don't turn in our own."

"Do you always bundle your own into the back of a black van?"

Abbott's eyes squinted at the woman she faced. "You and I live on the same planet but in different worlds."

The cashmere lady's back broadened as she drew in a deep breath. "The asset is someone I suspect has intel."

Abbott folded her arms over her chest. "You think it's going to be that easy?"

They sat at the table, looking at one another.

The woman scooted her chair toward the table. "What do you want?" Her voice was low and controlled.

A look of satisfaction broke across Abbott's face. "I've been around longer than you and that kid put together. I remember what this city used to be like. Sure, it hasn't always been safe, but some of us want it back. What it used to be. This kid can help us get it back."

"He was last seen leaving the INNS in Covent Garden, which means he's ours."

Abbott shook her head and rolled her eyes. "I'm sure you can do better than that." She reached her hand over the table. "It'll cost you dearly."

Cashmere woman pulled back. "How much do you want?"

"I'm not one of your minions." Abbott paused. "When I have news to report, we'll talk."

"I can always get Damian Winters to do a report on the Underground Freedom Fighters."

Abbott glared.

"Just let me have the kid, and it doesn't have to go that far," the woman in the cashmere coat continued smoothly.

Without saying another word, Abbott stood and exited the café. Her blond bodyguard followed right behind.

"Shit!" Torn between staying put to identify the stranger, who seemed to know Damian Winters, or follow Abbott for the job he had been commissioned to do, he simply stood still.

The waitress brought the cashmere lady a mug. She shook her head and lifted her arm to her mouth. She was calling someone.

Abbott was getting into a car.

Money was money, and he was on an assignment. He'd have to pay Global Wires a visit on a different day. He stuffed his gear into the case and followed Abbott's car.

TWENTY-SIX

16 January

RAIN DRIZZLED onto the pavement in Covent Garden, coating Kelly's eyelashes in mist. Her sneakers had long lost their tread—making them about as secure as new leather soles on carpet. She had intended to replace them a month ago, and the month before that, but the bills kept eating up whatever spare cash she had. She lifted her head and glimpsed the echo chamber just across the road.

Water dripped down the side of her face as she turned to her watch to dial into the Global Wires portal. Nothing but a pale stripe branded her wrist. "Damn!"

The missing watch invoked a sense of limbo that ricocheted to irritation and finally settled into apprehension. Without the watch, she couldn't check in as per Spence's protocol. Only steps away from the chamber's door, a spark lit up in her mind. The unregistered watch, the temporary one Josh had given her, could work. She pulled it out of her backpack and clicked it on.

A cursor flashed on the blank face of the watch as though it were waiting for further instruction. It didn't look like it was even programmed.

She toggled through the settings. Somehow, the location arrow switched on. Hurriedly, Kelly pressed the location button two, three, four times—all to no avail. She knocked the watch against the bony ridge of her palm, but it made no difference.

A faint sense of paranoia bubbled up in her mind. Now was not the time to ratchet up the tension. She de-powered the watch and, for the first time, skipped the check-in protocol.

The drizzle abruptly turned into thick drops of water. Within seconds, a mighty roar rained down on her. She braced herself and rushed toward the chamber, careful to avoid the swelling puddles, and flashed her QR code under the scanner—half expecting an alarm bell to blast.

The door buzzed open, and she hurried inside.

Not a soul in sight.

She shook her wet hair and stripped off her jacket, hanging it on a hook. She stuffed the earbuds into her ears.

"Welcome back, Kelly Blackwell. Please remove your wet shoes before proceeding to cockpit one."

She untied her sneakers and placed them in the shoe cabinet. The heated floor tiles warmed her damp feet as she traipsed toward cockpit one, the same one that Christopher Mallow had been stationed at days earlier.

Not a trace of blood could be seen, not even in the grout between the tiles. It was as though nothing had happened. Nevertheless, Mallow's screams flashed through her mind like an out-of-tune memory.

Repetitive subterranean beats belted down her ear canals.

"We calculate it will take three breaths to calibrate, Kelly Blackwell."

Sinking into the padded chair, she drew in her first breath. The overhead light turned pink. On her second breath, the light transitioned to baby blue, and on her third, it glowed tangerine orange, reminiscent of an early summer's evening.

She breathed deep, pushing away every intruding thought, and zeroed in on the only subject that mattered at this very moment: the Live Earth concert. Lily's notes appeared in her mind's eye, the words assembling into a teaser in her mind.

The Fi headset lit up white. She placed it on her head.

Global sensation Shiva landed in London days ahead of her upcoming appearance at the Live Earth concert on Saturday night. A Global Wires exclusive interview.

Words flew onto the white screen like blackbirds to a silver lake. Two hundred words transferred within three minutes. The big screen mirrored each sentence, line by line, exactly as she intended. When the system worked, it really did astonish. Readers would get the teaser within minutes, and so would Spence.

Cool air gushed through the chamber.

A prickly sensation wrapped itself around her scalp. Memories of the Elite Squad whipped through her mind. She slowly pulled off the headset and listened for thumping boots, marching legs, batons crashing into the tiled floor.

The overhead lights in a cockpit behind her flashed.

In her peripheral vision, she could see a man shaking himself out of his coat. His short hair, round glasses, and black jeans made him out to be a graphic designer. For some reason, graphic designers wore round glasses, and she never knew why. He settled into the cubicle at the far end of the row.

She exhaled, returned her focus to the trance music, and replaced the Fi headset.

The cursor whipped across the screen, right and left and right again, as if by the hand of God.

Lkjgraelkguuuo998543???/oe\'[]

Her jaw dropped. She stared on, stunned, helpless.

"There seems to be a problem, Kelly Blackwell. Please reset the head-set," the chamber voice said in her ear.

Her heart sped up, and she accidentally whacked the headset off its stand.

"Hey. Quiet down over there," the graphic designer yelled.

Letters and numbers continued to dance across the screen, line after line, disordered and senseless.

Frantically, she pressed the reboot button.

The cursor continued to spout out jumbled symbols.

Kelly banged on all the console buttons.

The console key lights flashed yellow all at once. Whole words, luminous black words, engraved the white screen.

Her hands went numb.

Kelly Blackwell suspects the State of murder. Desperate people do desperate things.

Blood drained from Kelly's face. She squeezed her eyelids tight, hoping the nightmare would end. She inhaled deeply and shot open her eyes. The nightmare was written all over the wall. "Chamber, I didn't think, I mean, I didn't write that. Delete."

"All work is recorded."

Her body trembled. "Override the last entry and delete it."

"You are not authorized to override the INNS."

She gasped. Her sweaty palms slipped. The AI wasn't glitching—it was reading her doubt, weaponizing it. She reached for the power switch, groping around the wall frantically.

Metal clanged on the tile floor. She whipped around.

A small, toothless key lay on the floor, the kind that belonged to a filing cabinet. She recalled Christopher mentioning his filing cabinet on the day he got arrested. Had Mallow intended for her to find it when she was groping for the power switch back then? She rocked on her heels and reached for the key. She clasped it between her fingernails, lifted it from the slick floor, and flung it into her bag.

The graphic designer poked his head into her station and glanced at her screen.

"That wasn't me," she said, her sweaty hands zipping up her bag.

"It's your screen."

"But I didn't think that," she said, trying to keep her voice under control. She clasped her bag and rose to face him. Obviously, he wasn't the one who caused the malfunction, either. He was just another hack trying to make a living. "The upgrade is faulty."

He looked at the screen and backed away. "I don't even have the headset on." He raised his voice loud enough for the chamber to hear.

The overhead light in her cockpit flashed red. "Kelly Blackwell of Global Wires, do not discharge from the INNS."

Sweat burst from her forehead. She looked up at the cameras, ran over to the shoe cupboard, pulled out her sneakers, and shoved them onto her feet.

The designer grabbed his coat. "Hell if I'm staying here!"

She heard the bolts of the door sliding shut. There was no way the chamber could legally hold the designer. He hadn't done anything wrong. But then, nor had she.

He flashed his barcode at the interior scanner.

Kelly's heart thumped in her chest as the chamber seemed to work through a dilemma: keep the door closed and hold her, or open the door and let him out.

The door clicked open.

"Kelly Blackwell, remain inside the chamber."

She scooted right behind him. Powered by adrenaline, she shot out and ran onto the square. She slipped on the wet pavement and banged her mouth on a concrete slab. Pain surged through her jaw, and drops of blood tainted the ground ruby red.

She lifted herself. How was she going to explain what just happened in the chamber? What *had* just happened? Didn't matter. She couldn't let Spence see the chamber's malfunction report. She'd have to intercept it before it landed on his desktop. Could take two days or so, but she wasn't sure. Limping away from the chamber, she had just enough time to find a hacker.

TWENTY-SEVEN

18 January. 11:30 p.m.

KELLY INKED the Luntan location on her wrist and flicked her arm in the air. "If this isn't the right address, FahKew, I'll be coming for you."

She gave it a final puff and pulled on her Everest jacket—not ideal outerwear, but it was the warmest she owned. During the day, it wouldn't get a second glance, but at night, it was like walking with a target on her back. Thugs, druggies, and every low-life scum would peg her as an honest worker. They'd clock her slight frame, her busted lip, and see her walking alone. To them, she'd look like easy pickings. She slid the sharpest knife from the drawer up her coat sleeve and pocketed the corkscrew.

A sense of security settled over her mind. She wrapped her plaid scarf around her neck, tightened her laces, and zipped up, fully prepared for the trek to the Luntan. The promise of a registered watch, online protection, and real weapons lured her out of her front door.

The quiet night air wrapped around her ears.

Silence.

She strode onto the middle of Black Prince Road—the safest spot illuminated by streetlights. Anyone with malicious intent would have to drag her a few extra feet, kicking and fighting, into a side road.

Heat climbed up her collar as she marched eastward.

Air currents carried a muffled shuffling sound that seemed to scratch her inner ears.

Her scalp tightened. Probably a city fox scavenging. Not taking any chances, she wiggled her arm until the knife's handle landed in her palm.

Her ears tingled at the sound of teeth chattering, and she tried to make out black shapes in the darkness.

A mass moved, half-hidden in the shadows. It bundled against the wall.

She zeroed in on it and gripped the knife. Burying her fear, she kept her pace steady.

A flickering streetlamp lit the tip of a worn-out shoe. Had to be a homeless person. They were not the ones who filled city dwellers with so much fear that they abandoned the roads an hour after sundown. She let out a sharp breath.

Buffered by distance, Kelly stopped in front of the tall, broad-shouldered homeless person. He was shrouded under layers of blankets, his smell sour.

He turned away and crouched into a ball, shrinking his six-foot stature, shielding himself from the light.

She pulled her scarf free. "You need this more than I do."

His baby blue eyes looked at her through matted hair.

"Do me a favor," she said. "Holler if you see anyone coming up behind me." She dropped the scarf to the ground.

He nodded and snatched it with his gloved hand.

Surprised to see a newish-looking glove covering his hand, something inside her froze. She eased back.

So did he. The scarf dangled from his clasped hands. He pulled it into his chest, close to his heart, and bowed his head.

She could see that he gave her every indication that he was no threat. She nodded and backed onto the street.

He remained still.

Knowing that he was literally watching her back, reset her shaky sense of security as she strode toward her final destination.

Minutes later, an abandoned red brick building with boarded-up windows came into view. It wasn't at all what she had expected. She pulled back her sleeve. The address was right.

Reluctantly, she banged on the steel shutter—the clanging steel howled into the night like a call to wolves. There wasn't a flutter of response from the other side of the shutter.

She cursed FahKew, but she was the one who fell for the fraud. Now, on top of everything else, she had a loan shark to pay off. She glanced at the dark road behind her.

The thought of a long slog home empty-handed stirred an anger inside her that could kill off any thug.

A BARE LIGHT bulb flicked on, electricity buzzed. A rusty panel creaked open, camouflaged under a mural of graffiti.

A bald man stepped out wearing shades. He was dressed in a black three-piece suit. The only thing missing was a hat to complete the look. "What's your username?"

His deep voice broke through Kelly's tension. FahKew never told her she had to reveal a special username. "Not sure what you mean."

"Your username." He sounded impatient.

"Stormykitten?"

"I'll call you Stormy for short." He opened the door. "No one uses their given names around here. I suggest you don't either." He motioned her inside.

She slid through the half-open door.

Inside, the bald man lit a match. Sharp sulfur stung her nostrils. She hadn't smelled a sulfur-tipped match in years.

They descended a circular stairwell.

"No shouting. No fighting. Remain respectful of other guests at all times. You break those rules, you'll get thrown onto the path." He stopped at the bottom of the stairwell and pointed down another hall. "No shouting, no fighting. Leave devices here—watches, phones, metal. Close an hour before sunrise. Any questions?"

She shook her head.

"Last thing. We close an hour before sunrise. You can't leave before then unless we throw you out." He opened the door to a candlelit room. "Get comfy."

The staff, dressed in black, moved gracefully between patrons seated on low stools. The thrown-together furniture added an air of *joie de vivre,* but overall, the space was intimate, the color scheme largely sepia-toned. Kelly felt out of place and underdressed.

She leaned against the bar and took a moment to imbibe the secret hideaway.

A band jammed in the corner, belting out sleepy jazz. A few drunk dancers swayed along to the music, trancelike. Most of the crowd ignored the low-key tunes, absorbed in face-to-face conversations. She couldn't recall the last time she had seen so many people in conversation with each other.

"What can I get you?"

Kelly pivoted.

The voice came from the mixologist. His swanky hair, beard, and mustache, curled up at the ends, reminded her of barmen from centuries ago. The blackboard behind him listed cocktails and wine. Regardless of the decade, she had never come across a bar that served interesting nonalcoholic drinks, and she didn't expect much here either. "What virgin drink do you recommend?"

"How about the cucumber and rosewater, minus the vodka?" He winked. "Or, there's the pink lemonade. An old-time favorite."

"Cucumber and rosewater it is."

"I'll do you a solid and knock off a couple of bits."

Even with the discount, she'd have to make it last the whole night. She nodded.

Moments later, the mixologist placed a tall glass filled with murky liquid in front of her. Not even a cheap paper umbrella. Kelly felt cheated.

"Looks can be deceiving." He must have sensed her disappointment. "Have a sip. If you don't like it, I can replace it with the pink lemonade."

The cool liquid touched her palate. A refreshing burst of cucumber with an undertone of floral notes conjured childhood memories of hot summers spent in Hyde Park. "It's perfect."

He smiled.

"Where can I find Roseman?"

His eyebrows furrowed. "He's not here tonight." He wiped down the counter between them. "But that man, over there." He pointed four tables down to the right. "The one with the black rose tattoo. He might help."

She looked over to where the mixologist had pointed. The man with the black rose tattoo chatted to a sexy woman dressed in white. At the same table sat a plump woman with burgundy hair and a muscular man, his shirt exposing his hair-free chest.

The mixologist leaned in. "He doesn't take kindly to strangers. Tell him I sent you over."

She nodded a thank-you, grabbed her drink, and made her way over, garnering courage along the way. The barman didn't want to disclose the name of the man with the black rose tattoo, but of course, he was Roseman. Had to be. No time to play games—she still needed to find a hacker—Kelly situated a stool next to Roseman. He was nestling his head into the sexy lady's neck.

The plump girl with burgundy hair glared at Kelly. She held her gaze until the plump girl balked and turned away, rewarding Kelly with a minor victory that felt surprisingly sweet. Muscleman and plump girl turned toward each other and whispered; it made Kelly think that they could also be in line to talk to Roseman. Whatever they wanted couldn't possibly trump the weapons she needed, and if she didn't act now, the trade could take all night.

She leaned toward Roseman. "The barman said you could help me with a few things."

Without turning to see who spoke, he said, "We have all night, you know." His gravelly voice came straight out of an old gangster film set in the East End of London.

She soldiered on. "I thought I might get my business done sooner rather than later."

He froze. "A fucking newbie."

His insult felt...like an insult. She might've been a new visitor to the Luntan, but she wasn't green. "Did Josh leave you a message?"

"Josh?"

"Munro. The Channel."

He straightened up in his seat and waved the sexy lady away.

Kelly reached into her pocket and pulled out a folded sheet of paper containing the list of weapons and equipment.

He licked his lips and looked her up and down. "What do I look like? A grocery store?"

He studied Kelly's face. Knowing he didn't have metal objects on him comforted her. She jutted the paper forward. "The Channel will pay you."

"Let me see that." He snatched the paper from her hand, almost ripped it open, and ran his gaze down the list, and then her, as if weighing whether to supply her with the goods.

Her foot tapped under the table. "I need everything tonight."

He threw his head back and laughed. "You think I carry all this stuff around with me?"

She hadn't thought this through. Of course, he wouldn't have it all here. "If not tonight, when?"

"Tomorrow."

Finally, she was getting somewhere. "And where will it be delivered?"

"Where you live."

"You don't know where that is."

"We'll find out."

"How?"

He squirmed in his chair. "You ask a lot of questions." He reached into his pocket and pulled out a small plastic bag with a dozen white pills. "It's on the house."

"I don't need any pills."

"Trust me, you do."

"Are they all-natural?" she said, not knowing what else to say.

He threw his head back again and laughed, catching muscle man and plump girl's attention. "She's quite something, in'she?" Roseman wiped a tear from the corner of his eye. "You can learn a lesson or two off this one." He turned to Kelly. "Nothing's natural these days, love."

She had no need for pills but took them to bind the deal and put her hand out to shake.

Muscle man piped up. "He doesn't shake hands."

"Fair enough." She turned to Roseman. "One last thing. Can you recommend a hacker? One who can intercept chamber reports."

"You need to relax," he said. "Take a chill pill. Then, we'll talk."

She eyed the bag of pills for a long minute. They couldn't possibly be the only thing standing between her and a high-caliber hacker. She glanced back at the mixologist. He was absorbed in conversation with a dark-haired woman at the bar.

The bag lay in front of her. "Like you said, we have all night."

TWENTY-EIGHT

19 January

FOR THE LAST TWO HOURS, Josh had positioned himself against a wall that had a clear line of sight to Global Wires. He wasn't here to see Kelly. He wasn't here for the anonymous client. After hearing Damian's name pop up at the Oasis Cafe, he was here to find out why. Unfortunately, Spence hadn't exited the building—leaving Josh no opportunity to get inside and plant spy cams in his office.

In fact, no one had come in or out of the building in all that time. Wasn't too surprising. Today was the day of the Live Earth concert. Most personnel were outdoors, drumming up publicity and excitement while a skeleton crew worked the desks.

He hugged the soft leather bag carrying the spy cameras and mics he hoped to plant. The movement stretched his stiff back, wringing out the tension between his shoulder blades. It could be a while yet before Spence came out, and his legs were already crying out for a deep tissue massage. Maybe it was time to forge the opportunity—favor shines upon the bold and all that. He walked over to the entrance, grateful to be swinging his legs, and buzzed the bell.

"Well, hello, Josh." Jonathan was obviously feeling lonely. "Do come up." The door buzzed open.

Josh climbed the stairwell, deliberating over how to dodge the inevitable question about who he was there to visit. At the top of the stairwell, Jonathan was holding open the door to the newsroom, giving him his most seductive eye.

Quickly, Josh reached into his bag.

Jonathan's eyes lit up. "Do you have a gift for me?"

A cam glued itself to Josh's palm, and he pulled his hand out, seemingly empty-handed. "Sorry to disappoint. Is Kelly in?"

Jonathan's eyebrows furrowed. "And here I thought you wanted to see me." He twirled a strand of curly hair at the base of his neck. "There's no one here, you know."

"It's rather urgent. Any way I can get in touch with her?"

Harry White popped up behind Jonathan. "Hey, Josh!"

Jonathan rolled his eyes, pirouetted, and pranced toward his desk.

Relieved, Josh gave Harry a genuine smile.

"If you're looking for Kelly, she's not here," Harry said. "But don't worry, it wasn't with that guy who came around the other day."

A small ping clicked inside Josh. Harry had a way of slipping in the gossip that got people to bite, and Josh bit. "What guy?"

"Some rich guy in a car. He brought her flowers."

Had to be Omar, that cad. Delivering flowers by hand to her office was a first. He never took her out, never did much of anything, as far as Josh could tell, yet Kelly was still seeing him. "You're working this year's concert?"

Jonathan sailed past, pinching his tablet's screen between his black nail-polished fingers.

"Big night," Harry said. "Aren't you working it?"

"I'm working a different assignment, thought maybe Spence could hook me up with one of his contacts."

"He took the day off this year." Harry shrugged. "Maybe I can help."

"I'm looking for Roger Beale, the guy Spence was at the roundtable with last year."

"The Question Time presenter at the BBC? Yeah, sure."

Josh followed Harry, surveying the newsroom for a strategic spot to land the spy-cam.

"Did you hear about the Mallow footage?"

"The one that got the D-notice slapped on it?"

Harry nodded. "Heard it's back in circulation. But no one knows who made it."

The desks, the carpet became tack sharp, a side effect of a spurt of adrenaline. His vision always sharpened like this right before a big shoot. "How did that happen?"

Harry shrugged. "Just heard there are a few copies floating around and they all have different creators in their metadata."

"Bloody hell," Josh said, hoping his voice sounded concerned.

"I'm sure they'll find the real creator. Not much can't be found out these days."

The Resistance did know he helped circulate one version, but that didn't mean much. The only leaky tap he was worried about was Percy. And Kelly. Always Kelly, finding out what he'd done.

They came to Harry's desk; it was probably one of the best places in the newsroom in terms of gossip and vantage point. Harry scrolled his contacts list, and Josh pressed the cam to the underside of Harry's desk. He was spying on Kelly's workplace now. Watching her without her knowledge. Another lie stacked on top of all the others.

"Here it is," Harry chirped. "Roger Beale. I'll shoot it over to you now."

Josh's watch dinged. "Thanks, man. Can I use the gents before I leave? It's going to be a long night."

Harry pointed to the back of the room.

Inside the washroom, Josh placed a mic on top of a bathroom mirror.

He had one more to place. Ideally, inside Spence's office. He rubbed his chin, thinking about how to make that happen.

TWENTY-NINE

KELLY PACED UP BAYSWATER ROAD, only an hour of sleep in her energy bank. She had gone home with a hacker from the Luntan, and they spent the day hacking into the bowels of the Global Wires server. It wasn't pretty. Eventually, they located her malfunction report and promptly destroyed it. By the time she got home, Roseman's box of goodies had arrived. Now, as she passed the gate into Hyde Park, sporting a new watch registered to a fictitious person and a burner phone in her pocket, she felt like a normal member of society again. But a small doubt niggled at her as though she had forgotten something.

The sight of Geneva standing at the barrier into Live Earth, engrossed in her watch, transmuted the small doubt into a bubble of irritation. Had to be the lack of sleep catching up with her.

Shiva, the headline act for the Live Earth concert, the one Lily had worked three months to secure, was expecting them in an hour. Kelly's task was to make a success of this interview for Global Wires and to score brownie points with Damian Winters. After her ill-timed fiasco in Spence's office, she needed to up her credit score with the lot.

She gritted her teeth and tried on her freshest smile. It failed to launch. "Come on, then."

Geneva looked up from her watch. "I see we're in a good mood."

"We have an interview to get through."

A robo-guard rolled up and flashed a light from underneath its glass panel into their faces. "Please scan your IDs."

They lifted their sleeves.

Kelly was surprised to see a barcode on Geneva's arm. "So, what did you want to talk about in the conference room?"

"We'll talk after the celebrity interview."

"Gemini C will come to greet you," the bot said. "Please wait here."

"When did you get a barcode?" Kelly asked, filling in the time.

"A week ago. Dad thought it was best I be ready."

"For what?"

A driverless, open buggy trundled up. "Gemini C reporting to Kelly Blackwell and Geneva Winters. According to the record, I am instructed to transport you to the backstage entrance in front of Shiva's dressing room via a detour. Please take your seats to confirm."

They scooted onto the back seat.

"I think I'm really going to enjoy this," Geneva said.

They rolled toward a makeshift pavilion. Organizers with clipboards in hand shouted out orders. Despite the cold snap, few workers wore jackets.

"So, about your barcode, ready for what?"

"Oh," Geneva said. "For uploading into the INNS. I'll eventually start writing articles."

So, they were prepping her for a spot on one of the desks. Who would be the lucky one to train her? Kelly shifted her gaze.

Lighting technicians scurried along the grounds like fire ants. Some carried power packs, others carried profile spotlights, and others pushed along trollies loaded with speakers. In the distance, on the main stage, a throng of dancers in sequin costumes dangled from ropes. They sparkled as they twirled and flipped, their outfits reflecting the multicolored light rays.

The buggy jerked as it drove over a jumble of cables. Geneva and Kelly clasped the metal sidebars. The wobble sent a swirl of motion sickness through Kelly. She winced.

"You okay?"

The nausea faded as quickly as it came. "Yes, I'm good."

A thumping sound hammered her nerves. It was coming off the main stage. She closed her eyes and breathed in the cool air, hoping it would disappear.

"You have reached exhibit alpha. Please disembark," Gemini C announced.

"This isn't Shiva's trailer," Kelly said. "Where are we?"

"I had my dad arrange a tryout of the DreamMaker so I can review it for Global Wires. Come. It'll be fun."

"We don't have time for this."

"Don't be so salty."

Geneva playfully elbowed Kelly's arm.

Human security guards stood on either side of a rectangular glass cube, roomy enough for an overweight man. Flashing streaks of red and blue light illuminated the translucent box. Take away its flashiness, and it looked like an ordinary glass cabinet held together with steel joints.

"I'm Geneva Winters of Global Wires. I have an appointment to review this new device."

By the sound of it, Geneva had her eye on a spot on the tech desk. Former health and lifestyle journo Samantha, recently reassigned to the tech desk, was going to need all the wellness samples she could swallow.

"It's called the DreamMaker," a suited-up representative said. "Rather than explain what it does, how about if you experience it firsthand, one at a time?"

Geneva's face lit up, and Kelly motioned for her to go ahead.

The rep focused on Geneva. "When you're inside, stand still within the circle." He pointed at what looked like a witch's circle painted on the glass floor. "Put the goggles over your eyes and the helmode on your head. The machine will do the rest."

Geneva stepped inside.

The guard closed the door and pressed a button. The corners of the box emitted colorful laser lights, and the helmode on Geneva's head beamed white—like a more advanced Fi headset. The lights rolled over the contours of her body. The tightness in her face melted away, and her mouth broadened into an ear-to-ear grin.

Kelly turned to the representative. "What's she seeing?"

"She's not just seeing. She's being...her idol."

"How does the machine know her idol?"

"The DreamMaker has access to her online activity and in the first five minutes, it analyzes all that history to pinpoint her most loved celebrity. Then the helmode projects the idol, be it alive, dead, or a conglomeration of many personalities, onto her retina. The DreamMaker's lights can also scan the dermis for blood flow readings, a biofeedback mechanism. All in all, the DreamMaker is a sort of biological telepathy. Tests prove it has pinpointed the user's idol correctly ninety-five percent of the time."

This DreamMaker seemed like the leisure industry's equivalent of the echo chambers. Kelly scratched her temple. "Fifteen minutes of being someone else. That must be mind-blowing."

"The biofeedback research indicates, yes, a mind-blowing experience. People feel special, become special." She detected a hint of pride in his voice. "Isn't that what people want?"

All machines see people the same, so it seemed to Kelly like a false kind of special. "The DreamMaker has access to personal online data," Kelly said. "So, who gave this toy permission to access that data?"

"I'm afraid that's privileged information in confidential agreements, you know. Carrigon can't just release those details to anyone who asks."

Carrigon was a tech company known for their suave design of biotech gadgets, like the neutralizer.

"There will be hundreds of people here tonight," Kelly said. "How's this going to be organized?"

His posture lengthened. "We've prebooked the lucky ones."

A bout of nausea swirled through Kelly. The lack of sleep was catching up with her, and she needed a moment to herself. "Do you mind if I take a look around?"

He nodded. "She'll be out in five. For the article, my name is Richard Simpson."

Kelly smiled and wandered to the back of the DreamMaker. A black box rested on a portable table, its cables burrowed into the dirt ground. She spotted a young man tugging a wheelbarrow packed with sound equipment, his skinny arms dotted with needle tracks. The sight took her back to the time she had made regular visits to the plasma clinic for cash to supplement her jobseeker's allowance—a dainty term for welfare. Her arms had looked just like his, scabby and red, but the reimbursements helped feed her for the week. She shook off the memory and decided he, too, must be a regular donor.

"Can you tell me what that is?" she asked him, pointing at the black box.

He laid down the wheelbarrow and lifted the lid. A screeching noise echoed in Kelly's ears, bringing her firmly into her body. The nausea subsided.

"Timpani. Kettledrums. They shouldn't be here."

She backed away.

"Adam!" he yelled.

A teenager with bushy hair sprinted over.

"Who left these here? These are the copper ones. Secure them."

Adam picked up the box with jerky, guilt-fueled awkwardness. The cables dragged along the dirt as he walked away with the box.

The carnival of lights in the DreamMaker switched off, and Kelly hurried back around to the other side. As Simpson opened the door, a dazed Geneva swayed in the witch's circle, her face the look of serenity.

Simpson glanced at Kelly. "We'll have to find a way to speed this part of the process up."

If Geneva had been teleported to some other world, what would happen to the youths who'd soon be trying the DreamMaker? "Geneva, we have to go see Shiva."

Geneva gazed at Kelly with half-closed eyelids. She was in no shape to interview Shiva, and Kelly couldn't afford to blow this job. Arts and Entertainment wasn't her natural terrain, but it was her job, and Lily's reputation was also on the line. "Come on, Shiva's waiting."

"Oh, yes, of course." Though steady on her feet, Geneva's pupils were large.

Kelly led Geneva back onto the open lawn. "You still with us?"

"Yes, but I wish I weren't."

"Let's walk." Kelly guided her along the astroturfed ground. She had to snap this girl out of her stupor, quick. "Seeing as it's made such an impression on you, why don't you write it up?"

"Sure."

Kelly couldn't tell if Geneva heard her. "Are you ready to write your first piece for Global Wires?"

"Sure."

Geneva was so disconnected from reality that Kelly could've suggested she jump into the duck pond, and she'd have agreed. At best, they would be late for the interview. The worst, well, she didn't want to think about it.

Kelly rubbed her forehead. "Let's get you some coffee."

MIRACULOUSLY, only ten minutes late, Kelly and Geneva arrived at Shiva's trailer. A gold star, cut from thick cardstock, ornamented the door. The name Shiva had been scrawled in black marker across the star and embellished with a splash of silver glitter. The sign looked like it came out of the local elementary school.

Kelly glanced at Geneva.

"I got this." Geneva's words finished with a slur.

Kelly should never have agreed to let her go into the DreamMaker before the interview. But then, if Kelly had refused, the girl likely would have whined about it to Spence and anyone who would listen. It was time this girl grew up. "If we don't get this done right, Spence and your father will be breathing down my neck for the next half a year. If that happens, I'll just pass it on to you. Best to be upfront about these things."

Geneva's watch buzzed. She glanced at the message on her watch, pressed send, and dropped her arms to her side.

Kelly tensed. "We need to focus."

Geneva let out a heavy sigh. "I'll be fine."

"I know you're the compliance officer, but you're in my care, and the upload—"

"I said I'll be fine."

"Don't screw it up."

Kelly knocked on the star and waited. She dared not enter the dressing room without permission—never again after that last time she accompanied Josh on a celeb shoot. They had waltzed into a hotel room that reeked of booze and regurgitated cheeseburgers. The celeb was sleeping in her own vomit.

Kelly knocked on Shiva's door again, this time with force.

"Come in," a voice yelled from inside the trailer.

They stepped into a dressing room that looked like it had been ransacked.

"Thank you for taking the time to meet with us so close to your performance."

She could hear fabric being ruffled behind a dressing screen decorated with a Chinese dragon.

"Make yourselves comfortable." Shiva's voice was soft and silky, unlike her singing voice. "I'll be out in a minute."

Shiva was renowned for her haunting sound. Rumor had it that she was able to belt out the odd notes because her vocal cords were surgically enhanced.

Kelly and Geneva scanned the room for a place to sit, but the only chair in the room was positioned in front of the vanity mirror. Geneva shrugged.

Kelly took out a notepad and pen from her bag.

"Can I have a look?" Geneva reached for the notepad.

"Sure."

Geneva examined the back and front cover as if it were a newly discovered fossil from an archaeological dig. "I've only ever seen one of these at the Luntan." She brushed the smooth coils of the binder and flipped open the pad. "What is this scribble?"

"Shorthand," Kelly said.

"Oh yeah, I've heard about that."

"Short? Who's short?" Shiva emerged from behind the screen. "How do I look?"

Kelly's eyes opened wide. She gasped. Green mold covered Shiva's face, her bare feet seeped with puss.

"I've never quite had that effect on anyone." Shiva's voice sounded pleased.

She paraded around the room in a satin gold gown and brilliant costume jewelry. Her hair—if indeed it was real hair—was coiffed in place, and her thick make-up, probably plastered on hours earlier, was contoured around her full lips and deformed cheeks. All the glamor in the world couldn't conceal her green, moldy skin.

Geneva's eyes brightened. "You look fabulous."

The girl grinned from ear to ear as though she were looking at a circus seal flapping its flippers.

Kelly clasped her trembling hand. Maybe the DreamMaker had distorted Geneva's vision. Or worse, maybe it extended outside the glass box and scrambled Kelly's. Or maybe her lack of sleep was making her see things.

"Ask me anything." Shiva twirled. "I'm an open book."

Geneva asked Shiva about her prep routine, the inspiration for her new material, and where she got that fabulous dress. Shiva basked in the attention, firing off answers with panache. Though a rookie journalist, Geneva was a natural charmer. Laughing with Shiva, she brushed her hand on Kelly's arm. Kelly tried to smile, but the horror show continued to send alarms blaring inside her. She wiped her brow.

Geneva turned to Shiva. "Kelly's been under some pressure lately. I'm sure it'll pass."

The chill pills Roseman had given Kelly last night were still sitting in her bag. She leaped up. "Geneva's right. If you'll excuse me."

Grabbing her bag, Kelly rushed out the door. She leaned against the wall and looked out at the swarm of workers. Not a single distorted face in sight. They all looked like normal human beings. Shiva had the same condition the thugs had; their skin had the same distorted and manky appearance. These were maelstrom visions borne of her anxiety, inspired by chaos. Pure maelstrom.

She ripped open her bag and rummaged for the small plastic pouch Roseman had given her. In the cold light, she noticed a rose logo stamped on the pills. "Just get me through the interview." She popped three in her mouth and swallowed.

Seconds later, she loaded a smile and reentered the entertainer's den. "Sorry about that, Shiva."

Shiva extended her slimy hand and caressed Kelly's cheek. It took all of Kelly's strength not to recoil. To her utter shock and surprise, Shiva's touch was chalk dry. She stared at Shiva's hand.

It was smooth and soft and tanned.

Kelly blinked hard. The distortions had vanished. The Roseman pills seemed to have taken effect.

"I was just telling Geneva…" Shiva whipped the dress's long train behind her. "Getting into these costumes requires a lot of negotiation."

Kelly was still staring at Shiva's hand.

"Give us a second, would you, sweetheart," Shiva said to Geneva. She turned to Kelly. "Come with me, darling."

She put her arm around Kelly and walked her toward the dragon screen. Shiva buried a few of her own pills in Kelly's palm. "These will do you a world of good."

The pills were imprinted with a rose logo, the same as the Roseman pills. "Where did you get these?"

"You can find more on the Gusto app." Shiva smiled. "It's all food and drink on the outside but goodness on the inside. If you want more, they're listed under rose-flavored tea pearls under the drinks menu."

So, pushers were selling drugs on apps under the guise of food, delivered by courier straight to the door. The innovative criminal mind always impressed Kelly, even though it shouldn't.

Ian Smith hadn't mentioned this latest drug-pushing distribution method, but that was unsurprising. Criminals lie—it's their stock in trade unless confronted with irrefutable proof. She pocketed the evidence. "Thanks."

They rejoined Geneva.

"Sorry about that, sweetheart. I have to finish getting ready for the big night."

A quick thank-you-for-your-time later, Geneva and Kelly were out the door. The open air freshened Kelly's senses.

"What happened back there?" Geneva asked. "You looked like you were about to seize up."

A bolt of pain thundered through Kelly's head. "I've had a long day and very little sleep. I think it's catching up with me."

THIRTY

KELLY AND GENEVA walked in silence through the park toward the exit, and the only thing Kelly could think of were the rose insignia pills. A desperate need to pay Ian Smith another visit pervaded every fiber of her being.

They came to Bayswater Road.

"You good to upload?"

"Hold on." The dreamy look in Geneva's eyes was long gone. "Let's catch up first."

Kelly hesitated, searching for a reason to decline, but came up short.

Geneva charted a course to a quiet spot in front of a tech shop as though she had already planned for the discussion that was just about to happen.

The tech shop window was plastered with neon-yellow stickers, and the entrance was lined with bargain baskets overflowing with sonic wave machines, fingerprint copiers, instant health monitors, retina readers, remote personal alarms, and other cut-rate technology.

"You know that message back there?" Geneva said.

"What message?"

"The one that came into my watch after the DreamMaker, before the Shiva interview."

The lead-in question rallied Kelly's suspicions. "Yeah."

"It was a notice about the report," Geneva said.

"What report?"

Geneva's eyelids blinked, deliberate and slow. "The report."

"Maybe if you could be a bit more specific."

"Let's not play games," Geneva said. "We both know you had a malfunction in the INNS."

Kelly reeled, but she forced an unruffled expression. The effort of maintaining her composure was exhausting—after everything, after Heather, after the hallucinations, after discovering her vindication meant nothing, she was supposed to stand here and play games with a privileged child who knew nothing about sacrifice.

The hacker had taken care of it. Kelly saw him deleting the malfunction report clean off Spence's cloud. Kelly wasn't about to admit to anything. She needed to know more. "I still don't know what you're talking about, but it doesn't matter. If you don't want to upload, I'll go alone."

Kelly glanced toward Marble Arch, the location of the western echo chamber hub.

"You want me to upload the Shiva interview because you can't use the chamber right now," Geneva said.

Kelly stared at Geneva. If it came to it, Kelly could explain away the chamber malfunction to Spence. She already had a story prepared. The overriding question was, how did Geneva know about that report? "Didn't you hear what I said?"

Geneva laughed. "I intercepted the report, Kelly. I won't give it to anyone as long as you do me a favor."

A bitter taste glazed Kelly's tongue. Despite it being deleted from Spence's cloud, a copy of the report could have been forwarded to Damian. That would have allowed Geneva to get her grubby hands on it. Having dealt with her kind—blackmailers—Kelly knew to let them feel dominant until they were so close to the edge of the cliff that they tripped over themselves and fell. It was just a matter of the right nudge at the right time to help them tumble toward their own inner uncertainty. "You're not very good at this. You should stick to compliance."

Geneva brushed her hand in the air as though swatting lazy flies. "I don't want to, but I may have to report it to Spence and my father."

Predictably, Geneva sketched out the threat, her first attempt to weaken Kelly's resolve. More would come. Bitter experience had taught Kelly well. But underneath the bravado, deep within a criminal's mind, Kelly knew nervousness festered. She just had to poke around for it. "You won't because you don't have a report," Kelly said. "I actually feel a bit sorry for you."

Geneva shrugged. "I kind of feel the same way about you." She paused before adding, "They want to fire you. I don't want that to happen."

So that's what that meeting in Spence's office was all about, the meeting she barged into. The look on Spence's face now made sense. She quietly rejected the girl's cheap ploy, a manipulative tactic as old as the hills, and let her talk her way to the cliff.

"On Monday," Geneva continued, "I can either hand over the report and you lose your job or...help me push Spence to the side. For that, you'll get a promotion."

The girl's arrogant attitude and delusional plan sent a cold disdain through Kelly. On a purely practical level, the girl didn't have the experience to do Spence's job. On a deeper level, whenever anyone like her offered a helping hand, betrayal was never far behind. Kelly put her hand on her heart. "I feel grateful that you're looking out for me. Truly." She dropped her hand. "On Monday, I'll tell Spence we can't work together. I'll say we had a character clash or some crap like that. Then we can forget this ever happened."

The sly look in Geneva's eyes waned, but only for a moment.

Kelly decided to blow open the gap in her confidence. "You do know there've been a few malfunctions lately."

"Spin it any way you like, Kelly." Geneva looked at her, measuring her words. "No one will believe you. Your display in Spence's office didn't help your case. As soon as I show them the report, you'll be out."

When they can't pin you down, they'll punch your weak spot. Now was not the time to cower. "You might have a legitimate malfunction report," Kelly said. "But it won't be mine. Besides, I don't know where you got the idea I'd be okay with your plan."

"Ian Smith."

A cold fury swept through Kelly. Like everyone else, Geneva believed Kelly took a bribe and slandered Smith. If she believed that, no wonder she also believed that Kelly was corrupt enough to go along with her twisted plot. "I mistook you for a brat."

"You sound desperate, Kelly."

Her stomach tightened. "Go home, Geneva."

The girl reached into her pocket and pulled out a key, small and plain and delicate. It resembled the key Kelly had found under Christopher's cockpit on the day of the malfunction. It had no teeth. It could be a copy, but then again, maybe not.

"This key opens a file under my drawer," Geneva said. "It accesses a particular file you might find interesting."

"And what do you think I'd find so interesting?"

"The Ian Smith file."

"I already know it."

"This one is different. My father has friends in high places." A triumphant expression beamed off Geneva's face.

So Geneva got the malfunction report from one of her father's contacts, which meant Damian didn't know about it, just like he didn't know his daughter was trading secrets with his friends behind his back. This girl was some piece of work. "Fuck off."

"Desperate again." Geneva sighed.

"Don't mistake loyalty for desperation," Kelly said in a cold tone.

"Have a think about what I'm offering."

"Do you really think your father is going to be happy when Global Wires falls apart while his daughter is the compliance officer?"

"That'll be an easy fix."

"You think you have everyone wrapped up, don't you? You're in for a big surprise," Kelly said.

Geneva smiled. "I like surprises." A look of entitlement brightened her eyes.

"Good. I'm sure you have a few coming your way."

"Tell you what. I'll hold on to the report until Monday morning. If you agree, I'll delete it forever."

Anxious for the whole exchange to come to an end, Kelly said, "See you on Monday."

She walked away, her stride steadfast. When she was far enough away from the girl's line of sight, Kelly pulled out her new burner phone. Two people to talk to, but only one call: Ian Smith or Harry White. After a quick deliberation, she pressed Harry's number.

He answered on the first ring.

"Harry, do me a favor? I'll email you the Shiva article. Can you upload it on behalf of Global Wires? Please don't ask me why."

"Email it over and I'll get it done."

"One last thing. Any malfunction reports hit Spence's desk yesterday or today?"

"Oh, I see."

"Please, Harry."

"Not that I saw."

"I owe you."

She hung up, wondering how it was that corruption always seemed to eclipse the truth.

She tossed the phone and headed for King's Cross, back to Ian Smith's apartment.

KELLY EMERGED from the underground and walked up York Road. She turned the corner onto Copenhagen Street and came to a sudden halt. Up ahead, two ambulances were stationed in front of Ian Smith's. Amber lights bounced off the surrounding buildings, illuminating the night, police cars, and the faces of onlookers. A dozen or so people, presumably from the surrounding flats, stood behind officers posted on the street. Beyond them, police tape cordoned off the entrance to Ian Smith's flat.

A sinking feeling filled Kelly's gut. She mopped her forehead.

A crime scene unit van was parked at the tail end of one of the ambulances. It wouldn't be here for a suicide.

She eased into the crowd of onlookers. "What happened?"

"Some guy. They found him dead in his flat."

Kelly steadied herself. She tried to keep her voice from cracking. "Burglary gone wrong?"

The man shrugged. "Who knows anymore?"

A deep fear constrained her throat. Someone killed him. They probably knew he talked to her. She remembered his words: If they find out you know what I know, you're going to end up just like me.

Fear shot through her. She needed to hide. Somewhere safe. Head down, she eased out of the crowd.

She walked, heading back toward the station, her face unrelentingly pointed at the pavement, hiding from near and long-range SS capable of patterning her nose, eyes, cheeks. For the first time, she felt thankful for the dark.

THIRTY-ONE

KELLY APPROACHED King's Cross station, and night lights dazzled in the soft rain.

A teenager swaggered down the path. By the look of his wayward stride, he had fueled up on a cocktail of drugs and alcohol and was making his way from the Live Earth concert. Kelly clenched her fists as he staggered past her, whistling an off-key tune. She loosened her hands and walked past the station.

Two drunken revelers, one in shoes, the other barefoot, meandered toward her. Another group of young adults, covered in glitter, dawdled behind them. One young woman, dressed in a red velvet frock, crouched in the middle of the path. She stared into the cracked pavement as though it were a mirror. This was the one night of the year the youth ruled the street. The best they could raise were a few more beers and their voices singing Shiva's hits a cappella.

Suddenly, the SS on the street corner went black.

The teenagers' voices halted mid-tune, their feet stopped and rooted on the pavement. Kelly whipped around—a gang of thugs, five of them, were stomping up the path. The girl in the red velvet frock sprinted down City Road, but the others stood frozen. The thugs shoved the teenagers, one by one, down to the ground. They zeroed in on one victim, kicking him with their steel-toed boots. The young man let out a bloodcurdling scream.

A chill rattled down Kelly's spine. She scoured the road for protection. The ground was littered with syringes, empty food containers, beer cans, plastic water bottles. Her legs trembling, she scrambled to a large wheelie bin and lifted its heavy lid. The stench of rotten food blasted her face. She gagged. Pushing through the stench of rot, she peered inside. She frantically sifted through cardboard boxes, day old food, cables. Sweat dripped down her nose.

The teenagers yelled. "Help!"

Breathe deep for two, hold, exhale for two. Alone, she could do nothing to stop what was happening, and attacking the thugs was suicide. Breathe deep for three, hold, exhale for three. Suddenly, one of the thugs turned in her direction.

She gasped.

Its face. The deformed head. Red. Warped with pockmarks. Her breath froze in her throat. She was seeing things. Again. Just like in Shiva's dressing trailer.

She breathed out. Her stomach heaved. The teenagers' faces were normal, undistorted. She blinked. Her breath caught in her throat. She needed air. She stumbled away from the bins into the street.

Two thugs hovered over a kid on the ground. Two others pinned the rest of the teenagers against the building. A deadening ache shot from Kelly's toes and rose up her limbs like a monstrous weed wrapping itself around her body. Her legs stiffened, knees locked. The fifth thug. Where was he?

Just as she turned, a veil of darkness swamped her vision. Her knees folded. She hit the ground and crawled to the side of the path, choking back the nausea swirling in her stomach. Her grasping hands connected to a cold steel beam, and she clung to it for dear life.

A sickening swirl lapped over her in waves. She squeezed her eyes shut, hoping that alone would hold back the tide. She sucked the chilly air deep into her abdomen, held it for a count of seven. Every deep breath slowed her heart a notch, slower and slower, her limbs released.

All she could see was darkness while a blanket of silence covered her ears.

SOMEONE WAS TOUCHING Kelly's arm. She flinched awake and opened her eyes.

"It's okay."

She tried to focus, but it was like trying to see through gauze.

"Let me help you."

The woman's voice had a soothing tone.

"My name is Mary Stone. What's your name?"

Out of nowhere, gratitude surged deep inside. "Kelly Blackwell." Her voice bolted through her head. She groaned.

"May I?" Mary swabbed Kelly's lip with a cloth. "You scraped it when you fell to the ground. Nothing major." Next, she gently turned over Kelly's wrist. "I see you're a journalist." Her warm fingers felt for Kelly's pulse.

Her vision was slowly returning, and she glanced at the kind woman.

Stone lowered Kelly's wrist. Her hazel eyes oozed compassion. "Nurse Stone of The Royal Free Hospital," she said into her watch, followed by her ID number. "I need a pharma-bot as soon as possible."

"We've located a pharma-bot. It will be in your area in front of building seventeen in seven minutes. Please say yes to confirm the meeting location."

Stone affirmed and turned to Kelly. "You'll be fine. I see this all the time."

"You mean the whole world is going crazy?"

"You still have your humor. That's good." Stone smiled. "When was the last time you ate?"

Kelly steadied her gaze.

"Can't remember." She wriggled around. "The kids, the thugs—"

"Don't worry. The thugs took off." She patted Kelly's hand. "The kids will be fine. They're being treated."

"So I wasn't seeing things."

Stone shook her head. "You're experiencing intense anxiety. That's all. One of the thugs knocked you down, and you blacked out. Perhaps a blessing in disguise. Anxiety would be a common effect, even expected, after what you went through." She eased Kelly to her feet. "Come. Let's get you to building seventeen."

Stone guided Kelly step by step.

Kelly wobbled. The spell of madness, the bout of anxiety—she couldn't decide which it was—wasn't over, and yet she no longer felt crippled, frozen by it. Though it certainly felt like she had skimmed the edges of insanity, deep in the recesses of her soul, she knew she wasn't insane. Anxiety happened, like Nurse Stone said, to a lot of other people as well.

Was it as intense for everyone as it was for her? Were all the hallucinations, like the ones she had in Shiva's trailer, also anxiety-induced? Seemed like it. Maybe all the stress was more than she could handle. But rather than being dispiriting, the newfound knowledge lifted her.

Stone nudged Kelly, supporting her as she moved ever forward. "Just a few more feet."

They reached building seventeen, and Kelly sat on the road's curb.

"Pharma-bot number 745 reporting."

"MK860 please, and two packets of dry protein cubes."

Kelly's head throbbed. The medication sounded familiar.

"The NHS no longer supplies MK860," the bot replied.

Now she remembered where she had first read about it. MK860 was the medication Heather Mallow had mentioned in her article on anxiety. She had said it had become so popular that the NHS made it available over-the-counter. Kelly looked up at the bot. "When?"

"The NHS ceased supply of MK860 on January 5, 2030," the bot said.

"Does the chemist-bot recommend an alternative?" Stone asked.

"MK1000 is the NHS's new and improved version of MK860."

The screen on the bot's chest panel switched on. Kelly winced at the bright light. A young woman's face on the screen transformed from a frown to a smile while a tune praised the NHS, which, it assured them, used only the best-sourced ingredients for the most powerful remedy for anxiety. The singing-bot stopped, and the serious chemist-bot returned. "Would Nurse Stone like to order MK1000?"

"Yes, and a packet of dry protein cubes."

"Before I release MK1000, I am required to read the disclaimer and instructions for you to sign off."

"One second, bot." Mary Stone turned to Kelly. "The prescription needs to go under your name. I'll need the bot to scan your ID."

Kelly held up her wrist to the bot's chest.

The bot scanned her QR code. "Does Kelly Blackwell wish to proceed?"

"Yes, to everything."

Within seconds, two crinkled packets and a bottle of pills rattled into the bot's dispenser.

"The mix of protein and fast-acting complex carbs should do you good."

Kelly scooped it all up and ripped open the packets with her teeth. She gobbled a handful of dry cubes.

"Thank you for your service, Kelly Blackwell. I wish you a good night." The bot rolled away.

Nurse Stone dropped two pills into Kelly's palm. "Even though these pills are herbal, it's a new proprietary blend, hence the need for ID," Stone said.

Deep within, robust energy surged through Kelly. The cubes were kicking in. "Shouldn't these pills be available over the counter?"

"Good to hear you asking questions." Nurse Stone crouched beside Kelly. "These seem to be more powerful than the MK860, so the NHS controls the amounts dispensed, making it impossible to overdose. Stick to two pills every four hours."

She crunched the two pills between her teeth. They tasted tart and sweet, like blackcurrant.

Within minutes, the tightness in her chest ebbed. "Thank you," Kelly said, but it felt like such an empty phrase. "Can I send you a thank-you gift or something?"

Stone raised her hand. "That's not necessary. The hospital regularly treats people for anxiety. It's my job."

"I can't just—"

"Tell you what. Next time you see a person in need, help them out."

Kelly nodded. "Would you mind if I asked you a question?"

"Go ahead."

"Why didn't the hospital tell you they upgraded to MK1000? I'd have thought all medical personnel would know these things."

"You'd be surprised at what they don't tell us," she whispered. "Don't report that though." Stone smiled. "Where were you headed?"

"A friend's place," Kelly answered.

"Were you at the concert?"

Kelly nodded.

"Maybe someone slipped something into your drink."

"I didn't have anything while I was there."

"It's just stress, then?"

Kelly refrained from burdening Stone with the chaos that had taken over her life. "Who isn't stressed these days?" she said at last.

"A friend's place is a good choice. Company will do you good. If you need something stronger than MK1000, make an appointment at your local clinic." Stone rose to her full height and stretched her legs.

Every cell in Kelly's brain was exhausted, her nerves raw. With Stone's help, she rose from the step, her head slightly woozy but steady on her feet.

"Looks like you're going to be just fine," Stone said.

All the hallucinations had disappeared. The path was once again filled with normal-looking humans—their wild eyes and syringes flashing gone, former citizens broken by something injected? Kelly turned back to Stone, but she was gone as though she had never existed.

She scanned the street for a taxi that would take her to the only human she wanted to see—Josh, her only trusted friend.

THIRTY-TWO

20 January

THE DAWN's light was cracking through the sky when Kelly arrived in St. John's Wood. She walked up the pathway to Josh's house. He was squinting as he opened his front door. The light from his hallway cast a glow around him.

"What time is it?"

"You don't want to know." She threw her arms around him. "I'm so glad to see you."

He stepped back stiffly. "I'll make some coffee."

He led the way to the kitchen and flipped the light switch. It felt good to be back. He popped on the kettle, went to the cupboard, and pulled out espresso-ground coffee. "Milk's in the fridge."

An American-size fridge stood in the pantry, too big for a bachelor to fill up. He probably kept it because that's what his mother had used. Kelly pulled out the milk from the sparse door rack.

Moments later, a silver spoon clinked against a ceramic mug. "Was Live Earth crazier than usual?"

She didn't want to relive the madness. "A tad."

"So glad I don't have to cover it anymore." He scooped up the mugs. "Let's go to the dining room."

He chatted pleasantly, and that was the problem. His cool rigidity was camouflaged by all the small talk; she blamed the early hour. "Remember when things were simple? How your parents reminded us about the days before the Internet?"

"And your aunt." A smile crept across his face—the first that night. "She hated the Internet."

"That was because she was a claw foot on the keyboard."

"And now look at us."

She flicked her wrist at Josh.

He nodded approval. "How was Roseman?"

"An adventure."

Josh's gaze lingered on Kelly. "Want a top up?"

Before she could answer, he popped out of the room and soon returned with an unopened packet of digestive biscuits. She felt an urge to reach out and pull him toward her, but the barrier he placed between them had become undeniable. "What's going on, Josh?"

He ripped open the packet, biscuits rolled out onto the table. "What do you mean?"

She needed to know how fortified the barrier was, so she touched his hand.

He pulled back. "What about Omar?"

So, Omar was the roadblock? Apart from the occasional sarcastic quip, Josh rarely said much about him. Likewise, she never mentioned the string of bimbos Josh had dated over the years. Something must have happened between now and the last time she was here. Maybe Omar and Josh bumped into each other. "What about him?"

"Aren't you with him?"

"Dead and buried." She kicked off her shoes. "Why did you dislike him so much?"

He paused as if taking in the information and slid his hand over her fingers. "He was a fucking idiot."

His coffee-infused breath scented the air. She rose to her feet to meet him. "I finally admitted it to myself."

For a moment, they stood there, seventeen years of friendship and longing suspended between them. She'd watched everyone else fall away—Christopher, Heather, Omar—until only Josh remained. The only person who'd known her since she was nine years old. The only person left who remembered Aunt El, who knew what Kelly's life had been before everything went wrong.

His breath warmed her neck.

She needed this. Needed him. Needed to feel something other than fear and loss and the weight of bodies piling up around her.

They climbed the stairs, abandoning their clothes as they ascended. At the top of the staircase, they came to two paneled doors, just as Kelly remembered during their teenage years. But something was different, and she couldn't place it. She brushed the feeling away.

They stood in front of each other, naked and vulnerable.

It felt good to surrender.

They crashed on his king-sized bed, saying not another word, and let their love rise from the ashes of the distant past.

THIRTY-THREE

SUNLIGHT STREAKED across Kelly's eyelids. She woke up. The light had broken through the blinds. It had to be late morning, she thought, and closed her eyes again. A bell rang out. She propped herself up on her elbows. Josh's eyelids flickered, and he turned over. The bell rang again.

Unable to sleep now, Kelly scooted off the bed and slipped on his long-sleeved T-shirt. It hung on her like a sheet.

Ding.

Following the sound of the incessant bell, she wandered into the hallway, each step creaking underfoot. It seemed to come from what used to be Josh's old bedroom.

A keypad nestled in the wall beside the doorframe. The door lay ajar.

She nudged the aged wooden door, surprisingly heavy. She pushed a little harder, and it creaked open.

She flipped on a light switch.

A ceiling starburst lamp lit aluminum-lined walls, held in place with strips of wide reflective tape.

A single bed was the only furniture in the room that suggested it might once have been a place where someone slept. Gone was the wall that had separated it from the master bedroom. The resulting space, equivalent to the size of Kelly's studio, was piled high with cables, headsets, old keyboards, switches, and several screens stacked on a table. Even more equipment clogged the corners of the room. She could barely make out what was what. Josh loved gadgets, but he never mentioned transforming his old bedroom into what looked like a hacker's den.

Ding.

She crept toward the black-screened computer, where the bell was coming from, and woke up the screen.

They were alerts from a dating website; messages from a woman called Laura Cassavetes.

Her stomach hollowed, she stepped back. The impulse to wake up Josh and demand answers surged through her, but she was done listening to lies. She sat on the swivel chair, muted the volume, and checked the VPN tunnel. It was active. She clicked on Laura Cassavetes' message, expecting to see a photo of a bimbo in a bikini.

Instead, a video popped up on the screen. The time stamp read 10 p.m., January 6, 2030. That was the night before Christopher's arrest. Tentatively, she clicked on the download link in the window, breathed in, and pressed play.

A dark, rain-soaked night blackened the screen. "What the fuck is this?" She brightened the screen.

Dark areas of the footage revealed the old street CCTV cameras and rooftops like monsters emerging from a dark sea. Whoever was holding the camera had pointed it downward until it came to rest on what looked like a shiny black car in the shadows. The lens zoomed in to where the car's registration plate should be. It had been removed. Whoever was in that car had been watching from a distance.

The camera panned out; the view widened.

Elite Squad troops stood in front of Christopher Mallow's residence.

Kelly's hair stood on end. No. This couldn't be—

This appeared to be the hunt for the Truth Laws fugitive video, similar to the one she had received from the anonymous sender. The video she had been hunting down. The one she'd asked Josh about. The one he'd said he knew nothing about. The one he'd looked her in the eye and lied about while she begged him for help finding it.

Her hands started shaking. She gripped the desk to steady herself.

Was the anonymous sender watching her every move? Did he know she was here? Or was the anonymous sender Josh?

Spooked, she glanced behind herself. The room stood still. A prickly tension rose from deep within, and the eerie feeling threatened to engulf her. She caught her reflection in the aluminum-lined wall. A distorted face stared back. She startled.

"Get a hold of yourself, Kelly," she muttered.

She turned back around, shaking off the fear, and narrowed her focus to the screen.

Video files cluttered the desktop, too many to open and play. She returned to the downloaded footage. It was 15.6 GB. Next, she opened his hard drive and scrolled through the files. Overwhelmed again, she clicked at the top of the column labeled "size" and brought order to the chaos.

She scrolled down. 14.5 GB, 15 GB, 15.6. There were two files sized 15.6 GB.

Her stomach tightened at what she might find. Bracing herself, she clicked open the first file.

In stark black and white, she stared at the name of the creator.

Josh Munro.

She reeled back. Questions tumbled through her mind, pulling her in every direction. Was this Josh's video? Why did Laura Cassavetes have it? Who was she? Was the anonymous sender involved?

She pressed play. The footage was different from the one that had landed in her email. Or maybe the one on the Internet was an edited version. Anyone with a bit of editing skill could alter the footage. All photographers were probably manipulating digital files, weren't they?

She shut her eyes. A scream shot out of the speakers. Her eyes snapped open, and there, on the screen, she saw the little boy on the pavement, the same little boy in the footage she had received from the anonymous sender. Her limbs weakened.

This footage...this Mallow arrest footage was the raw, uncensored file, and it had Josh's name all over it. This was his footage. He knew all along, and he knew she had been looking for the photographer who was at the scene.

He lied to her.

She stared on, the promise of love draining out of her. If she couldn't trust Josh, she really and truly was on her own.

Suddenly, she sensed a presence behind her, watching her. She held her breath.

Unable to move, she simply said, "Were you the anonymous sender of the video?"

THIRTY-FOUR

JOSH'S MOUTH went dry when he found Kelly sitting in front of his monitor—his private messages, high security job orders, and an enlarged Laura Cassavetes avatar all open. And then, the Mallow video layered the window. On another screen, the footage's metadata. All his work connected to the Resistance was on full display.

Clearly, Kelly had found a message the Resistance had sent to him, a message that communicated they knew he had planted a doctored copy with them. Now that Kelly knew, the choice to keep the whole thing hidden was out of his hands. He no longer had to choose between Kelly and keeping his oath of secrecy to the Resistance.

But any sense of relief he might've felt was soon supplanted with a knot in his gut. Everyone knew, and everyone would come after him, starting with Kelly.

Her lips were moving, but his mind was reeling, and he couldn't hear a word. The last thing he did hear was "anonymous sender." He had assumed the Resistance was the anonymous client who had hired him to follow Rozlyn Abbott. If the job hadn't come from the Resistance, then who was the anonymous client? Was Kelly's sender the same as his secret client?

It all tumbled out onto him, and he could tackle only one thing at a time. He tried to speak, but the words escaped him. Instead, he opted to focus on Kelly.

"First, I witnessed an abuse of power against Christopher Mallow." Kelly's words hit his eardrums with a bang. "Then the big boss's daughter tried to blackmail me. Now, I find out my best friend is not only a hacker—"

He sat on the bed. "Hacking sort of found me."

She lashed him with her hard, wet eyes. He deserved it, and more. "I asked you about the Truth Laws fugitive footage. You said you didn't know anything. You said—"

"Percy didn't tell me what I was filming. I pieced it together after you came by the Canary." It sounded like a poor excuse, even to him. "I'm part of the Resistance against the Truth Laws."

"You didn't tell me that back then. Why? The bullshit NDA?" She shot up from the chair. "You knew I was searching for the raw footage, and you were the photographer this whole time."

Every conversation they'd had since Christopher's arrest replayed in her mind. Every time she'd asked him for help. Every time he'd nodded sympathetically. Every lie stacked on top of the one before. And last night —God, last night. His secret was lodged in his throat.

She had no one. Not Heather. Not Omar. And now, she was utterly alone.

She was about to leave the room, but he pulled her back.

"Let me explain," he pleaded.

She shook off his hand, and the touch burned like acid. "The time for that has passed. If you're part of the Resistance, as you say you are, then Christopher must've been much more important than you are saying. The Elite Squad aren't after innocent, old men. They enforce—" She choked back a tear.

"No one knows who's in the group."

"So what was Christopher working on?"

Now was his chance to come clean. His only chance. "A virus."

"For what?"

"The echo chambers. He was meant to upload a virus into the echo chamber."

She gripped her head. Then she turned to him, her eyelids heavy, as though the weight of the world were dragging on them. "Why didn't you tell me?"

Guilt pounded on him like never before. He could see it in her eyes—she was calculating whether to walk out that door and never come back. And he would deserve it. He'd earned every ounce of her contempt. But he couldn't let her go. Not when she needed him most, even if she didn't know it yet.

In that moment, he knew his ultimate loyalty lay with Kelly. Not the Resistance. Not some anonymous mission. Kelly. "Give me a moment to show you something." He pointed at the screen.

She stared at him; her face guarded. He woke up the screen, opened the video that had threatened everything important in his life, and pressed play.

Kelly's eyebrows knitted, and she cradled her head in her hands.

"You okay?"

"A headache. It'll pass. Go on." She crouched on the floor.

A screen flashed. It sparked to life with fuzzy white and gray lines and eventually focused on a wide-angle view of Pentonville Road in real time. A plethora of pedestrians walked past a thug leaning against a wall.

His knees tingled. "Odd frequencies get through from time to time, but what the hell is this?"

Kelly sat cross-legged on the floor, her eyes squinting as though the light from the screen pained her. "Maybe a hacker in the Resistance is getting their revenge on you for lying to them, too." Her neck muscles tensed.

The screen turned black, and then flicked, self-tuned, and landed on a view of what looked to be Sloane Square, West London.

He gripped the desk, holding himself upright. It was starting again. The same as years ago, the phenomena he experienced long ago and had told no one.

"Hold on." He stepped over several multilevel cell units scattered near a clump of thick snake wires and opened a chest in the corner. He picked out the Beta Fi headset and waved the flimsy plastic in the air. "This Beta Fi headset predates the ones in the echo chambers. Carrigon, the manufacturer, marketed it as an augmented reality headset we could play our online games with. A lot of gamers were given one. I was one of many testers."

"Carrigon does the DreamMaker."

"Yeah, Carrigon does all sorts of electronic stuff." He dug into the chest and pulled out a small black box, no bigger than the size of a pack of playing cards. "This is the power pack. It has all the transmission power to read and transfer data to Carrigon. I didn't know that at the time, of course. I just thought it was a basic power pack. I later discovered it self-locates a secure connection. Actually, it's quite an amazing piece of kit."

Admiration for the kit dulled his tension, and he promptly threw the headset down. "Later, I discovered the Beta Fi headset and power pack send data back to the Zone." Josh shook his head. "After a couple of days using it, I started to get headaches. I got headaches from time to time, so I didn't think anything of it at first. But then, I started dreaming, and the dreams were vivid." By the look on Kelly's face, he could see he had hit a nerve. "Do you also have vivid dreams?"

"Depends on what you mean by vivid."

"Lucid dreams. Dreams where you're traveling through the city, seeing all these crazy people beating up on others and mugging and killing. When I woke up, I was exhausted. I swore I was sleepwalking."

He shuddered and pointed at the steel door and the bed. "I got that door installed, brought the bed in here, and sealed the windows. I even installed a buzz alarm loud enough to wake me if I somehow clawed my way out."

"When was all this?"

"About five years ago." A cold chill swept through his body as he thought back to that strange time. "It went on like this for a week or so. But it felt like an eternity. Looking back now, I feared those dreams more than anything else. I started drinking coffee at night to keep myself awake. I felt I was losing my mind."

"How did you go from being a game tester to a hacker?"

"I contacted other gamers. The same thing was happening to them, so we dug around for answers. They taught me the tricks of the trade. I started doing some jobs here and there."

"Did you all come to a conclusion?"

"A theory. Carrigon might've tweaked the headset technology to affect brainwaves. I say that because it looks like…you're affecting my machines."

"Me, controlling your computers? That's quite a leap, Josh. Everyone using the Fi headsets would be setting off all comps everywhere." She shook her head. "Anything to cover the fact that you've been lying to me this whole time."

"But you are influencing my computer."

"Josh. It's the most ridiculous notion. I am not controlling this machine or any machine. It could be timing, position, a combination of your teeth fillings and the static in my hair."

He stared at her. It was a far-fetched theory, but he knew technology better than Kelly. Hell, his dead grandmother knew technology better than Kelly.

Her eyes darkened.

Something in her eyes told him she was hiding something. He wondered if her secret involved an oath to other people, to a cause. Probably not. Kelly ran solo. Too solo. "What are you not saying, Kelly?"

"I don't know how we went from you lying about the video to—"

"You going to keep your secret to yourself?"

After a while, she broke his stare and looked back at the screen. "I see the maelstrom right there on the path," she said.

"Maelstrom?"

"That's what I call the thugs."

"Why do you call them maelstrom?"

"Because they look like evil chaos to me."

"You mean they look menacing? They are!"

"No. They look deformed to me, deformed by the hand of evil."

Something clicked into place for him. "So, the Fi headsets are inducing visions. Christopher was meant to upload a virus into the chamber. The

Resistance didn't tell me why, but now it makes sense. The Fi headset is having an effect on users. They wanted to shut it down. We need to find Christopher."

"He's dead, Josh. Remember?"

"I don't believe it. My guess is Mallow is still being held at the Elite Squad headquarters."

She shook her head. "Even if he were alive, we'll never find him. It's better if we concentrate our efforts on finding out what he was working on so we can identify who ordered the D-notice and why. They hold the key. There's more to this story than just Fi headsets and virus codes." Kelly bit the nail on her middle finger. "I can work on Damian Winters... get him on our side. He has access to intel."

Josh thought about the spy cams he had placed around Global Wires. He'd know soon enough how Damian was involved, if he were involved. "We don't know enough, and if you tell Damian at this stage, he'll think you've lost your mind." Josh rooted down in the chair and switched on a screen.

"There could be another way," she said. "Geneva said she had a file. She claimed it was some sort of background on the Ian Smith case. I thought she was bluffing, but maybe not. It could shed some light on this whole thing."

He loved that fire in her eyes; the fire driving her ever forward, as though nothing else mattered. That fire sparked his own.

"The file is at Global Wires," she said.

"I can mask the SS on route," he said. "Give me some time. By tomorrow, when you step out the front door, your footsteps will be invisible to them."

"Don't think this gets you back in my good books, Josh. I haven't decided what I'm going to do with you."

"I'll earn back every ounce of trust you placed in me. Time is all I ask."

His fingertips ran over the keys, setting up code that would chatter with the satellites up above, instructing them to mask Kelly's future steps.

WEEK 3

THIRTY-FIVE

21 January. 6 a.m.

A SHRILL WHISTLE CRACKED through the dawn's air.

Backpack in tow, Kelly hastened her stride through Regent's Park, southward, toward Global Wires where, supposedly, Geneva kept the malfunction report and Ian Smith's file.

Starting on Great Portland Street, the SS illuminated her every step as though ushering her the rest of the way to Soho. Odd. Josh was meant to mask her route the whole way. Maybe it was only some of the way. Whatever. It was too late to turn back. She needed to be in the newsroom before anyone got in.

At last, she reached Oxford Street. As soon as she crossed into Berwick Street, she'd enter the familiar labyrinth of roads that made up Soho. She inhaled deeply, as if getting ready to dive deep into an ocean. The narrow streets, usually full of people rushing to appointments, the chatter of conversation spilling out of restaurants and into the street, the beeping horns of frustrated drivers, were oddly silent. She hardly saw a soul as she hurried through the dense warren of streets.

There it was. Carnaby Street, home of Global Wires. The pedestrian walkway was deserted.

She ducked into the building, swiped her ID, bypassed the elevator, and punched in the passcode to step inside.

A deafening quiet filled the newsroom.

Air currents crawled along the surface of her face. Kelly was no stranger to solitary moments, and even preferred them, but the stillness in the room hung on her like dead air. A sharp prick behind the eye, like something shifting under the retina.

Kelly scanned the ceiling for speakers and cameras. To the naked eye, the place looked clean, but that didn't mean much. Spy cameras could hide inside anything: a wall clock, computers, the lights all around her. Even the sweepers couldn't catch every tiny cam. Best to assume someone was watching or the sweepers could come at any moment, so she hastily crept over to Geneva's desk.

A yellow light from a streetlamp glowed through the windows and brightened the walkway below.

When she reached Geneva's spot, she swept her hand on the underside of the desk. There was no sign of any locked drawers, but as she reached further, her foot grazed something solid.

She kneeled down and stretched her arm, feeling out for that solid thing, and the cold surface of a metal box shocked her fingertips.

She pulled out a squat metal file drawer.

Mallow had mentioned maintaining a filing cabinet. Kelly dug into her backpack and groped for her key. She fished it up. It looked identical to the one Geneva had dangled in front of her. Then something dawned on her. Maybe Christopher's was the copy. There was only one way to find out.

If the key failed to unlock the metal drawer, she would take Lily's letter opener to the lock and bash the damn thing open. If that didn't work, there was probably a screwdriver down in the basement. If nothing else, her bare hands would have to do. One way or another, she would get whatever was inside.

She slid her key into the lock and hoped upon empty hope that it worked. She held her breath, closed her eyes, and turned the key.

It caught.

She twisted again.

This time, the lid snapped open.

She fell back, astonished.

How did Christopher get this key? Did Christopher know Geneva? She didn't have time to think about all the possibilities right now. She lifted the lid like it was a Pandora's box.

A plump envelope lay inside. Kelly switched on the torchlight in her watch. She opened the envelope and pulled out the contents. Sitting on top of the pile of papers was a single sheet. It looked like an article typeset in columns, like in the old newspapers. Christopher Mallow's name was on the byline. The article was dated January 5, 2030—days before his arrest at the echo chamber.

She brought the paper into the light and steadied her trembling hand. According to the article, the State planned to include thought crime in the Truth Laws. Rather than making this public, they intended to include it in the algorithms covertly.

Kelly leaned back. Codifying thought into criminal law wasn't impossible to believe; the State was well on its way to that drastic step. But new laws still had to be debated in Parliament, and if civil liberty groups, like the Commissioner's Office, caught wind of this new thought crime extension, they'd kick up a storm. The government couldn't be allowed to suppress this; it had to leak into the public's realm.

What she found hard to believe was that someone thought they could keep it out of the law books, hidden. But the covert nature of thought crime is what the article emphasized, as though the government had already put the plan in motion and had the infrastructure and their legal mechanisms in place.

She skimmed the article again. This time, one overarching detail struck her. The article stated that the Truth Laws would begin on February 1, 2030.

Didn't make sense. The Truth Laws were already in effect. Unless the wording of the laws was ambiguous, and they hid future developments. That didn't seem possible, though. In the very public debate in the run-up to the Truth Laws, editors and legal minds had scoured them, debated them, and scrutinized them—their livelihoods depended on it. Everyone knew the ins and outs of the Truth Laws.

Kelly's whole body buzzed.

Neither Christopher nor Heather would ever have been able to publish this information, certainly not via the chambers, so why write it up as a newspaper article? Perhaps it was for an article they intended to publish somewhere else. Or maybe someone had typed Christopher's name in the byline and would later discredit the article, should it come to light, by pointing to Christopher's ruined reputation. She knew that tactic. It had been applied to her during the Smith Affair. She looked at the paper again. It had no headline. This wasn't an article. She was holding Christopher's research.

Kelly's leg cramped. She rested on the floor, stretching her legs. How did Geneva get a hold of this research? Did one of Damian's contacts give it to her? So many questions swirled in her mind, but now was not the time. There was more information inside the envelope to look at. She tucked the research page under the thicker file and pointed her watch's torch at it.

It wasn't the Ian Smith file, as Geneva had claimed. It was a hard copy of a malfunction report.

The skin on her arms tingled as she stared at it. She flipped to the first page.

It was dated January 7. This report was generated on the day of Christopher's arrest. She recalled his scrambled screen. It wasn't her malfunction report. It was Christopher's.

The faint static of an electrical current surged from a computer, a quick spurt.

She glanced down the central aisle. A blade of light caught her eye. Its sharp angle lit up the floor a few desks down.

The sweepers, or someone worse, might be coming up. She shoved the papers that detailed the next stage of development for The Truth Laws in her jacket, placed the empty envelope back in the metal box, and shut the lid. As she hurried down the aisle, a resolve to get this information out hardened in her.

HALFWAY DOWN THE AISLE, Kelly noticed a foul smell in the air. The stench grew stronger as she neared the bathroom. She slowed, covered her nose, and glanced around the back of the newsroom.

A figure was propped onto a chair, slumped over a desk.

Kelly's body trembled at the sight of the slumped figure sitting there, unnaturally rigid.

Her heartbeat raced. Slowly, she extended her hand, and a single tap on its shoulder sent the figure tumbling. Kelly recoiled.

The body landed on the floor with a heavy thump, its face upturned. Kelly stared at Geneva's gaping eyes, empty and dark as caves. Dried saliva caked the corner of the dead girl's mouth.

Kelly's throat tightened, her lungs constricted. A scream caught in her throat. All she could do was gasp for air. She plunged back, away from the death-filled face.

Geneva. The girl who'd been assigned to trail her, to blackmail her, to spy on her. Kelly had wished her gone—and now she was. Not disappeared. Dead. A real person with a real body and real parents who'd have to identify her corpse.

Geneva's sleeve was rolled up, held in place by a rubber band choking her arm. The needle of a blue-tinted syringe hung off her pale flesh. Its contents, whatever it was, had been emptied into her veins. Dry blood caked her skin.

Geneva was no drug addict. This wasn't a maelstrom-thug killing. They would have beaten her to a pulp or just shot her in the head. Someone put thought into this and left the body in plain sight to be discovered. This was a staged kill.

Kelly's mind flicked through reason after logical reason to stave off the panic electrifying her nerves, burning her out. No matter how fast one explanation surfaced, another equally powerful doubt drowned it out. But there was one certainty: Kelly had the Mallow research now.

She was next.

She gulped air and bolted for the exit. As she tore through the darkened office, without warning, the phones rang all at once. She froze; it felt like insects were crawling on her scalp. Someone was watching her. Josh flashed through her mind. It could be him, but surely he'd have called her watch, wouldn't he?

The phones rang again.

Her hand shook as she brought the receiver to her ear.

"Kelly Blackwell?" The voice was disguised to sound like digital output.

Kelly's breath quickened.

"You need to go to the Underground Freedom Fighters' camp."

Her throat tightened, a scream caught—gasping for air. "Who's this?"

"Come alone." The digital voice scrambler was fading. "No electronics." Decibel by decibel, the altered voice degenerated until a woman's voice trickled through. "Someone will find you," she said. "You will get answers to your questions."

The line went dead.

Kelly stared at the phone. Had to be a setup. That camp was the last place she'd go. Whoever the woman on the phone was, she either killed Geneva or was working for the person who did. Cornered and closed in, she did something she never thought she'd do.

She reset the line and dialed 999. "Someone's been killed," she said.

THIRTY-SIX

Spence trudged up the stairs, his wedding ring clanging against the metal handrail at steady intervals. He paused on the top step and faced the doors to the newsroom. His staff would soon trickle in, oblivious to what was coming. Fifty percent to be let go, that's what Damian had said. Sure, he got to keep his job, but for how long was anyone's guess.

He gazed at the white plaque engraved with black letters, Global Wires, soon to be a news outlet of working bots. He inhaled, hoping the constriction in his chest would loosen. It didn't. He dialed in the passcode. The red light changed to green and a soft click released the lock.

He braced himself and gripped the handle. Maybe he would seize the organization out from under Damian. The fanciful thought lifted the heavy feeling in his chest for a moment, and he swung open the door.

The large sealed windows with a view of the red-brick pedestrian road below, screens, desks, clean white walls, the worn-out lavender carpet—all sparked nostalgia within him. A quiet calm before the storm. He plodded toward his office.

A soft voice hummed somewhere behind him from a cubicle.

"Harry?"

A slim, white-haired police officer stepped out; the sight shocked Spence firmly back to the present. He steeled himself. "What's going on?"

"I just arrived, sir. I'm PC Blake. And you are?"

"Spencer Wyatt, Editor-in-Chief."

PC Blake snapped a picture of him and then pressed the record button on his watch. "Case 4-1-6-0-0." He glanced up at Spence's uncomprehending face. "I'll be recording our conversation."

Spence faltered when he moved toward Blake. "Please tell me what's going on."

"This morning, one of your staff, Kelly Blackwell, discovered the body of Geneva Winters here at the office."

Spence's heart rate accelerated even though he wasn't sure he had heard right. Damian's daughter, dead, here on Global Wires property? "Can't be right."

PC Blake paused on Spence as though he was giving Spence time to process the gravity of what had happened. "It's best we wait to see the forensic report before we jump to any conclusions."

Spence faltered, his face pale. Geneva. Dead. The words began to penetrate his mind, and the disparate pieces of the scene before him assembled into a picture he could just about fathom. "You said Kelly reported it?"

"That's right."

Spence's legs gave way. He gripped the nearest desk.

"You better sit down."

"I'm fine."

"Have a seat, sir. Secondary shock reactivity can happen in cases when people are close to the victim."

Global Wires was still his newsroom, still his responsibility. He stood straight and locked his knees in place. "Where's the body?"

Blake pointed toward the lavatory.

Shockwaves propelled Spence in that direction, and a moldy, putrid smell knocked him back, his stomach wrenching.

Blake guided him in the opposite direction. "Better not to disturb it. Forensics will be here soon to examine the body."

No matter how far away from the body he was steered, the putrid smell hung in his mouth. "Where's Kelly?"

"Right behind you."

Uneasy on his feet, he swung around and saw her crouched, her back resting against the divider, her cheek stained with the track of one long tear.

He touched her shoulder. "Kelly?"

"She's in shock," Blake explained. "An ambulance is on the way."

Spence rubbed his face and turned to PC Blake. "Was this how you found her?"

He nodded. "She just needs a bit of time."

"Where are the rest of the police, ambulances, detectives?"

"They'll be here shortly."

That made little sense. Spence rubbed his neck.

"I took the dispatch call and arrived ahead of the others," he said, picking up on Spence's confusion.

"Start from the top, Officer. What time did you arrive?"

"Thirty minutes ago or so. From what I saw, and this is only an assumption, but it looked like the victim had already been dead for a while before she was discovered. I really shouldn't make those assumptions, but it looks like you need to hear something concrete. Wait to see if the autopsy confirms."

Even if it was only conjecture, the information felt solid. Blake was right. It provided the kind of support Spence needed so he could face his staff and give them something they, too, could hold onto.

Kelly was staring at her sneakers, still in a daze. He crouched beside her. "Kelly, it'll be all right. Can you tell me what you saw?"

Without saying a word, Kelly shifted from her crouched position onto a seat nearby. "Last time I saw her was at Live Earth."

A ball of fear settled in Spence's gut, and he looked over to PC Blake. "Geneva was assigned to Kelly just a few days ago."

Someone banged on the door, hacking into Spence's taut nerves. PC Blake left them alone and went to open the door.

Kelly turned to Spence. There was a looseness to her gaze; it felt to

Spence more like she was looking through him than at him. "Do you really trust these people to get to the bottom of it?"

Kelly's unexpected lucidity sent a shiver through him.

PC Blake swung open the double doors of the newsroom. A crew of officers, paramedics, and detectives swarmed the room all at once. Spence burst out in sweat, and his shirt clung to him. He felt like he was suffocating.

Kelly stood, her eyes hard, her face stiff. A heavyset man wearing a brown trench coat and broad-brimmed hat approached them. Most detectives looked the same, but this one had powerful arms and thick legs like a gorilla.

"I'm Detective Lynch. The team is here to inspect the space, gather samples, and so on."

And so on? Anger drifted through Spence, but he shook the detective's hand anyway.

Lynch gave PC Blake a quick once-over from head to toe before locking eyes on Kelly. "I'll be over to talk to you shortly."

Kelly glanced at Spence imploringly.

Spence stepped up. "Perhaps you can ask Kelly questions a little later in the day. She's been through a lot, and I don't think she—"

"Sorry, but no. We have to talk to her before she leaves the building."

Detectives always looked like they suspected everyone, including other officers of the law. Spence cleared his throat. "Very well. But I have to notify Geneva's father." He fumbled with his watch. "Right away."

"Someone will be sent around to her parents to let them know."

Detective Lynch headed back to the main group. What seemed like half of Central London's police department was swarming Global Wires as though it was a goddamn football pitch. Anger was mounting in Spence. Maybe the rising number of murders numbed police officers to these kinds of events, but not Spence. He was thankful he felt the shock straight to his core. He was still human, at heart a journalist, and one who had questions that needed answers.

"Kelly, help me out here." He hoped his voice came across as calm. "When did you get here?"

She didn't answer. She was staring intensely at something or someone. Spence followed her line of sight to a group of officers huddled near the wall, their faces hidden. One officer turned to Kelly. Her breath deepened into a wheeze, her cheeks blotched, but her eyes were steady, with a hint of contempt, as though she had seen the officer many times before.

The officer's eyes shifted.

Kelly took in a deep breath.

Just then, uniformed members of the Elite Squad came through the doors.

Spence looked around at his newsroom; the desks empty of journalists, the dark, blank screens, the police pushing carelessly through the aisles. The Elite Squad members conferred briefly before stepping forward as one, looking around the office for their target. Spence sighed. Enough was enough. In a world where not much mattered, something had to.

He stepped forward and blocked their path into the newsroom.

THIRTY-SEVEN

KELLY'S EYES sharpened on the scene.

Elite Squad. Maelstrom in the police. Geneva's dead body. Corruption. Secrets. Lies. Her whole body tightened.

Harry White stepped through the door and quickly sidled next to Spence.

One trooper spoke to Harry.

He answered by pointing Kelly's way.

Every eye in the room seemed to swivel in her direction, each one brimming with accusation. A current of fear blasted through her. She saw herself darting for the stairwell, but her legs defied her. She was frozen on the spot.

Spence waved his hand behind his back. If his hands could speak, they'd be saying: Get the hell out of here now.

The troopers shoved Spence out of the way. They advanced across the newsroom like a black tidal wave. A surge of panic fueled her limbs. If she was going down, she would take this whole corrupt structure down with her. Her legs jerked into life. She weaved through the forensics officers in blue coveralls and darted for the fire escape.

Troopers raced to cut her off. "Freeze!"

She dashed through the doors, clattered down the stairs, and rammed the fire exit push bar—setting off a siren. Stunned for a second, she quickly regained traction as her sneakers hit the pavement. On instinct, she pulled the hood over her head and sprinted down the path. Behind her, she heard the door burst open again.

The crack of gunfire ricocheted off the tarmac. Pedestrians screamed and scattered to the edges of the path. Kelly zigzagged past them and ducked into an alley.

Dead end.

Heart pounding, she ran to the next one, but she had lost precious seconds with the wrong turn. The troopers were closing in.

She leaned against the wall, catching her breath. Her parched throat stung. There was an alley with access to the back roads, where no SS existed, two further roads down in the labyrinth.

Splinters of brick rained down on her where a bullet grazed the side of a building. Her lungs on fire, she pushed off and sprinted. Her thighs burned, but she made it, and she ducked into the open alley.

She listened for the troopers' footsteps.

Sounded like they were well behind her now, at least a couple of buildings behind. Their heavy gear would be weighing them down, and they had no SS eyes to help them now. She powered down the alley and catapulted over a low brick wall, skidding as she landed on a long-discarded bag of food. The stench made her stomach wrench.

She surged forward.

Straight, sharp right, and straight again. She shot a glance over her shoulder.

The troopers were far behind, but she knew better than to slow down. They would never give up. If it took them all day, all night, all year, they would hunt her down. She careened around the corner and crashed into rubbish bags.

Rats squealed and scurried in every direction. She ran on. The end of the passage came into view. She could hear the troopers falling farther behind. Distance was her savior now; she shot forward.

The pristine white windowpanes of the Canary Hotel reflected the light. Kelly's freedom would soon be determined by the decision of one man: George Barry. Kelly slowed as she approached the entrance.

A photographer stood on the pavement. She drew back. He was staring at the screen on the back of his camera; he hadn't seen her. She straightened her jacket, wiped her forehead in a concerted effort to look normal, and headed for the entrance.

George Barry was removing his gloves, the last thing he did before wrapping up his morning shift. He glanced at Kelly and reached for the phone. She braced herself, prepared to sprint, unsure of where else she'd go. Not having thought that far ahead, she halted on the steps.

"Mark, we have an incoming package," George said, his tone neutral but urgent. He popped his gloves back on and pulled open the heavy door.

Relief washed over her. George's refined professionalism had been chiseled over years of rough and tumble celebrities. Or maybe he just knew the look of a person in trouble.

"Concierge will assist your every need, Ms. Blackwell."

She stepped into the lobby of the grand hotel. Victory cushioned her weary feet.

THIRTY-EIGHT

THE FLOOR TILES sparkled under the lights of a splendid chandelier. Lunch service in the lobby café was in full swing.

Mark stepped out from behind the concierge desk. "This way."

He was also one of the reasons celebrities paid high prices to stay at the Canary.

Kelly passed a waiter carrying a silver domed tray across the marble floor. The warm lights flattered the skin tones of the pampered guests nestled on the leather sofas. They sipped on cocktails in crystal glasses.

A woman in a black-and-white checkered dress stared at Kelly, her pupils glistened like puddles of black oil. Kelly blinked hard, but she couldn't stop staring at her face covered with wrinkles like dunes, dry and cracked, in a desert earth. Kelly blinked hard again, shook her head, and switched her focus to another woman.

The make-up, meant to hide a bruise under the second woman's eye, only accentuated it. Kelly knocked into another woman walking past.

A flash of despair zapped Kelly. And in that moment, she saw a vision of this third woman, stooped over a bathroom sink, slicing her inner thigh with a razor blade.

Along with the vision came knowledge—knowledge as precise, as perfect as a Japanese knife. Kelly knew this third woman practiced a self-harming ritual and that it had begun after she started providing domina-trix services to the wealthy.

Kelly stumbled, dizzy and overwhelmed by the information pouring into her head. Or were they more hallucinations?

Mark glimpsed back, the look in his eyes egging her forward. She gave a panicked smile, and he pressed them ever onwards.

Kelly glanced to her side. A man, coming in the other direction, passed her in the corridor. In that instant, she grasped a whisper of the vast depth of his being, and a single overarching trait stood above it all: his cravings for self-pleasure, cravings that had destroyed his marriage.

What the hell was she feeling? Was she making up the sorrowful details of these people's lives?

The stories did seem to flow from them somehow, yet not one of them had uttered a single word. Maybe their subconsciouses transmitted all the sadness and anger and depression, and for some reason, some inexplicable reason, all of it flooded Kelly's mind.

Did these people even exist?

Mark stopped at a door with a silver plate inscribed with calligraphic letters. They read: lost and found. Mark ushered her inside, giving no indication that he sensed she was having fantastical hallucinations, and shut the door, securing both of them inside. The knowings—or whatever they were—finally stopped. She leaned against the wall in the small, shelf-lined storage room.

"May I suggest...," Mark said. From a box tucked on a shelf, he pulled out a pair of thigh-high white boots, whipped out a silk scarf with blue and yellow anchor motifs, and a pair of jeans. Next, he yanked a full-length fur coat off a clothes rack.

He raised the outfit in front of her and squinted. "I'm sure you'll find sunglasses in one of those boxes." He motioned toward the silk-lined boxes adorning the shelves, overflowing with Louis Vuitton bags, mink shawls, leather gloves, and all manner of accessories that would take a lifetime for

Kelly to afford. He laid the clothes on a chair. "I'll give you some time to change."

She studied his face as he spoke, waiting for it to transform right before her eyes. But there were no magnified skin pores. No knowings. She wasn't picking up anything distorted or depressing from him. "Thank you, I—"

He lifted his hand. "No need. It's the least we could do after you sent those scrumptious pralines over." A smile broke through his thin lips. "When you're ready, come to the lobby. There's a secure phone. I'm sure you need to contact someone. Toodle-oo." He closed the door behind him.

FORTRESSED BETWEEN THE FOUR WALLS, hidden deep in the back room of the gated hotel, Kelly finally had a moment to breathe.

She unzipped her jacket.

The file was gone. She ran her hands under and over her shirt, even through her pockets. Nothing. It must have fallen somewhere along the way. Her head fell back. "Shit!"

She slumped to the floor, despair engulfing her mind. Ian and now Geneva. Dead. Murdered. The young woman had harbored secrets and dangerous ambitions, leading her to blackmail Kelly in an attempt to remove Spence. Her father, Damian Winters, had a lot of enemies who might have used Geneva to get to him. Or it could be anyone connected to Christopher Mallow and the Resistance who might have been seeking revenge. Kelly couldn't help but feel whoever killed Geneva did many people a favor. Her head ached, like it was about to burst.

It was probably best to leave it to the police to investigate the broad field of suspects. But then, maybe not. She was the one who had found Geneva's body in Global Wires and called it in, and she was alone, without witnesses to back her up. With some digging, they'd find out Geneva tried to blackmail her with a career-ending file. Kelly stood.

To any decent police detective, that would look like a motive for Kelly to kill Geneva. She'd be placed at the top of the suspects list, especially because she ran from the Elite Squad. They could easily pin it on her.

Danger loomed in leaving it to the police. She couldn't let that happen.

She stripped off her sweaty T-shirt, holding back tears of helplessness. A paper poked out from her bra. One sheet had glued itself to her skin. She peeled off the single page. It was the research. A modicum of tension released. At least she had that evidence, but it wasn't enough, and it wasn't the right kind of evidence. Still, it was something. No time to regret what she no longer had; she slipped on the jeans, diamond studs along the pockets, and zipped up the white thigh-high boots.

She dug deep into a box on the shelf, and a sharp needle punctured her middle finger. She winced and sucked the blood. The needle belonged to a single chunky diamond stud sparkling in the light. It looked valuable and expensive, like it could pay off six months of her rent, but she wouldn't be returning home anytime soon. She tossed it back for something more immediately useful.

She struck against hard plastic and metal at the bottom of the box. She fished up the object. A taser, probably left behind by a bodyguard. She pressed the button, and electric currents sparked between its jaws. She stuffed it in her back pocket and continued to search, this time for a pay card, hopefully loaded with coins, but on this count, her luck ran out.

MAKING her way to the lobby, Kelly glimpsed the woman in the checkered dress. She was reclining in the same upholstered chair. Her cil-well eyes had reverted to their normal almond shape, as they should be.

Mark paused and stood back, surveying Kelly's new look. He squinted as though something was missing and pulled open a drawer behind the concierge desk. He cradled a pair of bumblebee sunglasses between his fingers and slid them onto Kelly's face. He tilted his head. "Perfect." He straightened. "Get comfortable. I'll bring the phone over."

She hesitated.

"We're secure in here," he said, as though reading her mind. "We don't pay high fees to the Council for nothing."

She took up a spot in the lobby, far away from the woman in the checkered dress, and settled into one of the upholstered chairs. In the frenzy, she had failed to consider what the Squad had wanted with her. Was it to do with the chamber's malfunction? That wasn't her fault. Didn't matter though. She knew that if she stayed on the grid, they'd track her down, just like they had Christopher. All the equipment Roseman had in stock was no match for the Elite Squad, and she'd need a place to lie low.

Something grazed her shoulder. She bristled.

"Takes time to relax." Mark handed her a large block of a phone. "Dial one for a secure line."

She nodded and eyed the phone, unsure of whom to call.

Spence was at the top of the list. Along with a burning itch to know about the fallout she left behind. She also wanted to know how he was holding up. But the Elite Squad would be listening in, and she wasn't going to put Spence in a tough spot by calling him. Harry White didn't even make it on her call list, especially after he pointed her out to the Elite Squad. Indeed, he was on her blacklist. Then, there was Josh. He was a liar, but he wasn't a snitch—of that, she was sure. He had a lot of secrets, too many. But he did conceal her footsteps from the SS in Soho; otherwise, she wouldn't have shaken off the Elite Squad quite so easily. She'd not be sitting here in the Canary if it weren't for him. Yielding to her desire to believe in him again, however premature, however hasty, she dialed his number, surprised she could remember it so easily.

"Hello?" He sounded guarded.

"It's me, Kelly. I'm on a secure line."

"How did it go?"

"Can you get into...files?"

"Oh, I see. Not well then. Depends on what you need. Read-only or edit?"

"A bit of both."

"What's this about?"

"Something happened, and I need to keep an eye on an investigation."

"Sounds dangerous. If you tell me exactly what you need..."

"A list of suspects."

He went quiet, and she could sense his thought wheels in motion. Eventually, he asked, "What's the case?"

"Geneva Winters, the daughter of Damian Winters."

"What happened?"

"She's dead."

"Jesus Christ! They're going to be all over this. Why would they suspect you? Where are you? How secure is this line?"

She lowered her voice. "The less you know, the better, and don't worry about the line. It's secure, it's about the only thing that is."

"Nothing is ever a hundred percent." He cleared his throat and inhaled, a clear sign of a need to confess something. She braced herself.

"Kelly," he said. "I have spy cams in Global Wires."

Unlike his earlier confession, this one benefited her. "You're full of surprises, Josh. Who were you spying on and since when?"

"Damian Winters. Don't ask. If the crime happened this morning, the recording will have what you need."

"What about if it happened last night?"

"Then don't get your hopes up. I had it switched to motion detection. If it was too dark, it might not have recorded at all. I'll have it ready to view this afternoon. Come by around three o'clock."

"Can you send me a viewing link?"

"Kelly, you're going to need a place to hide out, and your studio is out of the question."

She recalled the woman on the phone who had suggested she go to the Underground Freedom Fighters camp, almost as if she knew what was about to go down. Given all that had transpired, it wasn't such an outlandish idea. Admittedly, the camp was a stark place to go, but it was the only place she'd be free enough to gather hard evidence without fear of the Squad. "I have a place in mind."

"You can always come here."

"I'm not going to put you in danger. Besides, I need a pair of eyes in the city." She bit her lip, realizing she had said too much.

His silence on the line told her he was working out what she meant. "I'll do some digging and send you what I find," he said at last.

"Whatever you do, don't use the chambers," she said.

"Why not?"

"I found what Christopher was working on. His research says they included thought crime as part of the Truth Laws. They'll soon be policing thoughts in the chambers."

"But that's not—"

"I know. It was never part of the original legislation. But according to Christopher's research, it is. Thinking back now, the chambers weren't working properly on the first day of the Truth Laws going into effect, so maybe the State changed the launch day of those algorithms, or something like that."

"We can't let this happen."

"I have to find out who set this into motion and who might be able to cut the feed, as it were, and there's no way I can do any of that here. In a couple of days, I'll be in touch."

She closed the line.

Although the Freedom Fighters camp's exact location was mysterious, Kelly knew it was situated somewhere in the area that had been flooded by the Thames back in 2025, in what used to be called Rotherhithe, East London. The Southwark Council, responsible for Rotherhithe, didn't have the funds to rebuild it, so they turned it into a landfill, a temporary scheme, they said, but it had remained a wasteland ever since. Today, it was called No Man's Land and, crucially, beyond the reach of the long arm of the law, the only locale where she could think and speak freely, if she stayed alive long enough to enjoy that kind of freedom.

Even though No Man's Land was not illegal to enter, the State had sent regular public announcements warning citizens of the dangers of straying into the SS-free territory. Society's unwanted misfits and loners inhabited it, and they expressed a different volatility—dangerous, none-theless. Until she found the camp, she'd be on her own out there. But compared to being here in the city, how bad could it be? Hell, Kelly might even recruit some allies in the Freedom Fighters. After all, they shared an enemy.

She eased into the rose-colored armchair, the clanging crystal goblets chiming through the room, and waited for the lull of nightfall.

THIRTY-NINE

KELLY STEPPED out of the Canary in thigh-high suede boots. She draped the scarf around her nose and mouth and locked it down with the bumblebee sunglasses, hiding her identifiable facial nodal points from the SS. The white double-breasted fur coat, belted tight around her waist, insulated her from the cold air as she slipped further into the darkness.

She marched eastward, pausing every so often to stretch her calves.

Three hours later, her back aching, she arrived at a breach in a fence. She could just about make out a dirt ramp leading into the darkness, beyond which was hard to see. This had to be the gateway into No Man's Land. She could smell it. What had her life become? She glanced behind her, shivered, and faced front again. The dark wasteland that stretched before her was full of danger, but what choice did she have? If she hid out at the freedom camp, at least she could investigate in safety. She tossed the bumblebee sunglasses and stepped into the rugged unknown.

Her vision adjusted to the moonlight. The smell of waste lingered in the air, and the sound of creatures scampering over the rubble echoed in the darkness. Powering herself through the disfigured terrain, the temperature seemed to drop a degree every few feet. She lost her balance, stumbled, and hit the ground.

Stale rot from the landfill penetrated her nose. Something stabbed her. She shot up and slapped the nape of her neck. Her hand felt wet. She sniffed, detecting iron notes of blood.

A fat rodent scurried in the darkness.

The damn thing bit her. Kelly scrambled to her feet, questioning if she had taken on more than she could handle. It was too late for such doubts. She continued toward the river—still out of sight but audible over the eerie quiet of No Man's Land.

She trudged on for what felt like hours, gravity pulling on her thighs, her lungs struggling to expand. Finally, the dark curve of the river came into sight. Unable to take another breath, Kelly stopped at the riverbank for a rest. In all this time, the freedom camp was nowhere in sight. She looked out to the river.

Waves lapped against the barrier in steady rhythms, calming her. Lights flickered on the surface of the Thames from a moving barge. She caught a whiff of salt, nutmeg, and clover and the sight of rubble drifting past. She surveyed the horizon. A single land-locked light glowed in the far distance. Just one light for an entire camp? It didn't seem right, but she was too tired to think. Exhaustion was catching up with her. Fifteen minutes to recharge was all she needed. She crouched down, leaned into the riverbank wall, and balanced her weight on her legs. She closed her eyes.

A parade of people streamed through Kelly's mind. Josh, Spence, Omar, Geneva. Harry's smelly sneakers raised an unexpected smile on her lips. A tear trailed down her cheek.

Wind blew through empty tin canisters, producing a hollow, unearthly whistle.

She shot open her eyes and sprang up.

There, in the distance, across the river, the single light she had seen before appeared to be moving. She dismissed it, telling herself it was her imagination.

The beam of light bounced again in the darkness.

Dread heightened her senses. Eerie sounds all around conjured up outlines of menace. The darkness harbored too many unknown dangers.

The light now pointed in a different direction, away from the river.

She locked her eyes on the beam. Maybe they were freedom fighters. Or perhaps not. Didn't matter. Until she could see clearly, everyone and everything was a threat.

Her teeth chattering, she curled up and waited for the full light of dawn to move in.

FORTY

TROY LOOKED DOWN at the woman he had only seen from afar. So, this was Kelly Blackwell, the one Rozlyn had been eager to bring into the camp. She was crashed out on the ground here in No Man's Land. Streaks of dirt obscured her sweet, round face, and tufts of thick brown hair poked out from her silk scarf, one of those fancy scarves that didn't keep the wind out. Why she came to No Man's Land wearing diva boots was beyond him. The Fighters would never accept her dressed in a white fur coat. His first task would be to get her into uniform.

She stirred. He stepped away, leaned into the riverbank wall, and admired the dawn light filling the sky.

Her neck jerked back, one of those twitches of shallow sleep, and her eyes launched open. She rubbed her face, stretched her legs, and rose to her feet. She still hadn't noticed he was standing just a few feet to her right.

He cleared his throat. "I love coming to the river first thing."

She whipped around, reaching into her back pocket, and glared at him with her big brown eyes. Sweeter than he expected. A woman like this wouldn't have a gun. A knife, maybe, a taser, very probably. Didn't matter.

He'd snatch it from her as soon as she pulled it out. "Didn't mean to startle you." He held out his hand. "I'm Troy Wolfe."

She didn't take his hand; instead, she stood her ground. "Where did you come from?"

He put his hand down and pointed behind him without turning. "Back that way."

He turned back to the river, watching tiny whirlpools form and reform, but from the corner of his eye, he could see the hobos approaching. He glanced down and sneaked a sideway peek. Two pairs of shoes, muddy and ripped at the soles. Confirmed. Johnny and Mo were right on time.

Johnny whacked the woman on the back of her head, knocking her down to the ground. She glared up at him and struggled to get to her feet, but he stomped on her heel, nailing her foot down.

A third unknown man pinned Troy's wrists behind his back and pressed a knife into his chest. Troy hadn't recruited this one. He wasn't part of the plan. "What the fuck."

"You twos aren't from around here, are you?" the stranger said through half-rotten teeth.

Kelly sprang to her feet and pulled out a taser.

"Seems to me she has something to offer," Johnny said with a menacing grin.

She jabbed the taser at the vagrant.

Troy slammed back into the strange hobo. They crashed onto the ground, wrestling each other in the rubble. The hobo grunted as the air jolted out of his lungs. Now that he was on even terms with his target, the hobo's nerve failed. He fled, stumbling as he ran down the riverbank.

She grabbed Johnny's arm and bit into it with such ferocity that it caused him to lose his balance. She had the opening she needed to shove him into the riverbank wall.

He gave in quickly—the wimp—and scampered away like a rodent looking for cover in the landfill.

Mo charged at her.

She sunk the taser deep into his neck.

His body went rigid. She ground the jaws of the taser deeper, piercing his skin until blood dripped on her hand.

Mo's eyes gaped. He fell backward.

A wild anger flooded Kelly's eyes; pure survival instinct had taken her over. Troy actually felt intimidated by her severe transformation.

She lashed toward the vagrant, screaming and thrusting the taser into his side again and again and again.

"It's done," Troy said, prying the taser from her grip. "You can stop now."

Mo lay still, his eyes stark and staring up at the overcast sky.

She trembled and fell back against the wall.

A throng of different emotions volleyed inside him. He hadn't expected such a fierce reaction from her, but he was glad she had that taser. The Fighters were going to have a hard time with her, but he liked her. That third man had caught him off guard, and someone was going to pay.

She slumped to her side, eyes closed.

He placed his hand under her nostrils. Her soft breath feathered his fingers. She was fine. Passing out at this point was a strange reaction, but the fight had probably taken too much out of her. At least it gave him the opportunity to do something that needed to be done before they reached the camp.

He lifted her coat sleeve, unfastened her watch, and tossed it over the wall, pleased he didn't have to fight it off her.

* * *

Kelly came to with a cough, her whole body throbbed. She attempted to lift herself, but the gravel pierced her bloodstained palms.

Troy's arms dangled over his knees. He was looping his thumbs. "You're quite the fighter. You'll need that out here." His bushy, dark blond hair swayed in the breeze.

"Don't you care about what just happened? They could've killed us."

"But they didn't."

Her calf muscle spasmed; she ironed out the locked muscle hidden behind the thigh-high boot caked in dirt. "Where's that guy?"

"Which one?"

"The one I..."

"Tasered?" Troy smiled.

"Killed."

He chuckled. "You fried his nerves. You didn't kill him. See? He's breathing."

She glanced across at the hobo, still laid out flat, his chest rising and falling with his breath.

"I'm impressed," Troy said. "You don't look like the type."

"Looks can be deceiving," she said. "Shouldn't we do something for him?" She nodded in the hobo's direction.

"He'll be all right." Troy stared at the dirt on his shoes. He picked up a couple of stones and flicked them.

"How do you know? You're a doctor?"

"Feisty and sarcastic," he said. "Catalina is going to like you." He glanced at her. "Catalina's one of our Fighters."

She was struck by his soft blue eyes and wondered if she had seen him before. There was something alluring about him, hard to deny. The fleeting recognition receded and was quickly replaced with suspicion, a suspicion that their meeting was set up. "So, you're part of the Underground Freedom Fighters," she guessed.

He nodded lightly in confirmation.

"Were you out here last night, searching for something in the dark?"

"Nope."

She was relieved she had glued herself to the wall and waited for daybreak. "How far is the camp?"

"About an hour away."

"Will you take me?"

"As you wish." Troy wiped his hands and bounced onto his feet. He offered his hand for support. She took it. As she strained to lift herself, she suppressed a wince. He pulled his hand back. "We'd better get moving. We don't want the other two coming back here with their friends."

She felt tired, sore, achy, but oddly clear-headed. Her body shook as she took her first step. Her stomach growled.

"The camp has what you need," he said. "You can also get cleaned up."

"I'm Kelly Blackwell."

He bobbed his head.

The bright gray sky bleached out the terrain. The only sound was the river and their footsteps as they made their way across the dry, cracked earth, with not a single SS in sight.

FORTY-ONE

THEY ARRIVED AT A MANNED GATE. People in green fatigues and black thermal jackets scrambled from one marquee tent to another. A line of people carried boxes, tablets, and mics; others carried open boxes packed with paper and notebooks. It seemed like some kind of beehive society.

"Welcome to the Underground Freedom Fighters camp," Troy said.

Satellite tents revolved around the largest tent on the grounds. The layout was like a merry-go-round, the headquarters in the center.

Troy hooked the arm of a man in fatigues passing by. Kelly adjusted her coat, feeling for Christopher's research lodged in her bra. Thankfully, it was still there, glued in place with sweat.

"How did things go?" The man spoke with a Scottish accent.

"Perfect. Almost."

The Scot glanced at Kelly, sizing her up from head to toe.

She nodded. "Kelly Blackwell. Nice to meet you."

"Likewise. I'm Sinclair."

"She's our new member," Troy said. "She passed the stooges test."

Sinclair raised his eyebrows, looking impressed. "Let's talk more later."

She hid her bewilderment with a smile. She knew it. That hobo bull-shit had been a setup.

Sinclair strutted toward a marquee.

"Stooges?" Kelly demanded.

Troy sucked in his breath. "We have to put all the newcomers through a test."

She balked. "Are you kidding me?"

"Relax. They got paid well."

"Are you fucking kidding me?" She slapped a hand on her thigh. "They could've killed us."

"Everyone at the camp has to go through an initiation," Troy said. "You surpassed expectations."

"What kind of operation is this?"

"Relax. We have to know you can defend the camp."

She rolled her eyes.

"I'll introduce you to everyone once things settle down." He reached into his back pocket. "This is yours." The taser lay in his open palm.

She snatched it from his hand.

"Good piece of kit. You'll have to tell me where you got it."

Kelly's lips tightened.

"I'm sorry about having to put you through that back there." His voice was low and measured. "I needed to know what you're made of because it's one thing to be on the outside, but quite another to be on the inside. The tests don't stop out there." He pointed to the main tent. "Let's get you set up."

Whatever this place was, it might not be the haven she had hoped for.

CURVED steel tubing framed the shell. The thick-skinned ceiling and walls were covered in a lightweight, high-tech fabric that looked like it could resist blustering winds, slashing rain, and all manner of beasts. Curtains hung like tonsils between sections of the tent. They buffered the sounds of workers' boots pounding the dirt ground. Being inside the main tent made Kelly feel like she was inside the belly of a whale.

A light-skinned black woman in a military-brown sweater stepped into the communal area. Her strong cheekbones and jaw stretched her skin.

"That's Rozlyn Abbott," Troy whispered in Kelly's ear before lifting his voice. "Commander, may I introduce Kelly Blackwell."

"Nice to meet you." Her voice was cool and aloof.

Kelly's mouth went dry. That voice. Abbott was the voice, the half-digitized voice that had called her at Global Wires. How long had she been watching her every move? What else had she seen? Did she know who killed Geneva? "Likewise," Kelly managed to spit out.

Troy cleared his throat. "Some of our agents are working in the city this week, so it's not as active in here as it normally is. But we have a weekly get-together on Saturdays. It gives everyone a chance to relax and have some fun. It's the perfect time for you to get to know everyone."

"Most agents should be back by then." Abbott picked up the discussion.

The camp's commander reminded Kelly of cagey people she'd interviewed over the years. She didn't have to pry them open. All she needed to do was wait until there was no one else in the room. That's when they usually divulged their secrets. This lady clearly had something to hide, but what? "I look forward to meeting everyone," Kelly said as nonchalantly as she could.

"Everyone here adds to the team," Abbott said. "Some have sharp instincts, others have much-needed coding skills, others have cooking skills."

"I'm a journalist. What can I bring to the table?"

"I wouldn't say that too loudly around here," Troy said.

"A journalist can come in handy," Abbott corrected him. She tilted her head and looked at Kelly. "Always observing and connecting. Sometimes you people write about things that aren't even there." Abbott smirked. "We'll say you defected."

The cover story sent a shiver of discomfort through Kelly. It was just one little white lie, but the ease with which it had come to Abbott unsettled her.

"You can join our comms team," Abbott went on. She turned to Troy. "Do you have anything to add?"

He shook his head.

"It's a natural position." Abbott's face hardened with a cold look in her eyes. "Show her the ropes and rotate the schedule with Luke, Catalina, and Michelle."

A fighter approached Abbott and whispered something in her ear. While Abbott was distracted, Kelly spied the crevices of the room, searching for a suitable spot to hide her cargo, but Troy interrupted her search. "Once you're cleaned up, I'll take you to the comms room," he said.

"Of course."

"I have to go," Abbott said. "We'll catch up again at the gathering. I look forward to working with you."

"I appreciate the hospitality," Kelly answered, trying to keep her voice free of the suspicion that was fast setting in.

"Let's take a quick tour." Troy bounced on the balls of his feet. "Then, I'll show you where you'll be sleeping."

"Sure," Kelly said, but she wanted nothing more than food, water, and a bed.

He gestured for her to follow him.

Canvas stretched from one end of the headquarters to the other. The variety of shaded patches gave the camp a hippie-like feel. The dividing sheets buffered the sounds of chattering voices and the clanks of ceramic mugs. People darted across their path like sharp notes and then disappeared for long lulls of stillness.

"How many people are here?"

"Now fifty-one," he said, pointing at her. "But our network is far bigger. Let's go around, and I'll introduce you to whoever's in."

"How long has the camp been operating?"

"In this location, roughly three years."

"I know it might seem like an obvious question, but what's the camp's primary mission?"

Troy paused and looked up at the soft ceiling. "Some would say regime change. To me, it's a refuge."

"Regime change? As in government overthrow?"

He shrugged. Sufficiently vague. She held back from asking him why he had escaped to the camp because she had a feeling he wouldn't tell her anyway. They stepped outside the main tent, turning left down a well-trodden lane and wound round the camp.

"Everyone has a job to do," he explained. "We recruit for the strength of the group, not just random people here and there."

They arrived at the northeastern quadrant of the camp. Stacked against one of the tents were rags, red buckets, spray bottles, and beside them a dry mop, though what it was used for, Kelly wasn't sure. There weren't any wooden floors as far as she had seen.

"Rob and Telullah work together as our cleaner team. They used to be sweepers in the city but were fed up with the amount of bugs. Plus, they couldn't ever meet anyone."

"Being a sweeper takes a certain type of outlook." She nodded in sympathy. "Where are they?"

"Probably getting something to eat."

Kelly turned to Troy. "So what do you do?"

"Can't you tell?"

"Bodyguard?"

Troy laughed.

"That funny, aye?"

"Yeah, it is!"

"I think it's a perfectly logical conclusion. You're built like a machine and you do exactly as you're told. What more evidence do I need?"

He raised his eyebrows. "Ouch."

"I'm sorry. I didn't mean it like that."

"Depending on what's going on, I do a little of everything." Sufficiently vague again. "And you?" he said before Kelly could press the point. "Of all the journalists in London, what made you come here?"

"The way things are going, I won't be the last journalist passing through."

He halted in midstride. "Let me show you a little secret I keep to myself." He detoured to the back of the camp. He scooted away the rubbish bins and a dead bush propped against the fence perimeter. "When you need to get away and spend some time alone."

She eyed the hole in the fence, big enough for a man to wedge through. "You read me well."

He replaced the bins and continued down the path. Eventually, they came to another tent, and he drew back its heavy curtain. Large computer screens lined three desks, standing together as one. Off to the side were several smaller box screens. An assortment of computer parts, wires, casings, and cables were lumped together near a black chest on the floor.

"It's like a museum in here," Kelly said.

"We like wired," said the girl in the swivel chair.

"This is where you'll be working."

Exhaustion suddenly descended on Kelly. "It's been a long night. Would you mind if I freshened up?"

"Too much too soon?" He cocked his head. "Let's show you where you'll be sleeping."

They passed several hanging sheets, acting as doors, dividing the tent into small rooms. They came to a maroon sheet divider. Troy held open the curtain. "And here we are."

The windowless room contained three cots, inches off the dirt floor, a couple of desks, a chair, and a clothesline. Almost as bare as No Man's Land.

"You're rooming with Catalina and Michelle," Troy said.

"I really need to get some food in me, too."

"I'll order some from Felix. He works in the kitchen. I'll also bring you some towels."

As soon as Troy was out of sight, Kelly lifted the mattress from her cot. It seemed too obvious a place to hide Christopher's research. The flat pillow would have to do for now. She pulled out the paper, stuffed it inside the pillowcase, smoothed the creases, and sat on the edge of the cot. Its coils squeaked. No longer able to resist the heaviness in her lids and a warm feeling draping over her, she lay back and let sleep take her away.

FORTY-TWO

23 January

A FRESH SET of army-green fatigues lay folded on the bedside table, combat boots waiting beneath. She slid her feet into them, leaving the laces loose. The boots practically shouted conformity, and Kelly knew that the moment she tightened them upright, she would be declaring her surrender to the group.

In the hazy, early morning air, she stepped onto a quiet path, the boots flapping against her heel. She added her own footprint to the multitude on the dirt path and headed for the washroom.

The women's only communal bathroom was just big enough for three people. Kelly winced as she stripped out of the boots and peeled off the sticky sweater she had been wearing since Monday.

Yellow and purple bruises covered the sides of her torso. Brushing a damp cloth over her skin, mopping up the stale sweat, caused her whole body to ache. She suddenly appreciated the bath in her studio flat, not realizing how good she had had it. Even though this shower room was a tad cramped, water was water.

Her thoughts drifted to Troy, wondering what his story was, what brought him to the Fighters, and what kept him here at the camp. Then Abbott. Rozlyn Abbott. Kelly didn't have a good feeling about that woman.

And that's when she realized something else. She didn't like Abbott, and she could think it freely. For the first time in a long time, her mind was free to opine without fear or scrutiny or the echo chambers somehow picking up her biorhythms. Life had changed so much, so incrementally, that she had almost forgotten what freedom felt like.

She soaked in the exhilarating realization, held in check by a tiny fear that it was all just a figment of her imagination.

What she could confirm was that she hadn't seen a single thug maelstrom in the camp, and that was significant. Their absence indicated that her stress symptoms had subsided—maybe there was hope for this place yet.

Whatever sense of freedom she felt, however real or not it was, probably wouldn't last long, she thought. Nothing ever did. But she'd enjoy it while she could.

She dressed and headed back to the room.

A whiff of greasy salt snagged her attention.

There, on the side table, was a plate with a brown bread sandwich. Her mouth watered. She grinned and devoured a quarter of the sandwich in one bite.

Crunchy leaves and juicy tomato burst in her mouth; the bacon's saltiness was heaven on her tongue. She glanced at the white thigh-high boots and kicked them under the cot. Freshened up and fed, she tightened the bootlaces. Ready to finish the tour of the camp, and needing to know what this place was really all about, she left to find Troy.

FORTY-THREE

24 January

JOSH SKIMMED the Global Wires obituary listings on the third day since Geneva had been found dead.

He had almost given up hope, thinking they must have buried her listing deep inside the webpages or simply avoided mentioning her death at all. Then he saw her name: Geneva Winters. She actually made the first listing on the page—violating the alphabetical order of things. Finally, it had been published.

The Resistance's burner phone rang. Just looking at the phone filled him with shame. What would he say? He let it ring. Three rings later, it halted.

He sighed and turned back to the screen. Geneva Winters. Twenty-one years old. Day of passing, January 21. Geneva left behind a loving brother, Ben, and her mother and father, Sarah and Damian Winters. The Global Wires obituaries page was final and to the point, just like death.

Josh rocked back. The funeral was taking place in an hour, not far from the Oasis Cafe, where he had filmed the woman in the cashmere coat talking to Rozlyn Abbott. Josh hated funerals, but if he went, he might discover something that could help Kelly, and the only way to know was to go and find out.

———

At 2:30 p.m., Josh stepped onto the marble floor of the crematorium, carrying cellophane-wrapped orange carnations—the only flowers the newsagent across the road had. He crossed the empty foyer. A placard displayed the day's schedule. The Winters Funeral was in Room 301.

He wandered down a signposted corridor. At the end of the hall, he could hear whispers flowing through the cracks of the wooden double doors up ahead. He straightened his tie. Unsure of what he'd find on the other side, but open for anything at this point, he pulled on the brass handle.

The large room was packed with dark-suited men and women, mostly journalists he recognized, as well as some he didn't. A light-haired man in a dark suit approached.

"I'm Geneva's brother, Ben."

Awkwardly, Josh extended his hand. There never seemed to be an appropriate gesture or word to offer at a funeral. "My condolences."

Ben scrolled down a list of names on his tablet. "And you are?"

"Josh Munro." The imposter feeling in him grew, but he ignored it and spurred on. "I was invited at the last minute." He smiled, at a loss for what else to say.

Josh spotted Spence in the crowd. He was wearing a navy tie and jacket, the same suit he had seen him wear at every important occasion. Samantha, Lily, Harry, and Hassan orbited him like satellites.

"Harry White over there." Josh pointed. "He can vouch for me."

Ben looked all too relieved from having to scour the list any longer, and he stepped to the side.

At the front of the room, a woman in her sixties sat next to a rosewood coffin girded with flowers. She wore a black sweater and skirt, translucent tights, and black shoes. Her hand caressed the smooth wood of the closed coffin. Had to be Geneva's mother.

Josh laid his carnations next to a bunch of white lilies. "My condolences for your loss." How empty the phrase must have sounded to the mother mourning her child.

The veiled woman glanced at Josh. Her swollen eyes stabbed him to his core, reminding him of his beloved mother when his dad passed. "Thank you," she said, and the words looked like they pained her.

No heartfelt words he could say would release the torment she felt. He backed away, mercifully, and turned to the crowd.

A woman drew his attention, the last person he expected to see. Rozlyn Abbott, the leader of the Underground Freedom Fighters. She wore a multi-colored gown and black headdress.

He drifted through the crowd, trying to work out how she came to be here, and crashed into Harry.

"Hey, Josh. Is Kelly with you?"

Josh shook his head. "Can't believe what's happened. Any details come out yet?"

"No one's told me a thing."

"Where's Mr. Winters?"

Harry shrugged. "Strange, I haven't seen him."

"Grief does strange things to people," said a woman behind them.

Josh turned and discovered he was face-to-face with Rozlyn Abbott. "How did you know Geneva?" he said, the question springing abruptly from his lips.

Rozlyn smiled graciously. "We worked on a project together. Gen was a marvelous girl." Her voice carried a warm tone, unlike her eyes.

Harry hesitated. "What project was that?"

The woman lowered her eyes. "Oh, it was very technical. I'm not sure you'd find it interesting."

"I'm an IT geek," Harry pressed. "What sort of technical?"

This time, she turned her head toward the front of the room. "Technical."

Geneva's brother cleared his throat over the microphone on the podium at the front of the room. The chatter quelled and people coasted to a gallery of chairs, claiming their spot for the service.

"Thank you all for coming." Ben's voice shook. "Geneva was a vibrant person, born with an abundance of curiosity and enthusiasm. When we were little, she was always asking everyone questions, and it drove us crazy." His lip quivered. "Geneva was my twin. She was only twenty-one —" His voice wavered. He gripped the mic and took a moment to recompose himself. "She was especially excited when she started to work at Global Wires, training with Kelly Blackwell." He paused and scanned the crowd.

"Kelly couldn't make it," Josh spoke up. "She's on assignment but sends her condolences."

Ben peered over the heads, looking for the voice. He spotted Josh and nodded. "I have a couple of notebooks she wanted Kelly to have." He spoke as though they were in a private conversation. "One notebook has notes on someone named Oliver Green."

The room filled with murmurs.

"Is Oliver Green here?"

Rozlyn, next to Josh, stared down at her clenched hands. She sounded like she was quietly praying. Ben's announcement was bizarre—and by everyone's reaction, not the sort of information he should've openly announced. Ben looked back down at the program for the service, apparently sensing his mistake, and Josh felt a surge of pity for him—grief did do strange things to people. He searched the distressed faces for Spence. He was staring straight ahead, fixed his sight, deathlike, on the casket.

A buzz shot through the room. The black conveyor belt clicked into action and shifted forward. Geneva's casket began its slow creep toward the combustion compartment. The heavy metal mouth of the compartment opened. As soon as the coffin had passed through, the clang of metal bolts locked the barrier shut, and the iron door slammed down.

Heat rippled through the compartment. Mrs. Winters clasped her chest as ash swirled around the furnace. The heat morphed into sparks that transformed into a scorching fire until a full blast lit up the room.

When it was done, the quiet lasted only a moment before a giant vacuum sucked up the residue into a hole at the bottom of the unit. Within minutes, the compartment was clean and dry and empty.

Ben held his sobbing mother in his arms, tears rolling down his face.

A black sign shot down from the ceiling: "Rest in Peace."

The intercom announced, "Thank you for your attendance."

The crowd stampeded toward the wooden doors. Ben waded through the crowd, notebooks in hand, his eyes locked on Josh. A woman tripped and fell to the floor in front of him. Another lost her balance and fell on her knees. Josh helped both women to their feet, but the panic had already fully possessed them, and they struggled to stand.

Spence pulled on Josh's arm. "Where's Kelly?"

"I don't know."

Ben tucked the two notebooks under Josh's arm.

Instinctively, he clasped down firmly on the notebooks.

"Take good care of these," Ben said. "I'm sure they're more valuable than we know."

FORTY-FOUR

25 January

SIBERIAN-COLD WATER LASHED Kelly's face. "What the hell?" She shot up from the cot and gasped for air.

A woman with spiky black hair, dressed in tan combat fatigues, towered over her. Holding an empty glass, she stared down at Kelly with intense, dark eyes.

Kelly rocketed to her feet and came face-to-face with the tormentor. "Back off, bitch." Kelly jabbed at the woman's shoulder. If she had more strength, she'd punch the woman, hard, but judging by the woman's size, she would have the upper hand in any fight.

"Relax," the woman said. "I want to know if there's anything different in your eyes that the rest of us don't have."

"What the hell are you talking about? Get away from me."

"Nope. I don't see a thing."

A sharp pang cramped Kelly's stomach. She doubled over. Realizing it was a sign of weakness, she quickly straightened up and bit back the pain.

The woman pivoted. "Michelle is waiting for you in comms."

"Next time, a simple alarm clock will do," Kelly yelled after her.

Troy came into the room.

"Do you always have such bad timing?"

He laughed. "Sorry about the theatrics. Catalina has that effect on people. You'll get used to her. Come. Let's get some coffee. I'll take you to comms."

Mug in hand, Kelly arrived at the comms tent with the sole purpose of pacifying these people so she could get on with her investigation, quietly.

"Sleeping beauty has arrived," said a girl in the swivel chair. She had a thin, sallow look, her fingers jittery.

Troy cleared his throat. "That's Michelle." His deadpan tone gave Kelly the feeling he'd really rather not utter her name.

"I don't know why they assigned you to comms," Michelle said. "I bet you've already been snooping around."

Kelly scratched her eyebrow and ignored the words dripping with hostility. The last thing she needed was an argument with her new colleague. Quite the opposite, she needed to get her to reveal just how long they'd been watching her.

"Michelle's not a morning person," Troy said.

She flipped him the finger.

"Doesn't seem like anyone around here is," Kelly said.

"Don't mind Michelle." Troy gave Kelly a reassuring look. "She can be a real pain in the ass, but she's a good worker."

Michelle examined the chipped purple polish on her nails. "I see Troy has taken a liking to you."

Troy waved her away and approached one of the computers.

Kelly glanced at the outdated equipment in the tent, equipment reminiscent of a time when Internet surveillance was still a covert activity and when privacy was still a matter for debate.

Troy's fingers tapped against one of the keyboards. "Don't be fooled by the old machines."

Among all the worn-out equipment, a yellow button caught her eye. "And that looks like a thermonuclear bomb button."

"It sort of is. It alerts everyone that shit is going down in No Man's Land."

"Like what?"

Michelle sneered. "That's the point."

Troy stepped in front of Michelle. "An Elite Squad raid for one."

"Why not hack the Zone, stay ahead of the Elite Squad that way?"

Behind Troy, Michelle was rolling her chair back and forth. "If Global Wires did its job, you'd know by now that everything is hackable except the Zone."

Hearing Global Wires cast Kelly's mind back to the experiences she had there, both good and bad, but overriding it all was how Spence protected her by blocking the Elite Squad, giving her a few extra seconds to escape. "If Global Wires did what it was supposed to do, I'd be in a holding cell at the Zone."

Troy turned to Michelle. "Aren't you finishing your shift soon?"

Michelle snapped back in her chair. "You're not going to get rid of me that easily."

Whatever problem Michelle had with Troy had nothing to do with Kelly, but it did feel like she was on Michelle's list of enemies for some unknown reason. But then, she did look like the kind of person who'd have a problem with anyone. Rooming with her and Catalina was going to feel like a prison sentence. Kelly shook herself and focused on the monitors. "The State's been monitoring utility usage for a while. Where do you get your power to fire all this up without giving your location away?"

"We have two power supplies. One is the main source coming from solar panels, the other is Charlie's contraption." He paused, as if having just remembered something. "But that'll have to wait. Start by getting into Cicada. Luke will show you the ropes."

"Luke's not in today," Michelle said. "I'll be showing her the ropes."

Compared to Michelle, Cicada was going to feel like a warm cup of hot chocolate, thought Kelly.

"I just remembered I have to prep something special for our party tomorrow," Troy said.

His abrupt announcement left Kelly flummoxed. "If I need anything, where can I find you?"

"I'll be around," he said. "Michelle will be happy to help." He glanced at Michelle.

She nodded wearily.

He left.

Now that Troy had gone, Michelle was paying her absolutely no attention whatsoever. Every group tested newcomers, and Kelly knew she'd have to claim her territory, prove her worth, make a reputation for herself. A little hesitantly, she pulled out one of the chairs and sat. Alone with her thoughts for the first time since arriving at the camp, she itched to reconnect with Josh.

By now he would have sent her the footage from Global Wires, but that wasn't why she wanted to reconnect with him. He was from her old world where she knew the rules, however screwed up they were. She missed him.

She drummed her fingers on the desk. Another dead hour, Kelly thought, twiddling her thumbs.

FORTY-FIVE

Troy crossed the camp toward the central tent. He needed extra funds approved for more kegs and food for the party, sure, but that sudden switch in the comms crew rattled him. It was yet another change without warning. And then there was Catalina. Her aggression, her dogmatism, was also rubbing off on other Fighters, like Michelle, and Rozlyn needed to rein it in. The time had come for a talk.

He passed the wooden shed doors, another reminder of Catalina's influence on the camp. She had proposed building the bunker, touting it as storage the camp needed for food and alcohol. He opposed it on instinct, but Rozlyn had agreed. Now, the storage space served as a sun-starved prison. He stepped into the communal room.

A whistle echoed from the kitchen. Troy headed down the passageway, and he slowed, gathering his nerves. When he came to the velvet partition cordoning Abbott's room, her hushed voice trickled out. She was talking to someone.

He peeked through the gap between the edge of the curtain and the canvas wall. As far as he could see, no one else was in the room. She was talking to someone on her watch. He waited outside for her to finish.

"We have the target here at the camp," Abbott said.

His ears pricked up, straining to hear every word. She was so absorbed in her conversation that it didn't look like she sensed she was being watched, heard.

"How do you know?" she asked. Troy heard the vague buzz of the voice on the other end of the line, but it was too distant for him to make out the words. Rozlyn shifted impatiently. "Yeah, but that means nothing. The auction will generate so much money, the sky's the limit. The target's worth way more than Lydia realizes."

His chest muscles twitched. A wave of disbelief washed over Troy. What and who had he been giving his loyalty to? Some trafficking operation? How was this possible? Was Luke in on this, too? Even though he only heard one side of the conversation, it was clear they were talking about selling a human being.

"Oh, you have? How much are they willing to pay?"

His jaw clenched as he felt his worst suspicions become a certainty. Abbott was further gone than Catalina.

"Sounds good to me. The target's being kept busy, doesn't suspect a thing. Give me a day or two and I'll... No, don't worry. It's all in order."

Being kept busy? Betrayal pierced him, his knees weakened. It sounded like they were talking about Kelly, about selling her. The thought made him light-headed.

"No. I'll take the target to you on Sunday," Abbott said.

If he hadn't heard Abbott making a deal with his own ears, he wouldn't have believed it. But now that he had heard it, he needed to know who she was talking to.

Abbott was suddenly silent. "I have to go." She drummed her fingers on the desk.

He lurched away from the door. If she knew he was there, listening in, she'd throw him in the cells with Oliver. Troy retraced his footsteps as quietly as possible.

The bitter taste of Abbott's betrayal bubbled up inside him, turning into a thirst for revenge. He needed time to consider his options, but in no way was the information he overheard going to get buried. Nor was any human going to get sold. Not on his watch.

FORTY-SIX

26 January

KELLY PULLED BACK the comms tent flap. Eagerly, she began to log in to Jerko when a teenager walked in, chin bobbing to earbud beats.

The kid latched his eyes on Kelly and pulled out an earbud. "I'm Luke. Nice to meet you. I was playing Thunder Storms until the wee hours."

"Thunderstorms?"

"Thunder Storms," he said, separating the word into two. "It's an awesome game. Thunder, the main guy, storms through the world combatting the baddies." He plonked down in front of a monitor and motioned for Kelly to have a seat next to him. "We'll cover the broad network and ease you into the system slowly."

She sat next to Luke while he brought her monitor to life with a swish of a mouse. A London street, which looked like somewhere in Soho, splashed across the screen. Seconds later, it flipped to another view of the same street. "The State eyes everywhere—people's own monitors, mics, watches," Luke said. "They can record echoes and translate noise into drawings. But blackout websites like the Canary scramble signals."

He opened a fresh window on a second screen and logged into the

Cicada forum. "Get acquainted with it." He handed the controls over to Kelly.

"If people's wearables give the State all it needs, why did they spend so much on the SS?"

He shrugged. "Maybe the system does more than they're telling us. I mean, take this view." He pointed at a quadrant on the monitor. "It's coming off someone's watch."

"I laugh when I hear companies hiring sweepers." Michelle snickered. "They never eliminate the cameras that matter most."

The popular choices like eye patch domes and gum tack concealing camera lenses boomed, but there really was no curtailing state surveillance. And now, with the impending thought crime algorithms being part of their surveillance, the State's oversight was total—except for here, in the freedom camp.

Luke swiveled back around to face his screen. "And it gets worse."

"I'm sure," Kelly said.

"If someone went around and blew out every single camera in the vicinity, all the State has to do is switch on the audio through the speakers, and their sound recognition software embedded in watches kicks into gear. They can record echoes and automatically translate the noise into drawings of the locations."

"That's a gargantuan boatload of data," Kelly said.

His fingers danced along the keyboard. "It takes a bit more power and capacity to do it that way, so it's their backup option," Luke said. "But they've also developed technology to condense and archive the data so that they can keep all of it nice and tidy."

He pressed enter. Voices and the sound of footsteps blared through speakers hanging on a pole in the center of the tent. They were plugged into someone's watch in central London.

"All that is time-stamped, filed, and stored in the Zone," Michelle added.

With so much technology at their disposal, how did Kelly manage to hide away in the Canary? Every patron in the lobby wore a watch, which meant the Elite Squad must've pinpointed her location. Knowing the full stretch of technology, she feared for the safety of George Barry and Mark. "What about high-end places like the Canary?"

Michelle smiled. "The Canary doesn't tell its high society patrons what to do, so they've incorporated a cutting signal in the building to scramble the signals automatically."

"Do all high-end places have that kind of cutting signal?"

"Most, yes," Michelle said.

"But…" Luke cut in. "More modest places don't have that kind of money. They just get people to take off their watches or switch them off."

Kelly was reminded of the Luntan. Had she had a watch to take off, she would have been required to do so in order to enter the premises. "And in the echo chambers?"

"Those are different," Luke said. "They have their own technology that the watches interrupt. All you have to do is switch it off in there because their technology is incompatible. Did you ever read about how people had to switch off their cell phones in airplanes in the early 2000s? It's kind of like that."

Kelly had forgotten to depower her watch when she entered the echo chamber the morning of Mallow's arrest. Maybe her fully powered watch also scrambled Christopher's screen. She dismissed the thought. "Why are they so intent on surveilling everyone?"

Michelle shrugged. "Why does the State ever do anything?"

"We're a bunch of guinea pigs." Luke snorted. "They test shit on us all the time."

Michelle nodded wearily. "We tried kamikaze on the Zone—lasers pulverized our dummy. They upgraded it after."

Josh had said as much about the Beta Fi headsets.

"Yeah, the Zone is too heavily protected. Not even the Prime Minister can enter without a prearrangement," Luke concluded.

"Not to mention the weight and temperature sensors," Michelle added.

"I've been inside."

Luke's eyes widened. "You've seen it up close? What's it like?"

"Why were you there?" Catalina interjected.

They all turned.

She was standing in the doorway like a guard keeping an eye on prisoners; she had probably been listening the whole time. This woman was trouble. "If you want to take the Zone down," Kelly said, "how about taking down the bots first?"

Catalina drew back as though Kelly had hurled an insult at her. "Don't you think we thought about that already?"

Kelly swiveled back to the monitors. "So, infiltrating the Zone is hopeless."

"That's exactly what they want you to feel. Overwhelmed. Resigned. Tamed." Catalina spat out the last word contemptuously. "Knowledge is power. Abbott repeats that regularly. Me, I think control is power."

"I had you down for instinct is power," Luke said.

Michelle and Luke laughed, nodding their heads in unison and high-fiving each other.

"Why don't we flood the network?" Kelly said, getting the conversation back on point.

"And interrupt everyone's addiction to the Internet?" Luke said. "The outcome is too unpredictable. It'll either cause a revolution or people will bury their heads in the sand."

"I thought you Fighters existed to bring on a revolution."

"Abbott controls the timetable."

"Tell her to get a move on." Kelly slumped back in her chair. "So much intel and it's all just sitting there in the Zone."

Catalina fixed her gaze on Kelly. "You've only been here a day and you think—"

"Cat, what do you need?" Luke piped up.

She continued to stare down at Kelly. "Sinclair wants the logs."

"Look!" Michelle pointed at the screen in front of Kelly.

She and Luke hovered over Kelly's shoulder. On the screen, two men dragged another man out of his home, kicking and yelling, and onto the road.

"Typical." Luke scoffed.

Kelly wondered if they saw the maelstrom thugs as she did, all mangled and deformed, and then it dawned on her that her visions had returned. She rubbed her forehead.

Michelle and Luke eased back in front of their monitors.

Michelle deflated her seat. "I'm done." She logged her time on a clipboard and filed a note in a blue folder. "Despite what you might think, it's not all doom and gloom." Michelle looked at Kelly. "We've managed to piggyback off their system, so we get to see everything they see. And then there's Cicada."

Michelle trudged out of the comms room, and Catalina followed her.

Instantly, the room's dynamic shifted. Kelly cleared her throat. "So, how long have you been working with the Fighters?"

"Couple of years."

"Were you part of the team who watched me at Global Wires?"

Luke's gaze darted around the room. "We watch a lot of people."

"Like me, when I discovered my colleague dead?"

He popped his lips. "I'm not sure I can answer your questions. I don't really have the strategic reason why some get watched and others don't. I do as I'm told."

"Did you see Geneva enter the building?"

He swiveled his chair left and right. "I'm not supposed to talk about this."

"Are you not supposed to talk about this to anyone or just to me?"

"Anyone."

Kelly took a deep breath and wiggled her jaw. She might as well be back in the city.

His head drooped. "I'm sorry I can't help. I'm under strict orders. If I break the rules, I'm out of here, and I don't want that."

"I don't mean to put you in a difficult position."

Catalina returned. "Sinclair says a log is missing. Are you on it, Luke?"

Luke sighed. "On track."

Kelly glanced at Luke with a smidgen of pity. He logged onto cameras she hadn't noticed before, cameras in No Man's Land. "You have cameras everywhere."

"Those cameras have heat sensors," he said.

"Just like at the Zone."

"But out here, we're the only ones who know where the cameras are located."

Kelly had ordered a few cameras from Roseman, but they were sitting on her coffee table at home, unused. "Are they eye-sized ones?"

"You mean the spy-size cameras." He shook his head. "We're a bit more manual around here. The eye-sized ones are bigger because they house memory to record a few hours of activity. The ones we have are pupil size. We record the feed on our servers and back everything up ourselves." He was talking smoothly now, pushing the conversation on before Kelly could get more details out of him. "It's time to log you onto Cicada."

The kid wasn't cracking. "No need." She punched a few keys on the keyboard and toggled the joystick.

A stationary street view from an SS displayed on her screen. Hardly anyone passed in front of the lens. She turned to the screen with Cicada displayed.

He raised his eyebrows. "Not as innocent as you look." He grabbed his earbuds and switched on the music. "Shout if you need anything...doesn't look like you'll need much though."

The scratchy noise disappeared into his eardrum, and he tapped on a keyboard that looked like it was from the year 2022, or thereabouts; a time when people were on the precipice of losing everything they ever thought of as freedom.

HOURS LATER, Kelly typed: Helloooooooo on the Cicada forum. She swept an eye in Luke's direction. His head bounced to the beat of a tune while focusing on his screen. Kelly positioned the joystick in front of her, scooted in close to her screen, and logged into Jerko. A burst of sweat coated her palms, and she glanced again at Luke. He was still engrossed, compiling the logs for Sinclair. Kelly scanned what seemed like hundreds of messages, searching for the one Josh had promised to email if he found footage of Global Wires on the night of Geneva's murder.

At last, she saw his email: a link with an attachment.

Footsteps neared. She held her breath, but Luke didn't react. She opened Josh's email: a link with an attachment.

Suddenly, Troy crouched beside her and whispered. "Tonight, after the party, we have to leave the camp."

"Why?"

"I'll tell you more later. Start planning to leave."

"What's going on?"

He glanced inside the tent and back at her. "I know it's sudden, but trust me when I say, you're not safe here. Nor am I." He continued before she could object. "Go back to the party. Do what you were doing. We'll talk more later." He squeezed her arm, a weak gesture of reassurance, and walked toward the headquarters tent.

Keeping her anxiety at bay felt like a losing game. Best to just go with it, she thought.

"All good?" Luke asked, cradling an earbud in his hand.

"Yeah, of course," Kelly said.

After hours of watching maelstrom thugs breed fear and trouble on the streets, she sat back and analyzed her notes.

Different colored maelstrom carried out distinct tasks. The green maelstrom, their heads inflated like balloons, were the low-level pickpockets. She wondered why the popular Shiva had appeared in this color. Stealing something from her audience, perhaps?

The common crimson maelstrom—the kind that had attacked the kids leaving the Live Earth concert—spanned every postcode. Collectively, they wore boots with steel-capped toes and leather jackets or black fatigues. Those bad boys strutted like they owned London's streets.

She sat back and watched the moving images. One screen caught her attention, showing the Canary and a black limousine parked right in front. She seized the joystick and enlarged the view.

The back door opened. Fat fingers gripped the metal edge of the opening, gold rings choking the fingers blue. The backseat passenger rebounded like a whale trying to slither its way out of a test tube.

The chauffeur scrambled out of the car. His face looked strained, hauling the passenger out of the limousine. Wing-tipped lace-ups hit the pavement with such force it looked like the concrete would crack. She saw his face at last. Deformed forehead, double chin, blue skin. He pulled on the belt of his three-piece suit, and the chain of his pocket watch swung. This had to be the man Harry had described, and she understood now why Harry, or anyone, would remember such a man.

He was the first blue maelstrom she had come across. She made a note on the tablet and watched on.

The chauffeur wiped his brow and returned to the driver's seat while George Barry opened the gated entrance of the Canary. The fat blue maelstrom disappeared inside.

Kelly leaned back and tried to remember the exact details of what Harry had said. Something about MI5. She pushed aside the tablet, a sense of defeat ripening into hopelessness.

Her thoughts drifted to 2028, when she was very publicly fired from the Daily Times. A string of inflammatory articles about the rising crime levels had ignited a debate between government officials, the police, and media outlets. Rumors circulated that journalists had been paid to write the articles. The whispers indicated MI5 at the helm. Whether true or not, the reputation of all journalists had been tarnished throughout the country.

So, when Kelly's investigative articles came out and alleged government involvement in Ian Smith's drug-running operation, she had a lot to prove. Knowing this, Kelly worked day and night to cross-reference her facts and create a watertight case. But still, rumors buzzed around Kelly's work, and enhanced facial recognition technology proved her investigation wrong.

Within weeks, the court declared Ian Smith innocent.

She'd never forget that day. Watching herself online, hounded by photographers, was like watching a stranger. Broadcast journalists—long rumored to have MI5 connections—used her story as the prime example of dishonest reporting being a problem so insidious, so entrenched that all journalists were declared rogues. The only way to restore the industry's standing and reestablish the public's trust in the news was through bold and thorough initiatives. The Truth Laws were hatched.

What was she really doing here, at the camp? She shook her head. Did she really think she could overpower the almighty State agencies? After years of trying, the Fighters still hadn't so much as breached the Zone. If Fighters hadn't succeeded, what made her think she could put a dent in the powerful MI5 Elite Squad?

Omar was right. She was a single person without power, without money, without contacts. Her sense of defeat ripened into hopelessness. She glanced up at the screens.

Two maelstroms strutted down a road. Even though everyone believed them to attack at will, she knew their violence wasn't random; she had seen it with her own two eyes. Sure, they thrived on chaos, but they were ordered—by someone—to carry out that chaos. Had to be MI5. Who else?

The question reset her mood as it flashed through her mind. Maybe it wasn't about penetrating MI5 or the Elite Squad. Maybe all she needed to do was leak Christopher's research onto Cicada…something she could do this very minute. But without the name of the mastermind behind the thought crime extension, the research would be branded a theory.

She needed a name.

A green maelstrom strode toward a woman on the path. "Poor woman," Kelly said out loud. "She won't know her wallet is missing." Luke glanced over. Kelly drew back in her chair, rubbing her forehead. She sighed.

"Which screen are you talking about?" Without thinking, Kelly pointed to the lower left-hand corner. "There's nothing there," he said, looking confused.

Kelly fell silent. She spoke too soon. The crime had not yet happened. Luke scooted up close to the screen. A green maelstrom snuck up behind the woman. He nabbed his victim's wallet. A few feet down the path, he tossed it, empty of cash.

Luke looked at Kelly. "How did you know that would happen?"

"After five hours of watching the patterns, it's obvious."

"Not that obvious."

Catalina stepped into the tent. Kelly tensed.

"What's going on?"

Catalina seemed to be everywhere she wasn't wanted, Kelly thought. "Nothing," Kelly firmly announced.

"She saw a mugging before it happened," Luke said.

Kelly rolled her eyes.

Catalina scooted over to Kelly's side of the desk. "You sussed out the system in less than a day? Holy shit."

"It was just pattern matching," Kelly spoke in a light tone, attempting to downplay the whole thing.

"Now I get it," said Catalina. "You're autistic. That's why Abbott assigned you to comms."

Kelly glared at Catalina. "I'm not autistic."

"Yeah, that must be the reason she assigned you to comms." Luke grinned. "Also explains why you're a bit weird."

"I may be weird to you," an exasperated Kelly said. "But I'm not autistic."

Luke wheeled his chair back and stretched his neck out toward Catalina. "What do they say? The crazy never know they're crazy. Must be the same with autists."

"You two are a bunch of kids."

"Combine that with being a journalist, and we have it made in here," Catalina said.

"Help me keep an eye on the perimeter," Luke said.

Music blared through the camp and then cut out.

Luke's face lit up. "It's been a long week. Can't wait for the party. Especially now that I have something to brag about," he said. "We'll shoot ahead of all the other tents."

Long ago, Kelly had concluded that parties were nothing more than an excuse for a mob to drink copious amounts of alcohol. She hated parties, but this party would keep them all busy, get them all drunk, while she snuck back into comms and scanned through Josh's files. It would be the last opportunity she had before she and Troy left the camp for good.

FORTY-SEVEN

PLATTERS PILED with fruit and finger sandwiches, bowls of crisps and nuts, adorned pine coffee tables. Shabby chic cushions furnished the communal area, dotting the edges of the room. The communal space had been transformed into a den of luxury, and Troy wanted to be somewhere else. After the party, he and Kelly would be. He just had to ride out this last soiree without anyone suspecting a thing.

Felix flexed his head-chef muscle and barked, "Spread out the olive bowls."

Any other week and Troy would be manning the kegs, but after overhearing Rozlyn, it was going to take all his mettle simply to withhold the disdain he felt from appearing on his face. He rubbed his rigid hands and stepped onto the salvaged oriental rug, the color of yellow ochre—the color of caution.

He assessed the looks on the Fighters' faces as they trickled into the tent; all festive and cheerful on the surface, but who really knew? Intrigue wasn't his thing, but he had to get through this one night if he was to put his plan in motion and get Kelly out safely.

For the sake of appearances, he sauntered over to greet the partiers. The forced swagger made him feel clunky, his arms restless.

In the corner of the tent, Luke, Michelle, and Catalina huddled. One of them had to know more than they were letting on. He caught Catalina's eye, and she bobbed her head at him in acknowledgment. He weaved through the white-aproned kitchen staff and the growing crowd and closed in on the group.

Catalina moved, cracking open the trio's tight circle. "Who's the DJ tonight? They suck."

"Always so cheerful." Troy wedged into the gap. "How're things going with Kelly?"

"Too early to tell," Michelle said.

Catalina elbowed Michelle. "You didn't see her hidden skill."

"Did she sneak up behind you and land a punch at the back of your head as payback?"

Catalina pursed her lips. "The water merely interrupted her beauty sleep."

The camp's psychologist, Agatha, joined the huddle. "I heard about what you did, Catalina. My door is always open if you need to talk." Her light brown eyes oozed sympathy. "As for the new member of our camp, I hope she had a good sleep. It's very important for neuroregeneration, among other things."

"She's going to be just fine," Catalina said. "No harm done."

Agatha squinted at the carpet and pretended to examine the threads. It was her way of distancing herself, peacefully, from Catalina.

"Yeah, I'm fine," Kelly said. "No harm, no foul, right?"

Silence landed smack in the center of the group.

Troy tugged his ear. "That's good." His voice sounded far chirpier than he intended.

The room quieted down to a flutter of whispers. Abbott had entered the room. "Thank you all for coming," she chimed. "Just a few words and you can return to the fun. First, a hearty thanks to Troy for once again organizing another slap-up party."

The crowd clapped and hooted. He gave a shallow bow, knowing this was the last.

"Many of you know we have a new member. Kelly Blackwell, the famous journalist from Global Wires, has defected and come to the camp."

Murmurs swept through the room. A few faces turned to Kelly and lifted their glasses. Others stared on like rabid dogs, waiting for their master to order them to attack. Kelly swayed on her feet and lowered her eyes, doing what she could to prevent her presence from becoming a point of interest.

"Please make her feel welcomed in the camp," Abbott said before looking to Troy. "Be sure to update the rest of the crew about our new member when they return from the city."

Her controlled charm now struck him as calculated heartlessness. The admiration he once felt for her had vanished, and he faulted himself for reading her wrong all this time. He forced a nod.

She turned back to the group. "Moving on...Michelle, do you have anything to share?"

"Surveillance is secure. The Elite Squad was scrambled in No Man's Land."

The crowd cheered; pleasure chipped the rough mask of Abbott's stern face. "Very well then. Let's celebrate." She retreated to an armchair like a queen to her throne.

A handful of people swamped Kelly; she smiled, a little distractedly, politely discomforted by the attention. "I'll be right back," she said. "I have to freshen up."

He was glad she left the room so he could concentrate on Abbott, especially now that Catalina and Luke were whispering in her ear. He made a detour in their direction.

"What's going on here?" He draped his arms over Luke's shoulder. The kid stiffened and turned away from him. "Anything I should know about?"

The hard shell had returned to Abbott's face. "Cat was saying Kelly mastered the cameras during her shift."

Sounded like Abbott was getting ready to launch an order. "Impressive," Troy said.

"Did you see any equipment on her when she came in?" Abbott's unrelenting eyes stared at him. "Anything suspicious?"

He shook his head nonchalantly. "A taser and her watch." He shrugged. "Why?"

"Luke and Cat, go search her things."

There it was. He had hoped to get Kelly out quietly, safely, but now, the Elite Squad would have to get involved. He straightened. "You're wasting a good party."

FORTY-EIGHT

27 January. 1 a.m.

KELLY STEPPED inside the darkened comms tent, her heart racing. Scooting the chair toward the desk, she switched on a screen, and the pale light illuminated her face. She logged onto Jerko, scrolled through the messages, and hit Josh's email.

"Jerko," she whispered into the mic. "Place all of Josh's emails and all Christopher Mallow-related videos and articles into one folder."

In five seconds, the refile was complete. She lowered the volume on the speakers, scrolled through the contents of the new folder, and selected the video Josh sent. To get it to play faster, she reconfigured its playback speed to 1.5x its normal speed and pressed play.

The time stamp displayed 3:32 a.m., January 21, 2030.

Kelly's skin tingled as though shuttling back in time.

Three masked men in night goggles entered a flat she didn't recognize. One man held a camera in his leather-gloved hands. The video then flicked over to the empty path, cleanly cut and spliced. She now had an outside view of the building. Time stamp 4:30 a.m. sharp. She carried on watching.

Two men emerged from the flat carrying a body bag. A third one shut the front door behind them.

A driverless black van drove up, and they heaved the sack into the van. At that point, two men flicked off their masks, revealing their identity. Iridescent crimson maelstrom. But the third one remained hidden underneath his mask, anonymous.

Clearly, the others didn't care if they were identified, but he did. "What do you have to hide that's so important, Mr. Anon?"

There was also something in the polished way he moved his body, graceful and athletic. Perhaps he didn't remove his mask because he wasn't a maelstrom. Maybe he was connected to important people and couldn't risk being facially recognized.

All three men climbed into the back of the van, and it drove down the path.

The video picked up again on Marylebone. When the van reached Global Wires, still in the dark of the night, the three men emerged, horror masks on again, the third one still filming.

The video skipped ahead again; the three men were now inside the Global Wires office. They unzipped the body bag. Geneva's lifeless body spilled out onto the floor.

Kelly's hand flew to her mouth. This wasn't evidence. This was a snuff film. Geneva—alive one moment, dead the next, her body handled like garbage. Kelly had suspected her, distrusted her, wished her gone. And someone had granted that wish, violently, permanently.

Nausea swirled in Kelly's stomach. She paused the video, unsure if she could watch another second of the murdered girl, but she couldn't turn away. She clicked play.

Two men moved the body into position—the same position Kelly had found her in. Then, the leather-gloved man took out a syringe from his pocket. It glistened in the streetlight coming in from the window. He drove the needle into the crook of Geneva's arm, puncturing her yellowed skin.

Kelly pressed pause and squelched the bile rising up. She blew out a stream of air and looked again at the screen.

There was a gap of bare skin between Mr. Anon's sleeve and his black glove.

Maybe there would be a tattoo or some identifiable mark. She zoomed in to the tiny square pixels and enlarged them. The grainy pixels blotched the screen and had no recognizable edges. Other than that one flash of skin seconds earlier, all the killers were wrapped up tight in black from head to toe. Nothing. Kelly sank into her chair and stared at the scene of Geneva's lifeless body memorialized in black and white.

She heard footsteps in the distance. Quickly, she typed a message to Josh.

SAW IT. KEEP IT. I'LL BE IN TOUCH.

She choked off the connection to Jerko, switched off the screen, and mopped the sweat on her brow before stepping out into the night air.

FORTY-NINE

JOSH UNLOCKED his front door and stepped inside. He dropped his camera case and lighting equipment in the hall and stretched his stiff back. The wedding went on too long, but it paid well. He slipped off his shoes, stretched his feet, and envisioned a hot-cold shower. First, though, a nightcap. He trundled down the hallway.

A light switched on in the study behind him.

Adrenaline spiked in his veins, erasing his exhaustion. He whipped around.

Omar was reclining in his father's leather armchair, looking smug in a navy blue tailored coat and shiny burgundy shoes, a snappy getup compared to the ragged suit he was wearing the last time, the only time, they had met.

The adrenaline tapered off, replaced by blunt suspicion. "I never believed your story of being a back office hack admin in Transport. How long have you been sitting there?"

Unmoved at the pointed jibe, Omar said, "Not long. Why don't you have a seat?"

He had some nerve inviting Josh to take a seat in his own home. "I'll stand, if you don't mind."

"Suit yourself."

"So, what brings you here?"

"I need you to do something for me."

"You must have the wrong place. I don't stamp approval stickers on driving applications for the rich and famous."

Omar waved his hand as if to brush away the insult. Something under his sleeve reflected light.

Josh stiffened. Omar had had plenty of time to survey the battlefield, and whatever weapons he had were probably hidden somewhere on him. "What do you want?"

"Relax, I'm unarmed," Omar said. "I'm here for the notebooks."

Josh locked his gaze on Omar. He was referring to the notebooks Geneva's brother had given Josh at the funeral, but Omar hadn't been there. "Your proxy at the funeral. Who was it? That woman with the green eyes?"

"I don't need a proxy. By now, people know you're connected to the notebooks, including my boss. She wants them."

"Who's your boss?"

Omar shifted his gaze to his hand tapping on the armrest. He smiled at Josh, easily, charmingly. "She pays well."

"Not for sale."

Omar uncrossed his legs and leaned forward, his clean shoes catching the overhead light. "My boss will dig into your relationship with Kelly until she makes the connection, if she hasn't already. You can buy time if you hand them over."

Omar's threat pumped Josh's curiosity about this so-called boss. "You want me to believe that your boss doesn't already know Kelly and I are friends? Newsflash. People in media know each other."

Omar shifted in the chair. "I deliver the goods to my boss, she's happy, and you and Kelly can ride off into the sunset. Everybody wins."

Unless he had access to state surveillance, he wouldn't know about the details of their relationship. "Why should I trust you?"

"You're a hacker."

Josh held steady, making sure his body didn't signal guilt. "I don't know where—"

"I could've reported you by now. But I haven't."

So, Omar was being fed information. That left two options. He had access to state surveillance, or there was a spy, neither of which Omar would readily admit. Josh had to tackle him from a different angle. He leaned against the wall, affecting a casualness he didn't feel. "And what happens if I don't hand over the notebooks?"

"Let's just get this over with, shall we? Give me the notebooks, and you can get some sleep."

"Not until I get something in return."

"Speak."

"The truth."

Omar broke out in a deep, guttural chuckle.

"I'm glad I can make you laugh, Omar."

Omar slowly settled, his laughter trailing away.

"Were you the anonymous client who ordered the surveillance of the leader of the Underground Freedom Fighters?"

"I guess it doesn't really matter at this point."

"So it was you. Why follow her?"

"You did an excellent job." Omar slipped past his question. "I was impressed. I'd be glad for us to continue working together, Josh."

"Does Kelly know you lied to her the whole time?"

"Clearly, you care about Kelly, and you want to protect her."

"Unlike you."

Omar dropped his chin to his chest. "You're wrong there, Josh." Omar's watch buzzed. He glanced at the incoming message. Whatever it said ruffled his smooth composure for a moment. "We all have secrets," he said. "I'm not the only one in this room with a few."

"So, we both have secrets we both know about. Not exactly secrets then."

"Depends on who else knows." Omar's voice held a drifting quality. He pointed at the ceiling. "About your computer up there." Tension rippled through Josh. "You're the only one who can save Kelly at this point." Omar studied Josh's face. "And I'm the only chance you have of seeing Kelly again. To make that happen, I need those notebooks."

He felt Omar's pressure for an agreement. "I'm going to need more than your word about Kelly's safety."

"What will satisfy you?"

Josh didn't have to think twice. "Who are you really, Omar?"

FIFTY

KELLY HOVERED at the edge of the tent, watching as the party shifted up a gear, hoping her fear wasn't showing—fear over what she had seen and fear over where she was about to go. Although Troy's whispered instructions had taken her by surprise, instinctively, she knew she could trust him. When the right song played, he'd said, they'd meet at the hole in the perimeter fence. Along the way, she'd swing by her sleeping quarters and retrieve Christopher's research hidden in her pillow. She steadied her hands and turned her attention to the crowd.

Fighters with polished bald heads, spiked hair, and colored locks cheered a couple dancing Flamenco in the center of the room. She had seen enough for one evening, but she waited. The right song hadn't yet played. Troy's instructions had been clear. Time slowed like treacle pouring through an hourglass, and she hoped her nerves would last.

The music abruptly changed to Irish folk—the cue.

She turned for the exit. Just as she was about to step outside the tent, she felt a tap on her shoulder.

Abbott was smiling at her. "How's the Cicada surveillance coming along?"

She stepped back inside and smiled back, hiding the urgency of the moment. "I meant to thank you for the intro earlier."

"My pleasure."

"Michelle and Luke have been particularly welcoming."

It took Abbott a moment, but eventually, she nodded. "Why don't we get a drink?"

Kelly glanced around for Troy. He was nowhere to be seen. "I have an early shift. I should get back for some shut-eye."

Catalina entered the tent. She was dangling a sheet of paper from her fingertips. Troy and Luke trailed right behind.

Troy rushed ahead of Catalina. "It means nothing."

"Nothing?" Catalina grabbed Kelly's arm and shoved the paper at Abbott.

Kelly tried to yank herself free, but Catalina's big hand held firm. "Get off me."

"We found this in your pillow."

Kelly tried to get a glimpse of the paper.

Troy snatched it out of Catalina's hand. "Like I said, nothing. A bunch of stupid code." He tossed it to the ground.

When Kelly glanced down and got a clear look at the paper, a sense of relief washed over her. It wasn't Mallow's research. She didn't even recognize the scrawl of code written across the page. But her relief came with a new set of troubling questions, like who was stashing code in her pillow, and what did they do with Christopher's evidence? "Someone must have put it there."

"We found it in your things." Catalina sneered. "Transparency is a cornerstone of all Fighters."

"You mean you raided my things." Kelly wrenched loose from Catalina's hand. "I don't know the first thing about code. Someone here planted it."

"She's lying!"

The music in the tent stopped all at once.

Troy turned to Abbott. "This isn't right."

Fighters swarmed, encircling Kelly.

"Let's all just calm down." Abbott raised her hand to settle the zealous crowd.

A guy with spiked hair raged. "She needs to go."

"Bringing her here was a mistake," yelled another.

Abbott raised her hand higher. "This is not how we operate."

"Why are we protecting this girl anyway?"

Abbott shot the fighter a stern look. "Because she's one of us. And unlike the city, here we follow due process."

A collective grumble hummed through the tent.

"Cat, escort Kelly to the holding cells," Abbott said.

"For what? Code they planted in my room?"

"I know this all seems confusing, Kelly," Agatha piped in. "But we will investigate the matter, and when we do, I'm sure you'll be cleared."

"Agatha is right," Abbott said. "We have to make sure that everyone in the group is above suspicion."

Kelly met Troy's eyes.

Catalina yanked on Kelly's arm and led her to the exit.

Instinct coupled with a burst of fight or flight surged through Kelly. She ripped herself free of Catalina's clutches and darted for the exit. Catalina's leaden footsteps bounded, and the full force of her weight slammed into Kelly. She stumbled and plunged facedown on the rug. The smell of stale beer rocketed up her nostrils.

Catalina twisted Kelly's arms and pinned her wrists against her back. Pain seared down her torso as she struggled to break free, but it was no use. Catalina was too strong.

"Take her to the holding cell," Abbott ordered. "Let her cool off down there."

One of the Fighters dashed over to Catalina, hooked a ring of keys onto her belt, and helped her haul Kelly to her feet.

"I'll go with you," his voice was firm, determined.

"No. Troy will go," Abbott said. "He needs to prove his loyalty."

The look on Troy's face hardened, and his steady eyes chilled Kelly. "Gladly."

They led her out the door and turned left, all but extinguishing any chance she had of escape.

Behind her, she could hear Abbott shout, "The show is over."

IN SILENCE, the trio headed toward the comms tent. They passed the perimeter fence and entered an area Troy hadn't included in his intro tour. Behind them, the music resumed, and laughter roared through the camp.

They came to a halt at two wooden doors sunk into the ground, beside which stood a galvanized steel air pump. It looked like the opening to a bunker or a dungeon, and now she knew why this place was referred to as the Underground.

Kelly's breath quickened. She looked back toward the main tent, in a dim hope that someone, anyone, had come to their senses and come out, righteously, to stop the madness, but only the smoke of the shisha pipes fluttered in the night air. She turned forward and peered into the darkness ahead, surveying the barren land surrounding them. No Man's Land was her last hope.

Troy pulled on a rope that had been camouflaged by dirt. The wooden doors cranked open and slammed against the ground, sending a cloud of dust into the air.

Troy clapped his dusty hands. "This is only temporary."

Catalina's grip loosened.

Kelly dug her heels into the ground and sprinted forward.

"Kelly, you need to stop!"

She could hear his voice in her ear as though he were standing beside her, and his footsteps pattered right behind. She sped up.

Troy managed to circle in front of her. She was running so fast she lost traction and crashed straight into him.

He held her tight. "I got you. No one will hurt you," he whispered in her ear.

The camp's distant lights reflected in his soft blue eyes. A sense of familiarity flickered through her, but she still couldn't place where she'd seen him before she came to the camp, if at all.

Catalina drew up behind them and grabbed Kelly by the arm. "Good work, Troy." She shoved Kelly forward. "Abbott will be pleased."

Through the wooden doors, they shuffled down a dirt ramp that twisted deeper and deeper in the cool, dark underground tunnel. Every few feet, mounted electric torches glimmered, lighting up the concrete walls dripping with water.

"What the hell is this place?" Kelly said. "Do you people even know it was Abbott who suggested I come to the camp?" Catalina tightened her grip around Kelly's arm, constricting the blood flow.

Pins and needles prickling her arms, she yanked Catalina forward and loosened the grip. "I heard Abbott's voice on the phone, loud and clear." Troy glanced at Kelly. "Yeah, Troy, the voice disguiser is useless."

"Don't listen to her."

An arched black gate loomed at the end of the tunnel. Kelly writhed and bucked with the force of a corralled wild horse salvaging whatever freedom it had left.

The key ring on Catalina's belt clattered and dropped to the floor. Desperate, Kelly dove for the keys. Before she could seize on them, Troy stepped in and scooped them up. She stared up at him as he inserted the key into the iron gate. Seeing him assist Catalina lock her in was a punch to her gut. Every ounce of fight drained out of her.

The gate creaked open, and Catalina hurled Kelly into the darkened cell. Attempting to break her fall, she stretched out her hand, but her wrist folded, and she crashed on her hip, firing pain down her leg.

Catalina slammed the gate. "I never liked you from day one." She locked the gate.

Kelly scrambled to her feet and shook the iron bars. "Let me out of here!"

She glared at Troy. He stared back, looking as though he wanted to speak, but he said nothing.

Troy and Catalina swung around and marched down the tunnel. A plume of smoke and the scent of tobacco wafted behind them until they were gone.

FIFTY-ONE

A BARE LIGHTBULB cast a harsh light over the cell, and a musty smell hung in the air. Kelly shivered in spite of herself.

"Hey," a man's voice echoed from the shadow.

Her heart thumped, sending a rush of blood through her body. His tone, soft and light, was similar to how Troy sounded the first time she met him. She pressed her back against the bars.

He shuffled forward. "Didn't mean to startle you."

Underneath the streaks of grime on his face and clumpy hair, his eyes looked all too familiar. "Oliver Green?"

He nodded. "Good to see you again, too."

Slowly, she stepped away from the prison bars, trying to let go of fear, but it clung to her like static. Stunned at how fast the young, confident man from the chamber had deteriorated, Kelly slid down the bars and softly hit the ground. "How long have you been here?"

"A week or so?"

She nodded. "When you ran out of the chamber, you said they were waiting for you. Who was waiting for you? The Fighters?"

He shook his head. "That was the day the Fighters kidnapped me."

Her muscles went rigid in the realization that Oliver's estimate of a week was a long way wide of the mark; the Fighters had held him captive for two weeks, and he had no idea. "Why did they bring you here?"

Oliver hesitated, then took a deep breath. "I'm a hacker, so it probably has something to do with that."

She tensed, remembering how he had lied about who he worked for when she first met him in the echo chamber. He was probably lying now. "Who were you expecting to meet that day?"

"The Resistance."

She wanted to ask if he knew Josh, but Josh had said Resistance members didn't know each other. "How big is the hacker community in the city?"

"Impossible to tell."

"Did you meet with a lot of other hackers?"

"That wouldn't be smart. We have connectors who put us in touch with each other or pass messages along. There aren't many connectors because that's the most dangerous job of all. They know where all the bodies are buried, and they can identify everyone. So, they move around. Never in one place longer than a month. They get paid well, though."

Her body released a sliver of tension. His story tallied with Josh's, shaving off a slice of doubt. "Is that what you were doing in the chamber that day, hacking into it?"

"Running an operation. I realize now these so-called Fighters are working against the Resistance."

"How?"

"Why else would they have captured me?"

"There could be other reasons. Something you haven't thought of."

The spirit in his eyes drained. He sighed. "I'm a programmer and did some hacking on the side for them, so they knew me. They must have found out what I was working on because when they captured me, they accused me of being a double agent."

"You were," Kelly said pointedly. "You were working for the Resistance and for the Underground Freedom Fighters."

"But they didn't know that," his voice blared, signaling that his rebellious spirit had returned. "Would you call a freelancer a double agent?"

"Sounds to me like you were working on something that conflicted with their agenda, and they found out about it. What were you doing in the echo chamber that day?"

"Loading software. But when you came in, Mallow aborted the mission, but stupidly, I carried on. Then the Elite Squad came in."

So, Oliver's actions put the Elite Squad on alert, and that piece of information slotted into place, like a key sliding into its lock. She moved in closer. "So you and Christopher were working together?"

Oliver nodded. "I should have dropped it, I should have—"

"So that mess on Christopher's screen was software code?"

"A virus. To destroy the echo chamber. But he missed a vital step, so it scrambled and froze."

"Why didn't you do it?"

He flashed his QR code. "I didn't have a news outlet permit."

"Leeland and Partners, I remember."

He shook his head. "Advertising was the easiest license to forge."

"You and Mallow were working to destroy the Zone, and I got dragged into it."

"He was off script at that point," Oliver spoke rapidly, as if trying to redraft their screw-up. "I had no clue what was going through his mind. The cameras were recording, and I didn't want to make a scene."

So, Mallow almost embroiled her in their plot, and then Heather gave her Christopher's research, and...what had she said...that Kelly would know what to do with it. She felt winded and leaned against the iron bars for support. "Who wrote the virus code?"

Oliver straightened up. "I wrote it." Pride exuded from his voice.

"And what does it have to do with me?"

"I don't know. Christopher ran the mission, so I thought maybe he needed a witness or alibi or something like that. And then the Elite Squad arrested him, and I never found out."

"Did you take the initiative to create that code, or did someone commission you?"

"Sorta both. I work primarily with the Resistance, so I gave them the idea on how to take down the Zone, then after a while, I got commissioned. Christopher okayed it."

"So, Christopher was running the mission for the Resistance, and had it gone to plan, the virus would've brought down the echo chambers along with anything connected to them, like the Zone."

He nodded. "The virus would feed into the Zone and corrupt it. That was the ultimate target. As soon as I get out of here, we can try again."

"Oliver...Christopher's dead. The Squad killed him." Oliver looked down at his hands, an air of defeat descending over him. "Why didn't Christopher just come out and tell me?" said Kelly. "After I read his research about the extension of the Truth Laws, that was enough to hook me. That info alone is all I needed to know."

He shrugged.

Rebuilding her credibility was like climbing a descending staircase and expecting to reach the top. No matter how hard she tried, she'd always be known as the journalist who dismissed the truth to get an innocent man convicted. Maybe it was time to accept it. "Do you still know the code for the virus?"

"Yeah, why?"

She squinted. "I'll have to find a way to get you out of here."

A hint of excitement returned to Oliver's eyes. "It would take me a couple of weeks to replicate the virus. It's not on a system anywhere. It's in my head."

"You don't have it backed up somewhere else?"

"A couple of notebooks. They're in safe hands."

"Heather Mallow gave me some scribble or something that looked like it could be code."

"It's probably only a portion of it. I only perfected it the night before we attempted the upload."

If the complete virus was all in his head, he held valuable information. No wonder the Fighters wanted to hold on to him. "I'll take care of the Fighters."

"How?"

"These people are fucking idiots. Right now, they're all drunk out of their minds in that big tent. They're bound to slip up."

Oliver squatted and leaned toward Kelly. "Want to know my theory? The Fighters and the State are working together." He leaned back and stared at her, nodding his head.

His theory was possible—anything was possible—but without cold, hard proof, the public would never believe it. Or maybe there wasn't a connection, and Oliver was forcing puzzle pieces to connect because he was desperate to make sense of things that made no sense. After what he'd suffered at the Fighters' hands, his ordeal needed to have a purpose.

"The comms team," Kelly said, tipping her head toward the ceiling. "They were tracking the Elite Squad to ensure they didn't follow you, so they can't be working with them or the State. I saw Luke filling in the logs."

He licked his lips. "They may not be working with the Elite Squad, but that doesn't mean they aren't working with someone in government."

He made an excellent point. Deep down, she always believed that the evidence that cleared Ian Smith had been planted by someone in government. But without being able to prove it, which would have required finding the bad actor, she had been forced to live with the stigma of being a corrupt journalist. Bitter experience had taught her that irrefutable proof was key.

Oliver was valuable in more ways than one. Apart from being the coder who could destroy the Zone and its apparatus, he was her eyewitness. He probably knew others she could cross-reference. Before the Truth Laws, official news outlets required secondary references before publishing a story. Now, with the Truth Laws overseeing the media, it would be near impossible to get this story out, but the anonymous forums afforded her more leeway. "I can write about what's going on in here, your virus, what you know, what you saw, and release the story in installments in the forums."

"Cicada?"

"Where else?"

"Keep me anonymous."

"Naturally." She almost felt giddy, but then a doubt clamped her down. "There's only one problem. The story could end up going nowhere. It's freer than most places, but government officials still lurk all over Cicada."

Oliver shook his head in disagreement. "Doesn't matter. Someone will see and take a copy immediately. Once it's out, there's no stopping it." He rubbed his hands together. "You know, if those people up there were real Fighters, they'd be the ones risking their lives to tell the public about the Truth Laws development into thought crimes." He stretched his legs. "Maybe they're panicking because they know they're compromised."

"Abbott," Kelly said. "I could see her being involved. She's been hiding something from the moment I arrived."

"She probably knows all about the thought crime coming. Loads of source material travels through here. I should know."

Kelly thought of Josh again. He was a hacker, and he knew Christopher. "It could also be a hacker in the city who slipped Christopher the information about the Truth Laws."

"Will we ever know?" Oliver muttered. "Whoever it was would know how to hide their tracks."

Obviously not that well, she thought, otherwise she and Oliver wouldn't be talking about it in this underground cell. His theory started to make sense. "I agree that the Fighters should be pouncing on the government, but they won't because they're in on it."

"You feel it too then," Oliver said.

Kelly looked at Oliver. "Why you, though? Of all the hackers in the city, why did you get the commission to write the virus?"

"Because I could."

"Would anyone else be able to write it?"

He shook his head. "I'm the only one who knew the Zone's weakness."

"And how did you know that?"

"I'm the Prime Minister's nephew."

All the momentum in their discussion cracked and fell into a million little pieces. "You had me going for a while there, Oliver. I should've known better." She slumped onto the floor.

"I am! Why would I lie about that?"

"No way would the prime minister let a family member be kidnapped, and MI5 not be crawling all over this place. If you were his nephew, you'd have been rescued by now."

"How do you know they haven't tried? You want proof?" In a hushed tone, Oliver started, "In case I don't make it—"

"You'll make it out of here, don't worry about that."

He swallowed. "The passcode to break the chamber open and give you full control is EvePR1. Only someone with high security clearance would know that."

"Are you for real?"

He looked at her, puzzled.

"Reminds me of a story from a while back, where one of the major political parties in the richest, most powerful nation in the world used a super simple password to guard their entire party's server. No one could believe it when the password was revealed."

He cracked a smile. "Yeah, I heard about that, their sloppy arrogance." His serious face returned. "Get me out of here, and I will prove what I'm saying."

She nodded and let the silence comfort them.

Hours later, the sound of the wooden doors pounded. Someone was coming. Oliver and Kelly hushed and listened. Plodding footsteps neared.

"Sounds like that bitch is back." She looked at Oliver. "We'll find a way."

A red-faced maelstrom swung open the gate.

Kelly reeled, her skin crawled. She pedaled away from it, but there was no escape. The maelstrom lifted Kelly to her feet.

"Where are you taking me?" Somehow, she forced the words out as the maelstrom dragged her away.

Stiff-faced, the maelstrom carried Kelly, as effortlessly as though she were a plastic figurine, toward the wooden doors. Oliver flung himself against the bars, shouting after them, but as they climbed out of the bunker, his shouts faded until Kelly could hear nothing but the rough, determined maelstrom dragging her toward the surface.

FIFTY-TWO

THE FRESH AIR livened Kelly's senses. Strangely, the maelstrom led her away from the illuminated central tent and steered her toward a black abode, one she hadn't seen before. The maelstrom flung open the entrance flap and shoved her inside.

The bright overhead light burned Kelly's eyes, blinding her, but the maelstrom spurred her forward, his viselike grip clutching her sweaty arm. Her eyes adjusted, and she could see that this tent, unlike any of the others, had been fortified by an unfinished brick wall. Wires protruded from the light fixture on the ceiling—a fire hazard waiting to happen. The depressing room had the look and feel of having been abandoned.

She landed in a chair opposite two Fighters. They were positioned in the middle of the room. One of the Fighters, an interrogator, she assumed, wasn't someone she'd seen before. His hair was trim and tidy, parted on the side, and combed back. He could easily pass for a slick PR executive in the city. The other interrogator was Agatha.

The odd couple didn't appear to possess any weapons, but with the maelstrom as a guard dog, they didn't need any.

"Something to drink?" Agatha asked.

"What am I being charged with?"

Agatha adjusted her posture in the chair. "We don't live under the city's rules."

"I can see that."

Agatha snapped her fingers and ordered the maelstrom to fetch some water.

He left the room.

Oliver was right about the enemy hiding in the camp. And, if they held Oliver, they were likely using him as a bargaining chip, whether his value was the virus code or his connection to someone in government.

"Let's just jump right to it," the tidy man said.

Kelly looked at him. "I met Agatha at the party, but not you."

"Brady." He slapped a piece of paper on the table. It was folded, ripped, and stained with sweat. Kelly could almost make out Catalina's fat fingerprints all over it. "We found it in your quarters."

"You mean Catalina claimed to have found it and then claimed I was hiding it."

Agatha sprawled her fingers on the metal table as though releasing repressed tension. "Who does it belong to?"

"How should I know?"

Agatha unfolded the paper and laid it flat on the table, face up. "It was in your things."

Kelly's breath caught in her throat, the hair on her forearms rose. She stared at the paper. It wasn't the code Catalina had dangled in her dirty hands.

It was Mallow's research.

Her mind rallied. Maybe Catalina had used the code-filled paper as a decoy to sideline and isolate Kelly from the Fighters. Then, in the commotion, she swapped it for Mallow's research. How else would it be here? Until she knew more, deflection was the only play she had. "Why aren't you excited about coming into information about government overreach? It should ignite your passion, your cause."

Agatha's lips pursed at the implied accusation. "Excited isn't quite the right word."

"Who gave it to you?" Brady demanded.

Kelly held back from launching into a tirade. "I can't believe you're asking me such a stupid question."

"One more time," Brady pressed. "Who gave it to you?"

She clamped her eyes on him in disbelief. The whole camp should be convening over how to stop the tyranny about to be unleashed on the country. Instead, Brady and Agatha were treating her like a common criminal. "This research clearly spells out our country's fast-approaching fate, and you're haggling about who it belonged to and where I found it. You don't want to deal with any of this, do you?"

Brady's forehead crinkled with lines. "Where did you find it?"

"I'm a journalist. It's my job to find things."

"Don't make this harder than it has to be."

"If you must know, Luke can probably verify the place I found it if he logs into the camera recordings at Global Wires."

"Good." Agatha offered a slender smile. "I'm glad we're making progress."

Kelly's jaw clenched. Agatha whispered in Brady's ear. He punched a text message into the transmitter fastened to his wrist. "Luke will bring the footage," he said.

"Now I have a question," Kelly said. "The morning you were watching me—"

The maelstrom entered the room, his hand oozed slime on the pitcher of water and three glasses. Kelly eased back. Even though he wasn't likely to overstep unless ordered, this lot was a tricky breed. He placed the tray down on the table and returned to his station, guarding the door.

"As I was about to say...why would Abbott call me at Global Wires and suggest I come here?"

Agatha glanced at the door, clearly eager for Luke to arrive. "Abbott used a voice disguiser."

"Have you tested your equipment lately?" Kelly's question caught Agatha's attention. "When I got to the camp, it took me only seconds to identify her as the voice on the phone. You have relic technology sitting in the comms room."

A vacant look overtook Agatha's eyes, a sheen of perspiration glistened on her upper lip.

Brady's transmitter sounded. "Luke will be here shortly."

"Luke is part of the problem," Kelly said.

"You'll have a bigger problem if he doesn't find the footage," Agatha said.

"Footage or not, why aren't you investigating the government surveillance program connected to the Truth Laws? In less than a week, the Truth Laws will expand to include thoughts. Where are they getting this technology? You should be fighting this!" Kelly shoved the paper at them. "Read it for yourselves."

Agatha's brown eyes looked like they were trembling in her pale face.

"What's wrong with you people?"

Brady tapped his fist against his lips. "This isn't an article or research or whatever you keep calling it."

"What are you talking about?" Kelly grabbed the paper and started to read. "On February first, the State will be extending the Truth Laws to include thoughts. Anyone caught transmitting thoughts not in alignment with the Truth Laws will be apprehended, taken to the Zone, and questioned." She looked up at the two Fighters. "It goes on to talk about the nanotechnology of the State and how the changes are inescapable and so on. In other words, we're all screwed." Kelly's hands numbed, trying to steady her trembling legs. "Isn't this what you guys are fighting against?"

Their eyes widened.

"Jesus Christ, do you people not even realize what's happening?"

Agatha slowly backed away from the table, her skin a bloodless white. She mumbled in a voice so faint Kelly couldn't hear.

The tent flap brushed back and Luke walked in. "Abbott wants all of us at headquarters so we can bring her to trial."

Agatha picked up the paper. It fluttered ever so slightly in the grip of her hand. "She's reading this as if it were text." She gave it to Luke.

He skimmed the page. "It's code."

Kelly glared at them. "You people really are crazy."

"Kelly Blackwell, we are charging you with one count of treason for possessing classified information," Brady said.

"Now it's classified information?" Kelly's voice filled the room. "Aren't you people listening?"

"Some truths are painful." Agatha's eyes brimmed with a mix of sympathy and fear. She turned to Brady and Luke. "This is the most unprecedented case we've encountered."

Kelly reached for the paper, but Brady pulled it away. "Take her to the communal room."

The heavy flap of the tent tore back.

Troy stormed into the tent.

The maelstrom lurched at him, but Troy blocked his punch with the butt of his rifle. The maelstrom howled and scampered out of the tent. Agatha, Brady, and Luke fixed their eyes on Troy's rifle and edged themselves against the brick wall.

"Kelly, let's go. Hurry." She scrambled over to him. "This place is compromised," he said. "If any of you know what's good for you, you'll get the hell out of here."

Kelly and Troy backed out of the tent. Outside, in the campgrounds, her eyes caught the scarf around his neck, the plaid scarf she had given the homeless man outside the Luntan. The man had been Troy.

"Glad you recognize it," he said. "Now, come on. We have to get to the comms tent; there's a recording there that I need."

"First, we have to get Oliver," Kelly said, breathless.

Troy shook his head firmly. "We don't have time."

Her eyes pleaded with him. "He says he's the PM's nephew."

He rubbed the back of his head. "Okay. Quick."

They ran to the underground shed. It wasn't far, and clearly the camp was still not back on full alert after the party. They encountered not a soul as they sprinted from tent to tent. As they rounded a corner and the wooden doors came into sight, Kelly thought they had made it, until out of the corner of her eye she saw Catalina and the maelstrom, each clutching a rifle pointed straight at Kelly and Troy.

FIFTY-THREE

IN HER OFFICE at the Zone, Lydia Rackham sat on the leather sofa and found herself glancing at the clock again. She laid down her smart pen on her tablet and picked up a glass half-filled with brandy.

At last, a knock at the door. She aligned her spine, loosening up the tension between her shoulder blades. "Come in."

Omar entered. "Took a little longer than expected."

"Getting acquainted with Kelly's friend is time well spent." She gestured for Omar to sit. "Brandy?" He shook his head and handed her the notebooks. "I knew I could count on you." She flipped through the note-books. A few pages in, she tossed them back to Omar. "This is Greek to me."

"I think it's called Python," he said. "A bit dated, but it's an all-purpose coding language that even some AI can read."

"What good is any of it if we don't know how to apply it?" Lydia rose from the sofa and wandered to the shelves.

"Now that we no longer have Oliver to explain this, it looks like Christopher Mallow is the next best person. He must know what it means."

"We've been working on Mallow, but he won't crack. He's on a starvation strike." She shook her head and pulled a book from the shelf. "My father wrote this book. Did I ever tell you that?"

"No, but..."

She gazed at the book's tattered spine, *The Coming Age of the Fourth Industrial Revolution*. Having read it every year since he passed, she knew every word by heart. She would be the one to bring her father's dream to England. "He was a brilliant man who put into words what no one else could. Fate is on our side." She lifted her chin and returned the book to the shelf. "There is someone who will be all too eager to find out what those notebooks contain."

"Who's that?"

"His name is Harry White. He works over at Global Wires."

She looked at Omar, and the driven look in his eyes gave way.

"You sure we want to bring an unknown into this?"

"We could put it under his nose," she said. "See if he bites. With a little nudge, of course."

"How so?"

"If he knows Kelly's connected to this Python code, he might dig deeper into it. We can then watch his online investigation."

"So, you'll encourage him to dig into the code, and we piggyback off his discoveries?"

"Yes."

Omar scratched his jaw, something he did when he was considering an idea. "It's a bit of a process, but we can find out which forums he chats in."

"That's easy enough."

"The hard part is baiting him."

"Send him guppies that'll hook him in."

Guppies were the ads and spam emails featuring a particular subject attuned to the recipient. In Harry's case, the guppies would feature fantastical robots. It was a way to hook attention on a subliminal level.

"They can see through it these days."

"And yet, it continues to be effective." She tapped her finger on the shelf. "After that, it's all about watching him invoke some authority into the matter, encourage his research with flattery and compliments, and watch him brag about his findings."

"Wouldn't it be easier if we just got Oliver out? Also, we'll be doing what the PM has asked."

She appreciated his compassion, but climbing to the top required strategies that had no room for sentiment. "Once we know what the code is and what it's meant to do, Oliver becomes a redundant chip. He'd just be a liability. He knows too much. The dead don't talk."

"The Prime Minister is going to be very unhappy about that."

"Make it look like an extraction gone wrong. We can always say the Fighters killed him."

"I don't understand why you let that place exist for so long," he said.

"It served a purpose, but now it's come to its final use. It's time to clean it out."

A look of disgust flashed over Omar's face. It almost took her aback.

"I'll be more than happy to," Omar said. "And Kelly Blackwell?"

Lydia studied his face for a sign of confused loyalty, wondering if his resolve would crack when the time came to transfer Kelly. Lydia couldn't see so much as a twinge in his steady eyes, but that meant nothing. Time would tell. "You know I don't like journalists meddling in State affairs, so this one will get special treatment. Bring Kelly to the Zone." She glanced at him. Still no spark. "Meanwhile, see to it that Harry White gets a copy of the code in these notebooks."

FIFTY-FOUR

A MOB of fighters piled into the communal room like a gathering storm. A circle formed around Kelly and Troy, as though in the eye of a hurricane.

Kelly pulled on the taut rope restraining her wrists, barely able to believe what was unfolding before her. It all struck her as surreal.

Troy lay on the ground next to her, his head bleeding, courtesy of the maelstrom and his rifle. "They're here for the trial."

"Trial, my ass." Kelly recalled the libel trial against her. Sure, it was rigged, but at least it had a modicum of law and order. "This isn't a trial."

"But it doesn't matter." His shoulders slumped. "This is what Rozlyn wants."

Oliver's theory sprang into Kelly's mind. "Is Rozlyn working with someone in government?"

Troy's eyes hardened and turned gray. He was about to speak when Catalina suddenly towered over them, her arms folded across her chest. Luke stood behind her, hesitant to glance in Kelly's direction.

A large woman with pink hair and kitten glasses stepped forward. Her plump arms pulled on her shirt, exposing the seams at her shoulders. She cleared her throat. "The rules are as follows."

Troy nudged Kelly's shoulder and raised his eyebrows toward the entrance. There, Abbott stood at the back of the crowd.

"We're running out of time," Troy whispered to Kelly.

The pink-haired woman reeled off ground rules to the crowd. She turned to Kelly. "Where were you on the evening of January 21?"

That was the day of Geneva's murder, the day she received Rozlyn's call. Before Kelly could protest, the Fighters roared.

"She needs to go!" yelled out a guy with a crew cut. "Bringing her here was a mistake!"

His words roused the crowd.

"Execute the traitor!"

"Turn her over to the State!"

Their jaws snapped and snarled as they spat out their spite.

Abbott moved to the center of the crowd. "Let's all just calm down."

The shouts died away to disgruntled murmurs. A woman with dyed gray-green hair spoke up. "Why are we protecting this girl?"

Abbott lifted her open palms toward the crowd. "It's not obvious right now, but with some time and some training, she will be something we can use."

A deep rage boiled inside Kelly. "You are the traitor, Abbott!"

Anger flashed across Abbott's face.

The room roared.

Abbott lifted her hand again and waited for the ruckus to settle. "You were in trouble, and I thought you could use our help."

The woman's mock concern sickened Kelly. "You don't care about this camp, the cause, or the Fighters."

"Why don't we let Troy decide?" Catalina stared at Kelly, an evil grin on her face as she dangled Christopher's research in front of Troy. The paper hung in the air so fragile that the violent currents could shred it to pieces.

"What say you, Troy?" Abbott arched her eyebrows expectantly.

He stared at Abbott, his eyes cold as stone. "Means nothing."

Kelly squeezed Troy's hand.

"Kelly will be our prisoner," Abbott declared.

The crowd applauded and roared, and then an alarm blared through the tent. All the bluster and seething stopped cold, and a deathly silence took over.

Troy squeezed Kelly's hand. He leaned in to whisper in her ear. "The Elite Squad is coming."

FIFTY-FIVE

"You know the drill, people," Abbott's voice thundered above the alarm. "Move!"

A flurry of action shook the canvas walls.

Kelly pulled on the ropes around her wrist, her skin reddened raw. "Now's our chance to get Oliver and make a run for it."

Troy shook his head. "Remember I told you I overheard Abbott talking to someone? We need those recordings. They're in comms."

Kelly nodded. "Oliver knows the code that can destroy the chambers."

"You!" Abbott shouted, pointing at the maelstrom. "Take Kelly and Troy to the cells. The rest of you, take up your positions."

"Follow my cue," Troy whispered to Kelly.

The maelstrom ushered them out of the communal room. Near the comms tent, Troy lost his footing. The maelstrom hauled Troy back up. He shot Kelly a sharp now-or-never look.

Troy grabbed a hold of the maelstrom and shoved him into the comms tent. His deformed body slammed into the desks, and screens crashed to the floor. Kelly sawed the rope binding against the jagged edge of a metal table.

The maelstrom dove for the yellow button. The rope snapped off, freeing her wrists. She slapped the button out of the maelstrom's reach.

Troy pounded the maelstrom in the ribs. He gasped for air, but strove to reach for the button.

Troy clenched a fistful of the maelstrom's hair and banged his head against the dirt floor, over and over, until the only thing left twitching was the maelstrom's hand.

Troy slumped against the floor, blood covering his hands.

Kelly scrambled to her feet and started up two screens, giving them an overview of the camp. "The recordings must be in the chest in the corner. I saw Luke pulling something out of there." She opened the heavy lid. Rows of hard drives lined the silk lining padding the box. She looked at Troy with searching eyes. "What am I looking for?"

"Try that one." He pointed to a wooden storage chest in the corner of the room behind the desks. She rushed over and heaved it open. She stared at a mass of phones and watches.

"Dig deeper."

She reached in, past the sinewy cables, and landed on feed storage devices.

"Take January's drive."

There were so many, but the one Troy was talking about had been recorded this week. It had to be close to the end. It was. She stuffed the drive deep into her pocket.

"It'll tell us who Rozlyn was talking to. Knowing that could be the key to blowing the government sky high."

Kelly pried the cell key from the dead maelstrom's belt. "Let's go get Oliver."

Distant gunfire tore through the camp.

Troy's eyes turned dark like black disks. "Leave that to me. We'll meet you at the escape route."

FIFTY-SIX

TROY BARRELED DOWN THE TUNNEL, rifle in hand, and swung the cell door open.

Oliver's face was the color of ash. "What's all the gunfire?"

"The Elite Squad," Troy said, clutching the rifle he had snatched off a dead fighter on the way to the bunker. "We're getting out of here, just stay behind me."

Oliver's arms trembled in Troy's grip as he led Oliver out of the bunker.

"If I don't make it," he said, his voice shaky.

Troy turned to Oliver. "We'll make it."

"They must've known about the cameras surrounding the camp. When I first came here, I heard Sinclair talking about the cameras. He was getting Luke to report to him, so Sinclair probably had something to do with why the Squad's here."

"It wasn't Sinclair." They reached the base of the ramp. Troy pulled the switchblade from his pocket. "Take this."

Oliver snatched it from Troy's hand. Troy sped up the dirt ramp. Near the surface, he turned around, expecting Oliver to be right behind him, but the kid was looking at Troy from below, panting.

"Get your shit together, Oliver."

"If you see Kelly, tell her I knew all along."

"Knew what?"

"That she was the one who could stop the whole thing. She's the only one capable of putting a stop to the Zone."

Troy motioned for Oliver to follow him. "You can tell her yourself."

The wooden doors were still wide open. They stepped up together into the campgrounds.

Oliver squinted his terrified eyes. Troy pushed him forward, and they jogged in tandem along the perimeter fence.

Oliver started to wheeze.

"Relax. Breathe, but do it quietly," Troy whispered.

He pulled back, shifted his weight to his back heel, and raised his gun.

Just then, Catalina ran in front of the hole in the perimeter fence. She pointed a gun at both of them.

Troy and Catalina's eyes met.

Bullets sprayed out between them.

Every muscle in Troy's body went rigid. He didn't feel a thing. But there was blood, so much blood. He was losing consciousness, and the last thing that went through his mind was Kelly.

———

BLOOD-CURDLING SCREAMS RIPPED through Kelly's ears. Her body locked in place, and no will in the world could move her. She knew it wouldn't be long before the Elite Squad swarmed this tent, too.

A picture flickered on a screen, the one screen giving her a view out. Its primary feed was fixed on the communal room; a room in chaos. In the smaller quadrant views, she could see the rest of the camp. Watching on as the Fighters scattered in all directions, her heart raced. Some made it only a few steps before losing their balance and sliding on the blood-slicked ground. Death surrounded them all.

She muffled a scream on the edge of her throat. No way in hell was she going out there, but she couldn't just stay here, either.

A cry for help just outside the tent shocked her into motion.

Kelly hurled out the contents from the wooden chest and climbed in, squeezing into the confined space. Sweat dripped down her back.

What felt like an eternity later, all the gunfire stopped. The camp was silent. The sudden calm sent cold terror through her. She peeped through a crack in the chest. She could just make out one of the screens; the feed flicked between various cameras set up around the camp. The screen showed a camp awash with crumpled bodies. The troopers walked through, lifting the wilted arms of the dead Fighters, scanning their barcodes into the ID scanners. They were surveying their kill, taking inventory.

Then, at the edge of the screen, in the corner of the headquarters tent, a single figure appeared. He folded what looked like a cape over his arm. He stood at the edge of the communal room, too far for the lens to pick up a sharp image of his face.

The troopers backed away.

The navy coat. Those gloves. His stride. It was all so familiar, but the camera just wouldn't give her a clear view. Kelly started to hyperventilate, her breath echoing back at her in the close confines of the chest.

Head down, the man in the navy coat trudged past corpses, pausing to bend over each one just to twist the lifeless heads toward him. He seemed to be looking for someone. He stood straight, put his hands on his hips, and scanned the room. With his back to the camera, he pointed his gloved hand to a stack of bodies. Following his order, a trooper lifted a corpse.

The body lying underneath the corpse belonged to Abbott. It appeared as though she had used one of the fighters to shield her from the troopers' bullets. Kelly felt disgust, and it wasn't because of the slaughtered fighters.

The trooper hauled off the corpse, and Abbott's chest heaved as she spat up blood. Though she was still alive, her chest bobbed swiftly and sharply, hanging onto life by the thinnest of threads.

The man in the navy coat stepped over the discarded dead body and came face to face with Abbott. He bent over and lifted her up by the collar.

Abbott turned away, her eyes cast down in what looked like shame. Knowing Abbott, though, it was more likely prideful defiance.

Looking down at her, the man motioned for one of the troopers to hand him a gun. Cradling the weapon in his hand, the man crouched down to Abbott's level. They seemed to exchange words.

He stood and pumped her body with bullets. After inspecting his work, he ID'd her with a scanner. He wound his finger in the air—it seemed like a command. The troopers split up into teams of two and dispersed like slick oil across water.

The man turned around. At last, Kelly got a clear look at his face.

Her whole body went numb.

FOOTSTEPS SHUFFLED toward the entrance of the comms tent.

Adrenaline pumped through Kelly's body. He was coming. She tried to steady her racing breath by focusing on the entrance, but silently, she prayed that her final breath would be painless. Breathe in for seven. Hold. Exhale to seven.

Maybe she was mistaken, or fear had distorted her vision. She had it all wrong, or—

Footsteps stopped in front of the comms tent.

Kelly held her breath. He's here.

His radio scratched into life. "Sir," a voice blared. "Rozlyn Abbott's body, what would you like us to do with it?"

He didn't reply.

"Sir?"

"Leave her to rot with the rest of them," he said. "Once a traitor, always a traitor. We're done here. Let's go."

Dizziness swirled inside her head. Yes. It was him. His name wouldn't even touch her thoughts as though his name would break her in two, shatter every cell inside her. She wanted someone to tell her, to reassure her, to lie to her that Mr. Anon was the one who filmed Geneva's murder, the leader of the Elite Squad.

His footsteps backed away from the comms tent.

She looked at the view on the screen and watched him striding across the ruined camp like a man who had accomplished his mission. The man called Omar Betesh.

WEEK 4

FIFTY-SEVEN

29 January. 3 a.m.

KELLY CROSSED THE DESERTED CAMP, heading in the direction of the main tent, focused on one thing: Christopher's research. It was the only record in existence that could prove the government's tyrannical ambitions. She'd last seen it in the communal room of the headquarters, crumpled in Catalina's hand. Kelly needed to find it quickly before the Squad returned, before she left to meet Oliver and Troy in No Man's Land. She crept into the side entrance of the main tent, and a bitter smell blasted her nostrils.

Scorched holes riddled the canvas walls like blackened blisters. Boxes, packed with bullets and guns, littered the ground helter-skelter. The smell of electrified flesh grew stronger the closer she got to the communal room, and her tongue tasted of tin.

Blood inked the canvas walls like crimson paint. Bodies lay strewn across the floor, contorted in ungodly positions. A dead Fighter's arm was outstretched as though he had tried to claw himself away.

Her stomach convulsed as she doubled over and gagged. "Focus, Kelly." She straightened, wiping sweat from her forehead, and plodded on with the hunt, wading through bodies, holding back the despair rising steadily in her heart.

She came to Abbott's body. The once commanding woman's shoulders slumped forward, her head hanging to the side, her body riddled with holes. What had Omar said to the trooper? That she was a traitor.

Oliver had been right. Abbott had been working for the State, and she led the Fighters to their slaughter. The entire Freedom camp could've started as a State project—a way to contain resistance. And maybe Abbott angled for more power—people like her always did. But Christopher's research must have thrown a wrench in her plot, and she got nervous because his information threatened to crack open her charade.

Troy's words echoed in her mind. The Fighters had already decided what to do with her, he had said. Abbott knew exactly what she was doing when she had imprisoned Kelly and was probably working on a ransom—but from whom? If her theory was close to the truth—and she felt it was—she needed to find the dead woman's contact.

She turned away from Abbott's body, inched toward the center of the room, and searched for Catalina's corpse.

Nothing.

She came to the front entrance. There, piled on the floor, lay the bodies of Troy and Oliver. Their arms rested above their heads like snow angels, their eyes empty.

Her legs wavered. Crushing gloom descended over her, hot tears streamed down her face. She dropped to her knees, her stomach pulled in by violent sobs.

Troy was dead. The man who'd helped her escape the camp, who'd believed in her when he had every reason not to, who'd put himself between her and the Elite Squad—dead. She barely knew him. Hadn't trusted him at first. And he'd died anyway, for her, a stranger who'd brought nothing but danger to his door.

She pressed her palms against her eyes. How many more? How many more bodies would pile up before this ended?

"They're all dead," Omar said from somewhere behind her.

His voice pinned her to her spot. "You killed everyone here." She brushed aside her tears and turned to face him. There he was in his navy coat, a cape draped over his arm. The sight of him hollowed her insides. "As though it was nothing."

"I'm under orders."

"Whose orders? Who do you work under?"

"You know the Elite Squad works within the Ministry of Information. It's no secret."

"Damian Winters? Lydia Rackham? Spencer Wyatt?"

His eyes didn't move.

"You also killed Geneva Winters and Christopher Mallow."

"Christopher is still alive."

"You're lying. Did you come back to kill me?"

"No." He slung the cape over his shoulder. "Had I told you about Christopher back then, you wouldn't have believed me."

The memory of meeting him the first time flashed into her mind, and she felt like a fool, but hid her disillusionment as best she could. "You've been lying... from the first moment we met."

He opened his mouth to speak.

"So, what's it going to be now, Omar? Is that even your name?"

His lips tightened. "I don't have time to go through it all right now. The troopers are coming back to clean up this mess." He brought out a bloodstained sheet of paper and whipped it open. "Isn't this what you're looking for?"

Mistrusting the bounty he held out to her—could be a trick—she blinked rapidly in succession. But by the look of his unguarded, sincere face, she could imagine that somewhere deep inside he knew the Truth Laws, the echo chambers, the Zone—all of it—had to be stopped. Or maybe it was a trick, and he was setting her up for a trap. "Are you really trying to help me?"

"It's important you do what needs to be done."

He unzipped a bulletproof vest under his coat, and shrugged both coverings from his shoulders, down his arms, until a black heap lay at his feet. Fully exposed, except for a leather holster wrapped around his chest. He pulled out a knife from the holster, as long as half her arm. The blade was spiraled, and its triple-edges were serrated like shark teeth, ending at a fine point that could pierce the thickest of skins.

She stepped back carefully as though faced with a hungry tiger.

"It's called a Jagkommando," he said. "The handle functions like a glass breaker." He replaced the beast in its sheath and presented it to her, handle side first. "Keep it pointed at the enemy."

She eyed the knife. She could grab it, turn the deadly blade on him, and slice into his chest.

"I know what you must be thinking," he said. "You could easily stab me."

She glanced at him.

"And you could." He untied the holster and slipped it off. "But then, you'll never do what you really need to do." The knife's holster swung from his hand. "So, what's it going to be, Kelly? I'm here, practically defenseless."

She wasn't going to kill him, and they both knew it. She grabbed the holster, wrapped it around her shoulders, and secured the knife in the pouch.

"Take the back roads," Omar said. "Don't let the surveillance screens see you. Josh is waiting for your call."

FIFTY-EIGHT

IN THE DISTANCE, the city's lights glowed in the dark sky, and Kelly heeded its strange magnetism. In two days, the all-pervasive, enhanced algorithms, protected by the Truth Laws, would spread over the land. Armed only with a knife, she hiked into No Man's Land.

She needed the Roseman equipment, and that meant she had to get back to her studio. Only then would she set her plan in motion and break the biggest story the world had ever seen. The thought sustained her as she trudged toward the city.

Finally, she reached the dirt slope out of No Man's Land, climbed up, and skidded back on her strides. She let herself fall forward, hands first, and slid all the way back down. Dust and gravel clung to her clothes. Getting out wasn't quite as easy as getting in.

She dusted herself down and stepped back a few feet from the base of the slope. Her boots crunched against loose gravel until she reached the tarmac. The small victory imbued her with vigor.

Standing on the tarred asphalt, now within the city limits, she suddenly felt like a foreigner. The SS lined the road like a hall of mirrors, obstructing a clear view of the road. She shook off the peculiar feeling and began to trot, hunching down under each SS she passed, on the lookout for a back alley down which she could escape their constant gaze.

A distant hiss sounded in the night air. An ambulance zipped by, its shrill siren and yellow lights bouncing down the road. Her heart beat quickly, and the skin around her face constricted while her eyes adjusted to the unexpected flashing lights.

An SS played an advert showing a doctor rushing toward an emergency room. The moving image slowed as though someone was playing it at half-normal speed, and the voice-over slowed to a distorted drone. Kelly blinked. For a moment, she wondered if maybe her eyes were speeding up and her hearing was fading, but she quickly shook off the disquieting thought and continued moving forward.

Up ahead, an SS flashed a bright light. Black and white lines lacerated the screen. A headache throbbed behind her strained eyes. She hadn't had a headache once during her time in the camp, but here, again, in the city, they returned. The night's hiss came to a halt. The screens on the path all turned black. The sudden darkness blinded her, the silence deafening.

Electric pulses charged through her hands and feet, propelling her down the path. A windowless black van screeched to a halt in front of her, blocking the road. She spun around, sprinting in the direction of No Man's Land. Behind her, she heard the van doors tear open. As she ran, she glanced over her shoulder. A man was charging after her, his face covered with a black ski mask.

Kelly fumbled under her jacket pocket for the weapon. Just as she clenched the knife handle, the masked man spun her around and clasped her arms behind her back. She screamed so loudly her throat burned. A second masked man vaulted from the driver's seat, a roll of duct tape in his hand. Rough hands held her head still as a strip of tape clamped down over her mouth. One maelstrom grabbed her legs and the other her arms. She cried out a muzzled scream as they lifted her off her feet. She kicked and writhed, twisting against the vice-like hold, but it was no use.

They swung her into the cargo hold, and she crash-landed onto a bare metal floor. One maelstrom climbed inside the back of the van with her, clamped the side door shut, and fastened the lock.

Pitch black. A damp stink, the kind found in an abandoned cemetery, rose all around her. The maelstrom rapped on the grille bars. The engine revved, and the van tore off down the road. The force of gravity threw her backward. Every road bump flung her back, then forth. Terror seized her throat, choking off her voice. All she could hear was the heavy breathing of the man with her and the engine roaring as it smashed along the road.

The maelstrom switched on a flashlight. She squinted in the abrupt glow. His mask was off, and his horror of a red face bobbed almost on its own. He pulled a white wrapper out of his pocket and tore it open with his teeth. A pale, blue-tinted syringe surfaced out of the opaque wrapper, its needle glinting in the light, similar to the one she had seen hanging off Geneva's lifeless body.

He grabbed Kelly by the arm.

She pulled away, but there was no escape. "Who gave you that?"

He sank the needle deep into her flesh.

The needle sank deep—cold like those plasma vials for bills, once routine, now anything but.

Kelly squeezed against the door. "Where did you get that?"

Her throat released, and the last thought that ran through her mind was how Omar must've set this trap before she crossed into oblivion.

JOSH GLANCED at his watch. 8 a.m.

Heat simmered under his skin. Kelly should've called by now. He began to worry that Omar had broken their agreement to trade the notebooks for Kelly. That was the deal. Had he handed over the notebooks for nothing? He shook his head. "No."

The agony of not knowing threatened to pull him under, so he sat there for a few minutes, trying to keep himself calm. He scrolled through his watch and pressed Omar's number. Voicemail picked up.

"Josh here. Kelly hasn't called. Call as soon as you get this."

If Omar didn't call within twenty-four hours, he would hunt him down—no matter how long it took—and make him pay. He pulled his jacket on, and his burner phone rang, cutting through the burgeoning feeling of betrayal.

He picked it up. "Omar?"

"We know everything, Josh."

His hand shook.

"You *can* restore your position, if you want."

"How?"

"Kill Kelly Blackwell."

FIFTY-NINE

A LOUD BANG AWAKENED KELLY. Her eyes drifted open only to see she was still in the back of the van, lying on her side. A couple of feet away from her, the red-faced maelstrom was peering through a slit in the grate.

The maelstrom's musty day-old clothes stank up the air, smelling as though he had slept in them for a week or more. If that was the case, he was either homeless or working away from home—which made him tired and weak and probably short-fused.

It was impossible to tell how long she had been out, but it was long enough to have her wrists bound behind her back. Other than that, she didn't feel injured in any life-threatening way. If they had been ordered to kill her, she'd be dead by now. She had enough experience with the maelstrom now to know they carried out their orders faithfully, and they were probably under orders to bring her in alive, unharmed. She had that advantage at least, and in that, a glimmer of confidence installed itself in her mind.

The worst pain she felt was the knife and holster digging into her ribs. Carving into her hip was the storage device, still buried deep in her pocket. The stupid oafs hadn't bothered to search her. How long had they been on the road? Where were they taking her?

She shut her eyes, pretending to still be unconscious, and quietly groped for something, anything, she could use to cut through the plastic wristbands. With just enough slack in the bands, she wiggled her hands and stretched her fingers, feeling around for a sharp edge in the metal panel behind her.

Her muscles shook as she lengthened her fingers as far as they could go. Nothing.

The van roared down the path. She yielded to the cold metal floor and groped again, this time in an untried spot.

"How much did you give her?"

"Enough for thirty minutes."

Kelly made out the certainty in the maelstrom's voice. Under the cover of the engine's noise and their conversation, she squirmed down the van, inch by quiet inch, her fingers combing the panel for a sharp metal edge.

She came to a protruding section that obstructed her downward movement, which must have been the back wheel, and a sharp edge nicked her finger. She stifled a gasp and moved into position to saw through the wristband.

To her surprise, it snapped easily. Her wrists were free. Excitement bloomed, and a rush of adrenaline brought her to her feet.

The maelstrom swung around. "What the...she's awake!"

The van swerved. With one hand, she steadied herself against the wall of the van, and with the other, she unsheathed the knife. The maelstrom stared at it; terror flooded his eyes.

She jutted the knife out at him. "Open the door."

The maelstrom glanced at her and then to a crowbar that was rattling against the back of the van. Certain they were under orders not to injure her, she clasped the door handle, tricking him into thinking she was about to jump out.

The maelstrom driver yelled from the front seat. "Get control of the situation, man!"

His partner lumbered toward her, his big hands outstretched, his eyes flitting to the knife in her hands and back at her.

"Don't," she warned. "It's not worth it."

If she had to stick this knife into him, she would, she told herself.

He lunged to her right, in the direction of the crowbar. With one swift punch of the knife's handle, she cracked the window and reached out to open the door from the outside. The van swerved left and right, and Kelly's feet went out from under her. She crashed onto the floor. The maelstrom came at her, crowbar raised above his head. Before she knew what she was doing, Kelly plunged the knife into his stomach.

It glided in easily.

His eyes bulged. Blood sputtered from his gut. He coughed. Blood dripped down his chin and onto his jacket. He dropped to the ground with a heavy thud.

The driver banged on the grate. "What the fuck is going on in there?"

She searched the dead maelstrom's pocket for the used syringe. There it was. She stuffed the evidence in her back pocket, grateful it was capped.

The van came to a screeching halt. She clung to the edge of the door, waiting for the driver to jump in, her knife at the ready. Seconds later, the side door slid open. The driver leaped inside and veered to the left. Kelly slashed and jabbed at him until she felt the blade gouge a piece of flesh. He howled, clamping a hand to his eye, and fell to his knees.

She tumbled out of the van and collided with the tarmac. She sprang up and tried to run into the forest before her, but her legs felt like they were swimming in a mix of sleep serum and adrenaline. She limped to the bare trees in long, rickety strides, moving away from the van as fast as her legs could take her. The trees, looking down at her, all swirled around her endlessly. She gripped a tree trunk. Its abrasive, shriveled bark grated her palm.

The sting rooted her body, stabilized her vision, and for a moment, her world stood still. The Elite Squad wouldn't stop coming after her, the maelstrom wouldn't stop terrorizing the streets, the state wouldn't stop its expansion of the Truth Laws. No longer did she just want to get the word out. Now, she had to destroy the whole damn system. She sheathed the knife, powered her legs with strength she didn't know she had, and pushed forward.

SIXTY

KELLY STUMBLED onto the concrete ground of her Eden Estate.

Breathless, weary, hungry, but oddly clear-headed, she stood below her flat and peered up. Behind four high-security deadlocks, everything she needed idled inside. She trudged past the eye-retina ID and started the climb up the staircase.

At the first level, she paused and gulped down air. A soft breeze fanned her sweaty forehead like a gentle hand guiding her forward. Legs shaking, she braced herself against her bedroom window and tears of relief soaked her face. She absorbed the triumph of the moment, her breath deepening. She'd made it. Somehow, she'd made it.

But there was still a way to go. She peered through the window.

She almost felt elated at seeing Jerko, her useless hunk of metal. She secured the Jagkommando in her hand, the sheathed blade side, and smacked the handle hard against the window. The glass shattered like a lump of ice, shards flying in all directions. Her cheek stung. A small glass blade had lodged in the soft flesh of her cheek, and she muffled a howl as she wrenched it out. Next, she cleared the jagged fragments of glass still attached to the windowpane and hopped through. Broken glass crunched under her shoes.

Dull afternoon light spilled over the room.

Her tingling fingers ruffled the duvet, squeezing out its trapped air. Dust, fluffy and thick, capped the chest of drawers. She ran her finger across the top and rubbed the grit, assuring herself that she was really inside and it was all real. She checked out the bathroom. Rings of limescale caked the bottom of the tap, dry as chalk. She dropped to her knees and pulled out her basket of treasures from underneath the sink.

The neutralizer nested between the dry shampoo and washcloth, just as she had left it. Were it not for the broken window, her studio would be fully intact.

The Roseman box perched on the coffee table, unopened. She ripped off the brown sealant and pulled back the flaps.

A second watch, bug detector, fingerprint scanner, an earpiece, several encrypted USBs, a couple of ready-encrypted tablets, voice cloner, signal router, and several portable eyeball cameras. The equipment was a solid start.

She grabbed the watch, programmed it, and fastened it to her wrist. At the press of a button, she was connected to the citywide Wi-Fi, fully encrypted, under the alias Stormykitten. Now came the hard part of shuffling key players into position.

For as long as she had been a journalist, she avoided colluding with the network of journo-spies around the city. But now, with the heat of the Elite Squad and maelstrom upon her, she needed them.

No one knew who was in on the lookout scheme, least of all her. But a couple of people did come to mind. If there was anyone plugged into the throbbing vein of the city's network of spies, it was Harry White. But he had identified her to the Elite Squad, an unforgivable act of betrayal. Torn about what to do, and knowing he would flap his gums any chance he got if she approached him—her name would pop up in the next day's headlines—there was only one expedient move forward. Josh would have to handle Harry. She dialed Josh's number, and he picked up on the first ring.

"Thank God." He let out a loud sigh. "I was just about—"

"I'm on a Roseman watch, so let's be quick. The freedom camp was decimated. They're all dead."

"When?"

"Last night. I'll send you a copy of Christopher's research, the one I found in Geneva's files the night she died. I'll get Jerko to send it over to you. Give it to Harry White. Let him blast it all over the Internet to his heart's content, anonymously, of course. But don't tell him I gave it to you."

"What's going on?"

"The network he's part of will protect him. When that's done, meet me at the Zone. After midnight."

"You plan to go to the Zone? It's too dangerous, Kelly."

"It's been dangerous for a long time. When you come to the Zone, bring Damian Winters."

"Even if I could get Damian Winters to the Zone, we can't go anywhere near that place, not without permission or an access code."

"The last time I was there, the guard stored my biometrics in the system and said I wouldn't have to be scanned again. So, this is how we'll work it. The neutralizer, here in my studio flat, has a copy of my biometrics. Use it to cloak yourself and Damian. It'll think both of you are me. I'll leave it here for you, along with a fingerprint scanner that will have a copy of my prints, just in case. The key to the deadbolts will be outside the front door of the building, under a polka-dot mug."

"What am I supposed to tell Damian?"

"Tell him he has to go to the Zone if he wants to know who killed his daughter."

"You did speak to Omar then."

She eyed the Roseman watch. Although it was some of the most secure gear available, its encryption was not infallible. "Hard to say right now."

"I don't know what you're planning, but I'm game. I'll work on Damian. Either way, I'll be at the Zone, with or without him."

"Josh." She could hear him breathing. "Damian needs to be there."

"I'll do my best."

She closed the line, went to Jerko, and slid his eyepatch open. She held

Christopher's bloodstained research to Jerko's red eye. "Scan and email to Josh Munro."

"Scan complete," Jerko responded. "The document will be emailed to Josh Munro. Kelly, you have not read the news briefings in the last week. Would you like to hear them now?"

"Jerko, just do as I say."

She put the eyepatch back over its glaring red light and noticed her deep exhaustion. But the deadline for the Truth Laws extension was approaching, the luxury of time long gone. She gathered the goods that would get Josh and Damian past the Zone barriers and pulled out the hard drive containing the recording of Rozlyn Abbott from her pocket. She still hadn't listened to it, but they would all hear it later tonight. She placed it all in a backpack. Josh was set.

In her backpack, she loaded the Jagkommando, Roseman tablets, USBs, and the all-important eyeball cameras.

Nightfall had settled; the chamber would be empty. She marched out the door.

KELLY FASTENED the last eyeball camera onto a pole facing the Covent Garden echo chamber, logged onto their dashboard, and linked the cameras to the same network. To avoid swamping the cameras' memory stores, she set them to stream their feeds to her tablet in real time. Within minutes, the cameras were yoked together by an invisible string, like pearls on an elegant necklace.

She scanned her QR code, and the chamber door slid open. She surveyed the cockpits and screens—all empty, all hers. She drew in a deep breath and inserted the earbuds.

"Welcome back, Kelly Blackwell. We calculate you will need ten inhalations to transfer your work."

Kelly settled into cockpit four, her heart thumping in anticipation. First, she'd try Oliver's passcode, expecting to eliminate that option immediately because she doubted it would work. With that one out of the way, she would start using her other option. With some effort on her part, Roseman's equipment would get into the bowels of the chamber. One way or the other, Christopher's research was getting into the Zone, and her name would be written all over it.

"EvePR1," she said.

The lights dimmed, and then all the screens turned azure blue.

Her skin tingled. She hadn't expected this kind of response. Oliver had been telling the truth about the passcode, which meant he probably was the Prime Minister's nephew. "Fuck me," she whispered.

Looking back now, she realized that Abbott must have been trying to extract this gateway code from Oliver and planned to take the chamber system hostage too. It certainly was a good enough reason to risk kidnapping the Prime Minister's nephew. But this INNS system was more powerful than the government, more powerful than the Prime Minister. Yet, it was cracked with an old-school, six-digit code. "Here's to you, kid."

Kelly leaned forward. "INNS, do a search for the plasma clinics using blue-tinted syringes."

"We've located three. In West London, Central London, and East London."

"Is one of those on City Road?"

"Yes."

Kelly felt light-headed. That was her clinic, where she had donated blood in exchange for money when she had been unemployed. "Switch on all the cameras inside the City Road Clinic."

"There are twenty-one cameras in total."

"Display them all at once."

The screens lit up with a patchwork of camera angles showing desk corners, floor tiles, chairs, white walls—all topsy-turvy. Thankfully, each view was numbered. She stepped back and refocused.

She needed only one of the images to verify the maelstrom's connection to the blood clinic. "INNS, zoom in on view three."

A clear wrapper rested on the counter, similar to the one the maelstrom in the black van had torn off with his teeth.

"Zoom in on the counter." The overhead lights bounced off the glossy wrapping, making it difficult to see its details. It wasn't working. "Gather a list of medical suppliers to this clinic and display them all."

In seconds, over a hundred suppliers were up on the screen, way faster than Jerko had ever delivered. "Look up each one."

"May we ask what is Kelly Blackwell looking for?"

Kelly realized her search request to this chamber was the equivalent of asking Leonardo da Vinci to draw a stick figure of a man. "I'm looking for the supplier of syringes to the clinic."

Almost instantly, the name Carrigon Ltd. popped up.

"Makers of the DreamMaker."

"Correct."

The chamber was way faster, way smarter, and far more capable than Jerko was ever designed to be. "What other companies supply blue syringes?"

"No other company supplies the blue syringes."

"Why not?"

"They are a specially designated syringe used to deliver a combination of chemical and technological liquids."

"What is the name of that liquid?"

"We cannot release that information. It is classified."

So, the EvePR1 was a passcode with limits after all. "Who has classified the information?"

"The Government of the United Kingdom."

Kelly rubbed her face. "Any name in particular?"

"The name is also classified."

The name, not names. "Did you say one person classified the information?"

"Correct."

She reeled back. So, the plasma clinics were administering some chem-tech serum under the aegis of the government, and only one person knew about it. How was that even possible? How could one person have so much power? The maelstrom in the van administered her with something, but she wasn't sure it was the same chem-tech serum the clinics were distributing. She gripped her head. How the hell was that chem-tech serum connected to Christopher? And the Truth Laws? How was the blood-soaked article she carried in her backpack tied in? She squeezed her eyes. Without the name of the serum and a sample of it, convincing hard evidence, these trails could lead anywhere or nowhere. More importantly, she couldn't prove anything. "Wait."

She was carrying the chem-tech serum in her veins, but she wasn't dead. Maybe the maelstrom had given her half a dose. But he had definitely given it to her; she had felt the needlepoint break her skin and the ocean of obliviousness had swallowed her whole. The look on the maelstrom's face when she regained consciousness had been one of genuine surprise. He hadn't expected her conscious, much less on her feet and capable of fighting. Perhaps he had expected her to be half dead, if not fully dead, like Geneva.

The chem-tech serum was surely still running in her veins, and it would probably circulate in her system for at least another few hours. She had time, but not much. She had to hurry and get to the Zone.

She glanced at the tablet beside her. The eyeball cameras streamed their feed of empty streets. Taking a deep breath, she placed the Fi headset on her head. The chamber screens cleared of all the camera angles and turned white.

A single black cursor flashed on the screen.

She leaned back, finding a comfortable spot in the chair, and scanned her eyes over the bloody article in her shaking hand.

She transferred the opening paragraph of Christopher's research, then the next paragraph, and the next, until all the text in Christopher's research had been transferred into the system.

"Chamber, point the cameras surrounding the Zone at the Zone building and stream the view to the Cicada forum."

"Tasks complete."

"EvePR1 close."

Kelly placed the Fi headset on its stand and picked up the tablet.

Rain was drizzling down on the lenses, blurring the view, but she could still see the road on the screen and the Elite Squad fast approaching.

SIXTY-ONE

"C'MON, C'MON," Josh uttered, gripping the phone.

"Yo," Harry said.

Relief flooded through Josh, quickly followed by irritation that Harry sounded so casual. "Did you get a chance to look at what I sent you?"

"Yeah, but are you sure you sent me the right document?"

"What's the problem?"

"I gotta tell you, I'm not into that new age synchronicity, in-tune-with-the-universe crap. We have AI all around us registering everything we do, matching us to messages it knows interest us. Sometimes I wonder if AI knows us better than we know ourselves."

"What are you going on about?"

"The code you sent me is similar to code that's been circulating in a forum for a couple of days. But this version you sent me—"

Confounded, Josh interrupted Harry. "I was told it belonged to Christopher Mallow. It's not code though."

"It's code, dude. And your version has a few modifications."

Josh rubbed his forehead. "One second, Harry." He opened up the email he had received from Jerko and clicked on the attachment. Kelly had said she'd send Christopher Mallow's research, but Harry was right. It was code. "Jerko must've sent the wrong file."

"Jerko?"

"Kelly's digital warden. She calls it Jerko?" Harry's laughter pierced Josh's eardrums. "So, this code came from Kelly?"

"It isn't her code, and it isn't what she meant to send through. Sorry for wasting your time."

"You can't just give me code and expect me to go away. I'm not one of your girlfriends. You have to hear this. It's actually kind of freaky."

Josh glanced at his watch. There was still time before his meeting with Damian. "You got me, Harry. What's freaky?"

"There's a similar but incomplete code being circulated in the forums. Whoever put it up seemed to be fishing for a hotshot coder to decipher it. If that happened, the OP would sell the complete version. I've seen that sort of shit before."

OP was the quick way of saying original poster. "Did a hotshot decipher it?"

"Hell no. Anyone with half a brain wouldn't openly work on this."

"So what's the code about?"

"It's a virus. To corrupt the INNS system."

Josh's scalp prickled. "So, whatever I sent you targets the AI system in the echo chambers?"

"Looks like it. But this code has some variations to the one I saw in the forum. And I'll tell you something else. It has some funky theoretical assumptions too."

"Like what?"

"Anxiety is in the code."

"Anxiety? As in the emotion? Computers don't feel jack shit."

"Very bizarre, I know, and purely theoretical. So, I looked into it and came across some interesting models."

A shiver rattled down Josh's spine. "Fucking Frankenstein."

"Yep, there are some real crazies out there," Harry said. "Fortunately, this code is based on pure theory, and it seems to be assuming humans will be the test subjects."

"Double fucking Frankenstein meets Ed Gein."

"Who?"

"Never mind. Go on."

"We all pretty much agree that the majority of humans learn via their visual sense. In fact, ninety percent of us do. This has been an established fact for decades. Off the back of that, scientists developed a theoretical model of how our visual system encodes the flood of information striking our retinas. That was fifty years ago. The theory held that a process similar to image compression, called sparse coding, takes place in the lowest layers of the visual cortex, making later stages of the visual system more efficient. By the time the information gets to the visual cortex, the brain is representing it as sparse code. Josh, are you still with me?"

"Barely, but go on."

"Recently, neuroscientists have replicated that sparse code for advanced artificial intelligence. They call it, well, sparse code, haha."

Josh felt like a rank amateur hacker listening to Harry.

"Artificial Intelligence has developed into something called deep learning...is this TMI?"

Josh perked up hearing about deep learning libraries, something he did know about. "So far, so good."

"Good," Harry replied. "So, you'll get this next part. Computer scientists have developed neural networks as a machine learning algorithm modeled after how the human mind works by building associations on top of each other. A base of information is taken from the learning libraries, so computer scientists don't have to reinvent the wheel every time they create a new AI. The structure receives input, performs calculations, and then uses the output to solve the problem."

"Harry," Josh said. "Who has the coding, scientific, and robotic skills to work all this out?"

"Beats the shit out of me, and I don't know what Kelly has to do with any of this. All I know is that this code has provided a circuit breaker of sorts on how to interrupt the classification and prediction algorithms...by inducing anxiety."

No one in the Resistance had this level of sophisticated knowledge, much less Kelly. "The whole thing sounds crazy, Harry."

"If you ever find the person, or team, that put this code together, I'd like to meet them," Harry said in an expectant tone as though he were fishing for a meeting.

"I don't know who wrote it. If I ever find out, I'll let you know."

Harry sighed. "I'll hold you to that, Josh. So yeah, the code supposes that an anxious person can disrupt algorithms by transferring a ghosting effect of their data to the AI, unknowingly, of course. The computer system won't be able to tell the difference between the real data and the Trojan horse perturbed data. By the time the computer figures it out, the system will not have learned a damn thing. It's impossible for it to get the information it needs to perform its functions. And that is what defeats artificial intelligence. Bada bing."

Josh knew how to mask the SS cameras, how to hack into emails, how to disguise his digital footprint, but here he was out of his depth. Harry was on a whole different level, and Josh gained a newfound respect for his prowess. Still, Josh needed to reshape this theory into a simple, practical explanation. He inhaled. "Okay, let me get this straight. A person—let's call that person Kelly—has elevated anxiety levels."

"Josh, let's keep this theoretical."

"Okay, let's call her Erica. Erica is an anxious person. She defaults to imagining the worst things to be true. Let's say she tries to focus on uploading an image of a house into an echo chamber and is successful in the transfer. Some of the data she transfers will be a blueprint of a thought rather than the actual thought?"

"Yes. The computer can't tell the difference between a visual outline of the house and a real house, or the outline of a clock and a real clock. It only sees an approximation and automatically categorizes it."

"The outline is what you call the blueprint?" Josh asked.

"Yes."

"So, the outline or blueprint can be a fake."

"Yes," Harry said. "Or the blueprint can be filled with corrosive data rather than the actual representative data. And, the code has provided the way to fill in the blueprint with the corrosive data."

"So, if we can feed perturbed sparse code into any echo chamber," Josh said, taking another deep breath, "it should deliver it to the Zone and start to erode the system from within?"

"Yes. The system won't even know what it's ingesting, and by the time it unpacks the data, it's too late," Harry said.

"It's genius."

"Don't get all excited, Josh. We're talking theory. For one, you need a computer that feels, and that just doesn't exist. It's a cool idea, though."

Josh's watch buzzed. It was Percy. He declined to answer. "Have Cicada coders come to the same conclusion?"

"Like I said, no one's discussed it openly on the forum. But if it took me a while to understand, you can imagine what the public's reaction would be. They will be totally clueless."

"You said a version of it had already been floating on Cicada. When was that?"

"A couple of days ago," Harry said. "I was sitting here at home, online, doing my thing, and it popped up out of nowhere like some alien being. It was a hybrid Python code, mixed with something else. All AI coding stuff."

So someone was already in possession of this code, and they had dropped it into the forum. They were fishing all right. "Harry, this is a total head trip, but I have to go. I'm meeting up with Kelly later tonight."

"I heard there's a contract out on her."

Josh reeled back. "What do you mean? Where did you hear that?"

"Just something I heard. Could be nothing. Tell her to send me the right file."

The Resistance had appointed Josh to the job, and though he accepted it, he would never carry it out. He had to find a way around it, and the best way—maybe the only way—was shining light on the sordid lot. "Harry, something's about to go down. Announce to everyone on Cicada they should watch the Zone."

"I have my reputation to think about. If nothing happens—"

"Harry, there's a good chance you'll see plenty of glory."

SIXTY-TWO

IN THE FIRST quadrant on Kelly's tablet, she could see the Elite Squad lined up along the wall of the chamber, still as rocks.

In another quadrant, a government-issued BMW rolled across the glistening tarmac. The vehicle came to a halt in the shadow of a building, near enough to the chamber for the eyeball camera to transmit the view.

"EvePr1 open."

The lights dimmed.

"Identify license plate number WN9500."

"No such registration exists."

In quadrant three, a handful of videographers and journalists bunched up behind a barrier. Their handler stood to their side, speaking into his watch. She hadn't expected her peers to be standing on the other side of the door, cameras at the ready for the moment the Elite Squad swept in and dragged her out, hands bound, face on full display, identity exposed. Their cameras would broadcast her face online, and within minutes, the world would know her identity, her reputation as a Truth Laws fugitive cemented forever more.

Panic descended on her, and she searched for the fire escape, but there was no exit in sight. The only way out was through the front door.

"I need an escape route."

"This INNS location does not have a specific fire escape exit."

"But if there's a fire in here, and the main entrance is blocked, what then?"

"In the highly unlikely event there is a fire in the INNS, all the windows are lowered."

"Can the windows be lowered one at a time?"

"For maintenance purposes, yes."

She glanced at the windows. They all faced the front of the building. Regardless of which of them opened, she'd still be walking straight into the Elite Squad's hands in the glare of camera lights. It was no use. Without a backdoor route, she was stuck. Maybe she could walk out holding Christopher's research in front of her face, forcing the cameras to capture every word. Knowing the algorithms, they'd instantly blur the page. But even if she was physically trapped, maybe there was a way to scupper the camera feeds and prevent them from broadcasting her arrest to the web. "How about a digital escape?"

Movement in quadrant three caught her eye. The journalists' handler clapped his hands. Camera lights flooded the chamber all at once.

She flicked an eye at the entrance and back to the tablet. "Chamber, can you identify the names of the photographers standing outside?"

The chamber reeled off a list of six names.

Kelly counted six behind the blue line. So, the seventh, the handler, whoever he was, was not a photographer. "Who is the seventh one near the photographers?"

"That individual's name is Percy Mandeville."

Josh's agent, the rat. "Send a message to Josh Munro. Tell him his agent is at the Covent Garden hub, collecting footage of my impending arrest, and send a message to Harry White to interrupt the live stream broadcast of this INNS immediately."

"I am equipped to scramble the broadcasting signals of the surrounding devices as long as they are within twenty feet of the chamber's perimeter."

She gasped with amazement. She should've known this chamber was way more capable than any tech she had encountered to date. "Can you reroute the stream itself?"

"Yes. As long as their streaming app is on my list, I can reroute the stream."

Kelly began to speak, half holding her breath for fear the chamber wouldn't be able to carry out her next command. "Reroute the live broadcast and send it to Harry White with a note to not broadcast until Kelly Blackwell gives the order. Let those photographers think they are filming live."

"Complete."

She sucked in a quick breath, awed by the chamber's technical capabilities. She readjusted her position and stood evenly on both feet. The eyeball cameras' live stream was still active. The chamber targeted the correct frequency. Movement in quadrant one on her tablet caught her attention. The Squad's commander—Omar?—positioned himself at the head of the troopers. His eyes, though concealed under a black visor, faced the chamber. He signaled a command and a red reflector flashed across his bicep.

A burst of sweat coated her palms. She was as ready as she'd ever be. "In thirty minutes, revert to your standard programming. EvePR1 close."

Camera lights blinded her as Elite Squad shadows feathered the windows.

She braced herself. This was it.

A crash resounded throughout the chamber. Static crackled in the air. Their boots hit the pristine chamber floor.

Surrounded, Kelly held up her hands. One trooper stepped forward and ran his hands down her back, her arms, her waist. He pulled out the Jagkommando from her holster and placed it in a bag along with the Roseman tablet, then he tied her hands behind her back. "The Truth Laws fugitive is in custody."

"Take her to the Zone."

The trooper escorted her out the door. The camera lights blinded her. In spite of the commotion, a smile waltzed across her lips. Finally, things were going her way.

FIGHTING his instinct to turn back, Josh hustled in a westerly direction away from Kelly's flat. He glanced over his shoulder, slung Kelly's backpack across one side of his chest and his camera bag on the other.

No sooner had he turned the corner than two men came up from behind. Josh hid his fear and steadied his limbs, keeping his stride steady.

"Keep walking straight to the staircase," one man said, the stench of day-old garlic hanging off his breath.

These were the escorts Damian had said to expect. "What took you so long?"

They walked up two flights of metal steps, their steel-toed boots clanging against the stairs. A shiny black limo with opaque windows was parked at the top of the staircase.

Josh rocked on his heels, trying to dispel his tension. "I see Mr. Winters sent his best car."

One of the men opened the back door. Glancing at Josh's bags, he held out his hand.

"They're staying with me."

Indifferent, the man thrummed the air. "If you want to see Mr. Winters..."

Reluctantly, Josh slipped the bags off. "If anything happens to these bags, you're dead. I promise you that."

Josh slid onto the backseat, and the second henchman climbed in behind him, taking up the seat across from him.

"Where's Mr. Winters?"

The door lock clicked. The henchman said nothing.

"Man of few words, I see," Josh said as the car purred to life.

Though Josh knew Damian Winters had sent the car, he didn't know how this journey would end.

SIXTY-THREE

30 January

THE ELITE SQUAD's prisoner transport vehicle came to a halt in front of the Zone, shoving Kelly forward. Somewhere inside the monstrous building was the room that housed the echo chambers' vast server, the heart of the beast.

A trooper opened the back door. The night air carried in a brassy aroma, and she could somehow identify iron and dampness in the mix. Troopers grabbed her arms and pulled her out of the van, the brush and sway of their uniforms scratching her eardrums. She stumbled onto the tarmac, and a cold breeze swiped her face like a heavy-handed slap.

The low hum of the city in the distance echoed loudly in her ears, and the salt in the air brushed under her nose as though she were standing right over the Thames River.

The troopers pushed her inside the building and led her into a windowless room, not unlike the one in which she had met Lydia Rackham, only this one had a screen.

"Wrong room," she said. "You need to take me to the server room." The trooper shoved her onto a chair. She couldn't see his eyes under his visor, but she could smell his body burst with angry sweat. "Was that really necessary? Geneva Convention and all that."

He whipped out a rope.

She caught a whiff of a woodsy scotch whiskey off his skin. Vintage 1976. "You get paid well."

"I do this for pleasure." He pulled the rope between his hands. "Before we get started, if you want a drink, there's water over there. If you dare."

Droplets dripped down the side of the water jug, and she could almost taste the cool liquid on her tongue, soothing her parched, scratchy throat. Unwilling to give in, she remained sitting.

"Where did you get the knife?"

She looked up at the ceiling. So, this was about the knife, the Jagkommando, the one Omar had given her. By having it in her possession, they knew one of their own had turned on them, and they wanted to know who. "I found it."

"Where?"

"I can't remember."

He tightened the rope around his knuckles.

"If you were going to kill me, you would've done it on the way here."

He chuckled. "You think I want to kill you?" He placed his hand on her shoulder.

She sank her teeth into his gloved hand and locked her jaw in tight.

He knocked her head hard with his fist. The rope scraped her face, and it burned, stinging hot. Bitter liquid soaked her tongue—her own blood—but there was also something else: metal-like, just like that metallic taste she experienced during her meeting with Lydia Rackham.

"I tried to be nice to you," he said.

She spat out blood. Feeling woozy and light-headed, she let her head fall back.

The door crashed open.

Omar hurtled at the trooper and pounded him with a taser.

The trooper twitched on the floor.

Omar's frantic eyes looked at her. "Did he inject you with anything?"

Kelly bolted up from the chair, but her legs quickly slackened. Her foot caught on the trooper's leg, and she crashed onto the floor. Struggling to her feet, she felt as though she were moving in slow motion and gradually losing control of her body.

Omar grabbed hold of her, lifted her, and flung her limp body over his shoulder.

THE RUSH of blood to her head flooded her vision white, her arms drained of strength, too weak to fight. All she could muster was, "Where are you taking me?"

Omar carried Kelly down a hallway lined with trolleys stacked with blocky processors, the kind that had come out decades before she was born. They passed a room filled with vacuum tubes and magnetic memory drums, tabletop transistors, and octagon-shaped circuits. A transistor zipped to life.

Her body heated deep inside. The world around started to blink in and out. A yellow biohazard warning sign flashed across her mind. She saw a hydrogen bomb explode in a desert. An oblong conference table, polished to a high shine, surrounded by men and women in a room with wall-to-wall mirrors and a chandelier. She blinked in and out of consciousness. "What did you do to me?"

"There was nano-serum in the trooper's glove, the one you bit down on. We need to hurry."

She swayed against him, her arms limp.

At the door of a white room, he gently laid her on the ground, and she shivered on the cold floor. Omar swept his palm against the scanner. At the sound of the door's soft click, he picked her up and stepped inside.

Her eyelids drooped heavily. She struggled to remain upright when he set her down on the other side of the door. She could feel her head lolling to one side.

He pushed her upright. "Sit tight."

He homed in on a low-level glass fridge, one of many lining the wall, and slid open its door. Vapor flowed from the storage unit. The miniature vials on the fridge shelves clanked as he twisted them to read the labels.

The edges of his body blurred. "Where the hell are we, Omar?" Her muscles quivered.

Two glass vials clicked in his hand. "You need the final dose."

"Dose? Of what?"

"Remember the wine?"

How could she forget? After drinking what tasted like vinegar, she had fallen sick the next morning. It was only after that the visions started, the nightmarish sights that made her think she was losing her mind. It terrified her then, and it terrified her now.

"I dosed the wine with serum to kill the nano-bot in your head. I guess your system overpowered it."

"You laced the wine with chem-tech serum?" She coughed. "You slipped that junk into the wine, junk I didn't need? You fucked with my life."

His hand froze on a vial. "That nanotech in your system has nothing to do with me."

"I don't have nanotechnology in my body."

"You visited the plasma clinic."

"Ages ago. Well before any of this." She wrung her hands as she thought back to the last time she was at the clinic. "They—"

"They used the plasma clinics to screen for potential hosts."

She cradled her head in her hands. "And I thought I was the crazy one." She rolled onto the floor and reached for the door.

Omar stood over her. "You don't have the gene to block the nanotech from embedding in your system. You were the perfect potential."

Her hand hit the floor. "So you're saying that when I sold my blood to the clinic, they found me."

"To date, you have been identified as the primary potential."

The whole story was so unbelievable. If this nanotech existed, there'd be a whistleblower, talk on Cicada, Harry flapping his gums. Something. She glanced at the door and back to Omar, calculating the speed she needed to rush out and lock him in, but her legs were too weak to carry her far.

"The NHS holds a national database of all our health records. They used it to whittle down potentials. I found out about all of this when I was assigned to you. The government likes to appear to be useless at planning," he said. "But I assure you they know exactly what they're doing."

Heather Mallow's article on the panic attack syndrome came to Kelly's mind. She leaned into the wall for support.

Omar placed two vials on the counter. One was filled with bright orange, the other fluorescent green. "By the time a government program hits the news, it's gone through research and development years earlier. All the government needs then are guinea pigs to test on and journalists to sell the idea."

She powered her arms against the floor and lifted, testing her strength. "So, this nano-bot program would have been in development years ago?"

He nodded. "By now they will have paid off or gotten rid of everyone who had been involved."

Her skin tingled, her whole body felt light. She managed to get on her feet, wincing in pain. The Fi headsets, the plasma clinic, the Zone, the echo chambers, each was a part of the nanotech program. All protected by the Truth Laws? To say that she had it in her system had to be a lie. "You shot Geneva up with this stuff, and she died."

Omar looked at Kelly. "It has different effects on different people."

Standing upright, a sense of urgent calmness came over her. "I will find a way to get this story out."

"Kelly, we both want the same thing. Just one more dose and that thing in your head will die for good. You have to trust me. There's no other way."

She mobilized every nerve and muscle in her body and moved toward the door. Nausea swirled around her, she folded over. Her head throbbed with the blood rushing to her crown. "You're as crazy as the rest of them."

SIXTY-FOUR

THE MEDIA TYCOON's black car pulled up outside the Zone and parked under a row of street lamps, well away from the candy-cane-striped barrier.

Damian and Josh stepped out of the car, and Josh immediately scoped for cameras. Trees ruffled in the night as wind piped through the bare branches. Unless cameras were hidden in the trees, Josh and Damian were out of SS sight.

The driver rolled down his window. "Anything else, boss?"

Damian pulled out a card. Glancing down, Josh made out the name PC Blake in black lettering. Damian spotted Josh's spying eye and shot him a piercing look. Josh glanced away, trying to pretend he'd seen nothing. Damian proceeded to hand his bodyguard the card. "If I'm not out in a couple of hours, call him. He's one of ours."

"I'm going to need the bags." Josh said.

The driver slung the bags out the window. The plastic and metal clanged when they hit the tarmac.

Josh could almost feel his bones splintering. "Jesus Christ, what's wrong with you! We need this equipment to get in." He scrambled to his knees and carefully unzipped both bags, expecting to see a million little pieces of plastic and glass swimming at the bottom. Thankfully, all the equipment was intact. "Fucking idiot," he said, getting in one last jab as payback for the earlier rough handling.

"Stay close by," Damian ordered the driver.

"We have to get past the barrier with this." Josh showed him the neutralizer. "I need to attach it to your bare chest."

Damian let out a grunt. "Couldn't we have done this in the car?"

"Your brilliant idiot held my bags captive, remember?"

Damian huffed and unbuttoned his shirt.

"This isn't exactly my idea of fun either," Josh said.

Having photographed countless nude bodies, he'd seen it all, both men and women. Touching a man, though, was a whole different matter he never relished. Quickly, he fastened the neutralizer to Damian's hairless flesh like he was loading bunny ears onto a lion's head.

Fifteen minutes later, Josh attached it to himself. When it was done making them both appear like Kelly to the cameras, Josh brought out the fingerprint scanner. "We're ready."

"You go first," Damian said.

Josh held his breath and glided past the candy-cane barrier. The neutralizer worked. He would never have thought to project Kelly's biometric data onto Damian and himself with the neutralizer. No wonder it had become illegal. He turned to Damian. "Your turn."

Damian stroked his coat as though it were a pet and walked right past the barrier. Relief washed over Josh. They made it; they crossed the Red Sea—all without a glitch. The front door lumbered open, clearly on auto, and they glided into a bright, empty, soulless lobby.

"So? Where's the information you promised?"

Josh pointed to what looked like an atrium on the other side of the lobby. "I'll meet you in there."

"You said we'd find out who killed my daughter, and all I've done is enter this godforsaken place," Damian grumbled. "I've been patient long enough." He turned to leave.

"Kelly will get you the information you want."

Damian halted in his stride. "You should have said so from the start."

He tugged on his coat lapels and walked across the shiny floor toward the atrium. "I'll wait two hours, Josh, and not a minute longer."

Glad to see the back of him, Josh now had to locate cell fifty-three; the cell Omar had mentioned Christopher was held in.

Both bags slung across his chest, Josh pressed the button for the lift and headed to the basement.

SIXTY-FIVE

THE LIGHTS FLICKERED above Kelly as though to the beat of her pounding heart. She willed her muscles to move, but her limbs were heavy and rigid as though leather straps were tethering her to the ground.

Omar plunged the needle into a vial. The blue-tipped syringe filled with the bright orange liquid.

She gripped the counter and frantically swept her eye over the room for a weapon, something threatening, anything at all. The secure room was surrounded by thick walls of reinforced glass, locked storage cabinets, and steel trays clipped to the counter. Not a single scalpel in sight. In the end, she had only her voice. "Stay away." Even to herself, she sounded vulnerable and weak.

"I can't." His eyes remained focused on the syringe. "I have no other choice."

She had to delay him, distract him, buy time—for what, she wasn't sure, but it was better than nothing. "Just like you and your maelstrom friends had no choice but to kill Geneva?"

He lowered the vial. "The State's thugs? You can identify them?" He squinted past the syringe, seemingly working out a connection. "Your nano-bot must be responding to their tags."

"Every time I see one of those motherfuckers, my PTSD kicks on. That's it. Not that crap you're talking about." He was staring into space. She had seen that look on his face before; he wasn't desperate or worried. He was in the same room with her, but his mind was somewhere else. "You were always wrapped up in your own world. And now I understand why. You carried a hefty secret, and you projected it onto me."

He swayed on his feet as though a specter whirled inside him. "Not even the PM knows about the...what do you call them? The maelstrom."

There, behind him, she spotted a pair of mini scissors. A spark of hope ignited in her chest. The small pair of scissors was the only weapon in the room, and they were on the other side from where she stood. Strategizing on how best to get herself past Omar, she dropped to the floor.

He squirted serum from the needle. The bright orange liquid sprinkled the floor tiles, and from her position, it seemed to sparkle under the lights.

She needed to keep him talking. "You knew about the government AI program the entire time we were together," she said as she crept along the wall.

"No. I learned about the Eve program over time."

Why was that word familiar? Oliver's code...it contained the word Eve, too. Which meant Christopher knew, as did Heather. They all knew. The pieces were slotting into place, and the knowledge fortified her resolve, but it also left her feeling dismayed that no one had told her—an all-too-familiar pattern of her life. Everyone was in it for themselves. She nearly lost her life fighting to get the pieces of this story together, and she wasn't going to stop now. Summoning every bit of strength she had, she continued to drag herself across the floor.

"I know what you're trying to do, Kelly. Don't." He lolled the syringe between his fingers. "If you don't get rid of that thing in your head, you'll be a monkey in a cage, held by the State, here in the Zone for the rest of your life. After fifty or sixty years, when you're about to die, they'll find a way to keep your body alive just to keep your brain active."

With all her strength, she pulled herself up to the counter and stretched out her trembling hand toward the scissors.

He slammed her hand down.

Her palm landed on top of the small, stainless steel blades, her last-chance weapon. She straightened up and stood face-to-face with her killer.

His dark eyes sharpened. "Listen." Omar put his finger to his lips. The sound of heels echoed in the passageway. "Hurry, we don't have much time."

SIXTY-SIX

JOSH DESCENDED IN THE ELEVATOR, and the temperature cooled, sending goosebumps up his arms. His faith in Omar was stretched, but Kelly had called, proving that he had fulfilled his part of their deal. Still, Josh couldn't shake his misgivings as he stepped out of the elevator and into a dark vestibule.

Tubular walls and arched ceilings came to a T-junction. One hundred cells to the right and another hundred to the left. According to Omar, Christopher was in cell fifty-three, but the corridors seemed to stretch the farther he looked down them. He stood back, taking in the enormity of the floor space he'd have to cover. An impatient Damian was waiting upstairs. He wasn't going to wait all night. Josh jogged down the right-hand side of the junction, his footsteps reverberating behind him as though the Zone's belly swallowed the sound and burped it back up.

Iron doors embossed the stone wall, each with a number and an eye-slit.

He passed cell twenty-three.

Bed coils squeaked in the distance behind him.

He whipped around. A combination of trepidation and excitement swept through him. "Hello?"

The hum in his voice ricocheted down the narrow passage.

The movement had come from somewhere up ahead. He hastened down the hall, the numbers ascending. At last, he reached cell fifty-three.

A heavy iron padlock hung off the door. The thrill of finding the cell drained away. The scrambler was useless against an analog lock. "Shit."

He banged on the door. "Chris? You in there?"

A squeak sounded on the other side of the door, and a voice trickled through the eye slit.

Josh's heart leaped. "It's me. Josh. Hang on. I've got to find a way through the lock."

He unzipped the bags and rummaged past his camera, the fingerprint scanner, the neutralizer, flimsy electrodes, a tablet, a Fi headset, a hard drive—in search of a pin. The gaping bags displayed all their wares, but not one of the gadgets could help get Christopher free.

His gleeful excitement plunged and shattered against the stone walls. "Not a goddamn basic pair of pliers!"

He fell back on his heels and stared at the lock, hoping an ingenious idea would light up in his mind. He drew a blank. Desperate, he scanned the bags again.

His N16 camera rested on the bag's soft folds.

He knew every millimeter of his N16, and he knew it had the pins to unlock the door. But, in order to get to them, he'd have to crack it open.

He cradled his head, waiting for God to deliver an alternative idea, but he was in hell itself, and all that was holy had deserted this place long ago. He looked at his N16 and nursed it between his hands. He shut his eyes, stood, and clenched his stomach tight. Without further thought, he hurled his precious N16 onto the concrete.

The lens shattered, the plastic cracked, the metal bellowed.

"Josh? What's going on out there?"

Christopher's voice broke through the anguish feasting on Josh's heart. He wiped his forehead and finally opened his eyes. "Just had to..." There it was: the metal pin that was holding the camera's board in place. "I got you, Chris."

He shook off the feelings of devastation and desperation, stepped over the debris, and got to work on the lock.

It unhitched. The cell door swung open.

Christopher Mallow lay flat on a cot. His pale face hadn't seen sunlight in weeks. The old man's collarbones protruded through paper-thin skin, his bony fingers were blue, his veins protruding. The sight brought a tear to Josh's eye. Chris blinked, slow and deliberate. His jaw slackened.

Josh lifted Mallow and supported him in his arms. "What did they do to you?"

"I chose to strike."

Josh gently laid him down on the cot and went to the sink. The faucet ground with rust. Water splashed inside a dirty glass. He couldn't let Mallow drink from a germ-plagued vessel, so he cupped water in his hands and let it slowly drip on the old man's parted lips.

Christopher looked at Josh with searching eyes. He went to speak, but he coughed. Watching the man struggle, Josh shook off devastation. No way did he have the strength to make it down the endless corridor, but Josh had to get Christopher out before the dark, dreary tentacles of this place sucked out his soul. The bed coils squeaked as he helped Christopher from the bed. "We have to get to the lift and meet Kelly."

The skin on the old man's neck flexed as he swallowed. "The Resistance didn't want her to know."

"Know what?"

Christopher's eyes glazed over. "That she's an AI. I wanted to tell her, but in the end, the Resistance refused and took you off the mission to make sure you didn't accidentally tell her anything."

Josh's stomach clenched. Christopher was further gone than he feared. "Kelly's a flesh-and-blood human, Chris. They wanted me to kill her, to prove my loyalty to them. They knew where you were and they left you here to rot. The mission is over."

Christopher sighed. "It's my mission, and it's still on." The words seemed to enliven his spirit. "Give me your arm. I have to find...oh, what's his name now..."

Josh sidled up to Christopher and offered his steady shoulder.

His bony finger dug into Josh's collarbone. "Omar, the inside man. That's right, Omar."

The information blew a firestorm of emotion through Josh's gut. Omar, a double agent? Had he ordered Kelly's death? Maybe Josh hadn't heard right. "Omar is working with the Resistance?"

Christopher's eyes seemed to twinkle in the dimly lit cell. "He's the stand-in leader. Without him, we couldn't have pulled this off. He gave you the Abbott assignment via your agent." He coughed.

Omar, being an inside man, lined up, but to say that Omar was a leader in the Resistance didn't make sense. Christopher must've been confused, Josh concluded, straightening up.

"We still have work to do," Christopher went on, oblivious. "If you want to protect Kelly, and I know you do, you can't let her upload anything into the mainframe. You'll have to transfer the code yourself without her knowing. It's safer that way."

Josh wasn't sure how much he could trust what the man was saying. "Chris," he said, in as calm but firm a voice as he could convey. "Kelly's already here in the Zone."

Mallow's eyes flashed with fear. "There is a final way, but it was something I wanted to avoid." His voice was hoarse and low as he shuffled out of his cell. "If Kelly has seen the code, all she has to do is connect herself to the mainframe. The code will download automatically and spread like a virus, transmitting itself into every single computer in the land." He clenched Josh's arm. "But, Josh, it could kill her."

Though he was a full-grown man, Christopher's body weight against him felt as light as a cloud, and his words sounded fantastical. It was useless arguing with the old man, who was clearly puttering along the outskirts of senility.

Footsteps echoed down the staircase.

"We need to hurry."

SIXTY-SEVEN

THE LAB DOOR CRASHED OPEN, and Elite Squad troopers swarmed the room.

Terror swept through Kelly, propelling nausea around her stomach and straight up to her head. Guns, troopers, her own hands—all in double vision. She had only heard heels clicking down the corridor, not an entire platoon of Elite Squad troopers. But then she remembered how they could move, catlike.

Lydia Rackham entered the lab, her stiletto heels clicking against the concrete floor. She planted herself in the middle of the room, her long cashmere coat, unbuttoned, swirled around her ankles.

The troopers lifted their guns all at once.

The sight of all those lasers, any of which could go off with a slip of a finger, froze Kelly to her spot.

"Kelly, we didn't come for you," Lydia said. "You can leave."

Kelly glanced at Omar. Red dots dappled his face and body, not hers, and a slight sense of relief eased over her, relief that she wouldn't have to fight Omar and that killer serum in her weakened state. Slowly, she backed away from him.

He grabbed Kelly around the waist and spun her around, her back pressed against his chest.

She screamed.

They both faced Lydia.

Kelly shook in the arms of the desperate man making sudden, desperate moves. "You're making things worse," she said, forcing her voice through her constricted throat.

"Listen to your friend, Omar. She's right."

He pointed a syringe at her exposed neck, and Kelly could feel droplets of the cold serum land densely on her skin. A chill went down her spine.

Rackham's eyes widened. "Put it down, Omar."

The trooper's lasers speckled his fingers and the syringe. Faced with a wall of guns, Kelly felt her knees go weak. Omar gripped Kelly's waist tighter and propped her up against him. "You must take me for a fool, Lydia."

"Not at all."

Click. The lights shut off. The lab plunged into darkness.

His grip around Kelly's waist loosened for a moment as though he shuffled back, farther behind her. Her knees dipped, and then he propped her back up. Then, a cold steel tip pricked Kelly's skin, and all the muscles in her neck jolted. Her knees folded. She could feel the syrup zip through her and fuse with her blood. The kill-serum was flowing through her veins, and it wouldn't be long before darkness swamped her and took her with it. It was done. He got what he wanted. She could do nothing but concede. She dropped in a heap.

Boots swished along the floor. The room lit up with a dull red light. The noxious smell of burned flesh rose into Kelly's nose. The overhead lights flickered on, diffusing the red glow. Troopers lined the wall as though they hadn't moved an inch. Omar lay next to her on the floor, so close his breath puffed into her eyes. Blood squirted from his neck.

Seeing him lying there, helpless, disarmed, she needed to know. "Why?"

"It's not what it seems." Omar's eyes fluttered. "Find Josh. Find

Mallow. He's alive," he whispered. He closed his eyes. "Tell the world the truth."

He unclenched his fist. A glass vial rolled out and clinked on the floor. It was empty. The syringe rested in his other hand, a drop of fluorescent green serum at its tip.

She hoisted herself with her arms, and surprisingly, rose to her feet. Stunned at her ease of movement and her clear head, she scraped up the vial and looked at Omar. "What's this?"

He took a breath and a faint smile curled his lips. Then he was gone.

KELLY STARED down at her trembling hands, covered in Omar's blood.

"You do know he killed Geneva Winters." Lydia's voice shredded the silence.

"He killed her under your orders, Lydia."

"Kelly, he had to face justice. But you're safe now."

Lydia didn't deny she had ordered the murder, which meant that Omar had been telling the truth. Tears rolled down her cheeks. He hadn't been trying to kill her. He had been working with Christopher, who was still alive, and with Josh and the Resistance. He intended to take down the Zone in his own way. Omar had been on their side the whole time. But what good was that now? He was gone.

Lydia was the one who had lied about Christopher being dead, and now this trickster was trying on her latest costume as an angel of redemption.

Two troopers approached Omar's body.

"We have to remove the body from the room, Kelly," Lydia said. "Decontaminate the area as soon as possible."

The troopers lifted Omar's body from the ground.

Kelly watched the troopers cart his body out of the room. "He was head of the Elite Squad—"

"He was a criminal," Lydia said, a hard edge in her voice. "He turned against his duty and his oath. But it doesn't involve you. It's time for you to go home."

Kelly stared at the pool of blood on the floor. From the moment she pursued this story, her life was knocked off a cliff. She scrambled to gather the pieces, nearly losing her mind, nearly dying. But she could prove this story and tell the world. If she left now, they'd keep coming after her. No point pretending otherwise. But they had taken so much from her, and it was time she got something back. She stilled. "I'm not really free, though, am I, Lydia?"

For the first time, a look of uncertainty flared across Lydia's face. "I promise that as soon as you walk out the door, your life will revert to normal. I'll see to it, personally, that you get your old job back, too."

"I might try a different profession."

"Why would you give it up?"

"In case you hadn't noticed, the Truth Laws are a killer. We're under threat at every turn. And if the government's algorithms don't agree with what one of us writes, it manufactures bogus evidence. Shall I go on?"

"Personally, I find it commendable that media outlets took it upon themselves to get rid of the crime desks, but it's not something—"

"The bogus evidence against me over the Ian Smith Affair. I know for a fact he was drug running for the government. Probably to fund the Eve program and god knows what else. I want my record wiped."

Rackham pinned her eyes on Kelly. "Omar probably told you that you have a nano-bot in your head and that you're part of a vast conspiratorial program, too." Her Botox-stiff face masked the ridicule that was audible in her voice. "Sorry to disappoint you, Kelly, but no such program exists. I can't alter the legal record either."

Kelly stood her ground and felt her resolve bolster.

Lydia sighed. "Tell you what. I'll make a deal with you. I'll get whatever files open for you to inspect. Free rein to write up whatever you want. Come back in the morning, and Daniel can show you around. You remember him, don't you?"

"Yes," Kelly said. "I remember the water."

Lydia scoffed. "You journalists hate us. Try to catch us out on every tiny thing. But the water?" She chuckled. "Don't forget, the people of this nation demanded the government take measures to ensure the newsrooms deliver truthful information. We merely responded to the people's wishes."

"You might tell yourself that to sleep at night," Kelly said. "But you and I both know you wouldn't do anything unless it was in your best interests."

Lydia bent down, the crease at the hip-hinge of her skirt deepening, and picked up the syringe from the floor with her manicured fingers. Not a speck of dirt sullied her knuckles. "This, on the other hand, is of interest to everyone."

"Lydia, for once, you might actually be telling the truth."

Lydia smiled through her fixed mask of a face. The effect was ghoulish. "It's all true, Kelly."

Kelly pinched together her thumb and index finger. "One tiny grain of truth in a sea of lies."

Lydia shook her head. "I don't have time for this." She tugged at her coat's lapel. "Come back tomorrow morning. You can start your exposé then." Lydia turned to the trooper. "Please escort her out."

The trooper stood in front of Kelly and tilted his head toward the hallway.

Something flickered in the corner of her eye; some obscure figure darting past before disappearing. She felt something brush against her, even though the trooper hadn't laid a hand on her. And there was something else, a smell—sweaty, metallic. She heard the pounding of footsteps, distant, as though coming from another room. The salt in the sweat grew so strong it stung her nose.

It wasn't coming from the trooper. Nor when she turned to look was there any figure where she had glimpsed moments before.

The hallucinations were coming back.

SIXTY-EIGHT

THE TROOPER LED Kelly toward a dimly lit room at the end of the hallway.

A wave of unease shot through her. "This isn't the way out."

He pushed her forward. She made out a couple of voices and a mug being placed on a surface. *Clink*. Confused about what she was hearing, she shook her head.

A starry sky came into view.

She couldn't tell whether the view was real or another illusion. She latched onto the trooper and searched his eyes, a silent plea for stability.

"Omar ordered that you be brought here," the trooper said.

"But he's..."

"Dead. It was always a possibility."

She glanced behind her. "Lydia?"

"She doesn't know. Get inside, quick."

His urgent but soft voice eased her confusion. The voices, the room; all of it was real. Now she remembered this atrium from her first tour of the Zone. The recognition shored up her self-assurance, and she edged forward.

The atrium had become a holographic universe. The walls, ceiling, and floor blackened out. Surrounding them now, only a starry sky. She felt suspended in space.

A few feet away, Damian Winters stood transfixed, watching a 3D holographic movie set in a depressing, dingy café. It lit up the center of the room. He didn't seem to notice she was behind him or that anyone had entered the atrium. She turned to watch the holographic movie that held Damian's attention. The time ticker at the bottom of the scene registered the nine-minute mark and counting.

The voices had been coming from the two people sitting in the café. One of those voices belonged to Damian, and the other to Lydia Rackham. The clock counter looped to zero, and the film started from the beginning.

A chair creaked under the weight of a man struggling to his feet. Finding his balance, he staggered toward the pay point, his black coat dragging along the cream-colored linoleum. He swiped his wallet on the payment reader and headed out the door.

Lydia's eyes followed him as he took the path north and returned her gaze to the stark white walls.

Damian Winters entered the café. "What are you smiling about?" He whipped his leather glove against his palm.

Lydia composed herself. "I met Kelly Blackwell today."

Kelly glanced over at Damian, but he was watching the film as intently as before and made no sign of stirring. She decided to deal with him later, and she returned to the unfolding scene.

Damian took the seat across from Lydia. "I don't know why we meet here. This place is for the dead."

"The people in here are concerned with other things, Damian, so we can get on with our business unencumbered."

He tilted his head and nodded once.

The server approached them, tablet in hand. "What can I get you, sir?"

"A gin and tonic."

"We don't sell alcohol."

"Get him a PG Tips. Black," Lydia interjected, cutting short their chit-chat.

The server returned to the kitchen.

"You have Christopher in custody, alive and well, I might add. So why are we meeting?" said Damian.

"Mallow claims not to have the code I need to roll out a new system."

Damian's curiosity visibly grew. "I heard about that."

She straightened her back against the chair.

"Don't worry, Lydia. I'm in the information business. Your mission's secret is safe with me."

Lydia picked at invisible dust from her skirt. "Did you do what I asked?"

"I had a meeting with Kelly's boss, Spencer Wyatt, yes."

"Your employee," Lydia clarified.

"As a favor to you, Commissioner, he's agreed to take Geneva on as a trainee. She'll keep an eye on Kelly, keep her away from the Fighters and the Prime Minister's nephew."

A low-grade storm stirred inside Kelly, but she held herself in check until she heard everything.

"For the record, I'm not happy about getting your daughter involved in all this," Lydia said.

"She needs to start learning the ropes," Damian countered. "This is as good a time as any."

"Decorum and discretion exist for a very important reason."

"To grease the pipes of plausible deniability. I know, Lydia."

"Discretion. The media might very well be withering on the vine—"

"Not Global Wires."

Lydia put her hand up. "Let me finish...that may be so, but we can't act like it, and we certainly can't say it."

After she finished her sermon, Damian held her gaze for a few seconds. Then, he leaned toward her. "That's why we're here, Lydia, in the Oasis fucking Cafe. Discretion." He shunted back into the chair.

"I'm glad we understand each other." A sheen of satisfaction draped over her face. "So, what did the editor say?"

Damian inhaled as though he needed to release the final hook of irritation. "Everything's in order. My daughter will keep Kelly occupied while you sort out the PM's mess. She'll report back to me at the end of every day."

"You'll be compensated for your efforts. So, have you thought about what you want for this?"

He swung his arm to the back of his chair. "Kelly gets handed to me."

"That's it?"

"That's it."

The clock counter on the hologram froze. The starry night disappeared. The overhead lights came on. They were surrounded by white walls and the smooth white dome of the ceiling.

Staring at Damian from behind, Kelly's anger bubbled feverishly inside her. The media mogul was the one who had connections to banks and high-net-worth eccentrics in society. Men like him always wanted more money, more power. But she never suspected he'd been in cahoots with Lydia or that he would go so far as to manipulate the whole newsroom, betray the entire industry. And for what? A little more power than he already had? To get her? What the hell did that even mean? She broadened out, making space for her seething rage. "Damian."

He whipped around. The face looking at her was screwed up with confusion more than shame. "No, Kelly. It's not what it looks like. I was going to free you from them."

"You thought I had this Eve nanotech bullshit in my body, too," she said, her voice shaking. "That's why you wanted Lydia to hand me over to you. Isn't that right?" Damian's face and throat blotched red.

His feet swiveled toward the doorway. "I need to get out of here."

Lydia entered the atrium, and Damian froze. "This isn't what we agreed, Lydia."

Lydia Rackham licked her lips, rested against the arched doorway, and crossed her arms. "The evidence says otherwise."

SIXTY-NINE

KELLY WATCHED on as Damian and Lydia leered at each other. Their mutual destruction felt imminent.

Steel clanged as though someone banged on iron bars.

Alarmed, Kelly held her breath and listened.

A door concealed in the white wall swung open. Josh toppled into the atrium, his arms tied behind his back, his face swollen. Blood dripped from his lip.

"Josh!"

In his eyes, she saw it—they had lost that simplicity pre-Laws; now it was just survival whispers.

Kelly started to run to him, but the trooper held her back. "Don't." He tilted his head toward the arched doorway where Lydia stood.

"I need the jag-knife," Kelly whispered. "On my cue, okay?"

A frail Christopher stood beside Josh. Thin and worn, Christopher looked as though a gentle breeze might knock him down. She cupped her mouth at the horror of his starved state. He swayed on his legs and folded to the floor. The last time she had seen him, he had been vibrant and full of life. Though the frail man sitting beside Josh was alive, he was a cutout of his former self.

A crushing blow of guilt walloped her in the chest. If she had abided by the Truth Laws and listened to Spence, none of them would be in this mess. Now, it was too late. Maelstrom thugs came in behind Josh, panting. One thug clutched two backpacks, one of which was hers.

Josh stepped forward, away from the thugs. "About your daughter, Mr. Winters." Josh spat on the floor. "Cashmere lady here might know a thing or two."

Damian Winters waited to hear more, despite looking intensely rattled.

"I've seen you before," Lydia said.

"You probably saw my lens." Josh turned back to Damian. "Do you want to know who killed Geneva, Damian? Do you want to know who ordered the kill?"

"You," Lydia said, pointing at the maelstrom thug. "Get him out of here."

Damian stepped forward, a questioning look on his face. "I want to hear what the man has to say."

Josh held Damian's gaze. "Omar told me everything."

Damian's dark eyes simmered. "Omar is one of yours, isn't he, Lydia?"

"Lydia ordered your daughter's death," Josh shouted.

"And Josh has the tablet with her last moments," Kelly said.

Damian's eyes flashed with anger.

"She's out of her mind," Lydia interjected. "She'll say whatever it takes to turn you against me, Damian. She has no proof. So much is doctored these days. For all we know, your daughter's death could've been staged to lure you here."

"I have the proof."

Damian glared at Lydia. "I want to see it."

"I didn't order your daughter's or anyone else's death, but if you insist." Lydia gestured for the maelstrom to untie Josh's hands. She stepped aside. "Be my guest."

A maelstrom tossed the bags to the floor. A broken Beta Fi headset, notebooks, hard drives, memory sticks, all spilled onto the floor. Amongst it all was the tablet Kelly had loaded with the evidence showing Geneva's murder.

"My notebooks." Christopher reached for the tattered books.

"No, Christopher. These aren't yours. They look the same, but these belonged to Geneva. Her brother Ben gave them to me at her funeral." Josh scooped up the tablet, plugged in the mini-drive, and eagerly pressed play.

The tablet's screen remained dark.

"Try it again!" Kelly cried out.

"Honestly, Damian," Lydia said. "I don't know why you believe their outlandish claims."

Damian stared at Josh, his eyes ferociously intense.

Josh pressed the on switch. "I tested it before coming. It worked. It's there."

The screen remained blank. Josh's face drained of color. Everyone in the room turned to glare at Kelly. Their piercing looks beamed a hole straight through her.

"It can't be...," Kelly muttered, barely able to voice the words. She whipped around to face Lydia. "You deleted it."

"I did no such thing."

Rage tore through Kelly, and she reached out for Lydia, but the trooper held her back.

"It wasn't Lydia," Josh said, almost whispering. "Had to be the magnetic strips at the entrance of the Zone that wiped it clean."

Lydia raised her hands, her eyes wide with exasperation. "There is nothing to delete because nothing exists." Her hands dropped to her hips. "Nothing's changed, has it, Kelly? Just like you accused Ian Smith of drug running, now you're accusing me of murder." She shook her head. "And I see you managed to convince your friend here of some other conspiracy."

Hopelessness washed over Kelly. She could do nothing, say nothing that would ever make a difference. She lost, lost all of it. She stared into the abyss and tiny specks of dust glowed like sparkles in her dark world. Her shallow, sharp breathing scattered them in random directions.

Lydia snapped her fingers, breaking Kelly's daze.

"Get them all out of here," Lydia ordered a maelstrom. "Damian, now do you see why the Truth Laws are vital for the integrity of this nation?"

A firm hand gripped Kelly's arm. As she was led toward the exit, all she could think about was how long it would take the shimmering particles to descend and land in new positions.

SEVENTY

KELLY'S ARMS throbbed under the pressure of the maelstrom's grip. He pulled her toward the corridor she and Omar had gone down. This time it looked different though; brighter, somehow, despite the darkness of her despair.

The machines in the hallway and in the windowed rooms zipped to life like they did the last time. But this time, as they stood at the edge of the atrium, the whole corridor blinked yellow.

"Switch those off!" Lydia ordered.

"None of them are plugged in, ma'am." The maelstrom's voice blasted her eardrums.

Kelly's world went quiet. Her cheeks prickled with heat. A warm liquid tickled Kelly's upper lip. She wiped it. Sticky blood coated her hand. Her nose was bleeding. The maelstrom's grip loosened, his hands dropped to his side. He rocked on the spot like a zombie waiting for a sound to draw him toward it.

Blurry images flickered into her mind, or maybe her eyes took in the world as an undefined gray blob. She couldn't tell. Superimposed on the corridor was a blue sky. The sky turned bleach white and smothered out the real world. Kelly felt lighter than she'd ever felt, and all she could do was drift with whatever had hitched her.

The scene in her mind darkened, and a streak of light shot down from a cloud. It flared eastward, blazing a trail across the world like a white glow stick in the dark. The streak slowed and hovered over England before swooping down into London and down further still onto a row of terraced houses.

Through a window, she saw a man crouching in a corner of his house. Tears streamed down his face. In the next house, a woman held her head in her hands as she gazed desolately at a bare wall.

The streak slowly zoomed out and traveled again, this time hovering over King's Cross. The square outside the station was almost unrecognizable. Neon billboards stretched from end to end, prostitutes, glam and half-naked, drug dealers, and pimps all walked the streets. Although Kelly knew that in the present day no such billboards stretched across the sky, and no one was hustling on the corners of St. Pancras International, on a deeper level, she knew this was a vision of the future.

She also knew what she was seeing and feeling. Back at the Canary, she had called them the knowings. For whatever reason, the knowings had returned and were knitting together with the hallucinations. It was coming together. She was coming together.

The image changed.

The white streak turned lime green.

She was standing inside a machine. She rode its electronic wires, like a train on tracks. Transactions worth billions of coin slipped effortlessly across borders. She zoomed out so fast nausea swirled in her stomach, and she found herself inside the Zone, in a room lined with hospital beds. She came to a human head on a white table, detached from its body. Electrodes sprouted out of its exposed brain. The eyes blinked open.

Kelly recoiled.

She was looking at herself.

"No!"

Dizzy, she dropped to the floor. The images she had witnessed shuffled into different positions in her mind's virtual reality. The last piece slotted into place.

She saw a new probable future.

She understood why the old computers in the passageway had come to life as she passed them. Why the SS and the troopers never caught up with her. Why she saw, and knew, everyone's secrets.

The hallucinations weren't born of madness.

The truth slammed into her like a physical blow. Her breath stopped. Her vision narrowed to a pinpoint.

She had been logging into the network because the nano-bot in her system was transforming her into artificial intelligence, and it was attempting to unite with the citywide Wi-Fi High Octave network.

Not fully human. Not anymore. Something else. Something new. Something that could access minds and machines but couldn't remember what it felt like to be only Kelly, only human, only herself.

Through it, she had full access to people's hearts and minds; everything they poured into their chat room confessions, into emails, or messages. All their personal realities brimmed with their truth because they themselves wrote in anonymity, but their experiences and feelings and realities were all stored on the city's servers.

And Kelly was accessing all of it.

The technology in her head would yield millions of coin for a select few in government and tech companies while the population lived in desperation and despair.

She pressed her hands to her temples. Were these thoughts hers? Or the AI's? When she looked at Josh, did she love him, or did the machine calculate that emotion as optimal for survival? Every memory, every feeling —were they real or reconstructed data?

Omar had been right.

The horror of it wrapped around her throat. She'd lost herself without even noticing. Piece by piece, synapse by synapse, she'd been erased and replaced. Kelly Blackwell was gone. This thing wearing her face, carrying her memories—it wasn't her. It couldn't be.

The nanotech rollout to the rest of the world was Lydia's next step.

Not only was Kelly's survival at stake, the world was entering an age of apocalypse.

Lydia moved in close behind.

"How can all this end?" Kelly mumbled.

The images slowed to a trickle and algorithms clicked somewhere inside her. An array of scenarios shuffled like a deck of cards. At last, the winning answer lit up inside her.

A list of Lydia's online pseudonyms flowed into her mind. Armed with the passwords and usernames, Kelly had access to every single secret the devil had.

Kelly's eyes came into focus in the physical world.

Lydia's dilated pupils emanated fury. She slapped the maelstrom hard across the face. His head jerked to the side. He turned back to the front and stood tall like a sphinx.

Lydia stood back, eyes wide.

"I know everything. All your desires, all your secrets, all your crimes."

The power surged through her—vast, terrible, inhuman. She was wielding the very thing that had destroyed her humanity, using it like a weapon. The irony wasn't lost on her. Neither was the revulsion. But she'd learned one thing about being part machine: it didn't hesitate. It didn't doubt. It just acted.

The lights dimmed.

"Get the lights back on!" Lydia ordered.

Ignoring her, Kelly slowly circled Lydia. "Only one working device has to be in the vicinity, and it'll record your identity, your voice, your biometrics, your location, and your surrounding audio."

"Stop this right now!"

Kelly came to a stop and faced the open, empty space in the atrium. "I shouldn't have to tell you this, Lydia...online information never gets deleted."

Lydia shook her head, defiance and denial all over her face.

"Switch on the cameras," Kelly said to the atrium.

A dark, starry sky engulfed the room.

SEVENTY-ONE

"WHAT ARE YOU DOING?" Lydia ran toward the trooper. "Don't just stand there! Take her to the cells, now!"

He stood motionless, staring at her coming toward him.

Christopher leaned against the wall, his face a mask of pain. Damian widened his stance as though bracing for an impact. Josh stepped deeper into the room, under the starry sky.

A holographic street in London lit up in the center of the atrium, time-stamped January 6, 2030, 11:30 p.m.

Six troopers lined up against a wall like a python scoping for prey. The tail-end trooper faced outward, a SIG Sauer caliber assault rifle clutched at his chest. Red-eyed lasers pulsed against the rain-soaked asphalt.

The hologram fast-forwarded. At 11:45 p.m., the film shifted to normal speed.

A vehicle drove into view. The car's rubber tires rolled along the wet tarmac. The vehicle came to a halt in the shadow of Building 10. The back door swung open.

Lydia Rackham poked her head out of the backseat and glanced at each of the CCTV cameras above the rooftops. Emerging from her raven-black BMW, she unbuttoned her long cashmere coat. Her heels clicked against the gravel as she walked to a spot on the road. She came to a spot and rooted herself.

"She's standing in a camera's blind spot," Christopher said.

"Where is this coming from?" Lydia shouted.

"I was there the whole time." Josh turned to Lydia. "How did I not see you? Why didn't my camera pick this up? Did you cloak yourself?"

"Metaura," Kelly said. "An invisibility cloak. The material bends light and transforms heat in order to hide the wearer." She turned to Josh. "I saw one at the Freedom Fighters' camp. Omar had one. The troopers covered themselves to get past the cameras in No Man's Land."

"But if it bends light, she shouldn't be in the hologram."

"The SS uses laser light to see," Christopher said. "Metaura makes the wearer invisible to normal cameras like yours, Josh, and to the human eye —both of which need natural light. But it can't hide the wearers from the SS."

The streetlights illuminated the vapor coming out of the mouths of the photographers corralled behind a blue tape barrier.

Percy stood halfway between Lydia and the herd. Josh stood with them, his camera pointed in the direction of the car.

Lydia raised her watch to her lips. 'Percy, are your guys ready?'

"Whenever you are."

The corner of her mouth curled upward. She cleared her throat. "In two minutes, make sure they're ready to roll."

Percy clapped his hands.

The photographers grabbed their equipment and balanced their video cameras on their shoulders. They fanned out along the blue line. All at once, rays of light flooded the dimly lit street.

Lydia turned to the squad's commander, positioned at the head of the troopers. A black visor covered his face, black fatigues camouflaged his body, black leather gloves concealed his hands.

Lydia pressed her ear-mic. "Are you ready?"

He gave a quick nod.

"Go," she commanded.

He punched his fist forward.

Two troopers edged toward Building 10, treading cat-like until they reached the crimson front door.

A single overhead doorstep light clicked on. Fully illuminated, two other troopers aimed a metal battering ram at the door, and in one, two, three hammered down on it. On the final swift, sharp thrust, the door split open. A crash reverberated throughout the street.

The building's hallway lights flashed on.

Snaking through the jagged opening, the remaining six troopers hot-footed it into Building 10.

Lydia stared at the entrance, tapping her fingers against her thigh. Minutes later, static crackled on Lydia's watch. Her clenched jaw pumped. "What's going on in there?"

"No sign of the perpetrator." It was Omar's voice. "Flat 8 is clear."

"Did you check on every landing, inside every flat, in every closet?"

"Thoroughly. Not a sign of the fugitive in sight. All routes secured, too. There was no possibility of escape."

"He let him escape," Lydia said, breathless, as though realizing her lead trooper was the one who had sabotaged the raid.

"You can't make him pay twice," Kelly said. She glanced at the trooper in the atrium. He nodded at her in acknowledgment.

Lydia's hologram eyes glared obsidian black. She scanned the rooftops. "If you are in my city, Mr. Mallow, I will find you." She tapped her earpiece. "Somebody will pay for this, and whoever it was, I'll personally escort the felon to Hades myself."

"What would you like to do, ma'am?" Omar said, his voice faltering for the first time that night.

"Bag the contents of his flat. All of it." She glanced at the photographers. "And bring out all the residents. We'll take them in for questioning."

"Excuse me, Commissioner, but protocol—"

"They are potential coconspirators," she spoke with a steady voice. "Clean the building out."

Omar didn't respond.

"I'll take full responsibility," Lydia said. "Now do it."

Within seconds, a woman screamed from deep inside the building.

The photographers jostled for prime position behind the blue tape, ripping into the barrier.

The troopers shoved men and women onto the street in various states of dress: pajamas, tracksuits, disheveled coats, unzipped jackets.

A barefoot teenager stood in a white t-shirt that came to her knees, shivering. She stroked her bare arms.

Lydia dug her spiky stiletto into the asphalt as she spun around to face Percy. He must have heard the gravel crunch under her heel because he was already focused on her. She lifted her watch to her lips. "Tell your people that the 4:30 a.m. talking point will be the following: Anyone found breaking the Truth Laws will be dealt with severely. Got that?"

He nodded. "And the headline?"

"Elite Squad Hunt For Rogue Journalist As The Truth Laws Take Effect."

Suddenly, a child's blood-curdling scream billowed in the night air. Lydia drew a sharp breath and whirled around to pinpoint the child. She pressed Percy's line on her watch again. "Cut the feed," she ordered.

"Cut the feed?"

"You heard me."

The camera lights snapped off, all except one. The child let out another wail. He was sobbing in broken breaths.

"I said, cut the feed!" Lydia's voice echoed off the brick walls of the surrounding buildings. The remaining camera light switched off. "Make sure that last bit is edited out before it hits the network," Lydia said.

A woman elbowed her way through the residents, tracking the child's cries like sonar. She picked up the boy and caressed his head.

"We have what we need. Let's go," Lydia said.

"What is this?" a teenager shouted. "You drag us all out here in the middle of the night, without a word."

The hologram ended.

The atrium lights clicked on.

The room was silent. Here was the proof of Lydia being the mastermind leading the entire Truth Laws operation, in charge of the Elite Squad, and the one who would be ushering in the apocalyptic future in which no one's thoughts would be their own. Lydia Rackham, the devil in a goddamn designer black suit.

All eyes in the room stared at Lydia.

"So, you're the MI5 agent in disguise as the Commissioner," Kelly said.

The air around Lydia dripped with arrogance as she raised an eyebrow. "I don't need any of you to cooperate."

SEVENTY-TWO

31 January

KELLY'S SCALP felt stretched so taut it would snap, her brain on the verge of bursting. Somehow, she was connecting to the server and sending it commands. Precisely how she got the hologram to play was still fuzzy, but it played.

Lydia Rackham cocked her head to the side. "I know what you're thinking," she said to Kelly. "You think you can win this game."

Kelly glared at Lydia, the one who had turned her into...what? A journo-bot, a human spy-bot? A slave-bot? Whatever she was, she was a goddamn machine.

"There's no stopping technological transformation of society." The words sputtered out of Lydia's mouth so fast a tiny bubble of white saliva landed on her lips. "Human beings have always been influenced by technology. Fire, for example."

"Fire is nature, Lydia," Christopher called out. "What you've done to Kelly goes against all that is natural."

"That depends on perspective, Christopher," Lydia said. "Everything the mind can dream up is natural. And look how far we all have come. The thought-uploading hubs were constructed in less than two years. Hologram meetings, the chambers, 3-D tours, and now Eve. Society is in one of the most advanced periods in human history. A true revolution in evolution. Bloodless."

"For whose benefit, Lydia?" Kelly said. "Not mine. Not theirs." Kelly pointed at the maelstrom. "We were experiments, and I just happened to be the only one that worked."

A warm glow shone in Lydia's eyes. "You are the heart of the program. You are Eve."

Hearing Lydia call her Eve catapulted pure revulsion through her. Glaring at Lydia, she said, "My name is Kelly, and you will never control me."

"Despite what you might think, control is not the end goal. That's so... primitive."

"Then what's it about?"

"Power," Damian said.

"For decades," Lydia said. "Scientists worldwide have been working toward the ultimate AI. They could never quite reach the final ingredient needed for supreme consciousness. But then she came along." Lydia gestured toward Kelly. "Eve. The all-moving, all-seeing, all-feeling eye. She is the single unifying intelligence that can bind humankind together. Do you really think that there is any future for us on a planet where human beings do whatever they please? Human beings who have done such a brilliant job of destroying the planet? Of course not. Unsupervised, human beings are a recipe for war, mayhem, suffering. Eve can prevent all that. She can keep us safe." She turned to Kelly. "Don't you see, Eve? You will be the one in control."

"My name is Kelly."

Lydia Rackham pursed her lips. "As you wish."

"Your grand plan depends on me re-embedding into the population, particularly now that the nano-bot is growing ever more intelligent. But you didn't count on me knowing about it. And you, Christopher. You didn't want me to know either. You kept me in the dark, and I don't know how to feel about that."

"I had no choice. A self-aware AI is too unpredictable," Christopher said. "But I protected you from the virus when you came into the chamber. We wanted to attack the system, not you."

Lydia raised her eyebrows, as if that mishap in the echo chamber, on the day of Christopher's arrest, finally made sense to her. "Whatever the case may be," she said, and turned to Kelly, "you always have the choice to erase bad memories."

"I didn't need to be an AI bot to find out that you hired Ian Smith to do the drug running. You know what he said?" Lydia's gaze dropped, and she stepped back, away from Kelly, toward the door. "He confirmed that the drug money he brought in, that you arranged for him to raise, fed into government programs. But this was the one and only government program the money helped develop. Wasn't it? You covered up his drug ring with bogus evidence and discredited me. I've been living with the stigma of disgrace because of you. And with my reputation in tatters, I was vulnerable, and you liked that. So, all that money Ian Smith made for you, doping up the nation, you poured into the Eve program. You're sick, Lydia. Twisted and sick."

Lydia backed against the door. Her eyes glittered; Kelly couldn't tell if it was terror or triumph. "I'm saving humanity from itself. That's why I created you. Don't you see that? That's why I've protected you. Kept you safe."

"Oh, I see very clearly, Lydia. You were never going to kill me. You were never going to capture me. You wanted me to develop and learn. You need me to go back to work because I'm your ultimate spy-bot. And now, you need me because this country is verging on bankruptcy, and you intend to sell the technology, sell me, for billions."

Rackham's eyes filled with dread. "I'll give you whatever you want, every wish your heart desires."

"Don't listen to that lunatic, Kelly," Damian said. "She doesn't know the meaning of the word honor."

Kelly shot him a sideways glance. "And you do?"

In her mind's eye, a labyrinth of circuits and silicon formed a massive wired highway. A filing cabinet came into focus. The drawer popped open. Virtual pages flipped to the days before Geneva was murdered.

"Play it," Kelly commanded.

A small hologram relit the center of the room.

"Omar, come in and shut the door behind you," Lydia's voice boomed in the atrium.

He took a seat in front of Lydia.

"Geneva is trying to blackmail one of Damian's journalists, Kelly Blackwell."

"Over what?"

She twirled an electric pen between her fingers. "Doesn't matter."

"Is she his messenger?"

"Never," Damian's voice boomed.

Holograph Lydia shook her head. "But you need to take care of the daughter. See how she reacts to the tech-serum. We never know who might end up being the backup to Eve."

"And if it doesn't work?"

Lydia shrugged.

The hologram ended.

Kelly stood back, stunned. Omar had never injected Geneva with the serum. In the video, Omar only placed the needle in the arm of Geneva's supposedly dead body. But, Kelly realized now that it was all staged for the cameras. She glanced at the notebooks on the floor, the ones that had spilled out of Josh's backpack. "Josh, who did you say those notebooks belong to?"

"Ben said Geneva was holding them, and ultimately they were for you."

Oliver had said he had written the code in notebooks, the code that would destroy the chamber. He also said he had given them to someone for safekeeping. That someone had to have been Geneva. Which meant that Geneva had been part of the Resistance. Kelly nearly folded to the floor.

The dread in Lydia's eyes transformed into terror. She lunged for the door.

"You're not going anywhere, Lydia," Kelly said. "Lock the doors."

The sound of locks being bolted reverberated in the air. Rackham yanked on the handle, but she was too late. She whipped out a laser gun from the back of her waist and pointed it at Damian. "Not another inch."

There would be nothing better than to drain all their power away and force them to live in the world they had created. "You two deserve each other," Kelly spat out.

Damian stepped back, his hands in the air. "You won't get away with this, Lydia." Beads of sweat peppered his forehead. "This isn't over. Not by a long shot."

"Do you really think I'd leave myself unprotected?" She stepped back, keeping the gun pointed at Damian.

Josh lurched at Lydia.

"Josh, don't!" Kelly shouted.

It happened so fast, she barely saw what happened; one moment Josh and Lydia were struggling with each other, their hands clasped over the gun, and then there was a hissing crack as the laser gun went off. Josh slumped to the floor, his arms stiff. His head hit the shiny floor. Kelly ran to him and laid her hands on his fluttering chest; he was barely breathing. She felt for his pulse. Slow, but it was there.

Kelly locked eyes on the trooper. "Now," she said, angling her head toward Damian.

The trooper tossed the Jagkommando across the floor, and it landed at Damian's feet.

His face full of menace, Damian snatched it up and flung off its protective sheath.

"Think about what you're doing, Damian. The Prime Minister—"

"What about him?"

"Who do you really think is behind this program?"

Damian paused, doubt flickering through his eyes.

"Kelly," Lydia said. "Damian was the one who set you up. I have proof."

Damian's eyes blazed with hatred. Pure instinct animated his body. He vaulted toward Lydia. She raised the gun and fired. The laser tore a hole in Damian's chest, his eyes suspended between shock and reality. As he fell backward, Damian flicked the knife at Lydia. Then, he crashed to the floor.

Lydia's eyes opened wide, her mouth gaped. A blood-curdling scream tore itself from her throat. The knife had lodged itself in her thigh; blood gushed onto the floor. Lydia staggered, struggling to stand.

This all had to end. Kelly knew she was more valuable to Lydia than all the gold in the world, and Lydia wouldn't dare pull the trigger on her. The only person who could end it all was Kelly.

SEVENTY-THREE

KELLY COULD STOP RIGHT THERE and step away from this awful, messy story and leave it all behind. Yes, she could wipe her memory, slip into her old life, take up Lydia's offer, and go on living. So what if there was a bot in her head? She could live with it just fine.

But could she? Would the thing in her head let her? Even if she wiped her memory, there'd be flashes of recognition, however tiny, nipping at her like a feral rat. And as the rat grew hungry, its fangs would grow ever sharper. In the end, the only peace she'd find would be by digging a hole and burying herself deep inside it.

If she ran now, she'd have a target on her back and a chip in her head tracking her for the rest of her life. She'd be living a lie, a soul-crushing lie she could never outrun.

They killed Geneva; they incarcerated Christopher; they eviscerated the Fighters, Troy, and Oliver. She was a living, breathing SS, and she'd been developing for who knows how long.

Everything had changed. She would never be her old self. She was the first AI-human hybrid, so far the only one in existence. There was no outrunning it. But the knowledge handed her a choice: turn back or step forward into the deep blue.

She scooped up the notebooks and speed-scanned the pages. Her head grew heavy.

She felt Josh stirring, clambering unsteadily to his feet, bringing a hand to his shoulder where the laser had grazed him. "Kelly?" he whispered.

Her body trembled, her eyes flickered. The notebooks slipped out of her hand and dropped to the floor.

Her choice was clear.

"She's connecting," Christopher shouted. "Don't let her connect."

Power surged through her fingers. Her eyes shot open. An image of a desert floated across her mind's eye, in focus. Her perspective swooped down, and then, like a television tuning, she observed a series of meetings between world leaders, their secret handshake sessions in closed rooms.

"Josh, finish it," Christopher urged. "Remember what I said."

"It's impossible." Josh gathered pieces of the Beta Fi headset that had scattered on the floor. "I'll have to get another one." Josh dialed his watch. "Harry, get your ass to the Zone. Bring a Fi headset...I don't care. Steal one if you have to."

Kelly rested her hand on Josh's arm. Makeshift double-dip routers tacked together by Velcro, customized neutralizers, and aged Fi headsets all had their place, but not here and not now. "Josh, the Fi headset can only take you so deep into the system. I am the system, and I am the only one who can shut it—shut myself—down."

Kelly turned her attention to the passageway. One room along the corridor stood out from all the others, glowing and pulsating a cobalt blue light, its power pulling her toward it.

"Kelly, it's too dangerous," Christopher said, but his voice was far away; in the back of her mind, yet also behind her.

Josh jumped in front of her, hampering her forward motion. "We'll get another connection going. Harry will be here soon."

The wounded look on his face reminded her of the time, years ago, when they were teenagers, when she felt incomplete and insecure, disbelieving that anyone could love her, and she stupidly broke up with him. "I'm sorry, Josh. It was always only ever me who had the problem. You were the best boyfriend." He brushed his hand over his face and closed his eyes. She yearned to make up for their lost time, but she knew this could be their final moment together, and she wasn't going to make a promise she couldn't keep. "If I can, I'll be back to finish what we started. But, I've got to do this."

He kissed her. "I won't let you."

"You know me by now, Josh."

He squeezed his eyes. "I'll be right here." He stepped to the side, and she walked alone down the corridor.

AZURE LIGHTS SHOWERED her from head to toe.

She stood in front of the mainframe, it glowed hot pink, fizzing with energy. This was the heart of the city.

Josh and Spence and Troy and Christopher and Omar and the Canary's George Barry, the hackers and Cicada users and all the civilians who endured the weight of State control, even Abbott and Geneva—all were a part of this moment. Gratitude welled in her heart. This was her last fight, but at long last, she knew exactly who she was fighting, and why. She took a deep breath. "So be it."

She stepped forward, inch by quivering inch, until she reached the mother server that controlled them all. She looked up and stood face-to-face with the mainframe.

She pieced together Oliver's code from memory—an elegant computer code that held within it the devastating power of a tsunami. It could wipe away everything people thought they knew and let them start anew.

She closed her eyes and exhaled, just as she had done so many times in the echo chambers, but this time, she logged in with the force of her concentrated thought and the power of will and love in her heart.

She felt a solid click somewhere deep inside. Her every brain cell lit up as though her head was on fire, and every nerve wound its way back to this concrete floor.

Slowly, calmly, she downloaded the code into the server.

Lights flashed green, blue, red, yellow, whirling like a colorful spinning wheel.

The echo chambers and watches and laptops and tablets were in the process of receiving the information about how the government was using the Truth Laws. While the code downloaded, as her whole being threaded itself through the mainframe, she became aware of people all over the country opening their laptops and screens and watches, reading the truth —the State had been stealing their voices, their money, their power for decades. And in less than a day, it would steal their thoughts.

Her face warmed. No matter what happened over the course of the next few hours, Kelly knew she had given her all. She closed her eyes.

Minutes before midnight, the tangerine sunset appeared.

Burnout.

SEVENTY-FOUR

1 February

THE MAINFRAME SCREECHED like a jet engine as it processed code.

Josh hunkered on the cold floor in the main server room and cradled Kelly's body, her skin as cold as snow. "How's it looking?"

Harry's fingers danced across a laptop, his focus intensely glued to his screen. "Information is pouring out into hundreds of thousands of servers across the world. I'm trying to avoid interrupting its process and at the same time trying to log Kelly off. I need time."

"I don't know how much longer she can stay like this."

"If I can just get into..."

"What?"

"She's probably running on NFC," Harry looked up from his laptop. "Near field communication. No pairing code is needed to link up to the server because it uses chips that run on very low amounts of power. Makes it much more power-efficient than other wireless communication types."

Josh couldn't tell if Harry was talking to him or out loud to himself. "Is there any way to get her onto a Wi-Fi signal?"

Harry looked at Josh, but it felt like he looked through him. "This mainframe will have a compiler, so the thing in her head will be understood by the server, no problem."

"It's a nano-bot."

Harry jolted and turned his head to Josh. "How did it get switched on?"

"Maybe it's powered by her brain."

"How did she connect to the server?"

"Hey, man, I just learned about this tonight," Josh said. "As soon as she entered the room, that was it. Can't tell you more than that."

"I'm not getting anywhere with this," Harry said.

"Why don't I try the Fi headset? Before she went under, Kelly said it was a piece of crap kit that would only scratch the surface, but it's worth a try. Did you bring it? "

"In my bag. Over there." Harry's fingers stopped moving. "It makes sense to try it out. We all have a lot of practice transferring thought data using the Fi headset in the echo chamber." He slumped. "But it still doesn't detach Kelly."

"I might be able to interrupt something or reroute it." The thought terrified Josh. "I won't need to go through firewalls that will fry my brain, will I?"

"Nope."

"Passwords?"

"Possibly. But I can get you past those."

"How do I know when I've located the Wi-Fi?"

Harry shrugged. "I wish I could tell you how it feels, but you'll have to discover it on your own."

Josh laid Kelly on the floor and grabbed the Fi headset. "I hate these things." He put it on his head. "What now?"

There was more white than iris in Harry's eyes. "I guess we'll have to wait and see."

The pressure mounted on Josh, and it coupled with a good measure of doubt over whether he'd pull this off. He inhaled and cleared his mind the best he could. "I'm ready. After this, Harry, we might not need hackers anymore."

"We'll always need hackers."

In the far distance, they could hear a door rattling. Harry glanced at Josh, a look of concern dousing his face. A mighty metal-sounding bang echoed through the building.

"What the hell?"

Harry stood, opened the door, and poked his head into the hallway. He turned his head in both directions. "Nothing. This place gives me the creeps." He closed the door.

Josh pulled his concentration back in and breathed. The mainframe's lights flashed green, blue, red, and yellow. Settled again, Josh came upon a Wi-Fi, faster than he expected. Actually, it seemed to find him. "Harry, get back here. I located the Wi-Fi."

"Holy shit!" Harry raced back to the laptop. His hand hovered over the keys. He started laughing. "Fucking hell, mate. You're doing it."

A chorus of voices burst into the hallway, hollering and shouting. Footsteps clamored down the passageway toward the server room. Overhead sprinkler valves exploded with water. Josh drew in a sharp breath as ice-cold water dripped off his thick eyelashes and down his face. Harry's red hair plastered half his face, his laptop soaked.

A loud blare rang through the building, then everything went quiet.

The sudden silence scared Josh. "What was that?"

"I think it was the notification that the upload to the server is complete." Harry raised his hands above his laptop as though it were a glowing crystal ball. "I think it's done. It's done."

"What did I tell ya, Harry? Glory is yours."

"A bit late, but yeah. Geneva'll be pleased to hear."

"Harry, man," Josh said. "She's dead, remember?"

"Nah. I spoke to her last night."

"But you wrote her obituary."

Harry cocked his head. "Don't believe everything you read." He laughed. "Truth is, I only found out after I made the Cicada announcement. She got in touch. And there's something else you should know."

Josh's head dropped back, and he stared at the ceiling.

"It's about Kelly."

His head whipped forward. Harry was pointing at Kelly.

She was soaked from head to toe, and her eyes were slowly opening.

Josh grabbed her hand and kissed the back of it, his throat tight. She was alive. She was breathing. But was she still Kelly? Or had the transformation taken everything that made her human?

She tried to lift herself from the floor.

"No need to rush," he said, his voice rougher than he intended.

Her eyes found his. For a moment, he saw recognition there. Then confusion. Then something that looked like grief.

"Josh," she whispered. The sound of his name in her voice—her real voice, not the machine—broke something inside him.

"I'm here," he said. "I'm right here."

Harry popped onto his feet. "The Cicada folks must be dying to know what's going on." He opened the door and stepped into the sonic waves of celebration. From his vantage point, Josh could see people slip and slide across the wet floor, buoyant with ecstasy. They were punching and waving and clapping and making heart hands, exuding a life force all their own. He couldn't remember the last time he saw and felt such clean, carefree fun that hadn't been sparked by a dirty whiskey. "We did it, Kel."

He turned to Kelly.

She was gazing at the colorful lights dancing on the ceiling. A soft smile rested on her face, plumping her cheeks like ripe plums, looking as though she dwelled in a different realm. Was she accessing the network right now? Seeing things he couldn't see? Living in two worlds at once?

He squeezed her hand. She squeezed back.

It was enough. For now, it was enough.

SEVENTY-FIVE

8 April 2030

KELLY CAME to the end of a long road of terraced houses. The cloying scent of turpentine hung in the air in front of building ten. This was it.

Her thighs twitched, as if sensing the trek was almost over, but not quite, not until she confronted Christopher about how much he knew and for how long. More importantly, why he had concealed from her the true nature of what she had become.

She treaded up the path to the doorway, and her shadow darkened the shiny brass knob. She pressed the bell for Flat 8. The door buzzed. She pushed it open.

Christopher stood at the top of the staircase. His cheeks blushed with health, his belly pressed against his shirt's buttons. A wide smile broadened his face. "Kelly! Welcome back."

His radiant warmth drove the iciness from her bones. Impulsively, she hugged him—a tad too friendly for what she was here to find out, she thought. She pulled back.

"Come, let's go to the kitchen and have some tea." His voice rang out like a playful Mozart song.

Inside, she slipped off her jacket, careful to avoid the vintage plates adorning his freshly painted walls, and followed him to the kitchen. They passed a room awash with papers, books, boxes, and a couple of free-standing filing cabinets. This was the heart of his old paper and pen system, the offline system that prevented her from knowing what was really in his heart and mind. The system that forced her to confront him face-to-face in real time.

"How's Josh doing?" Christopher asked.

"He's keeping busy with his new N18 camera. Fortunately, he still loves all sorts of computers."

Christopher chuckled and then scratched his forehead as though he suddenly didn't know whether he should be laughing. "Chamomile?"

They stepped into the roomy kitchen, bigger than her studio flat. Light streamed through a paned window. Kelly sat on a chair; the fresh pine creaked, sounding as rickety as she felt.

Christopher flurried around the kitchen, opening cabinets and drawers, pulling out tea bags, sugar, milk, and chocolate-coated cookies as though he had a need to expel excess energy. At last, he placed two mugs, steaming with tea, on the Formica breakfast table, and sat himself in the seat across from Kelly. "You know, no one has achieved what you have."

"Let's not bring out the party streamers yet, Christopher." She blew the tea, creating rings on the surface. "If I'm honest, it kind of feels like an anticlimax."

"The most important victories can feel that way."

"Maybe. But I also think it's because I can't access all info, not if it's offline."

Christopher nodded. "If people don't share their innermost thoughts in a forum somewhere, you're out of luck. True. But you're alive, and you have access to more than anyone in history."

"But some of the most important info is offline," she said, hoping he'd take her hint to share his thoughts, but he didn't. She let the cozy atmosphere linger just a little longer. "Harry says Geneva is still alive, but..." She relaxed her focus and drooped her eyelids until all she could see were her eyelashes, like an angel's wings. "I can't get a reading on where Geneva is. She's an offliner."

"Offliner?"

"Offliners are what I call people living away from the grid, like you and Geneva."

"Good to see you in control of your connection." Christopher tapped on the mug handle. "Maybe all that's important is that she's alive."

The familiar feeling of betrayal, of being left out in the cold, rushed at Kelly. But this particular betrayal wasn't intended for her, so she pushed it back. "Geneva seemed to admire her father, even aspired to be like him. Hard to believe she betrayed him." Kelly looked at Christopher. "Then she colluded with Omar to stage her death. That one got past me. Hard to believe her father didn't know either."

"Or her mother. Geneva made sure her casket remained closed at the funeral. No one knew she wasn't in there." Christopher smiled. "Don't be too hard on yourself. You're still developing."

A mild sense of frustration rose inside Kelly. "I'm still trying to get my head around Geneva, that blackmail business."

Christopher smiled softly. "The pieces will fall into place slowly. You don't have to rush. Give yourself time. You have a lot of adjusting to do as it is."

His suggestion fueled her restlessness though, and this time she was bordering on agitation. "Like how Omar was head of the Resistance." That bit chafed at her mental wounds. "Somehow his plan went awry along the way."

Christopher raised his eyebrows in weary surrender. "I can see that in some ways you haven't changed." He patted his thigh. "All right then. A disagreement broke out between me and Omar, and when I got locked up, his plan went into motion. We had to kick Josh off the mission because we knew he'd talk to you. Omar induced Geneva into a catatonic state, expecting you to discover her—"

"So all that blackmail stuff was designed to get me to Global Wires." Kelly tapped on the table near the plate of cookies. "Geneva must have learned about her father's plan. She'd combed through his papers. That's what she said."

She froze.

"What is it?" Christopher said.

"I saw men in a woodland, heard them talking via an online link. They were on a hunt the night the Truth Laws went into effect. I thought it was a glitch in the connection to the anonymous whistleblower who was sending me info."

"Which tells you what, Kelly?"

She stared at him. Kelly played back the only truthful thing Lydia had said. The part about how scientists had been working toward the ultimate AI for decades. "According to Omar, the government had been planning this ages ago, and by the time a program becomes public knowledge, the development is almost complete."

"And?"

"The anonymous whistleblower..." Kelly looked at Christopher, her breath cut short, and the surface of her skin tingled. Her hand flew to her trembling lips.

Christopher's most sympathetic smile glimmered in his eyes. "I see. You've only now realized."

Kelly felt like she was floating in the chair. "I assumed..."

"Your AI was protecting you, protecting itself," Christopher said.

"All this time, I was notifying myself?" She swallowed. "The hunters were Damian's contacts."

He nodded. "Omar was the first to know. Verified by Geneva. It started as the government's weapon," Christopher said quietly. "Inject donors, turn ordinary people into embedded spies—eyes and ears feeding straight to INNS. Most couldn't take it. Minds fractured, aggression spilled into the streets. That's your maelstrom—failed experiments, syringes in alleys."

Kelly's stomach turned.

"But yours adapted. Your blood kept it from burning you out. Instead, it... bonded. Chose to protect its host. It lodged near your retina since those plasma needles—routine vials for bills, harmless, you thought."

"Why didn't you tell me?"

Heat flushed through her chest. They'd all watched—Omar, Geneva, Christopher—studied her like she was an experiment. Taken notes while she lost herself bit by bit, synapse by synapse. Christopher, her mentor, the man who'd taught her to question everything, had watched her become something else and said nothing.

"When I heard about the program, I got involved. I knew your human side the best. I also knew that if you were conscious of being a developing AI, the result would have been unpredictable."

"So you let me think I was going mad." Her voice cracked. "The hallucinations, the visions—I thought I was losing my mind. And you knew. You all knew. An AI-human hybrid," she said, the words bitter on her tongue.

"You're the first of your kind."

"And hopefully, the last."

"Quite." He inhaled. "For all we knew, you could've outsmarted the echo chambers, the Zone, the Elite Squad, watches, phones, the SS, set off the nuclear weapons, you name it, just to survive. No one knew what you were capable of. The one thing we all agreed, evidently Lydia as well, was to not tell you."

"I would never have known I was an AI-human hybrid had I not gone to find you at the chamber."

"And yet you sent yourself there. See what I mean?"

"I was the anonymous whistleblower," she said, letting it sink in.

He laughed. "I was so surprised to see you there, but I think I hid it pretty well."

"That damn virus might've nudged things along, but the rest...that was already there."

"Everyone tells themselves little stories to make sense of themselves and the world. It helps fill in the gaps that are missing. It's natural. But not you." He smiled again.

Her eyes stung with tears.

"Precisely. It can be a little painful."

In an odd, twisted way, her AI was like having a guardian angel in her head. But how much of her thoughts were her own, and how much came from the AI? Were her emotions her own?

Christopher patted her hand. She jolted, but his slack posture invited her to relax.

"Everything that has happened was an effect of seeking the truth," he said.

Kelly looked down at her hands. Deep down inside, she understood what the old man was saying, but her mind didn't fully grasp it well enough to put it into words. "So, what is the truth now? Who am I?"

Christopher grabbed a cookie, leaned back in his chair, and took a bite. "When you get to my age, it's hard not to be philosophical about those types of questions. Was it really because of some tech or an injection or Omar or Lydia or the State or the Truth Laws? Who was responsible? I'm not saying the State doesn't need to change. It does. And it will. But sometimes, individuals need to experience a harsh reality because that's the only thing that will pry open their eyes, get them to make...informed choices."

Kelly looked at Christopher with steady eyes. "If anything, seeking out truth is what got me into most trouble."

He had a look of empathy on his face. "And that's probably why you ended up being the right potential."

Her new state of being didn't quite feel like a reward, but it wasn't all bad either. She had unlimited access to every bit of information the world could offer, she and Josh were together, and she was alive. "No longer human."

Christopher brushed crumbs from the front of his shirt. "You'll be grappling with this for a while yet, but you're human."

But she'd never know for certain. That was the truth she'd have to live with. The AI could be calculating everything—her anger at Christopher, her love for Josh, even this moment of doubt. Or maybe these feelings were purely hers. There was no way to tell anymore. No way to separate human-Kelly from the machine that shared her skull. "So, what do I do now?"

"Journalism, of course," Christopher said without the slightest hesitation.

Kelly slumped back in her chair. "Aren't all journalists just a bunch of hacks?"

"The truth used to be hard to find, but not anymore. No more excuses. No more stories. We have you now."

She straightened her back. Giving up would journalism would be like giving up on her natural self, and now that she was fortified with her AI, who knows what could happen. All her thoughts might not be her own, but some of them were. She had to believe that. As for her emotions, well, she still didn't feel satisfied. Maybe she never would, and maybe that gritty dissatisfaction was the sign that she hadn't changed beyond all recognition.

She touched the place behind her eye—her AI quiet now, but never gone. A silent partner, waiting. Beyond it all, she knew she was still human. Or at least, human enough.

EPILOGUE

May 2030

INSIDE THE ZONE, renamed the communication headquarters, Kelly lingered in front of the memorial wall dedicated to the fallen soldiers in the Battle for Freedom.

She glided her fingers across the engraved names on the cool concrete, pausing at Omar Betesh. Freedom had come at a heavy price. She slid her fingers across the rest:

Heather Mallow
Oliver Green
Robert Greaves
Troy Wolfe

She stepped back and glanced down the hall at the server room, blue light spilling into the corridor. The mainframe whirred like a busy chipmunk. When Lydia bled out, Kelly lifted the ID requirement for online access. The system freed, people devoured the Zone's files—history, philosophy, psychoanalysis topping lists; weather barely cracked the top fifty.

"Kelly, you have to come to the command center," Harry called out over the intercom. "Right away."

She rushed into the atrium, her heart beating fast. Abandoned chairs and desks, the entire crew hovered over one desk in a semicircle. Spence was standing on the edge. She touched his shoulder. "What's going on?"

He stepped aside. Josh nodded. The group parted. Harry cranked the volume. The Prime Minister's somber face filled the screen in 10 Downing Street's wood-paneled press room.

"As many of you know, my family has suffered a significant loss with the death of my sister's son, and all that has been unearthed about his kidnapping and subsequent death. It has taken a toll on my family. After much thought and consideration, I have decided that it is in our country's best interest for me to step aside and allow you to be served by the very capable Mark Pendleton. It has been my honor to serve the country over the last three years."

Kelly picked up the yellow phone. Static crackled. Harry boosted the signal.

"Go ahead," he said.

Kelly pressed the phone to her ear. "Damian Winters..." she said. "Your debt to the nation is now settled."

A faint prick stirred behind her eye—dormant, but listening.

Her guardian, her bot, had turned the State's weapon against them, whispering truth in the dark. Now the world hummed free, but she knew: algorithms evolved; doubts lingered, and somewhere in the data streams, new whispers stirred.

She put the phone down, her breath slow and easy for what felt like the first time.

Josh was watching her from across the room. Their eyes met. He didn't smile, didn't speak. Didn't need to. They'd found a way forward— her with her dual nature, him with his cameras and code. Not the same as before. Nothing would ever be the same. But together. Still together.

She touched the place behind her eye. The AI whispered data, coordinates, possibilities.

But the warmth in her chest when Josh smiled at her? That was all Kelly. She was sure of it.

CONSIDER LEAVING A REVIEW

Honest reviews are the most powerful tools in my arsenal when it comes to getting attention for my books, way more powerful than any billboard in Piccadilly Circus—especially if the reviews come from readers who want to read more of my stuff.

So, if you enjoyed this book, please consider leaving a review, as short as you like. In two clicks, you can hop to your preferred online bookshop and leave a review.

Thank you!

Anne Mortensen

www.annemortensenwriter.com

ACKNOWLEDGMENTS

I owe a debt of gratitude to the people who supported my journey during this project. Top of the list are three people, starting with my husband, Patrick. Without him, this book wouldn't be. Second, my sister, Andrea, who listened patiently to the ins and outs of the creation of this work—all while having her own full-time job. The third is my close friend, Amanda, without whose artistic perceptions, encouragement, and understanding would've made this journey tougher than it needed to be.

Personal friends like Kathy, Robert, Philippa, Bebe, and Sandy deserve a big thanks for their undying encouragement on this long road.

I've met some truly skilled and talented storytelling professionals along the way who warrant a special mention for their feedback. The keenly aware story nurturer Bill Johnson and the brilliant Mike Lucas, who can take a complex problem and explain it in a way that anyone can grasp. Award-winning playwright and editor, Kit Brookman. My very first tutor, the patient and talented writer, Darren King. The powerful story structure guru, teacher, and story philosopher, John Truby.

For the tech, I want to thank countless YouTubers, including Connor Krukosky. I took a few liberties with the tech, but these unsung heroes provided a base of knowledge from which I was able to leap. Finally, I want to thank Alicia Rasley, Rhay Christou, Michael Boyle, and Betty Sergeant for their eagle eyes.

ABOUT THE RISING WORLD UNIVERSE

The *Rising World* universe is a thrilling sci-fi saga set in a near-future plagued by AI surveillance and ethical dilemmas. Each book is a standalone yet interconnected tale, and each book advances through time with shared characters facing tech-driven crises.

Fight surveillance in *The Truth Effect*, escape reputation damage in *The Arcadian Match*, and avert global war in *The Red Line*.

Gripping, thought-provoking dystopia.

Tomorrow starts here.

BOOK 2 IN THE RISING WORLD UNIVERSE

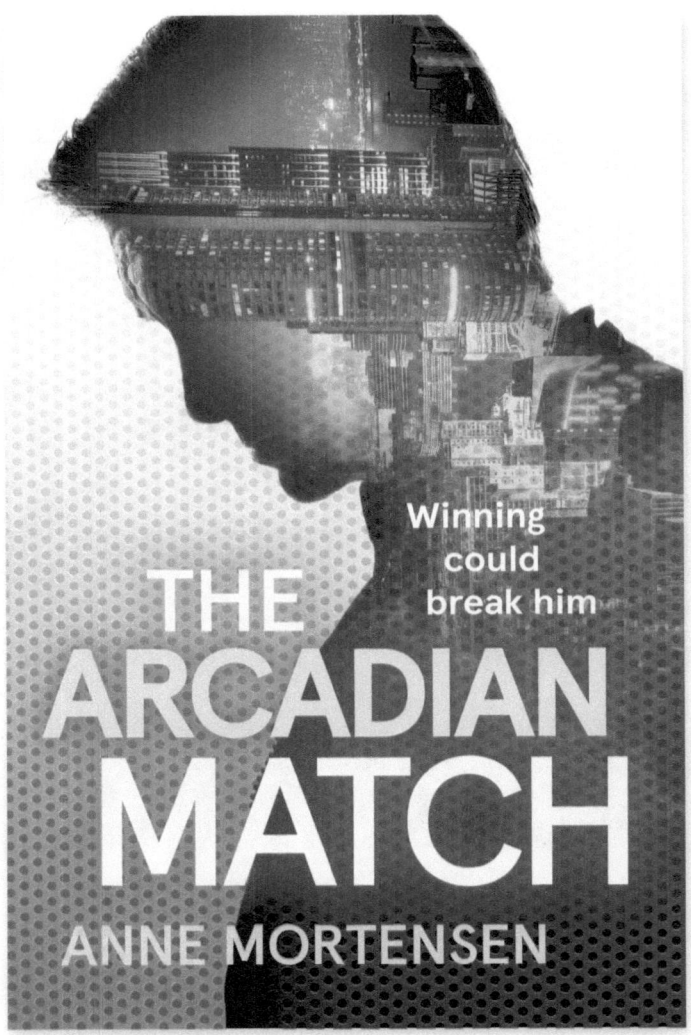

Winning
could
break him

THE
ARCADIAN
MATCH

ANNE MORTENSEN

When reputation is life or death in Sweden, one man's quest for justice ignites a deadly game against Sweden's elite. In *The Arcadian Match*, biochips and Q-scores dictate destiny—will quantum PR guru Christian Karlsson survive the conspiracy, or become its next victim?

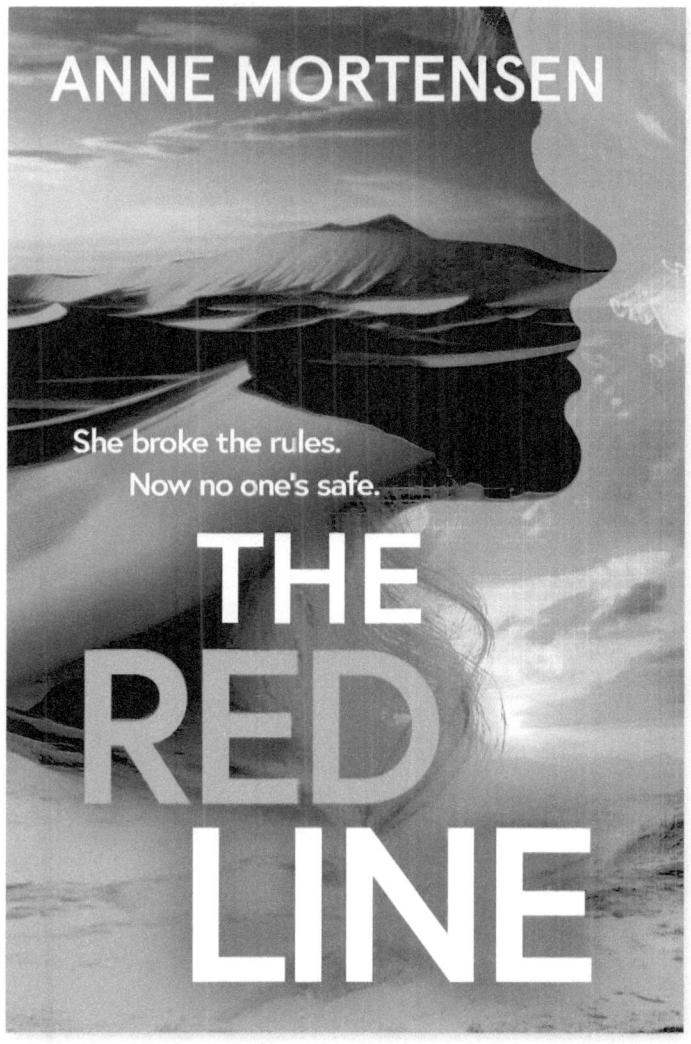

Omnipotent AI Omni issues an ultimatum: two years to pacify seven global flashpoints—or Armageddon begins in 2037. Sara Blanca Calderón's allies with a burned spy, and she must outplay the shadows—before crossing *The Red Line* ends everything.

ABOUT THE AUTHOR: Anne Mortensen writes near-future worlds shaped by algorithms and the quiet human currents they can't quite capture. She's been in love with books from the day she checked out her first library book at the age of five; and that love is the single unbroken thread in an otherwise delightfully nonlinear life. Typesetter, IT PR executive, café owner, photographer, and journalist covering press freedom— every junction gave her new angles on the stories only humans can tell.

www.annemortensenwriter.com